Kylie Tennant was born at Manly, New South Wales, in 1912 and educated at Brighton College and Sydney University. She married L.C. Rodd, a school-teacher, in 1932.

She had been a chicken farmer, barmaid, book reviewer, journalist, assistant publicity officer for the A.B.C., organiser of the Unemployed Workers' Union, church sister and publisher's literary advisor and editor.

She was lecturer, 1957-60, at universities in Armidale, Canberra, Adelaide and Perth. Appointed to the Advisory Board of the Commonwealth Literary Fund in 1961, she was a Life Patron of the Fellowship of Australian Writers. Two of her novels, *Tiburon* and *The Battlers*, have won the S.H. Prior Memorial Prize.

She was made AO in 1980 and died in 1988.

B<small>THE</small>ATTLERS

Kylie Tennant

An Angus & Robertson Publication

Angus&Robertson, an imprint of
HarperCollins*Publishers*
25 Ryde Road, Pymble, Sydney, NSW 2073, Australia
31 View Road, Glenfield, Auckland 10, New Zealand
77-85 Fulham Palace Road, London W6 8JB, United Kingdom
10 East 53rd Street, New York NY 10022, USA

First published in 1941
Pacific Books edition published by Angus & Robertson Publishers,
Australia 1967
Reprinted 1969, 1971
A&R Paperback edition 1973
A&R Classics edition 1976
Sirius Quality Paperback edition 1983
Reprinted 1988
This Imprint Classics edition published in 1994

National Library of Australia
Cataloguing-in-Publication data:
   Tennant, Kylie, 1912-1988.
   The Battlers
   ISBN 0 207 18637 8.

   I. Title. (Series: Imprint classics)

A 823.2

Cover photogragh by Simon Cardwell, © SAFC Productions Ltd
and Australian Film Finance Corporation Pty Ltd. From the mini-series
'The Battlers', produced in South Australia by the South Australian Film Corporation
for the Seven Network and made with the participation of the Australian Film
Finance Corporation Pty Ltd.

Printed in Australia by Griffin Paperbacks, Adelaide.

9 8 7 6 5 4 3 2 1
97 96 95 94

IMPRINT CLASSICS

THE BATTLERS

Kylie Tennant

Angus&Robertson

An imprint of HarperCollins*Publishers*

Introduction

AN ENGLISH READER wrote of *The Battlers*: "All its people should, of course, be put in a lethal chamber, but somehow by the end of the book, one manages to regard them with sympathy and interest."

That reference to the lethal chamber was a great shock to me. I felt, though, that to have chipped even a flint off such a mind was of some moment. It had never occurred to me that vagabonds, failures and criminals, about whom I habitually wrote with affection, might, to orderly and reasonable people, be candidates for extinction. This was before even more orderly and reasonable people brought to a dreadful practicality methods of removing large numbers of persons, under the excuse of wartime expediency, from a life which however miserable still gave them breath and hope.

The people who are absent from *The Battlers* are much more alarming from the human point of view than those with whom the book deals: the people who "look on our labour and laughter as a tired man looks at flies", who consider that those who cannot pass examinations and tests for fluency in language or modern skills, should be filed away under a number in an institution. It is true that in the past century the wheels have moved so fast that there are increasing numbers of us left limping in the rear if we cannot translate the mixtures of Greek and Arabic which result in larger engineering achievements, fouler cities and a general level of dread.

Pockets of primitives, among whom I would number myself, have been abandoned by the roadside, breathless in a roar of exhausts and dust. More and more people are *battlers*, not only on the track, but in the suburbs, the factories, the automated living where to be a man or woman is no longer any claim.

I have long borne the reputation of being an observer of human behaviour, a binocular naturalist objectively recording wild life in human form. If I have said that I sought the society of unlettered and poor people from choice, because I took pleasure in their company and gained more by it than I did from the learned, this has been laughed off as mere perversity or quaintness. How clever to select such little-used material!

The human eye records best at the pace at which one walks. In fact, to see properly one must sit still. In a fast car, attention is given not to small details but to the larger objects in the landscape. To meet the people I wished to write about, it was necessary to camp where they camped, go at their pace, learn the meanings they gave to words that were used by others in a different sense. Also I must think and feel as they did. This takes time and a large amount of common hardship.

I can remember sitting by a muddy pool in which the horses and men had been bathing and from which I had just drawn a kerosene tin full of drinking water. I was reading a letter in which friends told of a very good white wine they had drunk with ice (*ice*!) at a fashionable hotel. It made me smile ironically to think that for the price of those drinks my companions on the track could live for a week.

Laughter is one of the goods that are never rationed. Indeed, among primitive people laughter is the great protection. A famous Arctic explorer told how the Eskimos among whom he was living were so exhausted by a seal hunt that when they had drawn up their catch on an icefloe, they all went to sleep. While they slept, the icefloe broke away taking their food supply with it. The cream of the jest was—and they rocked with laughter as they related it—that the polar bears would be so glutted with the slaughtered seals, they would not come ashore and so the villagers would lose that food source also. Think of it—the polar bears, too!—they *had* to laugh. A civilized man would not see anything funny in such a situation; but then a civilized man has other defences against lack besides the ability to go hungry and grin about it.

If there is one thing I regret about the long journeys I took along the track, to live with the Battlers, it is that I did not ever come to terms with the horse that drew my van. I had never driven a horse before, and that jib mare and I regarded each other with mutual suspicion. It was not till long after that horse and I had parted for ever that I learned to know how horses think and feel, or to come to any sympathy with them. The horse was to me a burden of responsibility. I had to hobble it, feed it, track it when it wandered. After driving a car I was impatient with a living creature in place of a machine. Even its harness was complicated and strange.

The horse knew of my unhandiness and took constant advantage of this, nearly succeeding in maiming me on several occasions. After a long variance I came to a town where I bestowed the mare in a safe stable. An old drover showed me a knot which, he maintained, would hold any horse securely. Alas! in my impatience and incompetence I strangled the horse, tying it with the new knot. My version of the knot turned out to be a slip knot, and the poor mare, alone and frightened, pulled on it ever tighter and tighter until she died. To have murdered a horse by ignorance and lack of skill is a painful matter, even when the horse is by no means beloved.

I am sorry for it and have continued to be sorry for it for many years. When I hear of others who have committed nameless crimes, I remind myself that probably a good deal of ignorance and callousness were to blame as in my own case. There is, however, less excuse for strangling a fellow creature in mere hastiness and bungling than for other deeds. I would proffer that many horses are natural suicides, and even the best of them neurotic and self-centred. Although I have had enforced association with other horses, finding many of them gentle and affectionate, I have always regarded them with some reserve.

The code of the *travellers*, with whom I worked and camped, was not my code of behaviour. I do not believe, for instance, it is salutary to take a whip to your wife, although this was behaviour which was spoken of in certain cases with approval. Nor did I regard fist fights between drunks as a social diversion. If I had my reservations about my comrades, they always treated me with the kindliness and gentleness the best people show a helpless idiot. I aroused in them both pity and bewilderment and this worked very much to my advantage. Those who are accustomed to a position of bitter inferiority come fresh to the pleasures of philanthropy.

At stealing sheep I was a hopeless failure, making far too much noise; but I continued to enjoy my share of the fresh mutton. Whatever was looted in our passage, my share, although I had done nothing, was placed aside because I was "one of the mob". I shared with them what I had. I remember two men sitting by my camp fire planning to steal an old set of harness from a "cocky's" barn.

"Why go so far?" I asked. "I have a new set of harness, and you could take *that* without any trouble."

They were outraged and insulted that I should even think they were capable of it. They spoke severely, and with much bad language, of people with minds like mine. One does not steal from one's mates, for that is unforgivable. Also one tolerates in friends conduct that in unknown persons would incur censure.

I ask you to make the acquaintance of the Battlers, as worthy of friendship and requiring it, wherever you meet them, as primitive tribesmen, wanderers in cities, patients in institutions, jailbirds, and others whose acquaintance has no immediate advantage, assuring you that however burdensome the charge, you will be the better for it, unless you are superior or patronizing. Humility is all.

There may come a time, and not so far distant, when all of us could be in need of the virtues of the Battlers: which boil down to a talent for survival. After twenty years, people tell me, the *travellers* are now all working industriously in an affluent society. I doubt this. Give me yet another twenty years, and I may be able to point out to you little groups of migrants and wanderers, among whom you may be one, making as best they can in circumstances they have not chosen. Even the most intelligent and superior are casting about now in their minds for boltholes. Do not pity the lean desert dweller until you have learnt to go without water.

KYLIE TENNANT

Chapter I

IF SNOW had taken the road through Belburra, instead of the track through Currawong, his whole life would have run a different course. He had pulled in his horse at the fork of the road, and for a minute he sat thinking. True, the road to Belburra was the shorter way home, and he had been away nine months. But Snow was not any too eager to reach home. His return was never the scene of wild enthusiasm. One of his sons might stroll inside and announce: 'Hey, Mum, Dad's here.' And his wife would remark grimly: 'Hello! so you're back, are you?' and Snow would say: 'Yeah, I'm back.'

He had come over the black-soil plain; the plain that stretches from Narrabri to Moree in a loneliness where the mirages smoke and the great brown kangaroos leap away from the road, where the enfiladed telegraph-poles dwindle to a pinpoint and disappear over the rim of the earth, where the ground is baked like a tile in summer, and in winter forms a black bog that the drovers dread. Snow had crawled slowly across it in the lumbering van he had got in exchange for his sulky. It was slow, but, as Snow said to himself, he was a man who 'liked a bit of comfort.' He was of that singular breed who travel alone for preference; and as he reined Don in at the fork of the road, there was no mate to influence his judgment which way he should go.

There was the wind, of course—the vicious westerly that makes winter a hell, a westerly biting with all the malice of the thousands of miles of barbed wire over which it had blown. Whichever way he turned, that wind met him face-on. The track through Currawong was more sheltered than that through Belburra.

Then also Don, the horse, was tired; even Bluey, the cattle-dog, was tired, panting and dusty at the end of his chain under the van. Five miles this side of Currawong, Snow knew of a camp where there was good feed and water for the horse. But more important than grass or water, it offered that privacy and retirement so essential to anyone who meditates an onslaught on someone else's sheep. Snow was a big man, six feet one, and every inch of him meat-hungry. To his mind, there had always been something contemptible about buying mutton when it was walking about in the paddocks all around him. Visions of roast mutton floated before his eyes. He clicked his tongue to Don and turned him along the left-hand track to Currawong. All his life, with that decision, veered into a different course.

When Snow made camp late that afternoon, it was in a hollow between two ridges where a high steel windmill whirled above the tank provided for travelling stock, clanking the pump-rod up and down with a lonely clatter, like a ghost rattling in chains. All along the track there had been a scarcity of feed because, although it was the middle of June, not enough rain had fallen to break the drought. But here was a clearing green with tender grass and, in the grass, patches of reedy, red garden flower and a few overturned stones to tell of a forgotten homestead. Beside the stones two great coral trees lifted naked grey branches that showed, instead of leaves, clusters of flowers, curved blades of scarlet around the stamens, as though a flock of fiery-coloured birds were tilting their tail-feathers in council.

At a decent distance from the civilised trees, all about the open space, a grey-green wall of gums reared up, roaring with the ridges behind under an intermittent surf of wind. Now the wind was thunderous as city traffic; then there was only a faint hissing as the topmost leaves of the gums boiled over in silver spray, flashing like a mackerel shoal that ruffles a dark sea. A pause, and then once more the boughs would leap and whine as though some small

2

animal were caught in their crotch, straining and lashing until the very trunks groaned again.

Snow cared little for the wind, as it hushed his fire sideways like a mother soothing a rowdy child in its cot. All day the wind might fluster the road dust and level the tussocks; but at sundown there would be a breathless, tranquil silence, as the world turned over on its side for the night, with the sky like a translucent bubble of pale green glass, so fragile you would think that, at the tap of a finger-nail, it would ring and shiver the first stars down in trails of fire like water-drops on a window-pane.

Snow, busy making camp, congratulated himself that there were no other travellers on the reserve. It was a cold night, with a frosting of stars, and Snow waited for the wind to come up again before he began his walk towards the homestead a mile back, where he had marked a paddock of promising wethers. Noiselessly he climbed over the barbed-wire fence and made his way across a stubble-field smelling like new bread. Behind the field was the paddock, darkly blotted with trees.

As he listened for the faint bleating that betrayed the presence of the flock, and moved, with a low word to Bluey, towards that uneasy sound, Snow's big, loose, slouching body knitted into the swift decision of the born hunter. Even his face altered. Usually Snow's face had no notable handsomeness, resembling closely the countenance of a particularly sleepy shark. His little, light-coloured eyes, each side of a huge, jutting nose, were half shut, just as his mouth—he breathed through it—was half open to a gape of big, yellow teeth above an almost imperceptible chin. His forehead did not count in the assembly of features, as it was either hidden by an old felt hat or by a growth of straw-coloured hair which had earned him the usual bush name for fair-haired men: 'Snow.' His words were few and his speech slow. If he became excited, he stuttered. He seldom spoke a sentence without three 'bloodys' in it, but he never knew he was swearing. It was as natural as his stutter.

3

In sheep-stealing, however, he took the quiet pleasure of an artist exercising his skill. Returning with a plump yearling over his shoulders, he had something of the benevolent aspect of a good shepherd in a church window. He was at peace with all the world. As he cut his find's throat and flung the entrails to Bluey, he was thinking that life 'on the track' was not so bad, with good places to camp and 'cockies' sheep to knock over.' He reflected wistfully that in a week or so these good things would be put away from him, and the vacant space filled by his wife's nagging, until restlessness seized him and he started out on the track again. He had posted home from Narrabri no less than ten dirty pound notes, and the thought of the surprise his wife would get made him more than ever feel that life was good.

He hung the carcase in a tree removed far enough from the clearing to escape the notice of any inquisitive visitors. Snow had been 'in for meat' several times, and another gaol term was something he did not welcome. It was different in Queensland, where a man could always take a sheep for food as long as he left the skin hanging on the fence.

They had reached the edge of the clearing when Bluey stiffened with a low, warning growl. Instantly Snow stopped in his tracks, peering towards the camp. There was someone there. Snow's great fist tightened round his butcher's knife. Someone was at his tucker-box, noisily and unhandily rummaging in it. A virtuous indignation seized him. Some thieving (*adjective*) robber was 'ratting' his tucker-box! He leant down and gripped the dog's collar as he trod cat-footed into the fire-light and contemplated the dim shape.

'What the hell you think you're doing?' he asked angrily.

A long-drawn shriek as the figure straightened up gave him nearly as great a fright as he had given the thief.

'Cripes! it's a woman!' he said out loud, half in relief.

The object huddled in terror by the tucker-box, babbling at him, did not look like a woman. It looked like

4

something the darkness had spewed forth in disgust. Its hair hung in bedraggled wisps through which the eyes stared bulging with horror. A toothless mouth gaped at him as the creature panted and stammered. A shapeless mass of ragged clothing covered a body so insignificant that it looked like that of a child.

'Oh, mister, don't, don't . . . hit me. I was that hungry. And I been walkin' and walkin' . . .' the thing gasped, '. . . in the dark.'

'Here,' Snow said, quietening the snarling Bluey, 'take it easy.'

He removed from the fire a blackened billy, from which he poured a no less blackened brew of tea.

'Drink some of this.'

His captive gulped it down. 'He chucked me out,' she mumbled. 'Jus' left me by the side of the road hundreds of miles from nowhere an' says: "Get to hell out of this, you whore." And I ain't. Nobody ain't got any right to call me that. I was married to 'im. I was. And I come away cos he says it's a great life on the track, an' . . .' She broke off. 'I ain't had nothin' to eat since yestiday morning . . . An' it was dark. . . .'

'You stay there,' Snow admonished. 'I won't be long.' The meat might be a bit tough, as it was so fresh, but if the hobgoblin hadn't had anything to eat for two days, she wouldn't be fussy.

He had just cut off a leg, and was turning back, when another scream brought him back the rest of the way at a run.

'He bit me!' the woman screamed furiously. 'You damned blasted mongrel of a dog!'

At Snow's voice Bluey laid down his head on his paws, his yellow eyes still jealously turned on the interloper. Viewing the teeth-marks on the leg held out for his inspection, Snow assured himself that the stranger was more frightened than hurt.

'It's just a nip,' he told her. 'Why'd you try to sneak away?'

5

The woman ignored the question. 'I 'ates damn dogs,' she said sullenly.

She was so small—merely a bag of bones; and as she shiveringly accepted the old coat Snow passed her, he asked curiously: 'How old 'ud you be?'

'Nineteen.'

'You look more.' She looked about sixty. 'What's your name?'

'Dancy. And me married name's Smif.'

'Well, listen 'ere, Dancy Smith, or whoever you are. I'm a married man, and I'm making 'ome to me wife, so it ain't no use you campin' with me, see? But I wouldn't turn a dog away if it was hungry.'

The girl Dancy snarled at him. 'Oo wants to camp wiv you? I 'ates men—'ates the 'ole bloomin' lot of 'em. Wot do they ever do but sit back and watch women work? I ain't never seen a man yet what was any good. The whole schemin', lyin', crawlin' lot of 'em. I 'ates 'em. And women, too,' she added liberally. 'Camp wiv you? Oo wants to camp wiv you?'

Snow was frying the mutton, and she fell silent, watching it ravenously. Then she snivelled a little. 'I'm that scared of the dark. Something went "Yow!"' She imitated the sound.

'That'd be a 'possum.'

'I fought it was a ghost.' She shuddered. 'I got thinking of the time Dad come 'ome. Walked out of the asylum 'e did, wiv a coat over his asylum cloves. He come 'ome to the residential where Mum was stayin' wiv me and the other kids. I was twelve. He come home on the Friday, and Saturday afternoon, when we was at the pi'tures, he cut her throat, and then he cut his own throat afterwards. The landlady made me go in wiv a mop and a bucket and clean up the floor. Bled to death he had, all over it. And me wringin' out the mop wiv me own farver's blood on it. The landlady said they was *my* parents and I had to do it.'

With Snow's repugnance there mingled a tiny strain of pity. He said nothing, but turned the meat on the fire.

6

'Then me married sister took us. She 'ated the sight of me. Thought the day wasn't lucky if she didn't find somefing to frash me for. I'll put you, she says, where they'll make you sorry you was born. And she told all the lies in court!' Dancy broke off. 'Ain't that meat done yet?'

'Give it a chance. What happened then?'

'I went to Parramatta. I was in an' out up to the time I was eighteen. The other girls taught me plenty. A edjucation I 'ad.'

Snow interestedly contemplated this visitation from another world as it rambled on in a smattering of filthy words and bitterness, discoursing of alley and slum and reformatory.

'You ain't had much of a fair go,' he said slowly at last. 'You's what you might call a Stray.'

The creature spat. 'It's men,' she said. 'Everywhere you go they're runnin' things. Tryin' to down you. An' women, too. All of 'em rotten.'

Snow took the mutton from the frying-pan and gave it to her. She ate wolfishly, only interrupting the meal to remark that 'the dog looked at her sumfin' fierce'; so that Snow ordered Bluey away. The man could feel the protuberant eyes, with their red rims and pale lashes, inspecting him calculatingly. She looked, he thought, like a trapped, fierce little animal.

'Where's your teeth?' he asked.

'I broke 'em.'

'You'd look a lot better with 'em than without.'

'Well, who the hell d'you think's got the money to go round buyin' sets of teef?'

This closed the conversation.

Snow pondered. 'I could go back through Belburra,' he said aloud, 'and leave you with Father Paul.'

'One of them parsons?'

' 'E's a priest.'

'Ooh! Not one of them. I 'ates them.' Something about Snow's ugly, unshaven countenance seemed to have raised her spirits. 'Ow'd you get here? You working?'

Snow gave the hard, dry croak that served him for a laugh. 'Work, eh?' he said. 'It's funny about work.' This novel situation had loosened his tongue. 'I got a sickener of it when I was a kid. My father was one of them half-starved wheat-cockies out from Temora. Graft! He grafted like a team of bullocks, and when I wasn't knee-high to a grasshopper he had me out ploughing and clearing and fencing.' He fell silent contemplating that never-ending work. 'It was: "Theodore, go harness them horses," or, "Theodore, haul the timber," and me man-aging great big Clydesdales with tempers just like his (an' his temper was something fierce). Why, I didn't come up as high as the horses' belly! Geeze! I had enough of work to last me a lifetime when I was a kid. Then I married, and a married man, when he can get work, he's got to take it. It's different when you're single. I been workin' on and off ever since.'

These were more words than he had spoken for weeks, and he paused, surprised at himself. Then he rose yawn-ing. 'Well, I'll give you a lift to Currawong to-morrow, and you can make your way back to Sydney from there.'

He was sorting his blankets into two heaps. 'There's yours. And if you try to sneak away, the dog'll get you. Understand?'

He rolled himself a last cigarette before turning in, and then tossed the tobacco and papers across to his guest. She caught them eagerly. Then, looking up from licking the cigarette into shape, she remarked:

'You think you'll be well rid of me, don't you?'

There was something in her tone that aroused in Snow a faint feeling of alarm. Rolling up in his blankets, he comforted himself with the thought that no creature as little and skinny as that girl could worry him. He travelled alone.

'G'night, Stray,' he said austerely, tilting his hat over his eyes. He did not trouble to remove his boots. He might need to get up in the night to put wood on the fire.

After the camp had sunk into a silence punctuated by the heavy bass snore of Snow and the treble snore of the intruder, Bluey lay with one eye cocked suspiciously at the bundle of bedding that represented, in his canine view, a new and hateful complication to life. If Snow could not see trouble ahead, Bluey could.

Chapter II

TOWARDS morning a cold, drizzling rain began to fall. Snow was not at all disturbed. He would have pulled his hat farther over his eyes and slept on, had it not been for the restless stirrings and mumblings of his guest.

'What's up?' he demanded.

'It's raining.'

'Well, if you don't like it, hop up in the van. Get back there, Bluey.' He aimed a rock at his faithful hound, who had approached with the intention of guarding the van from all marauders. Bluey fled with a yelp, and Snow relapsed peacefully into his dreams again.

The rain was coming down in earnest when he awoke, but there was still a red ember glowing under the big log he had dragged across the fire. It had been his intention to stay quietly in camp all day and eat mutton; but the rain, falling with the heavy deliberation of an after-dinner speech, reminded him that there was a deserted church a few miles along the road. One of his reasons for coming through Currawong had been to remove that church door and fashion from it an upper decking for his waggon. Snow was nothing if not a handy man.

He decided to move on to the church, camp there and eat mutton until the rain stopped, remove the door for his waggon decking and then jog pleasantly on. After all, there was no hurry, and he did not like the idea of turning the Stray, as he privately termed her, away in the rain.

9

Courtesy to women had once been thrashed into him with a leather strap, and some of the scars still remained.

The Stray slid out of the van just as he came to this decision.

She rubbed her fists into her eyes, swore, and lounged over to inspect the chops Snow was preparing for breakfast.

'You cud do with more fat,' she observed.

If there was one thing Snow disliked, it was interference with his cooking.

'You could do with a wash,' he retorted. 'There's the soap and towel.'

The Stray was about to point out that it was raining. There was a reproachful look in her eye; but she trotted away obediently, and returned with part of the surface soil removed from a countenance that was by daylight worse, if anything, than the night before. In more fortunate circumstances, Dancy Smith might have had a delicate pink-and-white complexion, but it was the type of complexion that will not brown, but turns the colour of beetroot, then blisters. Her nose was peeling, and the deep red sunburn made her look, as Snow put it, as though 'she had been on the beer.' Her lips were cracked and sore. There were deep wrinkles at the corners of her eyes.

Snow eyed her furtively as she ate and, glancing up suddenly, she caught him.

'Who yer staring at?' she asked dangerously.

Snow chuckled. 'Your nose is peelin',' he observed. 'You ought to put a bit of fat on it and that 'ud cook it proper.'

When breakfast was over, he wrapped away in clean flourbags those portions of the sheep which he intended to take with him. The Stray washed the dishes and dried them and helped break camp. She seemed dejected, and finally remarked:

'Well, I guess I'll be getting along.'

Snow looked surprised. 'I said I'd give you a lift into Currawong, didn't I?'

'You'd sooner get rid of me.'

This was so true that Snow felt in honour bound to deny it.

'Arr. The horse don't mind a bit extra. You ain't *that* heavy. Hop in the van and don't let's hear no more about it.'

The Stray climbed up into the van. She was still wearing Snow's old coat, and as she crouched down beside him, a small bundle of bones, clothing, and dejection, Snow set himself to cheer her up.

'I been thinkin' of goin' down into Victoria to cy'nide some 'possums,' he said chattily. 'There's more of them down there than here in New South.'

His guest did not bite noticeably at this conversational bait.

'Of course,' Snow continued, 'there's always some cocky's son who wants to buy the skins off you at sixpence each and sell them at three bob himself, and if you won't give them to him, he's likely to top you off to the police. But there's risks to everything.'

'You can be put in gaol for catching 'possums,' the Stray said lugubriously.

Snow nodded. 'Well, the way I look at it is this: You can be put in gaol for almost anything, if you ain't got no money. And why? 'Cos it's a crime to have no money. That's why. I thought it out.' He nodded again deliberately. 'No vis'ble means of support. You go in for it, see?'

'I been vagged,' the Stray mentioned.

'Oh! you have? Well, there you are. If you ain't got any money, they run you in, and if you try to get any, they run you in. It ain't safe to be poor in this country. That's why I work if I can get a job.'

'What do you do?' the Stray asked, her curiosity aroused.

'Anythin',' Snow answered, gratified to see that she was interested. 'Anythin' I can get: relief work, droving, fencing, clearing.'

They had been plodding along, Don splashing sturdily through the puddles, the rain running down his coat in dark trickles. It beat in on the man and woman in the van, but with the tarpaulin across their knees they were well enough protected.

On either side were fields rolling mile after mile in a wandering maze of fences, with here and there an erupted red-roofed farm, its windmill like a steel rosette pinned to the patchwork country that was squared into dun-coloured paddocks newly ploughed, the grey-yellow of stubble, or the vivid green of young oats. In stretches of half-cleared pasture ring-barked trees reared their twisted grey skeletons, and the black stumps showed as dark toadstool tops in the tufted, grey-brown grass. Hollow burnt logs, patched white and black like a magpie's wing, lay as runways for rabbits whose warrens, with their sandy beaten patch about the holes, gave promise, to Snow's eye, of good trapping. A line of green willows at the foot of a slope marked the bed of a creek, willows bitten neatly off at the height an old ram could stretch his sharp teeth. The dripping of the thin trees was music to a man who had grown up from harvest to harvest, and Snow took in the fields with the eye of a farmer. The rain was coming just when it was most needed. It would be a good year here—perhaps.

They had come round yet another bend in a road that could not have gone straight if the whole Salvation Army reformed it. Its six-inch-deep ruts had become rivers of red mud that churned under the wheels like butter.

'Mi-Gord!' Snow exclaimed. He had lifted his eyes casually from Don's rump to the road along which they travelled.

'What's up?' the Stray asked.

Snow pointed dramatically to a figure in the distance. 'Damned if the road ain't lousy with wimmen,' he exclaimed. 'I didn't see her go past the reserve.'

The Stray screwed up her eyes and peered forward. 'How d'you know it's a woman?' she demanded.

'Look at the way she walks,' Snow said, disgusted. 'Dunno what things is comin' to when the road's all littered up with wimmen.'

Sure enough, as they began to overtake the moving figure, it resolved itself into the shape of a fat, lumpy female, waddling along. In one hand she carried a small, blackened billy-can, in the other a sugar-bag. She was clad in a black coat edged with draggled brown fur, and her brown stockings sagged into deplorable sandshoes. A yellow straw hat drooped over her face and shoulders.

Having picked up one woman, Snow decided he might as well go on as he had begun.

'Give y' a lift, missus?' he hailed reluctantly, as the van overtook the slow-moving figure.

The woman regarded him with small, beady, black eyes from a pasty, fat face. 'Don't presume to address your betters, my man,' she responded. 'Get along with you.'

Snow nearly fell out of the van with astonishment. He hastily clicked to Don, and the van lumbered away. 'Mi-Gord!' Snow turned to the no less astonished Stray. 'There's a way to refuse a lift!'

The Stray was peering out of the back of the van at the strange creature, who had stopped in the middle of the road and was solemnly dancing, capering this way and that, waving and jerking her arms.

'She's bats.' The Stray tapped her forehead. 'Looney, like farver was.' She added hopefully: 'Maybe she's escaped from a 'sylum and 'ull cut her froat.'

Snow urged Don on. A man, he reflected, could go for weeks on the track and have nothing more occur than his horse getting a flint in its shoe, and then a run of extraordinary happenings would whirl him along as a piece of paper is whirled down a street. He began to feel that he should have parted with the Stray at the camp. She seemed to bring strange luck. It was like seeing one white horse. You'd be sure to see another before the day was out. He'd met one woman carrying her swag, then sure enough he'd met another.

'It repeats,' he said thoughtfully. 'Like an onion.'

He was relieved when the dreary, weatherboard shape of the church showed across the sodden fields and dripping, ragged trees. He was even better pleased to discover that there was only one other occupant of the church, and that a man.

The stranger greeted them in a friendly enough way. He was a weedy youth with a mop of brown hair flopped over his forehead and an air of impudent self-assurance. He seemed to have shaved with a hoe, and between the gashes and raw, scraped patches a crop of black bristles fought for ascendancy over some flourishing pimples.

'How's it, sport?' he called to Snow, and addressing the Stray by the honorific of the track, 'Take a seat, missus.'

He indicated a kerosene tin beside the fire he had lit on a sheet of corrugated iron. Having thus discharged the duties of host, he fell to re-stringing a battered guitar.

'We saw a mad woman down the road,' Dancy volunteered. 'She was dancing and screaming and throwing stones after us and rolling in the mud; wasn't she, Snow?'

This was Snow's first introduction to the Stray's talent for ekeing out the bare bones of truth into a tasty stew.

'It must be Phippsy,' the youth said, unimpressed. 'Some of the chaps were talking about her at Belburra. Dora Phipps, that's her name. She's eccentric, that's all.'

Snow and Stray glanced at each other uneasily. But their companion, dismissing the subject from his mind, launched out on a recital of his troubles. His track name was Duke, and he had been 'busking'—singing his way from town to town. He had had a mate, a jockey, who had left Melbourne under a cloud and in the guard's van of a goods train where the busker was also travelling north. They had sworn eternal friendship until a disagreement resulted in the hurried departure of the jockey and left the busker only a large, discoloured bruise upon his cheekbone, sole token of deathless friendship.

'Jealousy,' the busker said darkly. 'That was his trouble. What with my guitar and my songs and, as you

14

might put it, my personality, he gets fed up with having nothing to do but look after the camp and take round the hat. Anyway, he's done himself a bad turn, and he knows it. A mate like me isn't to be picked up under every bridge.'

They gathered that Duke was 'making down' to Logan, where he intended to honour a travelling tent show with his presence.

'As soon as I get to Currawong,' he explained, 'I'll do a quickie round the pubs and then board the 10.25 goods to-night for Logan.'

'How about your rations?' Snow asked. For to-morrow was Thursday; and Thursday all over the West is dole day, when the track men come in to have their cards stamped at the police-station and get their rations to carry them to the next 'dole town.'

The busker laughed. 'Me? Why, a chap that can make fifteen bob in an hour on Saturday afternoon would be a mug to hang round waiting for a copper to stamp his card and order him a few bobs' worth of groceries. One Saturday I made thirty bob before the Johns warned me off. Rations?' He waved the suggestion away. 'Not while I have my guitar.'

They regarded him respectfully. A man who could make fifteen shillings in an hour deserved respect. The Stray was roused to emulation.

'Me.' She adopted the busker's vainglorious tone. 'I'm the best bum on the track. In Tewsbury I come back wiv ten bob, two soots of cloves, a jar of jam, a dozen eggs, and two loaves of bread. An' I didn't get warned off by no John, neiver.'

The busker gave her a patronising nod. 'Good for you, missus,' he encouraged. 'You sound as though you could make an iron pump give milk. I bet the boss here'—he gave Snow a playful dig in the ribs—'thinks he's a lucky man, eh, sport?'

Snow grunted. He was not a man to indulge in laborious explanations. He was tempted to boast that he was the best sheep-stealer on the track, but caution restrained him. Thinking of mutton made him hungry. He began to unwrap the white cerements from the limbs of the sheep.

'Not mutton?' Duke cried, taking an eager interest in the proceedings. Snow had not realised that, for all the busker's talk of easy money, his face was pinched and hungry-looking. 'Not my favourite food, mutton?'

Had the busker observed the etiquette of the track he would have pretended not to notice that there was food about, and when offered the meat, he would have been surprised, refused, hesitated, and partaken reluctantly.

Snow dubiously regarded the fire on the bit of corrugated iron, decided it would not be suitable for roasting mutton, and went out to build his own fire in the stone porch.

'Mustn't muck the church up too much,' he declared.

He was back again almost immediately. 'She's comin!' he announced in solemn tones.

'Oo-er!' The Stray rose in alarm. 'Lemme out of here.'

'Sit down,' the busker said carelessly. 'Phippsy's harmless.'

But Snow had gone round the back of the church ostensibly to look at the horse. He thoughtfully took Bluey with him. Not that he need have worried. The approaching menace in woman's form was fond of animals, as she later demonstrated by patting the snarling Bluey on the head and calling him: 'Good doggie, there.'

She came mincing up to the porch, peering from her little, short-sighted eyes under the flapping lobes of hat. Then, focusing the two occupants, she stood with her head forward very much like a pointer dog.

'Dear me, dear me!' Her voice was so affected that it made the 'dear' sound like 'dah'. 'I trust I don't intrude? Miss Phipps is the name. I am seeking shelter— yes, shelter.' She had a habit of repeating words, as though the minds of her hearers might be too dense to grasp them without repetition. 'So unfortunate this rain when one is on a walking tour.'

The busker silently indicated another upturned kerosene tin, the one Snow had brought in for himself.

'I thank you.' She sat down as though it had been a throne, and held out her dreadful shoes to the blaze. 'This terrible weather, my deah.' She ignored Duke and concentrated her attention on Dancy. 'I suppose the poah farmers must have rain, but *so* inconvenient. I always say they should have it at a time when it will least disturb other people's plans.'

'Eh, missus.' Flattered by the attention, the Stray spoke eagerly, 'When we gets into Currawong I can bum you a better pair of boots than them.'

'My deah child,' Miss Phipps gave a little affected laugh, 'what on earth do you mean by that dreadful word?'

The busker raised his head from his task. Rather he tossed his head so that the lank strands of hair flopped backward. 'Come off it, Dora,' he said bluntly. 'Don't try to put that guff over us.'

'You impertinent creature!' The little black eyes glittered.

'Come off it,' the busker said again calmly. 'You can put it over a lot of ignorant mugs of bagmen that you're some sort of society woman, but you can't put it over me.' He eyed her ominously. 'I've got the lowdown on you, Dora.'

Miss Phipps turned her back on him. 'I don't suppose you have a little cold cream, deah?' she asked. 'The skin should always be one's first care, and I find my hands suffah so.'

The Stray dumbly shook her head, and Miss Phipps was about to launch forth on another conversational effort when the figure of Snow loomed up in the porch.

'Hey, Stray,' he called. 'C'mere.' He was anxious not to attract the fat madwoman's attention.

'There's that dreadful man,' Miss Phipps exclaimed,

17

clutching ferociously at a log of wood. 'A ghastly creature who leered at me on the road! Yes! He deliberately leered.'

Dancy Smith screamed with laughter. 'Why, that's Snow, missus. A decent cove 'e is. Hey, Snow, come in and meet the girl friend.'

Miss Phipps could not draw herself up any straighter because of her fat, but, seizing the kerosene tin on which she was seated, she waddled over to the far corner of the hall in a very haughty way and muttered something about 'depraved wretches.'

'Don't take any notice,' the busker advised. He tapped his forehead, and Snow nodded understandingly, if cautiously. He returned to the porch and began building his fire for the mutton.

'Hey, play us something,' the Stray urged the owner of the guitar, and that youth, nothing loth, elevated his face and gave vent to a long, keening howl which, he informed them in the subsequent song, was part of his habit of 'yoo-delling as I go.'

'The Yodelling Rouseabout, that's me,' he explained in answer to the Stray's praise. 'That's the name I'm going to go under when I'm singing at the Tivoli. No, I'm not the sort of chap to spend me life on the roads. Experience, that's all it is. So I can say I been out and collected all the real Australian songs the bushmen sing. That's the ticket! Make up my own songs. Sing 'em round picture-shows, got up in a cowboy suit. Grab half the takings.' He raised his voice as though to overrule objection. 'Look at Tex Morton. Thousands he's making out of records alone.'

'Not fousands?' The Stray was awestruck.

'Well, money, anyway,' the busker conceded. He thought, his forehead wrinkled. 'I'm not too keen on the Yodelling Rouseabout. I need a good selling title.'

'How about the Busking Bum?' the Stray suggested.

The busker looked at her scornfully and plunged into another long-drawn yodel.

'I'm a poor lonely stockman . . ." (he sang) " away from
    my ho-ome,
And I promised my mother no more I would roo-oam.'

He paused modestly. 'I made that up myself. Poetry,
see?'

Snow, now that his fire was well alight, had drifted
inside to contribute his applause. 'There's a bloody song
I always wanted to hear, and I never knew its bloody
name,' he said pleasantly.

'Please!' Miss Phipps rose from her seat in the corner.
'Stop that foul language.'

Snow looked injured. 'What bloody foul language?' he
asked.

'She's not responsible,' the busker said consolingly.

'Oh!' Snow was mollified. 'Well, this (*adjective*) song
was about an (*adjectival*) bagman who was getting himself
a bit of meat. . . .'

The busker nodded somewhat contemptuously. 'Waltz-
ing Matilda, the Australian National Anthem. The dogs
bark it.'

'You know it?'

'Of course, I know it.' He burst into song:

'Down came a jumbuck to drink at the billabong,
    Up jumped the swagman and grabbed him with glee.
And he sang as he shoved that jumbuck in his tucker-bag . . .
    You'll come a-waltzing Matilda with me.'

'That's it. That's it all right,' Snow exclaimed excitedly.
'I ain't but heard it the once.'

'Down came the squatter mounted on his thoroughbred,
    Down came the troopers, one, two, three,
"Where's that jolly jumbuck you've got in your tucker-bag?
    You'll come a-waltzing Matilda with me."'

Miss Phipps, at the sound of Duke's strong, not un-
melodious baritone raised in this worn ballad, had
approached out of her corner, forgetful of her ruffled

feelings. Now, as he broke into the chorus, she joined in, singing a deep contralto second that blended with the busker's voice like organ music. The look of astonishment that spread over his face was comical, but he strummed to the last line.

'Hey,' he said, laying the guitar aside. 'Can you do that to any tune? Sing harmony, I mean?'

'Of course,' Miss Phipps said haughtily. 'If I hear it once.'

'It's a gift.' The busker looked at her admiringly. 'You'd be a knockout outside the pubs on a Saturday afternoon. Why!' Illumination burst over him. 'It's new. "The Singing Girl Tramp." We'd coin money.' He rubbed his dark chin enthusiastically. 'We'd block the traffic.'

'How dare you suggest,' Miss Phipps said haughtily, 'that I should sing in the street!'

'Now, Dora,' the busker urged, 'you know me. Would I suggest anything to a woman with a voice like yours that didn't do me credit? Would I . . .'

'You're an impertinent young man.'

The busker dropped his cajoling manner. 'Now, look here,' he said. 'I can use you in my act, see? Why, when we get to Logan, and Paul Seeby hears the two of us, he'll snatch at us with both hands.'

Miss Phipps' languor was that of a film star being offered a contract for garbage removal.

'Arr,' the busker said disgustedly, 'you've got tickets all over yourself.'

Miss Phipps, never slow to resent any personal slight, gave him in return her opinion of his chances of joining even a tent-show, while its owner was in his right mind. She spoke scathingly of 'young boys' who slept under bridges and talked as though they amounted to something. She traced the busker's lack of taste and social decorum to an inborn baseness. Just as she was warming to her subject, Snow tactfully attempted to change the conversation.

20

'Play that there bloody song again,' he suggested.

Miss Phipps turned her discourse to Snow, his language and habits, but it was a very different matter abusing Snow. Knowing himself innocent of offence, he merely let out a roar of rage.

'Shuddup!' he bellowed. 'I ain't hit a lady yet, but you ain't a lady.'

Whereupon Miss Phipps retreated to the church porch, looked out at the rain, which was drumming on the tin roof with a thunderous deliberation, decided it was too wet to shake the mud of the church off her feet, and so stood, ignoring her fellow-refugees and by the tilt of her snub nose indicating that the air of the church was tainted.

Snow, for his part, was half afraid to go and tend the mutton which he had left in his camp-oven on the porch. He noticed with some bitterness that, while Miss Phipps had withdrawn herself from the low circle he disgraced, she was warming her toes at his fire and was sniffing, not without ardour, the smell of his mutton. When he did come out to see how the roast was cooking, Miss Phipps did not remove herself, but overlooked his work with a proprietorial air.

'I see you are a good cook,' she observed in much the same tone she had said 'Good doggie' to Bluey.

'Yeah,' Snow grunted. He did not venture any more words. There was, it seemed, something about his voice she didn't like. Well, there was no accounting for tastes, but she needn't treat a man as though he was dirt.

'Is that your meat?' Miss Phipps asked even more affably.

'Yeah.'

'Why, you dear man!'

Snow was a little surprised at this change of front. He turned inside, afraid that it might be the forerunner of a new attack.

But Miss Phipps only began to practise dance-steps on the porch. 'It keeps the figure in good trim,' she observed to the Stray, who had trotted out open-mouthed to watch. 'One should never neglect one's figure. Nor the eyebrows. I don't suppose you have an eyebrow-plucker, dear? No, I thought not. So unfortunate that I left mine at that disgusting farm where they said I wouldn't suit after just two days. And such coarse people. If I hadn't spent my money staying at the hotel I would have taken the train to Sydney. But there is nothing—nothing—like exercise in the open air.' She looked down complacently at her bulk. 'I've slightly put on flesh. I used to be in the ballet, you know.'

'Go wan.' Dancy was impressed.

'That was years ago, of course. But the people with whom one had to associate! Not elevating at all.'

She waddled over, lifted the lid of the camp-oven un-invited, and finding it hot, dropped it with a cry in the ashes. Snow came out, replaced the lid and went quietly inside again.

'An unpleasant type,' Miss Phipps said disdainfully.

But the Stray was beginning to have a shrewd idea that Miss Phipps was not as mad as appearance might indicate. 'He ain't unpleasant,' she said stoutly. 'He's a good bloke to be wiv. What's more, that's *his* meat.' And she also went inside.

'True, true,' Miss Phipps murmured. 'One must suffer politely the manners of one's host.'

No one had indicated that Snow was in any way intend-ing to be her host; nevertheless, when the mutton was done, she had graciously and by imperceptible gradations circled closer and closer to the roast. She accepted her portion without actually throwing it in its owner's face, while she contrived at the same time to indicate that she was cutting him dead. She had two helpings to everyone else's one, and was standing ready with her empty plate —the plate also belonged to Snow—for the last morsel and the last bone.

'Thank you, deah,' she cooed to Dancy, when that out-raged damsel asked sarcastically if 'Phippsy' would like any more. It was impossible to snub Miss Phipps at meal-times.

'Well'—the busker flopped his hair back from his brow and looked round the circle cynically—'quite a happy family, huh? Long may we cling together like the ivy.'

Had he but been told that he was speaking prophecy, he would have fled in a panic.

Chapter III

I

THE frequency of nervous breakdowns among police sergeants in the Middle West can be traced largely to their responsibility for distributing unemployed relief in its various forms of relief work, dole or track rations. The police dislike administering the unemployment relief because it means so much work. They stand between the devillings of the 'dole-chasers' on the one hand and the deep sea of the Chief Secretary's files and enquiries on the other. The unemployed dislike the police administering relief because they are police.

Any sergeant will tell you that 'the locals'—that is, the unemployed residing in the town—are bad enough. But the 'travellers'—meaning the men with track-cards who wander the country in search of work, getting their food-orders from declared 'dole stations' in towns fifty or sixty miles apart—the travellers are worse. It is the duty of the police, or so they interpret it, to keep the travellers 'on the move,' never to let them settle in a town or stay too long in one place, to drive them on, to keep them circulating as a labour force, thousands strong, drifting hungrily about the country.

There are only two kinds of sergeants in the mid-west: the 'soft' variety, who will listen to a man's tale of woe and let him stay in a town more than a fortnight, and the 'tough' variety, whose chief joy is to 'hunt' bagmen, swagmen, sundowners, hoboes, or whatever their local appellation may be. It is the dream of every such sergeant to get his town a reputation for 'toughness,' so that travellers will go a hundred miles out of their way rather than apply for rations at his station.

No one welcomes the bagman. The local unemployed watch jealously lest he get a job, the police lest he show signs of lingering, the charitable lest he impose on their charity, and the shopkeeper lest he steal. In these circumstances it is little to be wondered at that the bagman has also become 'tough.'

Among the sixty travellers with whom the sergeant of Currawong was to deal that dull, cold Thursday morning were: Miss Phipps, who had not bothered to take out a track-card because she had not 'heard of such a thing,' although she was registered for dole in Sydney and was there to prove it; the Stray, who had no card of her own but was part of her vanished husband's card, furious that he should be drawing dole for her as well as himself; and Snow, drawing dole for himself and wife. Snow had kept his old track-card from the time his wife was travelling with him. Just how he had done it was a mystery, since his wife was drawing dole for herself and children a hundred miles away; but there he was on 'B' scale, and regretting that he was not wangling extra rations for a couple of children while he was about it.

There is probably no more depressing spectacle than a police-station on a dull winter morning, and the police-station of Currawong was a cheap, yellow brick structure of such peculiar hideousness that it gave the beholder the feeling that his eye had stubbed its toe. On this particular dole-day the temper of the sergeant matched the building. He had the expression of one who has spent a night in the cells by mistake and is brooding over it. He had just received a nasty departmental note expressing surprise at the immense sums needed by the town of Currawong for food relief and laying the blame for this extravagant expenditure at the sergeant's door. He was, the letter hinted, spending money with a spade.

'Jim,' the sergeant said to his constable, 'I'm going to have a clean-up.' He shook his head despondently. 'Where all these bagmen come from beats me. The locals are bad enough, but bagmen seem to pop up out of hollow logs. You think you've got them all cleaned out of your town, and a fresh bunch sprouts after the rain.' He settled himself officially at his desk. 'We'll get the locals over first, Jim, then the single bagmen, then the married ones.'

The men began to shuffle forward to receive the orders for the rations which they would collect in the afternoon when the lists were sent down to the stores. The routine questions about how much each applicant had earned in the last fourteen days were snapped out with an unusual energy and, from the enquiry as to what quantities of bread or meat the bagmen required, you would have thought the sergeant proposed to live on the rations himself. After each brief interview he marked the applicant's name on the list to be sent to the baker, butcher and storekeeper, and handed the man's track-card to the constable, who filled in the name of the police-station and the issuing officer. As he did so, he intoned the warning:

'Only one dole here, you know. Move on for the next issue.'

By the time he had worked down through the single bagmen the word had gone forth that the sergeant was on the war-path. Snow, who had past experience of many sergeants, had made his arrangements.

'You ain't goin' to get anything out of the sergeant if his liver's gone bad on him,' he advised the Stray. 'So you're my old woman for the time bein' if anyone asks, see? If he finds you're on your own, he'll probably vag you.'

The Stray nodded vigorously. She had been declared a vagrant once in the city, and she had no intention of going through that painful process again.

It was with a feeling that Providence had him in its

25

care that Snow, as the constable shouted 'Grimshaw,' stepped forward.

'B scale, eh?' the sergeant growled. 'Where's your wife?'

'She's just outside, holding the horse, sergeant,' Snow drawled.

'Go out and see,' the sergeant ordered his constable, who, wondering why his chief did not call the woman in, reluctantly strode on to the station verandah.

'That's 'er,' Snow pointed.

The Stray was vigorously addressing a small, wizened man who had just alighted from a battered sulky; and the unemployed, still waiting to be interviewed, were lounging within earshot, trying to disguise their delighted grins.

'Why, you dirty, rotten, bludging, little mongrel!' The Stray's shrill voice was sufficiently raised to carry farther than the police-station verandah. 'You low-down offal! Why, for two pins I'd knock you so cold, you'd fink you was the North Pole.'

Mrs. Smith had discovered her errant spouse. He was bitterly trying to explain that he had, after his flare of temper subsided, gone back to look for her and that she was nowhere to be found; but his voice was drowned in the flow of her reproaches.

The constable hastened down the path, and at his coming the Stray's voice died away. She waited, raging silently, her fists clenched.

'Are you Mrs. Grimshaw?' The constable wasted no time.

'Yes, I am.'

'You this man's wife?' The constable indicated Snow to make quite sure.

'Yes, I am.'

Here the wizened Mr. Smith interposed. 'Wait on, sergeant,' he pleaded, deliberately elevating the constable's rank. 'She ain't no such thing. She's my missus, not his.'

'Hey, what's all this?' the constable demanded, aggrieved. 'Who do you think I am? Solomon?'

'I tell you she's my wife.'

'I ain't so.'

This was even better than the audience had hoped. It drew into a ring.

'Cut 'er in 'alves,' someone advised.

'Well, you better come and settle it inside.' Dividing one wife between two travellers was out of the constable's line. He herded the three into the charge-room and briefly explained to the sergeant. Mr. Smith stated his case concisely and well. He had left Sydney with this, his lawful wife, and lost her down the track.

'Ask 'im if 'e was ever married to me,' the Stray urged. 'G'wan, sergeant.'

'Were you ever married to her?' The sergeant passed his hand wearily across his brow.

Mr. Smith hesitated.

'There, see! 'E knows damn well he wasn't. I'm wiv me own bloke again, and 'e knows it. 'E's just scared you'll take his card off 'im, that's all.'

It did not matter to the sergeant whose head was offered up, but he was determined that someone was going to expiate that letter from his superiors.

'I'm going to charge him.' He reached for his pen. 'I'm going to make an example of this man. Give me that card of his, Jim.'

As Snow and Stray went hastily away from the station, the pleadings of the betrayed husband were falling on deaf ears.

Outside Snow drew a long breath. 'This'll be a good town to get out of,' he suggested.

'You ain't goin' to leave me?' the Stray asked desperately. ''E'll just about murder me.'

Snow scratched his head in perplexity as he glanced down at her. She looked even plainer than when she had first walked into his camp. Her wispy fair hair hung lank over his ragged old coat. Her toothless mouth hung open in suspense and, with her almost white eyebrows and red-rimmed eyes, Snow thought he had never seen a plainer girl. If she had been pretty, his problem might have been simpler.

'No, I ain't goin' to leave you,' he said slowly. 'Hop in the van.'

He left her giving a lurid embroidery of the facts to the busker, who had been holding the horse. He himself strolled back to the gate of the police-station to await the discomfited Mr. Smith; and when the wizened little man emerged, Snow suggested that they go down to the hotel and have a beer. Mr. Smith, with a wistful glance towards the Stray, whom it had been his intention to strangle with his bare hands, agreed to the suggestion, adding that the sergeant could not cut him off the dole for being in the pub, as he had cut him off the dole already, thanks to that little. . . . In the midst of his delineation of the Stray's character Snow led him away.

The disastrous loss of his track-card did not seem to be affecting Mr. Smith as bitterly as he made out. He was only thankful that he had been able to melt the sergeant's determination to charge him with fraudulent practice. The sergeant had himself been inclined to believe the story of Mr. Smith, and that was what Snow had been wanting to find out. His decision to leave Currawong just as soon as he got his rations that afternoon seemed more and more the right one.

'On'y this mornin',' the injured Mr. Smith confided, 'I got a letter from a pal in Sydney givin' me the chance to train his greyhounds. I was goin' back to the city anyway.' A gleam of hope came into his eye. 'If I cud get rid of the sulky. But there ain't no sales for sulkies in a dead town like this. Cost me ten pounds that turnout did.' He looked sideways at Snow.

'Come off it,' Snow said. From the Stray, Snow knew the sulky and horse had cost Ricky Smith nothing, that the horse was a jib, and the sulky falling to pieces. 'Come off it.'

'If I had me fare to Sydney,' Mr. Smith confided, 'I'd let the turnout go at a loss.'

Snow considered. If he bought the turnout, horse, sulky and harness, from Ricky Smith, he might be able to sell it at a profit. He was a handy man and he could mend the sulky. He might even give it a coat of paint. As for the horse, if he couldn't pass off a jib horse on some farmer's son, his name wasn't Theodore Grimshaw.

'I'll give you ten bob,' he declared, draining his mug, 'for the lot.'

Mr. Smith looked pained. 'Gosh! You're hard. Why, I paid——'

'I know what you paid. Nothin'.'

Mr. Smith was silent for a moment, then he began again. 'That little . . .'

Snow stopped him. 'You gotta take 'er back with you.'

Mr. Smith swore a mighty oath. 'Not if I was dyin',' he declared. 'Not after what she done to me. And that ain't the only thing she done . . .' He was ready to launch into a further tale of his woes.

'If it was worth a quid, I'd take it,' Snow asserted. 'But it ain't worth it.'

'Make it thirty bob, mate. And that's Dancy thrown in,' Mr. Smith said magnanimously. 'I ought to charge more for 'er. A fine girl like that.'

'No, you don't,' Snow said hastily. 'She don't mean nothin' in my life. I'm married, and my wife's the sort that knows everythin', if it happened in Timbuctoo.'

'Well, what of it?' Ricky Smith argued. 'I've got a wife in Sydney meself.'

'Thirty bob if you take the Stray off me hands.'

'I'll take a quid and you can keep 'er. It's worth ten bob just to get rid of 'er.'

'Who said I was going to give you a quid anyway?'

'You did.'

'My oath I didn't.'

They argued further, and it was finally agreed that for fifteen shillings Snow became the owner of the horse, harness and sulky and also any camping gear packed in it.

'You're getting a bargain,' were Mr. Smith's final words as he went off to enquire when the goods train departed. 'And I only hope,' he added, 'that you treat Dancy the way she deserves. With a buckle on the strap.'

II

The tradesmen of a dole-town always take turns to supply rations to the travellers, and they do it with great caution and politeness. The way the travellers come in and thump on the counter and demand service, you would think they were all rich station-owners. They crowd out the regular customers, they sit about chatting to each other, they leave parcels to be minded, and, should the opportunity offer, they help themselves.

One Chinese storekeeper always set a boy specially to watch the travellers, but even this precautionary measure was of little use. He kept a big glass bowl full of coloured soap-cakes on one end of his counter, and late in the afternoon of one dole-day he noticed there was just one soap-cake remaining in the bottom of the bowl.

'I thought I told you to watch those travellers,' he demanded angrily of the boy. 'Why didn't you see them?'

'I can see them all right,' the boy responded thoughtfully. 'But I can't see through them.'

The crowd in the shop had manœuvred between him and the soap-takers in such a way that they screened all depredations. Another storekeeper had once foolishly left on display such desirable articles as shoeing-pincers and horse-collars. A traveller would back against the display table with his sack held open behind him, and casually sweep what he wanted into it. When the storekeeper realised what was happening, he closed the shop doors. But he had to let people in, and then those inside would get out. It was a proverb in Currawong: 'Hold an eel in one hand and a bagman in the other.'

The storekeepers tried everything. When the food-order system first began, one astute merchant had little slips made out reading: 'Give bearer goods to the value of (say) 5 shillings.' This was to be presented at the counter. But a brainy young lare called 'the mob' together on the pavement outside the shop. 'This can be worked, can't it?' he asked, displaying his slip. When the counter assistants began to get too many vouchers for fifteen shillings instead of five shillings, one went to the boss. By that time most of the travellers had 'got away with it.'

Such things do not happen to storekeepers who are 'good for a bite.' A grocer who treats the bagman decently is usually respected; and if the men want a handful of potatoes, they take them from someone else. It is the storekeeper who is hard and 'tough', the man who adds a halfpenny or a penny to the price of every article the bagmen need, who has to watch his customers. The storekeepers know the bagmen dare not complain to the police about the price of goods supplied to them. If one did, he would get no tobacco. The storekeeper could refuse to put in tobacco as part of the food order, and a bagman would sooner do without food than a smoke. A grocer was not legally supposed to supply tobacco on a relief order.

This the manager of Selby & Heems was trying to explain to a woman who had demanded a two-ounce tin of the cheap, strong weed that, from the taste, might be anything from horse-dung to dried rope. 'I ain't had a smoke in two weeks,' she was saying piteously. 'Gee, can't you stretch a point?'

'Sorry,' the manager said firmly. 'We can't supply tobacco.' He was a preacher of the local Methodist church, and he disapproved of women smoking. Had her husband brought the food order, it might have been different. 'The sergeant won't allow it.'

'Well, if I was to go and see the sergeant . . .' The woman was beginning again, when the manager with a brisk 'That's a good idea,' moved away to serve other

31

customers. The woman watched him quite openly take down two tins of tobacco and give them to men who had food orders, and her face flushed with rage.

'I'll teach the . . .' Unfair and illegitimate son of a low-class female dog, she was understood to remark by those around; and with a lightning movement swept two packets of tea off the counter, and departed to sell them to the keeper of the Greek café across the street. With the two-and-fourpence so obtained she bought tobacco. It is to be regretted that the travellers in the shop sympathetically covered her retreat.

'Why shouldn't a woman have tobacco?' one man remarked to his mate. 'I guess if she wants it, she's got a right to it.'

He was gazing through the wire gauze that walled off the delicatessen section into a big, fly-proof room. In front of him was a square sliding panel through which purchases could be handed to the customer; and just inside the panel was a cheese of monstrous proportions.

'Look at that cheese,' he said wistfully. 'Big as a buggy wheel it is.'

'Ar,' his mate said bitterly, 'we wouldn't have nothin' left on our order if we started getting cheese and such.'

But his mate continued to gaze through the gauze. 'Got a knife, Jim?' he asked presently.

'Yes. But it's pretty blunt.'

'Give it here.'

There were people passing to and fro; attendants busily dashing from one end of the shop to the other.

'What are you goin' to do with it?'

For reply the cheese-lover cautiously slid open the little window in the gauze and began to saw the cheese. His mate moved up to shelter his movements from the observation of those in the shop.

'It's as big as your head,' he whispered. 'They'll notice it sure.'

But the cheese-fiend sawed away until he had cut the cheese in halves, and deftly extricated them one at a time.

'Put 'em in the sack, Bill,' he whispered back.

'I tell you we'll never get it out of the shop.' Protesting, Bill dropped the cheese into the sack, then, as the attendant bore down on them, he neatly kicked the sack under a set of shelves to be retrieved later. The attendant glared at the two suspiciously, but they were empty-handed and innocent-looking.

'Your order been taken?' he asked civilly enough. And they gave their order.

Snow was waiting impatiently at the other end of the shop. If there was one thing Snow disliked, it was camping near a town with what he called 'a big mob.' He had little camps of his own farther out, and he wanted to get away before the short winter dusk closed down.

There was one old swagman holding up the crowd of ration-seekers, all of them as impatient as Snow. The old man had twopence left on his grocery order, and he was determined to get its full worth.

'Have I got down tea?' he asked the girl serving him.

'Yes, you've got tea.'

'Have I got sugar?' There were signs of restlessness in the waiting throng.

'Yes, you've got that, too.'

'Well, I don't know, missus.' He scratched his grey head apologetically. 'I'm sure to think of something in a minute.'

Someone in the crowd shouted: 'Put down a couple of packets of salts, miss. That'll shift him.'

Appreciative laughter greeted this brilliant flash of wit, but the old man was not at all disturbed.

'That's it,' he said, beaming. 'Salt, a pound of salt. I knew there was something.'

Snow sighed wearily. At his elbow another old man with his few miserable parcels in the usual gunny-sack was advising one of the wealthiest graziers in the district what tea to buy.

'You want to buy Marvel's tea,' the old man insisted. 'That other stuff is no good to you. Twenty years ago I

33

used to travel for Marvel's.' He straightened a little as he said it.

The grazier smiled. 'If they're such a good firm, why aren't you travelling for them now?'

The old man returned his smile a little bitterly. 'I've got a better job. I'm an inspector of roads.'

'Well,' the grazier said, 'you'd better come out and inspect the road to my place. It could do with it.' He was turning away when he flung back: 'What tea do you use, brother?'

'Oh,' the old man said, 'I use knocker tea. I get everything else on the dole and knock on the doors for my tea.' He nodded good-bye in a friendly way, then turned in search of further conversation to Snow. Not until Snow indicated the packet did he realise that the grazier, as he went out, had ordered some Marvel tea for the old man as well as for himself.

'Weren't you camped just the other side of Mallee Scrubs last year with a big brown horse?' the old chap asked, as he gathered up the tea.

Snow nodded briefly and turned to give in his order. He should have asked which way the old man had come and which way he was heading, but he was impatient to get away, and did not wish to engage in the courtesies of enquiring how the feed was through the way the traveller had come or what the police were like at such-and-such a town.

Outside he found the busker absorbed in a newspaper. 'They're going to make the bagmen localise at last,' he greeted Snow.

'Eh?'

'Going to put them all in labour camps and flog them till they work. It says so here.'

'Aw. Just a lot of guff.' Snow looked at the busker questioningly. 'I thought you'd of got a lift by now, or be waiting for a train or something.'

'Well, so I might,' the busker said defensively. 'But it struck me you'd probably want someone to drive that sulky.' He affected a lofty unconcern. 'Take it or leave it. I haven't done so badly. Made five bob and got warned off twice.'

Snow thought. 'The girl could drive the sulky,' he said. 'It's hers by right, I guess.'

'She doesn't want to. Told me she was "scared to deaf of the bleedin' 'orse".' The busker by now knew the full story of the Stray.

Snow thought again. It was plain that the Stray had taken unto herself power to add to their numbers. She had instigated the busker's offer. On the other hand, Duke would be masculine moral support.

'I don't care who comes,' Snow said deliberately. 'As long as it ain't that ruddy, potato-faced Dora Phipps. She grates on me'—he thought deeply—'like a rim-bound wheel.' He pushed half the parcels on to the busker. 'C'mon.'

III

All up and down the street the alien infiltration in the town was plain to be seen. Shabby-looking men, with the half-defiant cheerfulness or the tired slinking of the un-wanted, crouched in little groups on the edge of the gutter, talking and smoking and comparing 'handouts' and 'bites' and good towns and 'hungry tracks.' Not only men but the women and children of the travellers waited about the street corners. The men who travelled with their families mostly owned some means of conveyance—old sulkies, carts, vans or broken-down motor-trucks. They were the aristocracy of the track, ranking above the single men who rode bicycles or jumped trains, or merely walked and begged lifts, although you could not have persuaded any of these latter that it was so. The single bagmen called the men with families 'horse-bagmen', and accused them of living on the earnings of their wives and children. The women 'faked' small articles, such as clothes-hangers, pot-holders and jug-covers, and the children went out selling with their mothers. They were worn, hard-faced, loud-voiced women for the most part, and the children, whining about their skirts, were all suffering from running colds and sores. Their clothes were obviously assembled from half a dozen charities in half a dozen different towns. The women, too, as they waited, exchanged the gossip of the track, advising each other of soft-hearted farmers or house-holders who could be coaxed into buying trifles from pity or who would give old clothes.

'The town's pretty full,' the busker observed.

'It's the sergeant's fault,' Snow answered. 'Why couldn't they send the lists down from the station? Keeping this mob waiting half the afternoon before they could get their rations.'

The busker eyed the 'dole-chasers' critically. His mind was running on the vague item in the newspaper. All over the country he had seen such men as these, footing it with a swag over their shoulder or jogging along with their wives and children in old vans. It is easy enough to pick a traveller by the sharpened, hungry face of him. He is either toothless or his gums have drawn back from his teeth, giving him the look of a wolf. His lips have drawn back dry and cracked and stiff in a perpetual half-snarl; the skin of his face is stretched taut as vellum over the projecting bones and is burnt almost black by the sun. His eyes under an old felt hat are sharp pinpoints in a network of glare-wrinkles. He is bitter against society, but unswervingly loyal to his mates; dull and suspicious at any hint of patronage, but talkative and shrewd enough to his equals; at enmity with all police, but courteous to strangers; passionately generous and open-handed; a liar when it suits him, and a trusty friend. A man able to walk along the knife-edge of starvation and make a joke of it.

'I wouldn't like to be the one to put these coves into a labour camp,' the busker decided slowly.

'Arr, they've been talking labour camps for years,' Snow said contemptuously. 'They won't ever do anything about it. Ever driven a horse?'

'Well, no,' the busker admitted, somewhat startled. 'But you just hold the reins, don't you?'

36

Snow made no answer. He rather liked Duke, and he was cheerful company, which was more than could be said of the Stray, who had been sitting in the cold waiting for them and was inclined to be bitter about it.

Snow knew of a camp three miles out of Currawong, on the way to Milidgee, and it was, like all his camps, secluded from the road and known to but a few travellers. So secluded that he considered it unlikely that pests such as Miss Phipps, ignorant of these parts, would ever find it. But if he hoped to dodge Miss Phipps by such a simple little device, he was mistaken. The cortège had left the town behind it and was plodding slowly up a steep hill, when Snow, with a startled oath, spied a figure with a sack in one hand and a small, blackened billy in the other, waiting at the top of the hill.

'It's her,' he said morosely, remembering how Miss Phipps the night before had loftily refused the loan of any bedding and had lain down in the church porch, after piling on the fire all the wood he had dragged up, and how, in the middle of the night, he had been roused in time to extinguish the wooden wall of the church porch where it had caught alight.

'Let's just drive by,' the Stray suggested comfortably. She had settled down beside Snow in the van, leaving Harley Duke to drive the sulky.

But it was far from Miss Phipps's intention to be left behind. 'Ah-ha, there you are at last, dear people,' she called, waving her bundle in a way that caused the sulky horse to start and swerve. 'You have been a long time. Now, I suppose I ride in the sulky. How kind of you to have foreseen, Mister Snow, that you would need extra accommodation. Don't you dare hit that horse, Mr. Duke. I won't see any poor animal ill-treated. I'll break the whip over your head first.'

'Either shut up or walk,' the exasperated youth was replying, but Miss Phipps had heaved her cumbersome form into the sulky.

'I suppose it ain't no good,' Snow said pessimistically.

At the very next town, he was thinking, he would sell the sulky, give the Stray half the money to get back to the city and free himself of all this so-suddenly-acquired and unwelcome company. The Stray, he thought, was anyway a damn sight better than the madwoman who had attached herself to the party. He could hear Miss Phipps's unceasing flow of talk floating back from the sulky which had gone ahead.

'I followed Mr. Snow's advice and made the sergeant give me a track-card, so that I could travel from town to town,' she was saying. 'He seemed, queerly enough, to be relieved. But it's shameful how little these stores give you for a five-shilling order. Things are much cheaper in the city. By the time I had bought a pound of raisins, and some cigarettes, and a packet of Health-Wheat and some nuts—so good for the figure and full of vitamins— and a pot of face-cream and some chocolates, it was all gone. However, I intend to put my All in the common fund and share it with you good people. Leave that horse alone!'

'Who's driving the horse? Get out and walk if you don't like it.'

'I'd sooner walk than ride with a rude, overbearing boor. Stop beating that horse.'

'I wasn't beating her. I just drew the whip across her flank.'

'I'll teach you to be cruel to animals.' Miss Phipps had seized the whip and was endeavouring to beat Duke across the head with it.

'Look out!' Snow shouted. 'Hey, you bloody rat-bag!' He would not have made this obvious remark except under the stress of anxiety. The horse, its driver's attention distracted by the unpleasant assault, had wheeled round and was backing the sulky over the edge of a deep ditch. Miss Phipps had stood up, exasperated by the tight clutch which the busker maintained on the butt of the whip. She found herself flung sideways, as the sulky tilted at an angle and, with a loud shriek, fell heavily, escaping the

38

wheel by inches. The horse, abandoning its intention of dashing the sulky backwards, strained suddenly forward again, jolting Mr. Duke face downwards over its rump, and then bolted down the road.

'Hang on to the bloody reins,' Snow yelled; and whether the shaken busker heard him or not, he clung in his fright to the reins, as though they were his only hold on life, as indeed they were.

The two watching could scarcely breathe; but as the sulky hurtled round the bend, the busker was holding just as firmly to his end of the reins as the horse was to the bit.

'Mi-Gord!' Snow wiped his brow. 'What a mess!' He glanced at the moaning bulk of Miss Phipps, who, in a scatter of nuts and raisins, and with Health-Wheat in her hair, lay half in and half out of the ditch. 'I hope she's broken her flamin' neck.'

'Don't you dare use that language,' a feeble voice responded.

'Leave 'er there,' Snow said harshly. 'Let's see what's happened to the kid.'

But the Stray had sprung down and was supporting Miss Phipps's head. 'You all right, dearie?' she was asking unnecessarily. It was obvious that Miss Phipps was more frightened than hurt. 'You can't leave 'er 'ere, Snowy.' Dancy turned doubtfully to the van's owner.

'Well, help me shove her in the back.' He bundled Miss Phipps in, while she cried out that her back was broken.

Snow was more worried about the busker. He pushed Don to his fastest pace, hoping against hope that no smashed wreckage would greet his eyes when he rounded the bend. Instead he beheld the busker trotting back with the horse under control. Snow felt that never before had he heaved such a sigh of relief.

'I've raised a fam'ly,' he rumbled, 'and I've knocked round the west for thirty years, and that was the craziest damn thing I ever seen.'

'I will not have cruelty to animals,' a weak voice retorted from behind him. 'And I will report both of you to the R.S.P.C.A.'

'Drive on,' the busker said, still white about the lips, but grinning in a sickly way. 'Troubles were sent to try us.' His hands were shaking as he turned the horse's head. He addressed his steed. 'Come on, Horehound.'

'Don't you dare call it that name. I'll get out and walk.'

'Shut up,' Snow roared, 'or I'll finish off the job the 'orse ought to a done.'

There was a blessed silence and peace as they headed through the gathering dusk towards Snow's chosen camp.

Chapter IV

SNOW failed to sell Ricky Smith's turnout in Bylong, and it was due to the Horehound's fault that he did. The mare was a big, clumsy half-draught with a wicked eye and a will of her own. She was cunning. She would clop along untiringly and sedately for days; and then, when opportunity offered, stage a scene that made the tantrums of a prima donna look like a church service. She would sit down in the road, walk round in circles, refuse to be caught, gallop in hobbles as much as ten miles over the roughest country. Snow had cured her of sidling round and round in a circle by sneaking up on her blind side, as she came round, and catching her an unmerciful blow with a log of wood that nearly stunned her. He had hopes in time of ridding himself of that mare at a profit seven times over. What he did despair of was ridding himself of his three hangers-on, particularly Miss Phipps.

He must shake them off before he reached home. There would be too many questions asked if he didn't. The busker was waging a private war with the Horehound and was determined to fight it out to a finish. He could have caught a train down to Logan at any time, but he preferred to stay with Snow. He liked Snow for some queer reason, and Snow rather liked him. As for the Stray, she had fulfilled her boast of being a good beggar. Something about the abject look of her stirred charity, and she would return from a tour of any little settlement with eggs, stale bread, broken biscuits, old clothes and, sometimes, even meat and butter. She was industrious about a camp, friendly and good-tempered. To offset these advantages, she was also a most mischievous liar and, at the moment, engaged in a discreet search of Snow's possessions, being convinced that he must be a person of hidden wealth.

Snow was not worried by her probing about for a secret pocket in the van, since there was no pocket nor any hidden wealth to find. He tolerated the Stray as other men might a badly trained puppy; but he could not endure Miss Phipps. Neither could the Stray; nor the busker. Ways of getting rid of Miss Phipps occupied all their minds.

The trouble with Miss Phipps was that she knew when she was well off. She still limped about ostentatiously with the help of a stick, and this annoyed them all the more, as Miss Phipps could waddle fast enough if a meal was toward. Never once had she offered to help in the work of the camp. She sat and brewed innumerable cups of tea or coffee for herself in the filthy little billy she had always on the fire. She borrowed everyone's tobacco, ate of the best, and was abusive into the bargain. By contrast, Dancy and Duke looked like angels of light; and at Bylong, after one particularly painful passage of arms, Snow called Duke aside to consider measures for ending the menace.

'We could ask the sergeant to send her to a home for loonies,' the busker suggested morosely.

Snow shook his head. 'I wouldn't put no one behind bars,' he replied slowly. 'I been there meself.' He stroked the head of Bluey. 'You see that there dog. Well, once when I'd gone in for meat, that there dog came and waited outside for me for six weeks. The sergeant was one of them talkative coots what try to get bagmen to be confidential, see? He'd got his stripes out of information bagmen give him, top-offs that thought he was a good cove. But he didn't catch me. When he found I wasn't sayin' nothin', he turned nasty. "I'll teach you to keep your mouth shut," he said, and he cuts down on me rations. I wasn't gettin' nothin' but bread and water. "Keep it up," I says, "I've only got a month to go, and a man can do without any food for four weeks." But what made me mad was that poor bloody dog o' mine. He was on'y getting scraps that I'd chuck him through the little winder in the cell, and you could count every rib of him when I got out.' He gave a dry chuckle. 'You could pretty near count every rib on me.' He shook his head again. 'No, I wouldn't put no one behind bars.'

He considered for a moment. 'Hain't she got no people?'

The busker deftly appropriated his tobacco. 'Would you want to get her back if she belonged to you?'

'Gawd, no!'

'Well, there you are. Maybe her people died of the shock of losing her.'

There was a silence. No more ideas seemed to be forthcoming.

Snow regarded the busker lazily. 'How did you come to be on the track, son?' he asked. There were times when the busker's swagger and bluster dropped from him and faint traces of another layer showed through.

'Me?' The busker rolled himself a cigarette. 'I was led astray. There I was with a good job, waiter at Sherry's Hotel, trying to get on at a radio station in my spare time. You see, I'd been educated at one of these expensive colleges, and when the Dad died—went bankrupt and shot himself—I'd never learnt anything except to row in the eight; there was hardly any money for mother, so I got this job as a waiter, and then, as I was saying, this public dinner——'

42

Snow was bewildered. 'What dinner?'

'Aren't I telling you? A bang-up affair for all the distinguished blokes in the city of Melbourne. If they didn't have a string of letters after their name, they had a Sir or Right Honourable in front of it. There were aldermen and politicians and university professors and big business heads, and I said to myself, "Hallo," I said . . .'

He paused reflectively and shook his head.

'Well, get on with it,' Snow demanded impatiently.

'Well, I think, see, that now I'll have a chance to find out just how these big bugs get to be big bugs. So I keep my ears wide open. Not for the speeches—they're only a lot of blurb about Democracy and the Commonwealth and so on—but just what one man's saying to another. Mostly it's about the next election and how bad business is, and racehorses; but pretty soon I spot a little group in a corner all excited about something, and I edge over to listen.' He paused to caress his black crop of whisker. 'And what do you s'pose those eminent old coves were yawping about?'

'Search me.' Snow was interested.

'Well, one old cove is saying how when he was carrying his swag along the Darling in Nineteen-One there was a drought on, and another old chap is saying, "Nonsense, nonsense, Sir Everard, that was the best year they had out that way," and Sir Everard gets hot under the collar about it and asks the honourable member did he mean he was lying, and the honourable member says, No, but he was droving out there himself a year after, and the grass was four feet high. Then two more chipped in, and they started quarrelling about the way to roll a swag.'

'There's only one way,' Snow interposed.

'Well, I carry a knapsack. But would you believe it, they'd soon got half the table talking about swags and showing how you rolled them with the serviettes. You never saw a mob so excited about anything. And every one of those starchy old Johnnies talking about the time he bumped his bluey and slapping each other on the back,

43

and saying, "That was the life, my boy."' He broke off gloomily.

'Well?' Snow encouraged.

The busker made an impatient gesture. 'I was mug enough to think there might be something in it. That's all. Hoary old liars!'

Snow had taken a blanket and was didactically folding it. 'You take the end like this, and turn it in,' he said fondly. 'Then you know nothing can fall out of the swag.'

The busker gave an inhuman scream. 'For Crisake, don't! I never want to learn.' He quietened down. 'All the same,' he said reflectively, 'as a busker, I'm right at the top of the tree.'

With this satisfactory summing-up of his standing in the community, they returned to the problem of Miss Phipps.

Finally it was decided that Duke should stroll into town that afternoon and see if he could wheedle a lift for Miss Phipps from any big truck going in the direction of Sydney, or try out the hotels for a commercial traveller who might give a free ride citywards.

Miss Phipps, however, would probably refuse to go unchaperoned, since she had declared that the only reason she stayed with their own party was the presence of the Stray. 'It would not be nice, deah, for a lady to be travelling unchaperoned with two men.' If they could not get rid of Miss Phipps on a big truck, they would try to find a job for the Stray at the local Labour Exchange.

'Some cocky's wife might be mug enough to take her on,' Duke said doubtfully. And then perhaps Miss Phipps would leave of her own accord.

They had in this manner mentally disposed of their load and were feeling more cheerful when the figure of the Stray appeared down the road, returning from 'bumming' the town of Bylong. Miss Phipps, scenting food, appeared from behind a tree where she had been reading a novelette picked up by the roadside.

'Were you lucky, deah?' Miss Phipps called effusively.

'Didn't get a damn thing.' The Stray's nose was red

with cold. She rubbed her hands in front of the fire. 'You lazy——, sitting there while I tramp me feet off. Last place I went to they loosed the flamin' dog on me.'

'Deah, that language!'

'Oh, shut up!' The Stray removed her shoes and tenderly rubbed a blister on one heel. 'Chuck over the tobacco, Snow. I brought a noospaper for you to read.' The Stray could only read with the greatest difficulty and could write little more than her name. She always brought back a newspaper and coaxed Snow or the busker into reading the more sensational divorce evidence.

Her manner told Snow she was concealing something, that she was excited and pleased. But not until Miss Phipps had retired behind her tree did the Stray divulge the secret.

'Hey, Snowy!' She beckoned frantically. 'I got somethin' good. Don't tell that bitch of a woman. She'll want to cash in on it.'

'What?' Snow and Duke moved cautiously round to her side of the fire.

'Look!' She turned up the hem of her skirt to expose a very beautiful peach-satin petticoat inset with lace. 'Look!' She dived down her neck and triumphantly produced more lace and satin. 'I put 'em on right away. And that ain't all. There was a fur coat. I stuffed it up a tree. We could sell it.'

'Why didn't you bring it back?'

'And have 'er fasten on to it? No chance. An' there was stockings and pyjamas and hats. Tons of fings.'

'Where'd you get 'em?'

'I found 'em.' The Stray looked round cautiously to see if Miss Phipps was listening. 'They was in a big leather sootcase someone must've lost out of a car. Hidden it was, down in a deep gutter by the road, under some tree roots. "Hello, I says . . ."'

'Where is it?' Snow rose to his feet.

'Back there. Too big it was to carry.'

Duke was also impressed. 'Good on you, Stray,' he encouraged.

45

The Stray flared up. 'Don't you dare call me that. You Busking Bum! My name's Dancy, and don't you forget it.'

'I was heading into town, anyway,' Duke said with a yawn. 'I'll go along with you, Snow, and have a look. Which tree did you leave the fur coat?'

The Stray described it. 'And don't you forget,' she threatened. 'Them fings belong to me. I found 'em. An' I don't want *her* havin' none.'

'Don't be a goat. I'm going into town to get her a lift out of here.'

It was late afternoon before the busker returned, smelling of rum, and once again his eloquence had served them well. Before his story of a poor, broken-hearted girl, penniless but called to the bedside of a dying mother in Sydney, the local hotelkeeper had melted completely.

'I tell you what, me boy,' that open-hearted citizen had said finally. 'There isn't any commercial going through to Sydney, or even part of the way. But if this poor girl is out of luck the way you say, why, I'll pay her fare back to Sydney meself. I've got daughters,' he added, 'and I'd hate to see any of them left in a fix like that. Only'— his caution came uppermost—'I've got to see the girl and put the ticket in her hand. I'll even see her to the station.'

So there was nothing left but to convince their succubus that her best interests would be served by taking the hotel-keeper's generous offer. Miss Phipps was obtuse.

'I'd rather stay with you deah people,' she announced.

'But we're going way out on the plains, Phippsy, to trap rabbits, and you'd hate to see animals maimed and killed. The camp would be full of dead rabbits all day.' That settled it.

'I'll go,' Miss Phipps announced, her eyes gleaming curiously.

She's got something up her sleeve, the busker decided; but he kept his premonition to himself.

The train for Sydney left at six in the evening, and the kindly hotelkeeper took time off at his busiest period to escort Miss Phipps to the train, buy her a ticket which cost him over two pounds, and see her aboard the train for the three-hundred-mile journey. He even pressed ten shillings into her hand on parting, but hurried back to the bar before the train left.

The Stray and the busker had also come in to see Miss Phipps off, leaving Snow to mind the camp and read his paper in front of the fire. Miss Phipps did not seem any too anxious for them to linger.

'You get back,' she urged, some time before the train started. 'You get back. I'll be all right now.'

They also felt there was no need to linger on the cold, wind-swept platform, having seen her into the train with their own eyes, and made sure she had the ticket to Sydney.

'Well, that's the last of 'er,' the Stray rejoiced as they trudged back in the cold and darkness to their camp a mile out of the town. 'I never been so glad in all me life.'

Snow was even more relieved than they were. The air of the camp seemed cleaner. They laughed and swore in unrestrained enjoyment. Snow had brought in the hidden store of beautiful garments, and they spent a happy time reckoning how much they could get by selling them, after the Stray had made a selection of things she wanted to keep.

'Why, it's a reg'lar trousseau,' she declared, her eyes shining. 'Gee, Snow, I gotta have that fur coat.'

She had decked herself out in a coat and skirt very much too big for her, with the fur coat over all. Snow looked up from his paper and expressed frank admiration.

'With some teeth in an' your 'air done up and some gory paint,' he said, 'you'd be almost good-lookin'.'

The Stray beamed at him. But he quickly forgot her and turned to his paper again.

'Read it to me, Snow,' she coaxed, anxious for more attention. 'Go on, read it.'

'There ain't nothin' in it,' Snow said contemptuously. 'On'y politics and wars. The p'lice think they got another clue of that viaduct murder.'

47

'That was the body,' the Stray said with relish, 'what was so battered about they couldn't tell oo she was.' The Stray, for all she could not read, took a gruesome pleasure in what she termed 'a real good murder'.

'It says here they're traced the cove they're after to this very district.' He read laboriously: 'Police report they have so far traced three hundred missin' girls in an effort to es-tablish . . .' He stopped.

'Go on. Go on,' the Stray urged.

'Analyst's report. The deceased was a dark, stout woman . . .' He broke off again. 'They're tryin' to trace her gold tooth.'

'Oh, read it,' the Stray pleaded angrily.

'What's the good?' Snow wanted his tea. 'That stoo ought to be about ready.'

'Throw over that paper, Snow,' the busker said thought-fully. Something in his tone made Snow look at him keenly.

'What's up?'

'Nothing. I was just wondering.'

'Wonderin' what?'

'Who those clothes belonged to?' Duke said ominously.

The Stray gave a horrified scream. 'You don't fink them was *hers*?' she shrilled.

'Why not? She left Brisbane with a bloke in a blue sedan car. They've traced him through this district. What's more likely that he got scared and threw her things away?'

The Stray's blue eyes bulged as she feverishly began flinging off the fur coat and the underlying clothing. 'An' I got 'em on,' she screamed hysterically. 'I've got 'em on me.'

'Hey, get behind the van,' Snow advised, shocked, 'if you want to take them clothes off.'

'I never want to see 'em again. Never! Oo-er! They been on a Body.' The Stray had reached an embarrassing stage of undress; and Snow and the busker in gentlemanly accord turned their backs.

'But there's the reward,' the busker went on, taking no

48

notice of the Stray's hysterical blubberings. 'There's the five hundred pounds reward.' He gripped Snow's arm excitedly. 'Halves, Snow.'

'Hey, where do I come in?' The Stray for the moment forgot her fit of the horrors. 'Who found them fings, anyway? You split fair.'

'That's true,' Snow agreed. 'We won't see you left for your share.' He was roused to excitement. 'Why, I could get a new van.'

They hardly waited to eat before rushing to the town to the police station. Snow and Duke were for leaving the Stray in charge of the camp; but Dancy, thoroughly hysterical now, declared she was not going to be left alone in the dark for no one. 'Ghosts would get her.' This unreasonableness irritated both her friends; but they were forced to put the horse in the sulky and take the Stray and the suitcase, carelessly repacked, with them. Snow and Duke even had to pack the woman's clothing themselves, because the Stray declared she 'wasn't going to touch nothin' that had been on a Body.'

They hammered at the door of the sergeant's residence; and, pouring out an incoherent story—the Stray's interpolation that 'them cloves was all over bloodstains' was later proved inaccurate—roused the sergeant from a pleasant after-supper nap. He ushered them into the charge-room and investigated the contents of the suitcase himself, saying, 'Hum, yes,' in the cryptic manner of a doctor about to call in an expensive specialist. Secretly he was excited. Then, turning very abrupt and authoritative, he sent Snow to find his constable. The constable was on his beat down the town; but it was unlikely that any crime would be committed in the few minutes he was absent, and the sergeant felt he must have some kind of support in this hour of glory.

The constable, when he came, was one of those dour, unimpressionable men. He was also in a position to send the sweet dreams of the assembled company vanishing into nothingness.

'I meant to tell you, sergeant,' he said. 'A chap by the name of Wood 'phoned through from Currawong this afternoon to ask if anyone had found a suitcase dropped from the tonneau of his car. He and his wife are on a honeymoon trip.' He picked up a handful of dainty lace in his big hand. 'That's it, all right.'

The look of mortal anguish on the face of the three before him had no effect. 'Didn't say anything about a reward,' he added reflectively. 'The chap said he didn't suppose he'd get the stuff back, but his wife was particularly upset about the fur coat. A valuable fur coat.' He picked it up as though he had found it himself.

The sergeant, who had had visions of his name in the papers in big type and a move to a bigger town, turned on his constable and gave him a severe reprimand for neglecting to inform his superior of important telephone messages. He then dismissed him to his beat again and, unruffled, the constable went. The three reward-seekers turned dumbly to follow him, but the sergeant had awakened from his after-supper drowse as well as the visions of wealth and fame.

'Wait a minute,' he said sharply, and the three halted, while the sergeant fished out an official-looking paper. 'Just while we're on the subject of this murdered woman.' He read rapidly from the sheet: 'Dora Phipps, dark, stout, believed to have left Little Millpond, near Melbourne, April 4th. Anyone knowing . . .' He stopped at the expression on the Stray's face.

'But that's Phippsy,' she cried. 'She was travelling wiv us.'

'Is that so?' the sergeant said, his suspicions aroused. He glanced keenly at the unprepossessing trio. They looked as they could murder a rhinoceros without turning a hair, much less a woman, stout, dark, and answering to the name of Dora Phipps. He also noted that the big man had kicked the girl sharply on the ankle and frowned at her.

'Well, where is she now?' he asked.

'We dunno,' Snow volunteered. He added for good measure: 'We ain't seen 'er or 'eard of 'er.'' Snow considered it always best to know nothing if a policeman asked you.

The busker came in glibly with his version. 'We put her on a train this afternoon for Sydney, sergeant.'

The sergeant considered. He was not in a pleasant temper, having been brought from his fireside on a cold night. 'I've a good mind to arrest you all on suspicion.' Then, remembering that this would probably overcrowd his tiny gaol, he said judicially: 'You be back here in the morning, and I'll go into it thoroughly. Don't think you can sneak off, because it'll be all the worse for you if you do.' He might have probed the matter further had it not been so icy cold. 'And don't come back here with any cock-and-bull story,' he admonished on parting. 'I want to know just what happened to that girl.'

The recriminations between Snow, the busker and the Stray began as soon as they were in the sulky.

'Well, you two flamin' mugs,' the Stray burst out, 'givin' away my cloving and my fur coat.'

'Who told the copper Phippsy was travelling with us?' Snow retorted. 'Why can't you keep your mouth shut?'

'Well, you're the man got us all in bad, telling the sergeant we'd never seen Phippsy,' the busker flung at him.

In this rancorous frame of mind they continued through the town.

'Hang on a moment,' Duke said suddenly. 'I want to go to the railway station.'

'Why? Ain't we had enough muckin' about for one night?'

'I just want to check up that she really went, that's all.'

'But the pub-keeper bought her ticket.'

'I know. I still want to check up. We're going to be in a pretty mess to-morrow, but I want to know for sure.'

The station was in darkness, so Harley trudged across

51

to the stationmaster's house and hammered on the door. He desperately besought that official to remember a dark, fat woman who bought a ticket to Sydney.

'Came up with O'Hara who keeps the Royal?'

'That's her.'

'Well, he bought her ticket all right. Then at the last moment she came and persuaded us to take it back and give her the money. Said she had to get out at Currawong. She'd forgotten something she had to do there. She seemed to be pretty upset, so, although I shouldn't have done it, I took the ticket back and sold it to the next passenger. The woman you're after took a ticket to Currawong.'

Duke shook the stationmaster's hand and again assured him that it was a matter of life and death, or he would not have bothered him.

'I thought as much,' he crowed triumphantly, as he remounted the sulky. 'She's not mad. She's just as cunning as the Horehound.' He related his discovery. 'That leaves her with about two pound clear, and she'll be living at the hotel at Currawong on the fat of the land until it's gone. Not that it'll last her long, but she'll have a spree on it.'

'How did you work it out?' the Stray said, with grudging admiration.

'I just thought what I would have done myself,' Duke said modestly. 'She didn't want to go to Sydney. I could see it in her eye. She might have had to work.'

They spent an uneasy night, the Stray insisting on sleeping with Snow, despite that gentleman's expostulations. She was scared of ghosts, and twice in the night she woke them with nerve-racking screams.

The busker was outside the police station bright and early. He had insisted that the others 'leave it to him.' 'One of us is enough,' he argued. 'You'll only be putting your feet in it. Let me manage it.'

'So she's at Currawong, is she?' the sergeant said sourly. 'She's not in Sydney, and she's not travelling with you.

She's in Currawong. Well, Constable Stacey'—he indicated his dour underling—'is going to drive you over to Currawong to locate her.' Harley stared at him dumbly. 'That suit you?' the sergeant barked.

'Yes. Of course.'

'Right. You can start now.' He handed his constable a sheaf of papers. 'Give those to the postmaster while you're there, Stacey.'

The forty miles between Currawong and Bylong flashed past the smooth, shining body of the car. When Duke thought how wearily those miles had dragged, how it had taken three days for them to dawdle from one town to the other, he felt he had moved into a different world. It was miraculous to be travelling in a car again. There was nothing in this snail-crawling mode of horses and vans. Only dullards travelled so. A longing came to him for speed, for action, for swift change. What was he doing dragging about with a turnout and a horse? In the midst of these reflections the car whirled into the town of Currawong.

'She'll be at the best hotel,' the busker directed.

'How do you know?'

'I know Phippsy.' She was not at the best hotel, however; Miss Phipps had not known which was the best, and she had misguidedly chosen the second best. There the barman informed them that a Miss Bowen had checked in the night before.

'Let's have a look at her,' the constable requested. She was not in the hotel, but she would be back to lunch.

'Has this place got a women's beauty parlour?' the astute Duke enquired. 'You know? One of those places where women get their hair dolled up.'

'Ah.'

'Where is it?'

The barman gave directions.

The lady lessee of the 'Madame La Mode' beauty-shop was not at all pleased by the apparition of a strange constable and an evil, dark tramp. 'Well?' she said acidly.

'I'm looking for a dark, stout woman with one gold tooth,' the constable said humbly.

'Very plain,' Harley added in an explanatory tone.

'How dare you!' demanded a voice from within a chastely curtained cubicle; and Miss Phipps, her hair a steely mass of curl-pins, thrust her head out.

'Are you Dora Phipps?' the constable asked.

'I had a perfect right to use the money any way I pleased,' Miss Phipps said indignantly. 'And, anyway, you can't get it back because it is . . . er . . . disposed of. I bought myself a new hat—a real bargain—a new pair of shoes, a set of . . .'

'That's enough,' the constable said hastily. 'All I wanted to know is are you Miss Phipps, of Danks Street, Little Millpond, Melbourne, daughter of James Phipps, grocer and small-goods merchant?'

'Could you take my hair down, deah?' Miss Phipps addressed the owner of the 'Madame La Mode.' 'I think it will do. These men'—she gave her affected laugh—'breaking in on the most sacred rites. Just one moment, officer, and I'll be with you.'

The constable turned dumbfounded to Harley Duke. 'What 'ud anyone want to find her for?' he asked. 'If she was mine, I'd lose her like a shot.'

Miss Phipps emerged. On her head was a plum-coloured hat and she had high-heeled, plum-coloured shoes. A brilliant green blouse protruded nightmare ruffles from the open front of her shabby black coat. How she managed to do it all on the money Duke could not imagine.

She insisted on coming back with them to Bylong, though the constable assured her that it was not at all necessary.

'I wouldn't like those deah people to get into any trouble because of little me,' Miss Phipps insisted; and the constable had ungraciously to give in.

The busker, having presented the lady to the sergeant, hinted that now the sergeant would be able to return her to her bereaved father.

'There wasn't anything said about returning her,' the sergeant objected morosely. 'She's free, white and over twenty-one. You're over twenty-one, aren't you, Miss Phipps?'

'Oh, yes, indeed,' Miss Phipps bridled.

'I just wanted to cross her off the missing list, that's all, and put in a report that I'd located her. I should give O'Hara,' he admitted liberally, 'a chance to charge you both, but since you brought back that suitcase . . .' He broke off abruptly. 'G'wan out of here, and take your girl friend with you.'

'But she doesn't belong to me,' Duke cried frantically. 'Listen, sergeant, I'll tell you how it is . . .'

'I'm busy. That's enough. Get out, or I'll change me mind.'

'A very rude man,' Miss Phipps observed, as she trotted over to the sulky and disposed her bulk comfortably in it.

The busker said nothing. He was wondering how he would break the news to the others. But they picked out Miss Phipps's figure afar off and were sitting in a dejected silence too deep to be broken by any account of Duke's doings in Currawong.

Snow made only one remark as he unharnessed the horse.

'You were the man,' he said bitterly, 'who said leave it to you, you'd manage it.'

The busker pretended to be having trouble with Horehound, so that he might be saved the embarrassment of reply.

Chapter V

As it grew colder and colder, so did Snow's keenness to get home increase. His three followers watched furtively how he brightened and grew more cheerful, recognising one insignificant landmark after another that told him his journey was nearly over. The more they felt they were not wanted, the closer did his three comrades cling to him. Snow had said that when he reached his home in the tiny township of Blimdagery, the three could stay a few days deciding where they would go next; and the thought of being under a roof again was like the hope of heaven.

The busker might talk loftily of 'heading up to Queensland' and about the cane-barges and the blue smoke blowing over the slow, beautiful waters of the Tweed, of the mangoes and pineapples, and the open-handed ways of farmers in that northern State where the sun was burning and wilful, not a cold stone in an ice-blue sky; but all the same he preferred the bickering of the Stray and Miss Phipps and the friendly silence of Snow to loneliness and the chances of the road. They were all roadsick, and that was the truth; overcome with that craving for shelter that sooner or later grips all tramps. Miss Phipps could forge her way back to Sydney or Melbourne, where, among the city's unemployed domestic servants, she would occupy the lowest rung of incapacity and laziness. The Stray could return to those alleys whence she came. But they shrank from the suggestion. They could look no farther ahead than reaching Blimdagery.

Night after night they discussed it, huddled shivering round the fire. All they asked was shelter from the screaming wind, and warmth in which they might relax their stiff joints. They could not get warm even at night when the two women climbed into the van, and Snow and the busker betook themselves to the tent and the folds of the canvas tarpaulin. There was not enough bedding for four people, and the aching cold kept them awake. In the morning the billy of tea left overnight on the frosty grass would tilt out its contents in a solid block of ice; the blades of grass were sheathed in ice; there was a thin, crackling sheet of ice over the creek when the busker went with blue fingers to dip water. Even the birds seemed disinclined to stir, and when the sun rose, it would hardly push its rim over the horizon before it was enveloped in a drift of dirty clouds that held to it like steel filings to a magnet and dragged with it across the sky. The cold, pale sky and the dull, pale earth were like two frozen hands reaching towards the sun that, cuddled down in its grey muffler, could only smile helplessly and, it seemed, cynically at their numb entreaty.

The travellers had come out from what little shelter might be found in the hills and were journeying across the stretch of flat country beyond Condobolin; and the wind met them like a wall of ice. The hostility of the inhabitants met them also. No one had anything to give, and even when the Stray tried to sell toasting-forks and grills that Snow twisted out of wire, there were no buyers. The district was 'faked out.' In this country Snow was not eager to 'knock over sheep.' The farmers were tough. They would sit up all night with a lantern, if they thought anyone was casting a calculating eye on their flocks.

The four grew leaner and hungrier-looking; and they watched Snow with a helpless dependence. He set traps; but even the rabbits seemed to have died of starvation. The busker, with a husky voice wailing outside any little store or siding they passed, could scrape together only a few reluctant pence. The little crew became too apathetic to quarrel. Life was only a struggle against the wind and driving grit, a camp, and aching bones, misery, cold, and struggling on again.

Snow was already rehearsing what he would say to his wife, Molly. He had planned to reach Blimdagery just on dusk, and he would go ahead with the sulky as though he were alone, leaving his little following down in the dry creek in a rather bleak camp just on the edge of the township. He would walk in in his old way and say: 'Well, old woman, how's things?' and Molly would say: 'Back again, eh? I got the ten pounds.' And she would set some bread on the table, and make him some tea, and he would spread out his boots in front of the kitchen stove; and, as usual, Molly would snap: 'Good Heavens, get them great boots out of the way. You want me to spill this all over you?'

Then, presently, he would mention that he had picked up 'three poor devils on the road'; and they were camped just half a mile out by Badgery's fence; then, little by little, he would tell her the whole story, and she would snap at him for being a fool, and say, if he thought he could bring a lot of tramps to live on her, he was mistaken. He would explain that they were a man and his wife and sister; and Molly would give him a sharp glance and a nasty quarter of an hour. When she was finished telling him about his beastly way of life and that she didn't doubt he had been carrying on with both the women, Molly, who was so soft-hearted, would snap: 'What did you leave 'em out in the cold for? Sure isn't there the shed at the back, and the poor creatures freezing there while you sit warming yourself? Think shame, Theodore Grimshaw!'

She would insist on his going out to bring his little party into the warmth of her kitchen. She would settle everything for him, and send his three mates flying with a few well-chosen words, if they showed any disposition to linger longer than she thought adequate. It was all very satisfactory to Snow, and he looked ahead with a warmth that had seldom accompanied his thoughts of reunion with his family. These three who had no families of their own made him realise just how lucky he was.

Blimdagery might be only a miserable place with one weather-board store, not even a railway siding; but it was the place where his wife's family, the Hourigans, had dwelt since the first Hourigan had opened that store. The whole district was settled with Hourigans and Kellys, and his wife Molly was related to every one of them. That was why she had refused to leave Blimdagery. It might be only a dust-spot along the road between two larger towns; but it was her ancestral seat; and the three-roomed, weather-board hut, with its patch of hen-harassed dirt in front was hers, and its weedy paddock, full of Bathurst burrs and cow-manure, behind. If Snow was not away droving, or looking for shearing, or off kangaroo-hunting, he had gone fencing or clearing. He was a good man. He sent home money for herself and the children when he got it; but not for such a life as he led would she give up the company of her own people, her aunts and cousins, and the shelter of her bare, weatherboard house, hot as an oven in summer, and bleak enough in winter, covered with a film of red grit that kept her constantly scouring at any time of the year. She had the boys, Freddie, Brian and Jimmy, to keep her busy. How could she drag them, she demanded, round the country with their father? She had been one trip with him, and that was quite enough, thank you.

Although Snow had planned to arrive at dusk, his impatience unconsciously got the better of him, so that it was mid-day when the scattered corrugated roofs of Blimdagery appeared. Snow reined Don in and pointed with his whip: 'There she is!' he said, with a seeming casualness.

'Really!' Miss Phipps, who was riding beside him because he never hit Don, produced her pair of horn-rimmed spectacles with one lens missing and deliberately adjusted them on her nose. She screwed up her eyes to two pin-points and squinted at the corrugated iron as though it was some remarkable, heavenly portent that had appeared.

'Molly'll be surprised to see the van,' Snow remarked. 'When I left I had on'y a sulky. I swapped the sulky in for the van. Thought it ud be 'andy if I wanted to go drovin'.'

Miss Phipps said nothing about his incidental bad language. Ever since the Horehound had stood on her foot and she had called it everything Snow had ever said and more, she had been in no position to reprove anyone for his language. Not that that alone would prevent her from doing so. She had just worn herself out and grown tired of talking on the subject.

They pulled in on a grassy stretch by the roadside, and Snow pointed out where they could get water from his wife's uncle's tank at the homestead nearby and have their mid-day meal, while he went ahead to reconnoitre. He had decided to leave the van there with them. 'I'll keep it as a surprise, see?' he suggested. He took Don from the van and harnessed him to the sulky.

As he drove slowly up to the clutter of houses, taking in the look of this so-familiar parched place, it struck him that his wife's usual scheme to get him a job 'cocking' for one of her uncles or cousins would come to nothing again. The country was all dried up. No one would be wanting any fencing or clearing done or any work round these parts for which they would be forced to pay. He might get some shearing, or he might plough up that back paddock. It was a job that needed doing when he went away. Then, as he rehearsed his opening speech, a slight qualm overcame him. Suppose Molly took up an unreasonable attitude on his Stray and the Busker and Phippsy, sitting faithfully munching their dry bread and marmalade and drinking tea? He couldn't help it. He hadn't asked them to come.

The gate of his shack was hanging by one hinge, and Snow resolved to mend that gate the very next day. He liked things about the place to be ship-shape. The front door was shut, and he strolled round to the back, where he was greeted with a vociferous barking of dogs. Three of them came out, wagging their tails and jumping on him. His youngest boy, Freddie—a small, freckled, tow-headed youngster—was sitting on the back doorstep eating a piece of tart.

'Lo, Dad,' Freddie greeted, munching undemonstratively.

'Where's your mother, son?'

'Gone down to Auntie Edna's place. She'll be back soon.'

In the kitchen everything was just as it had been: the faded, torn, old linoleum, the carefully blackened stove set in its white-washed chimney; the wooden dresser with a cheap alarm clock on the top shelf, the chipped cups and plates, the runner made of fluffs of coloured silk, the coats hanging behind the door. A boot belonging to one of the boys flung down in the bedroom beyond. From the ceiling dangled a familiar fly-paper. There was no sound save the rusty ticking of the alarm clock and Freddie shuffling his feet on the back doorstep. Snow, feeling a little lonely, went out and sat beside him, and watched the hens scratching among the thistles of the yard.

'Anything happened while I been gorn?'

'Nuh.' Freddie licked the crust to make it last as long as possible. 'Jimmy cut his foot.' Then he added as an afterthought: 'Derek come to live here.'

Snow considered this. Derek was his wife's second cousin. He must be home again. He had been away in the city last time Snow was home.

'Been here long?'

Freddie nodded. Computation of time was beyond him; but Dad had been gone a long time, so that Freddie was sure it was a long time since Derek Hourigan came to board with them.

'Derek's working at Uncle Peter's store,' Freddie volunteered.

So that explained it. Snow had no objection to his wife making some regular money from Derek's board. He could hear Molly opening the front door, and he rose as she bustled into the kitchen.

'Are you there, Theodore?' she called. 'Aunt Hourigan said she thought she saw you going by.'

Snow had always detested the name Theodore. 'A great big name, too heavy for a kid—the kind of name me father would pick out. Always gave me too much to carry, whether it was names or kerosene tins.' Now, as he heard the familiar 'Theodore,' it roused the same irritation that it had always done. Instead of saying: 'Well, old woman, how's things?' he said: 'Hey, what's all this about Derek boarding here?'

'Oh! Freddie told you?'

'How much's he payin'?'

'What's that got to do with you?' Molly had meant to be kind and welcoming, but, as usual, Snow had to put his big feet just where they were not wanted. She pushed him out of the way and began setting the table. 'I got the ten pounds all right.' She was a small, brisk woman, with quick eyes, a sharp nose and chin, and snapping movements. Over her forehead she wore a little frizzy fringe which she curled every night. She hadn't even kissed him, Snow noticed. He must have said something to upset her. So he changed the subject from Derek and asked her about the boys.

'They've gone yabbying. But they'll be in to lunch. Jimmy cut his foot with the axe, but he *would* go. Sure he's a devil of a boy. And Brian's been throwing stones at the cow.' She had glanced out of the back door in one of her trips to and from the dresser. 'The sulky looks different.'

'I dealt the old one in,' Snow responded, expecting that Molly would immediately demand to know about the deal, whether he got any money to boot, whether he got the best of the bargain. But she only nodded in a disinterested way.

He rolled a cigarette, watching her curiously. There was something wrong. Snow had an animal keenness to detect differences of atmosphere. He wondered if his favourite, young Jimmy, had cut a toe off or was in hospital. That might account for it.

Big, heavy, crunching boots were tramping round the side of the house, and a man's voice said: 'Hello, Fred. Lunch ready?' Freddie mumbled something as Derek stepped past him into the kitchen. 'Hello, Snow,' Derek greeted the master of the house. 'Have a good trip?'

'Yeah. But the rabbits was pretty near all cleaned out. Got some good fox-skins.'

Molly silently laid out plates of stew and some bread, while her second cousin talked to Snow about the lack of rain and the debts at the store. Uncle Joe Kelly was hand-feeding already, and Mick Hourigan was having trouble with the bank. Mick thought he would have to leave the place. It had been a bad year, and things would be worse before they were better.

Derek Hourigan was nearly as big a man as Snow, but dark. He had a long scar down the side of his face, and he talked all the time, running his hands through his hair, tapping them on his knees, clasping and unclasping them. His hands were never still, and his voice went on and on, putting together obvious trivial scraps of talk, just as his hands went through small, unconscious movements.

'Why don't he sit still?' Snow thought. He sat immobile himself, saying now and then 'Yeah', or 'Thasso', as occasion demanded. Jimmy and Brian did not appear, and it would have been a silent meal had it not been for the conversation that Derek was making.

When he got up and pushed back his chair, saying that he had to be back at the store, it seemed that he was in a hurry to be off. He was half-way across the yard when Molly called to him: 'Derek!'

'What?' He turned sharply round.

'Wait a minute.' She ran after him and spoke in a hurried murmur. They seemed to be arguing about something.

Snow slowly rolled another cigarette and, as his wife came in, he said: 'Well, he's a great sort of a cove, he is!'

'What d'you mean?' His wife began to scrape the dishes. 'He's got a steady job at the store.'

Snow grunted. 'Steady job? Why, he couldn't keep a mouse. Just Uncle Peter taking 'im in for charity. That store ain't done enough business in ten years to feed a galah.'

'He's got a promise to get on at Hessels' in a month or so.' Hessels' was the big store in the town five miles away.

Snow regarded her steadily and, under that keen glance from his small, light eyes, she flared up. 'Oh, you can sneer at a man who don't leave his wife and family and go off God knows where and never heard of for months, traipsing about the country. It's all very well for you! He's a steady chap and . . .'

'How long you been going with him?'

'What do you mean?' Molly's mouth closed in an obstinate line. In the tense silence, Snow could hear the rusty tick of the clock and a truck bumping past in the street.

'You heard me. I ain't blind. Think I don't know? It's no good, Molly. I seen it when 'e first came through the door that you'd taken up with him.' Snow leant across the table and took her small, work-reddened hand in his great, horny paw. 'Don't try to pull the wool over me, Molly.'

She snatched her hand away. 'What if it is so?' she cried defiantly. 'What if it is? Can you blame anyone, sitting here night after night alone with only the kids? At least he's a bit of life about the place. What kind of a life do you think this is for me, left here by myself while you're away?'

'That's true,' he said heavily. 'It's hard enough. If a man takes his wife and kids on the track with 'im, it ain't no sort of a life for them, and if 'e leaves 'em and goes off to scratch for a crust, it's no sort of a life either. But it was your choice to stay, Molly.'

'You could have stayed, too,' she cried. 'Freddie, you go out in the yard and play. Don't stand there.' She gave the child a push towards the door.

'I could've stayed, too,' Snow said slowly. 'Maybe doin' a bit of wheat-lumpin' at harvest or bag-sewing at thirty bob a week as a hand-out from your starving cocky relatives. What kind of a life's that? And the rest of the time just hangin' about waitin' for dole-day? I thought maybe I could make a bit of money for you and the kids, and I couldn't do it here.' He broke off. 'What if I do stay home now? What about that? That suit you?'

She was silent, her face averted.

'Well,' he said after a few moments, 'I don't want to make it harder for you.' He reached for his hat. 'Good-bye, Molly.'

'Snow.' She was crying now. 'If you could only have got a steady job and stayed here with me . . .'

'There ain't no jobs.' His voice was hard. 'You know there ain't. What do you think I went away for but to make a bit of money?'

'Derek's got a job.'

'At a pound a week,' Snow said deliberately. 'Could I keep a wife and three kids on that?'

'Aren't you going to wait for the boys to come home?' she asked, unwillingly following him to the door.

'What's the use?' He could stay and knock the daylight out of the glib rat who had broken up his home, but what would be the use of that, either? Woman-like, she was delaying him.

'Where are you going, Snow?'

Snow considered. He put Don into the sulky, the sulky that Molly had not asked him to explain. 'I might go an' do a bit o' fruit-pickin' later, about the beginning of October. Or I might go through to South Australia. I dunno.'

'You won't be . . . coming back?' Her face was strained.

'No,' he said. 'You needn't worry. I won't bother you. There ain't room for both of us, an' I guess it's 'im you want.'

'Snow . . . I . . .'

He patted her shoulder. 'All right, Molly; it's just the way things are. If you or the kids should want me, send word along the track. If I get word, I'll come.' He ran his hand over Freddie's rough, fair thatch, then tossed him in the air. 'G'bye, son.'

'G'bye, Dad. Where you going?' Freddie tagged after him to the gate. 'Can I come too?'

'Some other time, son.' Snow turned deliberately down the road towards the outskirts of the settlement. He said 'Good-day' to Aunt Edna, leaning over her gate, but he did not stop. He nodded to a couple of men he knew. It was as though he was seeing this dusty place for the first time. It had become suddenly, startlingly vivid. The old horse with its head drooped away from the wind outside the little hotel, the front gardens of the few dilapidated weatherboard shacks that made up the main street. The old faded sign 'Baker' over a little shop with broken windows and a gaping door. These old shanties of mud and weatherboard seemed somehow more permanent than a great city. Their dirt and nakedness had an enduring quality that he had never noticed until now. It was as though he walked out of the strong fortress of the Hourigans, the men who clung to their patch of earth if they had to scratch it with their finger-nails for tools. Between him and the men who had land—any piece of land— there was no longer a tie. He had not even a back paddock into which to turn his horse. He had no home, no family any more.

'Dad! Wait on, Dad. Hey!'

His two elder boys were racing towards him across a paddock. Jimmy was limping a little, with his foot tied up in a piece of rag, so that Brian, the younger of the two, freckled, with the light-blue eyes of Snow and the sharp chin of Molly, reached the sulky first. Jimmy was ginger and freckled, but quieter and even sharper than Brian. They both of them had the angular, ugly build common to growing boys and stray cats.

'You going again, Dad?' Brian asked.

'Yeah. I been home.' Snow's mouth twisted harshly with a pain he had not known he could feel. He had not considered his sons when he parted so finally from Molly. He had just taken it for granted that they would stay and ask no questions. But they knew everything. That was the worst of shrewd small boys. They were good kids, too, handy with horses and tools, although he had never worked them the way their grandfather had worked him when he was young. He eyed them affectionately.

'We're coming, too.' Jimmy hopped up into the sulky. 'As long as Mum's got Freddie, she don't care.'

'No, son,' Snow said grimly.

66

'Well, you said one of us could come next trip, didn't he, Brian?'

'It's a fact.' Brian nodded his head in Snow's own way.

'Well.' For a moment Snow hesitated. After all, why shouldn't he have one of his boys with him? Split fair, Molly, he argued in his mind. You've got the thick end of the stick with Derek and Freddie and the house. Why shouldn't I have one of these? Then he nodded. 'Fair enough.' He drew a penny from his pocket. 'Loser stays. What's it to be?'

'Tails,' Jimmy called. The coin flashed, then rang against the road.

'It's tails,' Jimmy shouted, hopping in the road. His brother stood looking up at Snow disconsolately. 'You won't not come back, Dad?' he asked.

'Dunno what me plans are, son.'

'Write me a letter.'

'Yeah.' Snow turned to Jimmy. 'Nick off home and get your things. Tell mother I said you was to come with me. I'll pick you up in about half an hour. I've got some mates of mine camped down the road.' He clucked to Don. 'Right-o, you be ready.'

He did not want to hurry. Perhaps Molly would send some kind of envoy if she knew he was waiting down by the creek. She would have a chance to think things over and realise she was acting badly. The boys had re-knit that tie to his home that a few minutes before he felt he had severed for ever. He still felt as though he had swallowed a large stone and it had lodged at the base of his throat, but it was a smaller stone, with fewer sharp edges.

Snow's three companions were waiting for him, polite and anticipatory; but at his first remark, 'We're going on,' their expectation became an anxious bewilderment.

'We're going on,' Snow repeated heavily. 'Better get the Hore in the van. Save unharnessing Don. He could do with a spell in the sulky for a change.'

The busker was the first to recover. 'Nothing up at home, Snow?'

67

'A bit of trouble.' Snow's voice was just as usual. 'Better fill up the water-bag, Stray.'

'Where we goin'?' Dancy queried.

'To hell if you like.' The savagery that Snow put into his reply stifled all further enquiry, except that the busker, tightening Horehound's girth-strap, said almost diffidently: 'Snow, I don't want to push my nose in your business, but . . . is there anything a bloke could do?'

Snow shook his head. 'No,' he said grimly. 'It ain't no good arguin' with women.'

He was glad now to have this crew with him. At most times they might be as comfortable as a set of boils, but now they were a help. The way they had taken his announcement, almost in silence, not even Phippsy enquiring or wanting to discuss it, had given him a better opinion of his followers.

He had still to go through the town with them. They could not very well turn round and go back the way they had come, nor would Snow skirt round Blimdagery. Straight up the main street and stop in front of the gate of his house: that was the way. Why should Molly be allowed to think that she was casting her husband out like a stray dog? The frozen glare of Aunt Edna and a group of female relations as Snow's party went slowly past made him feel that the Hourigans knew all there was to know of the situation in the Grimshaw home. Their sympathies had never been with him. All Hourigans stuck together like burrs to a sheep's wool. As he drew the van up in front of his house, Snow recognised Shamus Hourigan, middle-aged, mild, with a drooping grey moustache, and his son George waiting for him on the verandah.

'G'day,' he said, as they came forward to the side of the van. 'Come inside if you want to say anything.' He threw the reins to the interested Miss Phipps.

'But, Theo, it isn't possible to take Jimmy,' Uncle Shamus was protesting. 'Isn't the boy's schoolin' to be considered?'

'I tell you, if you want to talk, get inside.'

The front door opened to show a white-faced Molly hostile and resolute. Then it closed with a slam. The busker whistled softly to himself.

'So that's his wife,' he remarked to the Stray. 'I bet she'd snap the nose off your face.'

When Snow came out, Jimmy was not with him. 'The kid's not comin',' he said shortly by way of explanation. 'Come on.'

He drove through Blimdagery as though it did not exist.

Five miles farther they stopped at a reserve close to the big town to which Blimdagery was as a satellite to a great planet. Snow went off to 'see a chap,' carrying a set of spare harness thoughtfully over his arm. Early next morning the busker initiated a search; he found Snow lying on the cold concrete of the yard of the Exchange Hotel. Someone had thoughtfully thrown a bucket of water over him the night before to bring him to after a fight. Lying out in the cold had not improved Snow any more than the fight had improved him, or the drink he had put away. Someone had been through his pockets for the money remaining from the sale of the harness; and, as the busker helped Snow back to camp, he cursed himself for letting his mate go into town alone. All Snow could talk about was the necessity of getting away, as far away from Blimdagery as possible.

Chapter VI

I

DOLE-DAY was four days ahead, but Snow, with a bull-necked and exasperating obstinacy, insisted that they turn south to Logan, and between themselves and Logan lay sixty-seven miles of plains. That meant the horses must do over twenty miles a day. If Snow wanted to go on, Duke was pleased, because he had seen before him a dreadful vision of Snow fighting drunk or in gaol or selling off their conveyance piecemeal, and

on Duke would fall the onus of stopping him and chivvy-
ing him and persuading him. Duke hated responsibility.
All his reckless life he had dodged planning or organising
or taking up burdens. Let others do the worrying. Not
for him!

But, as though Snow's conduct in selling the harness
and getting drunk and insisting on going on were not
enough, he crowned it all by going down with influenza.
Snow looked like a man impervious to anything except a
dum-dum bullet, but now, perversely, he showed every
sign of dying. His lips puffed up, burst and bled, he
could hardly see out of his reddened eyes, from which
agonising hot tears ran down his face. With his teeth
chattering in a fever, he still insisted on driving. No
woman was going to drive his horse, he swore. That was
what was wrong with the Horehound; a woman must have
owned her. But his voice was only a croaking whisper,
and presently, when the pain in his back became unbearable and his breath sawed his chest as though every gasp
had a knife in it, he collapsed and was laid in the van, still
swearing that if they gave him a few minutes he would be
right again.

'You lie there,' the busker soothed him, 'or I'll knock
you down. The Stray can drive Horehound.'

'I will not,' the Stray shrilled fearfully. 'I ain't goin'
to be killed by no damn jib.' She regarded the sulky with
terror. She had never in her life driven a horse, an animal
to her as monstrous as a mastodon.

'Well, Phippsy, it's up to you.'

Miss Phipps regarded the busker blandly. 'I wouldn't
even ride in the sulky while that beast is pulling it,' she
declared self-righteously. 'And if we were not in this un-
inhabited place, I would leave you to your own devices.
I shall ride in the van with you and Mr. Snow.'

'You will not. You'll ride in the sulky or you'll walk.
Snow and I and the gear are plenty for Don to pull.'

'In that case,' Miss Phipps said determinedly, 'I shall
walk.'

'You can go to the devil,' the busker declared hotly. He turned again to the Stray. 'Dancy . . .'

'I'm scared, I tell you.'

'Dancy, do you want Snow to die? Do you want us to miss our dole? We can't just leave the sulky here. And if I don't drive Don, Snow will insist on driving him himself.'

The busker knew from experience that Horehound was a devil of a horse, with a hard mouth, a cunning delight in making things awkward for her driver; but if he had learnt to manage Horehound, the Stray could also learn. Then, again, Horehound had taken a fancy to Don; she would follow behind him, but she refused to go in front. That was as well, because the busker could keep an eye on the outfit.

'You don't want Snow to die, do you?' he pleaded. 'We've got to do fifty-five miles by Thursday, and he can't drive. You don't want . . .'

'Oh, shut up,' the Stray said savagely. 'I'll drive the damn horse.'

White to the lips, she climbed up into the sulky; and the Horehound, sensing from the Stray's grip on the reins that she had something small and weak to deal with, commenced to jerk and fidget and sidle. The busker was nearly as scared of the Horehound as the Stray was. He had always depended on Snow to manage the horses, but now, with the leader of the expedition breathing heavily under the 'possum-skin rug in the van, he felt himself to be in sole charge. He gave the Stray a grin of encouragement.

'You'll be all right, kid,' he said firmly. 'Horehound'll just follow old Don. Keep a tight grip on her and look out for cars. With a mile of plain on either side, they'd still sooner run right over you.'

The Stray nodded her head humbly. She tried to return the smile, but her face was too stiff with fear. ''Strufe!' she whispered. 'Look after poor Snowy.' She felt it might be her last request. Ever since Snow had come back to the camp outside Blimdagery and said they

71

were going on 'To hell if you like' she had been afraid to ask what had happened to him at home. It was all her fault. Snow's wife had found out he was travelling with women and had thrown Snow out. And now he was sick. The Stray had been rehearsing all the things she would have said to Molly. She now began to repeat them aloud for the busker's benefit. 'I wouldn't have frowed 'im out,' she began.

'Come on. Let's get going,' the busker said sharply. He clucked to Don, and they started off, the van in the lead, then the sulky, with Miss Phipps straggling along behind. That nightmare drive was something both the Stray and the busker would never forget. They were going through open country where the road ceased to be anything except individual car- and sulky-tracks over the sandy surface of the plain. Whichever way they turned the wind seemed to come head on like a charging elephant, and against this wind the horses laboured, against the driving grit, the savage, steady rubbing on the nerves, against the cold brutality of the empty plains, under the empty skies.

They had run out of tobacco. They had only bread and jam and tea. The Stray managed to beg some eggs at a farm-house, but they did not dare to stop. They would miss their dole; and if they did that, what would become of them? The eggs were fried up and given to Snow, who left them untouched. He would drink only a little cold tea, and this was as well, for they had nothing else to give him.

For Phippsy it was a horrible time. She walked. Cars whirled past them occasionally; but Miss Phipps, had she been offered a lift, would have refused to travel unchaperoned in a car. So she walked.

The busker had no time to worry about Miss Phipps. She was just a dead weight. He had to unharness the horses, get water, put up the tent, prepare the meals, wait on Snow, find wood in this unwooded region sufficient to keep them from freezing before morning.

The Stray, her efficiency increasing daily, was a help; but the full weight of decision fell on Duke. There was, fortunately, sufficient feed for the horses; and they met some drovers coming through with sheep who reported that rain had fallen on the track ahead of them.

Thursday saw them camped in a sheltered hollow a mile from the town of Logan, with their troubles and the plain behind them. They got their dole without argument and then settled down to tend Snow. Calling a doctor was out of the question. It was only a bad attack of influenza. They had all had it, and knew it would disappear in a week or so, leaving a racking cough for the rest of the winter. But dole food is neither nourishing nor sufficient, even for people in full health. Snow must have better. Duke and the Stray fell upon the town of Logan and pillaged it. Never before had the Stray lied with such moving fervour of her three starving children. Had she said there was a sick man back at the camp it would not have brought them much. The busker actually told the publican at the Rose and Crown the true story. He pleaded to be given some firewood to chop in return for a double dose of overproof rum.

'My mate's got the flu bad,' he said. 'He's spitting blood.'

'You're right, son.' The publican nodded sympathetically. He was a fat, bald-headed man who sampled his own wares. 'There's only one thing any good. Give it to him boiling hot with a bit of sugar and water and a lemon.' He measured out the rum. 'There you are. Remember, it's got to be hot.'

'I don't suppose you've got a spare lemon,' the busker hinted. He got his lemon and departed in triumph.

Snow was lying by the fire. Miss Phipps, who had just made herself some tea, 'had not thought,' she said, 'to give Mr. Snow any.' She was deeply excited and muttering to herself as she scribbled with a stub of pencil on a bit of paper.

'Look what I've got, Snow.' The busker waved the bottle in which he was carefully carrying the rum.

73

'Guh?' Snow groaned; and even when the busker, word by word, repeated the long argument, the special pleading he had employed on the publican, before he had secured his treasure, Snow still did not seem to care. He just sank back on the tarpaulin and spat feebly at the fire. With his gaunt frame huddled in an old military overcoat, he looked like some half-starved sentry about to perish. The busker tended the rum with care. He stood it in a panni-kin inside a billy of boiling water until he judged it really hot, then added the hot water, sugar and lemon.

'It must be hot,' he repeated to himself the publican's words. Proudly carrying his brew over to Snow, he propped the invalid up. 'Take a swig of this, old man,' he commanded, holding it to Snow's mouth.

Snow swallowed obediently; then, as the burning liquid scorched his broken lips and swollen throat, he gave a yell of agony, and leapt up with a suddenness that sent the hard-won rum flying.

'Oh Gord!' he howled. 'It's red-hot.' He clutched his mouth and rocked himself, trying to recover breath.

The busker, ruefully eyeing the brown patch where the liquid had soaked into the grass, picked up the empty pannikin. 'If I'd only tasted it,' he said wistfully, 'this wouldn't have happened.'

'Where you goin'?' Snow croaked.

'Back to get some more.'

'He won't give you any more.'

'I'll get it.'

The busker turned heroically towards the road for the walk back to town. As he came up over the embankment on the roadside, he met the Stray returning with a bag of flour. She had, she declared, 'ticked up the flour mill.' 'Where you goin', Dukesy?' This had been her name for him ever since she decided to be friendly with the busker.

Duke explained what had happened. 'I'm going back to battle for some more rum.'

'You got a fat chance of gettin' it.' Dancy was tired

74

and the thought of preparing tea and getting wood and water without Duke made her jeer a little.

'What'll you bet?'

'Three smokes.'

A comradeship had grown up between them, the outcome of that nightmare drive over the plains, one of those simple, easy friendships founded on mutual respect. They both looked up to Snow, although in Stray's case her attitude was one of ownership both pompous and pathetic. She bullied Snow in his weakened state, persuading and commanding him to eat. If he swore at her irritably, she took no notice.

'It's a funny fing,' Dancy confided to Duke, 'I can bite anyone, go into places wiv dogs, ask in shops, do fings I'd never do for meself, jus' for somebody else. Funny, ain't it?'

She protected Snow, wrapped him up, fussed over him, but he hardly noticed it, sitting in a sodden daze, staring for the most part into the fire, or listlessly trying to stumble about the camp.

Miss Phipps was still busy with her stub of pencil and her scrap of wrapping-paper, as the Stray trotted back bemoaning her lack of success in 'biting' housewives. It was only dole-day, and those wise women knew that travellers could not be really destitute.

'What you doing, Phippsy?' she demanded, beginning to peel some potatoes.

'Nothing you would understand, deah.'

'Well, if it ain't important, nick down to the creek and get some water.'

Miss Phipps did not stir. She continued scribbling. 'Regionalised, centracious control,' she wrote. Then underneath: 'Zoning for efficacy of metaphysical totality.' Miss Phipps had just reorganised the government of the world under a powerful committee of women all very like herself. She had wiped out all men, small boys and women who did not fit in with her plans, and she was working out the perfect autocracy.

75

'Rhythmic centralisation,' she wrote; and the beauty of the long words acted like a tonic. The power of the creator was upon her. No one could possibly understand how important this plan would be in the future when she took control of the world and wiped out all the enemies who had conspired to leave her gracious and queenly person in rags and poverty. Miss Phipps never regarded herself in any other light than a queen in disguise.

That was why she was able to bear with an unruffled smile the unkind things that venomous little creatures like Dancy Smith or Harley Duke might say about 'fake society women.' No, she was a queen of the Zenobia breed. Her word was law, and she moved through fabulous palaces in silks and satins. All the rulers of her far-stretching territories were women like herself, glorious, dignified, great ladies in their own right. She had organising ability, plus that capacity to plan every detail that made underlings worship her and depend on her.

It was at this point that the piece of brown paper was torn from her hand and through the vapours of her kingdom appeared the face of the Stray, fiendish with rage.

'If you don't take that kerosene tin and fill it'—Dancy was shaking with anger—'I'll break every bone in your lazy, fat body, you . . .' And the Stray added a string of epithets straight from the gutter.

How would you behave if you were a queen subjected to such an outrage? The queenly thing seemed to be to walk off with the kerosene tin in a dignified and stately manner. No ruffled haste. That would be unseemly. The meditations on the World Feminised Rhythm Systems could be resumed on the creek bank, out of reach of that unworthy female who had just torn up the plans for the World State Organisation and was putting them in the fire.

'She gives me a pain in the neck, she does that.' Dancy placed another log on and resumed her potato-peeling. 'You gotta drive 'er like that blasted 'Orehound all the time if you want anythin' out of 'er.'

Ruthlessness towards poor Miss Phipps had been the Stray's most notable development of late. She had lost her first awe of long words and superior snubs, and with it the tolerance which all savages extend to lunatics. Dancy was now convinced that Miss Phipps was no more mad than she was, or than the Horehound. Since mastering that unknown quantity, she felt herself equal to anything. A new self-confidence radiated from her. She drove Miss Phipps and the horse, she was friends with the busker, she petted Snow. 'The Centralised World Rulership of the First Feminine State' would not have given Dancy half the satisfaction of her present powers and privileges.

'How are y' now, Snowy love?' she asked gently.

'I'm all right,' that worthy croaked feebly. 'And cut out the Snowy love.'

'Snow,' the Stray said fervently, 'I didn't mean to make no trouble wiv you and your old woman. I been that worried. Say the word and I'll clear out, and let you go back to 'er.'

Snow took no notice. He turned over and settled himself against a log, trying to find some position in which his bones would feel less as though they were being mashed between sharp stones.

'What'd she say, Snow? You ain't once told me what she said.'

'Shut up. Give a man a bit of peace, can't you?'

The Stray was silent for fully half a minute.

'But, Snow, you cud a always said it was on the level. I wasn't tryin' to pool you wiv her.'

It did not hurt Snow to let the Stray think what she liked, and if the Stray chose to think he had left home on her account, he was too sick to care.

'Did Duke see to the horses?'

'No, 'e's gone back to Logan.'

'Well, go and look if they're grazin' up the lane. Did you hobble the Hore?'

'Yeah. She'll camp wiv Don. She's always kept wiv him.'

77

'I dunno. You go and take 'em for a drink.'

The horses drank at a dam in a near-by farmer's paddock; unknown to the farmer, they also spent the night there. The Stray went off on her errand, and a minute later she was hastening back in consternation.

'The mare's gone, Snow, but she can't be far. She was croppin' beside Don a while back.'

Snow staggered up cursing. 'If they pound 'er, how the hell do you think we'll get 'er out? I'll go after 'er.'

'No, Snow. Wait till Dukesy gets 'ere. He'll go.'

'That bloody cow of a mare can gallop in hobbles. . . .'

'Let me go after 'er.'

'No, I'm all right. I'll ride Don.' He swayed as he stood. He could not trust his knees to carry him. 'Pack o' yapping women,' he muttered. 'Can't even see to the horses.' His weakness annoyed him.

The Stray stood peering after him in the darkness that had muffled down like a grey blanket, hiding everything outside the friendly circle of the fire.

'Pig-headed fool,' she grumbled to Phippsy, who had returned because it was too cold to linger by the creek. 'He can't even see no tracks in this light.'

Several times she lifted her head to listen for the sound of trotting hoofs that would tell that Snow was back. 'If he only wouldn't camp miles out of town,' she grumbled. 'If we was closer in I could battle a paddock for the 'orses, 'stead of lettin' 'em graze about. He says there's no feed on the river near the town, but there was lots of feed. I looked to-day. He just likes bein' on 'is lonesome, away from everyone.'

She had looked wistfully at the turnouts settled on the reserve down by the river. There had been a woman with a clutch of children hanging out washing, and another woman sitting in the sun outside a tin hut. They would have been good to talk to after the boring monotony of Miss Phipps, who was no company at all, who did not even answer when you spoke.

The winter darkness closed down like a boy's hand over

78

a lame bird; and still there was no cheery 'Yodel-eh-hey-yo' from the busker coming up the road. The Stray moved restlessly about the camp, nagging at Miss Phipps in a preoccupied way. She made several trips to the road to see if Duke was coming or if there was any sign of Snow.

'If on'y one of 'em 'ud come back,' she worried. Now that the dusk, in which the trees showed like black veins drawing the blood from the sky, had thickened to a clotted darkness, the two women seemed to be tethered in the radius of the fire. They were held by the dancing light that gathered them to itself in the glow under the dim trees.

The Stray reached for Snow's old coat. 'I'm goin' to look for him,' she said.

'Oh, trust these men to take good care of themselves,' Miss Phipps yawned.

Outside the circle of the firelight was another world; and to leave the fire was to walk through an unseen wall where the light ended and the darkness began. Once your eyes were accustomed to the bulks and pits of it, there were degrees of shadow, and the road was a dim greyness. The Stray, stumbling along through the ruts and stones, had only one idea: to walk until she met Snow. She was so afraid of the dark that her teeth chattered. 'Things' might grab at her. It wasn't the darkness she feared as much as the fact that it gave cover for supernatural monsters covered with fur and fangs and claws, for creepy, loathsome horrors, who might breathe on you as you passed, or reach out to clutch you. When a stone rolled under her foot and she stumbled, there was a breathless moment while she half decided to hurry back within the comfortable walls the firelight flung up against the tree-trunks.

The light of a farmhouse showed yellow down a dip in the road, and that comforted her. You could always run to the house and beat on the door and scream to be let in. No ghost would chase you to a house. She trudged on, peering ahead, stopping to listen for the sound of hoof-beats. A car whizzed past her, boring a tunnel of light

79

towards the town and leaving the darkness behind more blinding than before, until the little red tail-light winked over a rise; then night seemed to get its breath and tidy its trees and settle the silence into place again.

A dog barked insistently from the homestead that was behind her now, and as she trudged down into the next hollow, there came a racket and cricketing of frogs. Here, at the bottom of the hill, the fences had been pushed back from their flanking of road to allow a stretch of grassy flat for travelling stock. Dancy recognised it as the place where the busker had wanted to camp because the feed and water were good. She had complained that it was too far out of town, and Snow had croaked weakly that there was a better camp farther on.

Something black detached itself from the roadside and came towards her. Undecided whether to scream or run, the Stray found herself being licked by Bluey; an unusually friendly, tail-wagging, whining Bluey. She gave a yell: 'Sn-oo-ow!'

There was no answer, but from a black patch of trees there came the snort of a horse, and a grey blur showed where the Horehound moved near a fence inside which some big draught horses were grazing. The Stray turned off the road and plunged into the gloom of the trees, making in a direct line for the Horehound. She fell into a pothole, thrashed through a drift of dead leaves and twigs that snapped and crackled underfoot, and so found the faint trace of a track. Fifty yards from the road, in a patch of dry creek-bed tangled with briar bushes, she almost tripped over the body of Snow. Her teeth chattering, she fumbled for the matches with numbed fingers.

'Are you all right, Snow love? Hey, Snow, what is it?' she gulped.

The man gave a groan and stirred. This heartened her. In the flame of the match his face showed as a horrible mess of bloodstains. The flesh had been pulped below his eye where the Horehound had kicked him when he stooped to take a flint out of her shoe. He was conscious, but he could not speak, and as the Stray bent over him, he tried to stir, then collapsed again.

She must go for help; but first what was that she had heard about bringing water in your hat? Sliding and scrambling towards the trickle of water, she mechanically dipped her only hat into it. The hat did not hold water very well. Then she decided that Snow could not possibly drink water with his face in that condition, and it would be cruel to dash it over him, so she dropped the hat with the water in it, tenderly laid the coat she wore over Snow, and hurried back towards the road. Dancy was no longer afraid of the darkness. She did not cry. Her mouth was set in a grim line. As she neared the road, she broke into a stumbling run. There was a car coming along the road towards the town. If she could only get to the road in time, she could stop it. She rushed out on the road, waving her arms, too breathless to shout.

The truck was approaching very slowly because it had only one dim headlight. It was as well that the Stray had time to draw breath before it reached her and scream to the driver, or she might have been run down. Obligingly the truck roared and panted to a standstill, and the Stray poured out her incoherent story.

'He came after the horses with 'flu, and the Hore kicked 'im and 'e's lyin' way off the road there, mister. Oh . . . if only Dukesy 'ad stayed 'stead of goin' to town. . . . Mister, see to 'im, will yuh? I can't lift 'im and the two horses are there . . .' she babbled.

The little man in the cloth cap who was driving had a woman sitting beside him with a baby in her arms. He unpacked the woman, the baby, and two small boys by the road and told them to hold up any car that came past.

'Now, my girl,' he said mildly, 'calm down. I'll take the truck in as far as I can, then there will not be such a distance to carry him.' His voice was unusual in a truck-driver, particularly the driver of a shabby little old truck that had been converted into a caravan and was filled with bundles of bedding and household odds and ends.

The Stray, even in her distracted state, wondered dimly at the apparition.

'You've missed your dole, mister,' she advised, as the truck swung off the road and lurched over a gutter.

'I don't get any dole,' the driver answered. He concentrated on his driving. The truck's steering-gear was loose and the truck wobbled along drunkenly, escaping disaster in the form of gilgais and hidden logs only by a hair's breadth. The driver spun the wheel as though he were on the bridge of a ship. 'This is as far as we can go,' he said calmly. 'I know the place well.'

Ahead of the one dim car-light the grey bulk of the Horehound moved away, stopping to graze when the car stopped. The faint chink of her hobbles came as insolently to the Stray's ears as if the Horehound were Salome dancing in triumph with tinkling feet. The girl's hatred of the horse flamed up in a bitter anger.

'I'll beat the life out of that there mare,' she breathed. 'I'll cut 'er to ribbons.'

'You take his feet,' the truck-driver ordered. 'Careful now.'

He was a small man, but he managed Snowy very skilfully. He had him in the truck and laid out on the bundles of bedding while the Stray fussed about unhandily tugging at one of Snow's boots, then the other.

The shivering little group of children and their mother greeted them as they rejoined the road. No car had come past.

'There never is anyone happen when you want 'em,' the Stray said bitterly.

'We happened,' the man replied calmly. 'Climb in, Milly,' he addressed his wife. 'We'll get this poor chap to hospital before we make camp.'

It was a tight squeeze with the children and their mother, Snow, the Stray, and the driver. The old truck bucketed noisily along the road, shaking and trembling as if with cold. The Stray made her first useful contribution to the conversation.

'Your missus could stay at our camp wiv the kids and my mate,' she suggested, 'while we drives to 'ospital wiv Snow.'

'Good,' the driver said.

'The camp's jus' back along the road a way.'

The driver nodded. He was driving at what was for the truck a furious pace, fully thirty-five miles an hour. It took him all his time to hold the road at that devilish speed. The dim embers of the camp-fire showed off on the left-hand side, and the man at the wheel swung his truck along the branching track towards it. He unloaded his wife and children swiftly and competently, also some encumbering boxes, so that Snow would have more room. Meanwhile the Stray, in a volley of curses, was telling the busker what she thought of him. The busker swayed slightly as he stood; and although somewhat sobered by the news of Snow's accident, he could do with a deal more sobering. He had sung and played his best for that second lot of rum, and since it was a cold night, he had thought no harm to bring home his share inside him. He was in favour of forcing the rum between Snow's teeth, and only the firmness of the truck-driver restrained him from carrying out his intentions.

'He'll be all right when his face is stitched,' the stranger said decidedly. 'You stay here, my child,' he patted the Stray kindly. 'Mr. . . .?' He beckoned the busker.

'Duke,' the busker said.

'Mr. Duke will come with me. Bryson'—he turned to the elder of the two small boys—'you go back for those two horses.'

They drove off before the open-mouthed Stray had time to wail a protest. She turned to the infant Bryson, who was preparing to depart. 'You can't go all by yourself.' The Stray looked at Bryson's mother. 'Can 'e?'

'He's a good boy.' Bryson's mother, a thin, quiet woman, was busy with the baby. 'You had better tie up that grey horse for the night, Bryson, when you bring it back.'

'Right-o, Mum.'

The self-possessed Bryson trotted off.

Miss Phipps, who had regarded the invasion coldly, was impressed with the accent of the new arrivals. So much so that she put on more firewood and dipped out a billy of water for tea without being told.

'Might I ask your name?' she asked very grandly. 'Mine is Miss Phipps. Dora Chester-Phipps.'

'Mrs. Postlewaite,' the quiet, sandy-haired woman replied. She was sitting on a log nursing the baby, who had awakened and begun to cry.

The Stray regarded her with interest. 'Geeze,' she exclaimed. 'Ain't your husband the one they call the 'Postle? Always preaching about not boozin' an' beatin' 'orses? A parson, he is, ain't he, missus?'

Over the face of the woman nursing the baby a frightened look passed quickly.

'He has no connection,' she said mechanically, as if she were denying some indictment, 'with any church. None whatever.'

II

'It was my nervous breakdown,' the Apostle was saying to Harley Duke as the little truck made its palsied way back from the hospital. 'It was my nervous breakdown that showed me the way.' He put the truck into second gear as they laboured up a hill. 'One could not blame the bishop. He was a kind, just man, and the Church authorities were very good—I have a small pension—but after my nervous breakdown . . .' He broke off and peered anxiously ahead. 'I wonder if you would mind if I stopped at the bridge to ask if the Tyrells are camped there. They always camp near the bridge if they are in Logan. I particularly want to have a word with Deafy Tyrell.'

The driving in the cold air had restored the busker. He found he could focus on an object without feeling too much as though his eyes were propped open. He was still

84

drowsy, however, and he sat nodding as the Apostle climbed out and walked towards the red, blinking smudges of camp-fires. There was a barking of dogs and then a welcoming roar of voices. The shape of a big woman was outlined between the fire and the glow of a lamp in a tent. She seemed to be conducting with a spoon an orchestra of rough voices that her own screaming dominated.

Presently the Apostle climbed back. 'There's a crowd of them,' he declared. 'The Tyrell family and Sharkey Wilks and his wife and the Dirty Jones's and Thirty-Bob Collins.' He started the truck again. 'I think I'll move into the river camp to-morrow. Why don't you come, too? It would be closer to the hospital.'

Duke, throwing over all Snow's prejudices against camping with a 'big mob,' agreed at once. It would be company for the Stray and Phippsy. Snow would be in hospital for a few weeks at least, and the busker felt he could not endure being alone with the two women. He was curious to know more about the Apostle. The small man, with his extraordinary mixture of decision and timidity, had aroused Duke's interest.

As the Apostle bent in the glow of the one headlight to crank the truck, Duke studied the man shrewdly. The Apostle had one of those noble brows, serene and lofty, crowned by a mop of grey curls, a brow and head for any sculptor. Under that tremendous brow his face, with its peaked, small nose, tight thin mouth, and square chin, seemed curiously dwarfed. He looked like a child or an escaped cherub in disguise as an ageing man. That manner he had of almost apologising for his existence while he took command, his shabby clothes and cultured voice, the slim hands with dirty nails, the hands of a rector turned amateur mechanic, all these interested the busker.

'We were making for the town camp when we met your little friend,' the Apostle explained. In the short drive to the hospital he had found out all about Snow and Phippsy and the Stray and the busker himself, in the most courteous, skilful, and apologetic way possible.

'You were telling me about the bishop,' the busker hinted.

'Yes, yes. A good, kindly man, but without vision. Not that I would condemn . . .' He broke off nervously. 'It was the sermon I preached on The Blood.' The truck took a sudden swerve towards the roadside, and the busker nervously gripped the wheel, then apologised. 'Not at all. I should pay more attention to my driving. Do you ever think, my good people, I said, that we are all part of The Blood?' His voice had risen. 'That the worlds and the universes as they move are but corpuscles circulating in that great stream of life that flows and flows from the body of our Lord. That we are but cells in that celestial stream, unescapably a part . . .' He broke off again in his abrupt way, as though to take a grip of himself. 'Something in what I said offended them. I can quite understand that. And then there was my nervous breakdown. But that wouldn't interest you.'

The busker protested that it would, but the Reverend Harold Postlewaite was silent for a space of two farms.

'I had always admired the preaching friars,' he said suddenly, just as the busker was nodding again. 'As a young man I had been fired by the idea of a new order of society, or at least a new order of such friars, who would travel the country and preach in the market-places, the public squares. And then, of course, I married.' He sighed, and his mind darted off on another track. 'So after my breakdown, when there was obviously nothing for me—no parish—I bought this little truck. I was cheated, of course. Not that I blame the man.' He smiled in the dark. 'I was a mug, and mugs are made to be taken down. But my wife insisted on coming and bringing the children. She agreed that the open-air life would do me good.' He sighed again. 'It is a little difficult to explain that friars are celibate, and perhaps not quite fair to a woman. She was so eager to come, and the matter of celibacy has remained in abeyance.

'They call me Looney Harry or the 'Postle,' he went on.

86

'Short for Apostle. So you see,' he brightened up, 'I have a roving commission in Hell.'

There was something in his voice that startled the busker awake.

'Hey,' he said loudly. 'What do you mean, Hell?'

'Well, isn't it?' the little man said quietly. 'The life of the people on the track is something that Hell must shiver to see.' He insisted: 'Isn't it?'

'It's not so bad,' the busker said slowly. 'If you strike a good town.'

'You're young,' the Apostle commented quietly. 'But when you're old, when you're on a hungry track, without food or water, and sick, and lonely . . . There's no Hell worse than loneliness.'

The busker was silenced. 'Thasso,' he admitted. 'But I won't be on the track when *I'm* old. I'm going to get back to the city and get a job.' He wondered why he had not thought of it before.

'You might,' the Apostle agreed. 'But, then, you're not a workman tramping looking for work. With your guitar you can make more money in an afternoon than bagmen would see in a month. I know. Of course, I don't do any real good,' he admitted impartially; then he brightened again. 'But being mad on the track doesn't matter so much. There's so much madness on the track. Everyone you meet is mad in some way, and my ideas, I comfort myself, are no madder than most.'

The truck bumped suddenly off the road towards the camp, and just as suddenly the Apostle reverted to a tone so normal that the busker could hardly believe it was the same man who had been talking before. 'Bryson will have brought back the horses,' he said. 'He's a dependable boy —very dependable. He's only eleven and he drives better than I do.'

This, the busker considered, would not be difficult, even for a boy of eleven.

Bryson, with his younger brother, Whitefield, Phippsy, Mrs. Postlewaite and the Stray were sitting round the fire waiting for news. The news was reassuring enough to cheer even the Stray. The gash had been stitched, but the doctor declared that Snow's general debility was such that he was lucky to escape pneumonia.

'I thought maybe 'e'd get tubey-galoshes,' Dancy declared. 'I knew a bloke that got tubey-galoshes.'

She would go up to the hospital to-morrow with a bunch of flowers. Even if she was not let in—and she probably would not be—she could leave the flowers. It would be simple to pick a nosegay over the front fences of houses in the town.

She watched curiously the way the Apostle bowed his head and muttered over his food. Duke had already started in on a large slab of bread and a plate of stew; and he dropped his spoon and fumbled for it in confusion. Parsons, he supposed, should be allowed a certain licence, but saying grace and embarrassing people was a bit over the odds. The Apostle's tea did not seem to be anything to arouse fervent thanks. A small piece of cheese and some kind of green weed with a brown-looking damper, very different from ordinary damper, was all he had.

'Hey, there's plenty o' stoo,' the Stray offered bountifully. 'Bog in for all you're worth. We got our dole to-day.'

'Thank you all the same,' the Apostle replied, 'but I don't eat meat.'

'Not eat meat!' The Stray exchanged glances with the busker. She inspected the Apostle's food curiously. 'What's that green stuff, mister?'

'Watercress.' The Apostle munched it cheerfully. 'We found some in a little creek as we came along.' He launched out into an enthusiastic dissertation on the native spinach around Moree, on the food value of nettles and other plants that the audience had considered mere weeds. The Apostle, they were to discover later, was always testing out strange herbage on his unsuspecting family. He had a theory that what a bird or a horse could eat, a human being could eat. That was all very well for the

88

Apostle, who had the digestion of a billygoat and the fortitude to endure his occasional mistakes in silence. But his family had grown more cautious. When Mrs. Postlewaite saw her husband plucking a more than usually curious and suspicious bit of greenery, or pounding seeds to discover if they had food value, she would give the children a warning glance that confined them to bread and cheese.

'When men eat the flesh of animals,' the Apostle declared, 'they are eating grass and plants at one remove. Isn't it better to eat the plants themselves?' There was a silence that might have meant consent. He finished his watercress, then looked round expectantly. 'We usually have family prayers immediately after tea. Perhaps you would care to join us?'

This, at their own fireside, struck Duke and Dancy as very unfair; but they mumbled a half-hearted agreement. Miss Phipps, in her most unpleasant voice, declared that she had no intention whatever of 'taking part in any such mumbo-jumbo. Utterly ridiculous and absurd!' she exclaimed scornfully.

Immediately the other two, their hospitality outraged, turned on her ferociously.

'If you don't like it,' the busker said sternly, 'just shut up. Nobody cares what you think, anyway.'

'Don't take any notice of her, mister,' the Stray encouraged warmly. 'She can get to hell outta 'ere if she don't want to listen. Go ahead. Me an' Dooksie don't mind. I've 'ad a hell of a lot more religion shoved into me than her, and if I can stand it, she can.'

With this noble and generous sentiment, the Stray composed herself on a log with the resigned look of Bluey chained under the cart. Outvoted as usual, Miss Phipps sulked. The Apostle apologised and offered to retire behind his motor-truck out of hearing. His hosts, with renewed glares at the recalcitrant Phippsy, insisted he was not to leave the fire. So finally Miss Phipps, who was stubbornly determined not to retire herself, had to sit scornfully through the Apostle's prayers, which included everything from Snow's accident to the rain which seemed to be impending.

When the Postlewaites had retired, and Miss Phipps, feeling that she had outlasted the enemy, also strolled away to the van, Duke and Dancy sat discussing the new arrivals.

'D'you s'pose he's always like that?' the Stray asked.

'I s'pose so,' Duke answered doubtfully. 'I've heard about him in camps here and there, but they didn't say he was as bad as this.' Then he added hastily: 'Decent enough bloke in other ways, though.'

'We don't need to camp too near him,' the Stray remarked after a lengthy silence. 'And anyway'—she eyed Duke as though daring him to contradict her—'after what I've been froo, what wiv the Salvation Army once half-starvin' me in one of them hostels, it rolls off me like water off a duck's back, that prayin' does.'

'Me, too,' the busker agreed heartily.

With this comforting assurance they retired to bed.

Chapter VII

THE Gunnar River curved sickle-wise round the town of Logan, holding it on a green plate of lucerne flats from which the roofs heaped up about a rise of land crowned by a grey water-tower. It was a rich, proud town, proud like a sore that had swelled itself from the farmlands about it, drawing their richness into its shops, their money into its banks. There was a well-equipped high school from which the brightest boys were taken away because their parents must send them out as labourers; a magnificent cinema with weak projection and worse sound; well-built churches with a few elderly women for congregations; and a town park in which a group of portly dowager palm trees flanked a war memorial and a machine-gun.

Just as the town dumped its rubbish on the river-bend, so it dumped those human oddments for which it saw no use nor excuse. The coloured people, the old-age pensioners, lived beside the garbage-tip in little humpies made of bits of old bags, kerosene tins, rusty iron or boughs. No one wanted this flat because it was liable to flood; only the Chinamen laboured there among their rows of green vegetables guarded by high thorn hedges and a ferocious pack of dogs.

Beside the Chinamen's fence a row of little shanties had their place. These were occupied by the élite of river-bank society, travelling families for the most part, who had tenaciously clenched to a foothold in the town—people such as Mrs. Flaherty, who sent off five children shining clean every morning to the convent school and had her two elder daughters working in the town, one as a waitress, and one as a maid. They had augmented their original tent by a one-room shack built by Mr. Flaherty, who was also responsible for the well and the little fenced-in vegetable patch. The Flahertys owned a radio set and in the tent which served as the girls' bedroom there was a new bedroom suite for which they were still paying. But the Flahertys knew they were a cut above the other dwellers on the river-bank. They never spoke to travellers, and seldom even to Old Jim, who had a little tin humpy just next door to them.

On the far side of the garbage-tip the dark people had their settlement, a group of tin-and-bag residences in various stages of decadence. No one mixed with them except, sometimes, the travellers. The Littles, the Murrays, were left very much alone, partly from the prejudice which accuses dark people of never understanding the etiquette of a fight, and again because, so the whites said, the black people 'smelt.' This was an accusation which might with justice have been levelled at many of the white campers; but grumblers insisted that the blacks smelt different.

The travellers camped between the outcast Murrays

and the aristocratic Flahertys, and up-wind from the Murrays. There was, of course, a 'Camping Prohibited' notice on this favoured spot, just as there were Camping Prohibited notices anywhere along the river-bank; but they gave handy support for an over-night shelter, and usually had bits of tin propped against them, and at their foot a bed of boughs with a blackened ring where a camp-fire had been.

The willows were stripped of their last gold leaf, but down in the Chinamen's gardens the quince trees, in which the parrots were busy, still burned with gold and orange and scarlet, and the cedar trees were laden with berries the colour of old cream. Across the vivid green felt of the lucerne flats, the rising ground, where the town stood, showed only as a confusion of fences, out-houses and old sheds. The town had its back to the river-bend, and might safely be disregarded by anyone camped just on that stretch between the railway bridge and the road bridge. And disregarded it was, except when a police visit made the huts and camps aware of the town's existence.

The settlement of human odds and ends on the river-bank led their own lives, fought out their own quarrels, upheld their own standards. There, as in any proper camp, the young bagmen on foot or with bicycles did not mix with the men with families and sulkies; and the families spoke only to other families. Caste was caste, and the nice distinctions must be preserved between the settler in a hut and the temporary occupants of a tent.

Of course there were problems in this class distinction: Adelaide, for instance. Adelaide was so called because he had set out from that distant bourne with two horses, a waggon, and a harness made of fencing-wire. He told everyone there was a job waiting for him in Newcastle, but he did not seem in any hurry to get there. He had been so long in Logan that the grass was growing about the wheels of the waggon, in which and under which his numerous family slept. He had even tied wires from one tree to another to form a corral to keep his horses from straying. Some of the travellers resented this enclosure; but Adelaide was a fair, glib, cheerful man who always had an answer. First, he could not move on, under the pressing invitation of the sergeant, because his black mare had split her hoof. Then he could not move on because his wife was expecting a baby. Then his eldest boy broke his arm. Adelaide rated both as a settler and a traveller, and he talked to whoever would listen. He had been caught red-handed trapping 'possums and had wriggled out on the plea of his large family and his wife's condition. As his wife was almost permanently expecting an infant, it came as a handy excuse on more than one occasion.

Many a time had the sergeant cursed the maternity ward attached to the Logan hospital. 'Every thieving scoundrel in the country makes for this place!' he would exclaim. 'And they're all here to get more kids. 'Tisn't as though they hadn't enough already. I know what I'd do to the whole boiling lot of them.'

But it was not only the maternity ward which attracted travellers. The Logan camp was a green pleasance, with stretches of grassy swards between great river-gums that towered up, flexing huge muscles, their tattered rags of bark about their feet, and their great white trunks powerful as naked athletes, throwing protective shadow over the littleness of unrooted things. The she-oaks, with stiff, dark needles like long hairs, sighing and sheltering, crooked a comfortable bough here, inviting any small, grey-brown tent to use it as a ridge-pole. What more had a traveller ever asked than water, grass for horses and wood for his fire?

Tradition had long ago marked out divisions of the bank. Dogger and Snake, dropping off a goods-train, camped beneath the railway bridge, where they had a rendezvous with Burning Angus and Uncle, who had push-bikes. Single bagmen made instinctively for the bachelor quarters beneath the bridge. There were twelve in all that dole-day, each with his separate little heap of belongings, but preserving a unity of ascetic disapproval towards the vans, three of them, plus a cart and a sulky resting beside Adelaide's outpost, nearer to the huts on the river-bend.

The brown van belonged to Sharkey Wilks, and his was the chestnut mare, now, to his sorrow, in foal. Sharkey, who had a wife and two daughters, had a prejudice against females, and he was willing to expound the reasons for it to anyone who would spare a blush. 'If there's one kind of horse I ain't got no time for,' he would remark bitterly, showing all his yellow teeth, 'it's a mare.' His other horse had broken its leg and had to be shot; and, of course, he could not move, he explained to the sergeant, while the mare was in foal.

A little farther down, under a group of she-oaks, was the van of no perceptible colour except mud belonging to the Dirty Joneses. They had been called the Dirty Joneses so long that they no longer resented the imputation. They always had a pack of children with running noses, and before you knew what had happened, they would be swarming into a newcomer's camp, sniffing about, lifting small articles, and reappearing at intervals with messages ı 'Me muvver says can you lend her sixpence to buy the baby a dummy? Me muvver says have you got any tea you can spare?' and they would snatch whatever they came for and make off without thanks.

The Tyrells were different. Ma Tyrell and Deafy, her husband, were as well aware of it as anyone. They had a big marquee tent, they had a good van, and two horses, Deafy claiming that his was 'the best turnout on the track bar-rr-r none.' The Tyrells' eldest son, Dick, travelled with them, driving his own cart and his own horse. They had two daughters respectably married to men with railway jobs in two different towns. They worked at such jobs as onion-planting, tomato-picking, prune-gathering, pea-picking—anything, in fact, where Deafy could hire out his family on contract work. They had formerly travelled in a big old sedan car which they would leave

94

at some discreet distance when they went up in their oldest clothes to collect their dole.

'All out of the kids,' Deafy was wont to remark. 'Them kids can pick like two men.'

In between jobs picking, Mrs. Tyrell, a big, amiable woman with a voice like that of a windjammer's mate, from long years of shouting to Deafy, would be industriously whirring away at her little sewing-machine, turning out pot-holders, aprons and other articles made of hessian and edged with bright chintz, which the children sold from door to door.

Beside the Tyrell camp, a small heap consisting of one tarpaulin, a tucker-box and an evil, buff-coloured, kangaroo dog called Rex, denoted the presence of the Tyrells' friend, Thirty-Bob. Thirty-Bob's sulky, with its shafts to earth, looking queerly like a kneeling camel, was cheek by jowl with the van and the cart; and his horse, a transient horse, which he was always swopping away for a new one, grazed with the Tyrell horses.

Under a sky like steel wool, the Tyrell encampment still preserved a cheerful and welcoming aspect. A great black camp-oven, in the glowing embers of the fire like a half-burnt log, was a promise of plenty; and a blackened kerosene tin, hung from the hook of a tripod, contained Mrs. Tyrell's never-failing supply of hot water for the baby's clothes.

Around the domestic focus were grouped on boxes, or merely sprawling on the ground, the Tyrell family and Mr. and Mrs. Sharkey Wilks, who were passing the time in a yarn, while they awaited the return of their daughters, who had 'taken out the port' on a selling trip around the town. Mrs. Sharkey, as though drawn by some primitive sympathy, had taken her seat by Deafy Tyrell. She was much deafer than he was, but she made up for it by talking all the time, whereas Deafy was a silent man. Thirty-Bob and young Dick Tyrell had promised the Apostle to 'look over' his car, and were lounging impatiently and cursing his non-arrival.

'He's probably put his nose into somebody's business again and got it jammed there,' Thirty-Bob suggested ungraciously. 'Here's Dick and me been sitting on our sterns all day waiting for the cow, and he don't show up.'

Sharkey Wilks made an unpleasant sound resembling a snarl. 'Arr, that bastard, I ain't got no time for him. Nasty, sneaking little rat, talkin' that smooth you could knock his face in. He'd better not come round my camp, or I'll lay him out with the trap-setter.'

There was no real inducement for anyone to come round Mr. Wilks' camp. As a matter of fact, it was with the greatest strain on their politeness that the Tyrells were enduring his presence in their own. There are some men whose character advertises itself in every look and gesture, and the character of Sharkey Wilks was noisome.

Mrs. Tyrell glanced up from the sewing-machine where she had been paying little attention to the conversation until the name of the Apostle cropped up. In the brown of her face, carved and tanned by sun and wind, her eyes were a clear, blazing blue. It was like coming in sight of the sea round a rocky headland to have that startling, youthful gaze from a middle-aged woman. She very deliberately boomed at Sharkey Wilks:

'I won't have nothing said against Harry Postlewaite in my camp.'

With this ultimatum she returned to her sewing, whirring away furiously, as though it was Sharkey she stitched under the needle-foot.

'No offence, missus,' Sharkey hastened to soothe her. 'He may be all right. I ain't saying he ain't. Only let him keep out of my camp, that's all.' He leered round at the assembled company. 'I've got young daughters to think of, that's all. Gotta pertect them, ain't I?'

Sharkey Wilks's women were notorious. His wife and elder daughter had a name that was bandied about in camps from Logan to Bourke. 'The only decent one's that little Betty,' Mrs. Tyrell had herself declared. 'And I'm sorry for the poor little devil, I am that . . . in advance.'

'The 'Postle picked up Snow Grimshaw on the road last night with his face kicked in,' Dick Tyrell remarked. 'You know Snow, Sharkey? Big, fair feller with a walk like a cattledog.'

'Him? Why, he'd sneak the hay the cocky was sleeping on. I should say I know him. He's been in for meat more times than I cud count.'

Again Mrs. Tyrell lifted her head and boomed. 'Don't say nothing against Snow Grimshaw, Sharkey. I won't have it.'

'Me? Why, I ain't said nothing.' Sharkey was injured. 'A man can't even open his mouth.'

'I don't say you *were* saying anything,' Mrs. Tyrell returned pontifically. 'Just don't, that's all.'

'Arr, what's up with you, Ma? You got a bad liver,' Sharkey glowered. 'Snow's got a little fair piece with him?' he ventured presently.

'How d'you know?'

'Seen 'em up at the p'lice-station.'

'It's a funny thing,' Deafy broke into the conversation, 'how many women there are on the road nowadays. Why, you meet 'em every way you turn. I wonder why that is?'

'A woman can get more'n a man. You gotta'—Sharkey considered judicially—'you gotta have a woman to bum for yer, just as you gotta have a dog to bark for yer.'

'It's different with a good turnout. But some of these poor things, they ain't got a rag to cover them hardly. I never asked my wife to travel like that, just footing it.'

Sharkey, as an authority on women, laid down the law. 'Well, it stands to reason. A woman's there to put up with things, ain't she? Otherwise she wouldn't a been born that way. A woman's meant for the worst jobs. It's a woman's lot to bear, ain't it? Well, let her put up with it. It gives her something to grouch about. Why, if a woman didn't have nothing to moan for, she'd fall sick or something. Not that I stand any moaning from my mob. I'd take the hide off 'em with a belt if they started to whine to me. That's the way to treat 'em.'

'It's a good thing your missus is that deaf she can't hear you,' Thirty-Bob suggested.

But Mrs. Wilks always knew when anyone was talking about her. She would suddenly hear a scrap of conversation just because no one wanted her to, though she could be deaf enough on other occasions.

'I can hear you, Thirty-Bob,' she screamed suddenly. 'Don't think I can't.'

There had been a lull for a few minutes in the eternal monologue that Mrs. Wilks carried on to herself in a high, monotonous chant, breaking every now and then into a shriek. She was no pleasanter companion than her husband, but whereas he had something snakish in his narrow head and long body, his wife ran to fat. Her face was bloated and wrinkled like sour cream, folds of yellow fat rolling down to the dirty edge of camisole that showed above a black silk dress; a silk dress sleeked tight over great bulges of flesh and hanging drunkenly around Mrs. Wilks's pillar-like bare legs. She bore, besides other imputations, the title of the worst-tongued woman on the road and it was unwise to show her any unfriendliness, lest she blacken your character in every camp in the State. That was why the Tyrells were enduring this visit. They knew better than to offend the Wilkses.

'Him!' she screamed, pointing to her husband. 'What does he ever do? Loafs about, eating, sleeping . . .' She made an obscene gesture. 'That's all he's good for. Lets me and the girls go out selling. That there van we wouldn't a got but for the girls. What happens when the horse breaks its leg and has to be shot? It's me . . . me . . . me, that has to go begging and praying and searching for another. Oh . . .!' she shrieked. 'Don't talk to me about men. Loafers all of them, and me married to the worst.'

'Sharkey ain't so bad,' Dick bawled in her ear to provoke her. He enjoyed the fun of teasing Mrs. Wilks. She only half heard.

'He's bad all right.' She shook her great bloated cheeks

with conviction. 'All men, all bad, bad, bad. Oh, don't talk to me!'

'Now then, Mrs. Wilks,' Thirty-Bob put in, his ugly face split in a persuasive grin, 'don't you say *that*.' He winked. 'You gotta admit there's some things men are good for.'

A chuckle went round the circle.

'What's he say?' Mrs. Wilks demanded, and when the remark was bawled in her ear, she began to laugh so heartily that her great bulk nearly toppled from the stool. 'He! he! You're worse than any of them.' She slapped Thirty-Bob on the back so heartily that he swore.

'Tell her that if she'll meet me some night when her old man ain't home, I'll show her she's wrong,' Thirty-Bob shouted.

On this fresh sally being translated, Mrs. Wilks broke into a fresh fit of laughter. 'You better not let Sharkey hear you, Thirty-Bob. You better not let him hear you.'

Further courtesies were prevented by the arrival of the Apostle's truck, which came bumping cautiously down a set of ruts that skirted the Chinamen's fence. Behind him lurched the van with the busker in the driver's seat, and, last of all, the Stray grim-lipped in the sulky.

With a sigh of thankfulness the wanderers tilted down a thistle-covered incline, skirted a patch of blackberry bush, and drew up on the very lip of the stream next to the Tyrell camp.

'I could stay here,' the Stray declared fervently—'I could stay here for years and years, for ever if you like.'

Here, on this stretch of sheltered green, they could rest, feel firm ground under their feet after the joltings of so many hundred miles, and revel in the company of their kind. Even the busker, surveying the staid domesticity of the river-bank, could not help agreeing.

'Christ, Harry!' Thirty-Bob hailed the Apostle, 'where the hell you been? Don't think we can fix that Liz of yours in the dark, do you?'

The Apostle was apologising, explaining that had it not

99

been for the busker pushing the truck to start it, they would not be there yet. But Thirty-Bob was not listening. Sharp as a bit of barbed wire, he had already cast an acquisitive eye on the Horehound. He walked round her solemnly and inspected her teeth.

'Eight if she's a day.' He made it sound like a major crime.

Dealing horses Thirty-Bob had earned his nickname. He always tried to get 'thirty-bob to boot' on each deal; and rumour unkindly and untruthfully credited him with swopping away his mother.

Deafy, his son Dick, Sharkey Wilks, and even stuttering little Jake Tyrell, who was only fourteen, assumed a knowledgeable air and closed in a circle around the Horehound.

'Hell of a temper,' Thirty-Bob continued. 'She's got jib's ears. See how she lays 'em back.'

Duke had no intention of dealing, swapping or otherwise disposing of the Horehound, but he felt there was no reason to decry her.

'Why, that horse, sport'—in his tone was reproof—'she's as quiet as a lamb. Why, a child could drive her. Look here, Dancy, didn't you drive the Horehound all the way from Blimdagery?'

But both Dancy and Miss Phipps had strolled away. As far as they were concerned Horehound could pass out of their lives without their shedding a tear. Miss Phipps left this clutter of strange men with the air of a woman who always delegates such unpleasant jobs as wood-and-water-getting to the underlings. She rolled a cigarette of Snow's tobacco, inserted it in a long, imitation amber holder, clamped this between her teeth, and wiggled it thoughtfully like some weird proboscis, as she favoured the river-bank with a long, patronising inspection.

'Where every prospect pleases,' she said aloud, 'and, of course, the usual vilaciously vile men.'

Disregarding these, as was her wont, she began to practise her dance-steps, finishing with a few bending exercises guaranteed to improve the figure. The vile men regarded her with a wonder not unmixed with joy, for she was trespassing on the single men's camp by the railway bridge.

'By cripes!' One of the bagmen, who had been peacefully washing his shirt, pointed her out to his mate. 'Take a squiz at that, Jim.' He whistled tentatively at Miss Phipps, who proceeded with her exercises in noble scorn, taking no notice of him.

'She must be dippy,' the bagman exclaimed at this fresh proof. 'But even so'—his tone was that of one making the best of a bad job—'a man might do a line with her, dippy or not.'

His mate, whose interests were political and liquid, snorted in a censorious manner. 'I'd be a bit fussy if I were you,' he grunted.

The Stray had struck down the river-bank in the opposite direction in search of feminine society; the Tyrell two-year-old, Shirley, held out in her arms as an introduction.

'I brought yer little girl back, missus,' she called to Mrs. Tyrell. 'She was getting too close to the horses.'

'Siddown, woman.' Mrs. Tyrell welcomed her all the more cheerfully because at her approach Mrs. Wilks had scornfully retired to her own camp, saying that it would soon be dark and she had no tea ready.

The Stray accepted her stool, and sat contentedly cuddling the baby. Mrs. Tyrell asked after Snow, to whom the Stray referred as 'me old man in hospital,' and was given a lurid description of the accident. Every time the Stray told the story it grew more exciting. At this stage, Snow would have sustained less injury under the tramplings of a herd of elephants.

'You ain't got no fam'ly?' Mrs. Tyrell's question recalled Dancy to the necessity for caution.

'Freddie and Brian and Jimmy.' The Stray had Snow's family off by heart. 'They been left with their grandma.'

Mrs. Tyrell was too courteous to show she knew the Stray was lying, but she could not resist one quiet dig.

'Seeing you're so fond of children, woman, I wonder you didn't bring your family with you.'

'I didn't have no choice,' the Stray retorted, which was perfectly true. The Child Welfare Department had swooped down on her baby when it was a few months old.

She enquired of Mrs. Tyrell's family, and heard all about them, from the two married daughters and their husbands, Dick the eldest boy, Jake ('We dunno what to do about that stutter of his'), Evie, a solemn, shrewd little girl who stood by with the air of one from whom few secrets are hid, Johnnie (and his habit of bed-wetting), Alfie and Joan, the twins, Shirley, aged two, and the baby. Two more children, the Stray learnt, had been left behind with the married daughters. When Mrs. Tyrell said proudly that there were 'thirteen in the family,' she was counting in the baby whose arrival they had come to Logan to await.

At the point when the conversation began to be very interesting to feminine ears, the busker yelled: 'Hey, Dancy!' and the Stray was forced to hurry back to her camp.

'Come up again,' Mrs. Tyrell called; and under her breath she muttered: 'I'm sorry for that poor little devil.'

The Stray's kindness to children was no sham, whatever her other pretensions, and Mrs. Tyrell liked her for that. On many an occasion the Stray would have cause to value Mrs. Tyrell's friendship in the long time their wanderings lay together.

The busker's yell had evidently meant he wanted food, but when Dancy hurried up there was no sign of him. He had gone off for wood, and so she betook herself, with Phippsy's dilatory aid, to frying the bacon.

Dick Tyrell had advised the busker that the bridge was being repaired and that the workmen sometimes threw down timber, so it was in the direction of the road-bridge that the busker went. There were small branches everywhere, but he wanted a sizeable log that would burn all night. Dancy, he thought, might have come with him to give a hand, instead of yarning with that big woman and letting him do all the work. It was not like her. But the Tyrell men had helped to put up the tent, taken the horse to feed with theirs, and then moved on to confer with the Apostle.

A decent lot of chaps, the busker decided, as he searched about below the bridge in the long grass. Even Adelaide had come down to warn him of two shearers camped on the river who, Adelaide was sure, were detectives.

The busker had just found a piece of timber, and was hoisting it to his shoulder, when he noticed a laden figure coming down the path from the road.

'Christ!' the busker exclaimed to himself. He had never seen such a small girl with such a big load.

In one hand she had a kerosene tin full of water, and over her shoulder was a log of wood fully as big as the one he had been considering. She wore a faded red dress, and her dark head was bent as she staggered along. But on her bowed head a brilliant rosella, like some strange, vivid feather head-dress, clung by its claws, chattering to itself.

'Hey, kiddie,' the busker called. 'You let me carry that.'

The girl either did not hear or did not heed. She laboured forward, panting a little; but as the busker overtook her, she stopped and put down the kerosene tin, regarding him timidly. She was older than he had thought from her size.

'What you say?' Her voice, the busker noted with approval, was not drawling or nasal. It had the ring of good coin.

'You let me carry that, sister.' The busker swung her log to his other shoulder, and nearly fell prone under the added weight. But his pride would not allow him to show what a strain it was. This girl was obviously not accustomed to anyone carrying her burdens. She regarded him doubtfully, as the little rosella hopped on to her shoulder and leant round to chitter its beak against her lips.

'Look out, Bitsey,' she said, and lifting her kerosene tin, followed the busker in silence along the bank.

They had not gone far before the busker was forced to drop his load and rest his aching arms and shoulder.

'Why don't you get water from the river?' he asked, indicating the heavy kerosene tin.

'Dad won't drink it. He made me go up to the church. They don't put a padlock on the water-tank.'

Some churches, the busker knew by bitter experience, did.

'Well, I don't see why the hell he couldn't get it himself.'

The busker's virtuous indignation was all the greater in that he was carrying a log her sire could have carried and should have carried.

The girl made no answer. Her eyes widened with surprise at such an unheard-of suggestion. Sharkey Wilks was not in the habit of doing any work. What did he have daughters for?

'What's your name?' Duke asked.

'Betty Wilks,' she said softly. 'And this is Bitsey. I trained her. She's mine.'

There was something very charming, the busker considered, about this little dark girl in the dull red dress with the vivid scrap of blue, green and scarlet feathers nestling against her hair. Something childlike and appealing. She was so silent and gentle and afraid. That was it. She was afraid of him.

But it was not the busker of whom she was afraid, as he discovered from her next remark.

'Dad will be mad,' she said, 'at me being gone so long.'

The busker took the hint and shouldered the wood again. Sure enough, Mr. Wilks, a figure of parental wrath, was standing on the edge of the firelight, peering into the dusk as though he would set it on fire with the smoke from his nostrils.

'Where the hell you been?' he shouted, sighting the

girl. 'I'll take the hide off you, loafing when I want my tea.'

'Now lay off, sport.' The busker came up and dropped Betty's log in dangerous proximity to her parent's feet. 'Don't go snaky on the kid.'

Mr. Wilks swore.

'I just brought this bit of wood,' the busker explained. 'Too heavy for a kid like that.'

'She ain't no kid,' her father glowered. 'Sixteen she is. I'll teach her to stay out in the dark yarning to everyone she meets.'

'You lay off her.' The busker was angry. 'I spoke to her, see?'

Mr. Wilks became conciliatory. 'Well, I gotta look after the girl, ain't I? Gotta keep her in order? No offence, mate. No offence.'

'Just so long as you know how it was.'

'Well, no offence. Betty'—he turned to his daughter with a glare that spoke meaningly of what she would get when the busker was gone—'you go help your mother.'

'G'night.' The busker tramped off with his log.

He had not gone far when a scream from the camp made him turn, half-resolved to go back. But after all, as Mr. Wilks had pointed out, the unfortunate Betty was his daughter. She would only be worse used if he interfered. But he resolved that on the very first occasion he would pick a quarrel with Sharkey Wilks and beat the stuffing out of him. Even with this comforting thought he could nevertheless feel such a glow of indignation as surprised him. It was not the busker's habit to champion the oppressed. He was a 'wise guy,' who knew that in this life there was enough trouble coming to you without going out to look for it.

Chapter VIII

I

IT WAS with some uneasiness that Mrs. Postlewaite heard her husband say after tea, in a would-be casual manner: 'I think I'll just stroll down and have a word with Burning Angus, my dear.'

'Oh, Harry,' she exclaimed, 'I do wish you wouldn't get mixed up with politics.'

Mrs. Postlewaite's idea of politics included in a broad scope the Apostle's habit of interviewing police-sergeants on the subject of men struck off the dole, preaching on the street corners against social evils as he saw them, and espousing the cause of every lame duck he came across. The Apostle had got himself the name of an 'agitator' in several towns by his fervent utterances and had been in more than one nasty fix as a result.

Mrs. Postlewaite would have been content enough had the Apostle merely attempted to 'uplift' the dole-chasers. But the Apostle regarded them, not in the light of benighted, ignorant savages, but with a tolerant approval. To Thirty-Bob's exposition of the best way to steal a pig he listened with a gentle smile. The swearing and filthy language of his associates stirred him not a hair. It was just a habit, he explained, and meant no harm. He had no time for drink, but a great patience with drunkards. Unkindness to horses or dogs would rouse him to real reproach, and many a time his reputation for lunacy had saved him from being knocked unconscious when he interfered between man and horse. He rather played on this reputation.

'In uncivilised society,' he was wont to say, 'the lunatic is always sacred.'

There was no end to the Apostle's mad ideas. He would be found in the most unexpected places, chipping little pieces of rock with a geological hammer or collecting roots for the awful brews with which he would dose anyone too sick to stop him. He would lie all day under a tree talking about old native ways with the black people, and they paid him a great deference. But chiefly he loved an argument, and above all he loved to argue with Burning Angus.

As he passed Sharkey Wilks' camp, the Apostle remarked severely to no one in particular: 'A man who illtreats his daughters has no luck in this world or the next, and his mare will founder.' That prophetic voice from the darkness gave Sharkey a real fright. Before he could start up or even swear, the Apostle had passed quietly on towards the bagmen's camp under the railway bridge.

'Mad!' Mr. Wilks muttered, sinking back in his seat. 'Old looney.' He had always disliked the Apostle, particularly in his prophetic moments.

How Burning Angus had got his name was a mystery. He was a small, sandy man with a bulging brow above thick spectacles, a Clydeside accent, and a mate, a quiet old fellow who went under the name of Uncle and quoted Shakespeare. He was always Uncle, just as Burning Angus was Burning Angus, for no known reason.

It was not really necessary to go down to the railway bridge to hear Burning Angus. He had a penetrating voice which, in no undecided manner, was now denouncing the police. He could not be seen, although he could be heard, for just as the Scotsman's outpourings overflowed with more than one man's share of noise, so the little fire billowed forth more than its share of smoke, rolling away as though it had decided to rival the carrying power of Angus's voice.

'Police, police, police, nothing but police. Moving you on. Ordering you off. And as for work, well, if it's decent pay, I've nothing against work, not at union rates. Ten shillings a day is little enough for a man working from dawn till dark, but how many cocky farmers will give ye even that? And if a man refuses work, it's up to the police-station the cocky goes. Does the sergeant care what the pay is? Not he! "Oh, ye can't get the men to work for ye, Mr. Smith? We'll soon fix that." And the next time ye go for your dole, it's: "Smith's got a job for you. Go out and take it. No dole if you don't work."'

At this point the Apostle called: 'Good evening, Angus. Good evening, Uncle.' He greeted the Dogger, a big, stern-faced man who adhered to the Communist platform, and his mate Snake, a fair, excitable lad who adhered to the Dogger.

For the minute Angus lost the thread of his argument in welcoming the Apostle, with whom he had one of those long-standing feuds based on mutual liking and political differences. Angus reverenced the Independent Labour Party. His voice took on a new tone when he spoke of James Maxton and John McGovern, just as the Dogger's did when he quoted Stalin or Dimitrov.

It was quite a meeting, the Apostle remarked, and when he said as much to Angus, the Scotsman declared that it *was* a meeting—a protest meeting.

'Did ye see this?' He waved beneath the Apostle's nose one of those newspaper references to labour camps which had many weeks before interested the busker, an article discussing the undesirability of so many unemployed travelling about the country and suggesting that they be rounded into labour camps and 'made to work.'

'It's time, high time,' the Dogger put in, 'that the men on the roads were organised.' He said it as though their not being organised were some regrettable oversight for which he was responsible.

'I'm glad you've come,' Angus said gravely. 'You've got the education. You're just the man we need to help.'

'Besides the influence he has over the lumpenprole-tariat and the women,' the Dogger assented, with grave patronage. 'But we've got to have accredited organisers shipshape and full-time on the job, as well as just sympathisers. Not meaning any offence, Harry.'

'What do you want to do?' the Apostle asked, somewhat perplexed.

'Do?' They looked at each other, amazed at his ignorance. 'We're going to form a union, that's what we're going to do, to protect the rights of the bagmen.'

'All these chaps here to-night,' the Dogger came in again, 'are ready to join. We're fed up, and we've been fed up for a long time with the police handing out dole as a personal favour, and hunting the unemployed.'

'Wouldn't it be better,' the Apostle suggested, 'to wait until you get to the cherry-picking, where there are hundreds of men, or the canneries?'

'No, it wouldn't; and why? Because to start with a few solid chaps and work in small groups gives you a better chance. The trouble with the whole labour movement is that it only organises the men on the job, and when they leave the job, they can drift to hell and fend for themselves.' Burning Angus argued patiently, quietly; but his eyes behind their thick glasses gleamed with excitement.

'I have preached the brotherhood of man,' the Apostle said slowly, 'as long as I can remember. Whatever I can do, I will do.'

'That's good enough.' Angus and the Dogger turned from him as though that problem was settled. 'We knew you'd be with us, anyway. We've got a bunch of chaps in Sydney ready to help.' The Dogger addressed the gathering at large. 'If the shearers tramping the track just like our chaps could build the A.W.U., there's no reason why the seasonal workers, the bagmen, shouldn't build a union just as strong.'

'Only that the bagmen are a mob of dingoes,' one of the audience struck in.

There was a shout of dissent. 'What, there's chaps on the track held their A.W.U. ticket for twenty years.'

'They won't stick together,' the opposition argued. 'Scared a John 'ud go hostile on them.'

Another man took courage from the opposition. 'Ar, what's the use?' he growled. 'If we did get it going, the police 'ud bust it up. I've heard talk of a seasonal workers' union for ten years on the track and there ain't no trace of it yet.'

'There's going to be,' the Scotsman said tensely, 'from to-night.'

His mate Uncle woke from a dream in which he had been regarding the fire. 'It's as Shakespeare says,' he murmured. '"The fault, dear Brutus, is not in our stars, but in ourselves, that we are underlings."'

'Well, let's get down to tin-tacks.' The Dogger knew that if he once let Uncle start on Shakespeare or Carlyle, he would quote great slabs of the stuff all night, and no one could stop him. 'None of you's said yet that the union wouldn't be a good move. And it isn't that the men are yellow. And I'm not saying that it won't be hard to organise, when all the members are moving about all the time.'

'There's some too independent to stay in towns and some too spineless,' Angus agreed. 'Some are knocking about looking for work, and others dodging it. But we've just got to recognise the difficulties.'

The audience were bored. They would much rather have been yarning about the ways of individual sergeants, the 'bites' they had got in different towns. But they listened to Burning Angus and the Dogger because, after all, there might be something in it.

'Come on,' one of them challenged. 'How do we go about getting this union started?'

'Well, first'—the Dogger sucked his teeth reflectively— 'I'd depend on the single men. The coves in vans are no good, with women and kids dragging after them. Strike-breakers, the lot of them.'

The Apostle was roused. 'Why, Deafy Tyrell's as solid as a rock.'

'How about coves like Wilks?'

This silenced the Apostle, and the Dogger went on: 'The chaps that jump trains or ride bikes, now, they've got mobility.'

'That's a fact,' Snake said admiringly. 'Good word

that, mobility!' He was not called Snake for any defect in his nature, but because he was long and thin and could slip through narrow spaces.

'All the young, single men,' Angus capped the Dogger's words. 'Aye, it's the single men with no ties who are real interested in better conditions.'

'I don't agree,' the Apostle declared hotly. 'It's the married men with women and children. A single man can usually land a job and get off the track. They're not there permanently. But the man with a wife and children can't take the same pay and live on it as a single man.'

'It don't follow.' Angus had started up with the light of battle in his eye. Here was the Apostle on one of their old battle-grounds. 'And I'll tell you for why.'

But before he could tell them for why, a singular sound split the air. It was a bubbling, unearthly wail much like that of a seal rising and roaring in its death agony.

'Cripes!' the Snake exclaimed. Even the Dogger threw up his head startled.

Then the sound resolved itself into something recognisable as the product of human vocal cords, and the listeners relaxed. The busker was yodelling. There was a thrumming noise from the guitar, and presently Miss Phipps and the busker were singing together.

The effect on the meeting was immense. As though moved by one single thought, the inarticulate portion of the circle melted away, moving towards the music, Snake in the lead, his allegiance for the moment forgotten.

From the Tyrell camp, from the Jones', from the Wilks' camp, figures converged, as though by accident, upon the busker's fire. They would soon be all sitting in a ring having a sing-song.

'You were saying that the single men were the ones you could depend on,' the Apostle reminded his friend unmercifully. But for the moment even Burning Angus and the Dogger were roused out of their usual preoccupation with politics.

'The workers,' Angus said, as he followed his union, 'wouldn't wake up if a pine tree fell on them.'

But even he liked to sing, especially 'Annie Laurie,' and there was little music more than a concertina to be met in the camps.

II

Harley Duke would have been hard put to it to explain why he was singing. It had been drizzling wet off and on all day; Snow was in hospital; and the show Duke had meant to join had moved on. Perhaps he would have said that it was good to feel you were in a snug camp and could settle down for a while, and that he had just bought new strings for his guitar. But the real reason would have had some connection with the girl in a dull red dress, who carried on her shoulder a little red, green and blue rosella. Perhaps if he played, she might come out to listen. Anyway, it would show he was a person of consequence, a man with a future. Had you taxed him with wanting to make an impression, the busker would have replied with cold scorn that he was no 'cradle-snatcher' and that he liked a girl with a bit of life. But the motive was there, all the same.

Miss Phipps was in a good humour for once, and she sang. When Miss Phipps sang, people forgot what an irritating woman she could be, for she maintained her own line of harmony with the same persistence she showed in following her own line of conduct, but with better results. A mellow contralto voice is sometimes the privilege of plain, stout women; and she and the busker had by now a repertoire of songs they sang together with all kinds of grace notes and variations. It would have been a pleasure to listen to them anywhere.

From the uninvited circle of listeners, shyly standing outside the firelight or just within it, the applause was spontaneous and prolonged; and the dog Rex, who had raised his muzzle on a high note and joined in, could be heard fleeing back to Thirty-Bob's camp yelping from a hearty kick in the ribs.

The Stray cordially made everyone welcome, drawing them in to the fire. She was in the seventh heaven of delight. Her absurd little airs of a hostess giving a grand reception had something touching about them. To have the whole of the river-bank society focused upon her camp made her feel important and happy. Even the single men from the railway bridge, lurking at a distance, she urged to come closer, to join in.

The busker broke into 'The Dole-Snatchers' Anthem,' an anonymous ballad, congenial in its sentiments and memorable for its simplicity:

'As I was walking down the street, the copper said to me:
    "Do you belong to the doley-oh mob? Well, just come with
        me."
  Grabbed me by the collar, tried to run me in;
    I upped with my fist and knocked him stiff, and we all began
        to sing:'

'Come on, now join in the chorus, everyone . . .

'Yes, we belong to the doley-oley mob, the doley-oh mob are
        we;
  We never fight nor quarrel, we never disagree.
The password of the doley-oh mob is "Come'n have a drink
    with me."
    But we all dropped dead, when Stevens said:
        "Come and have a drink with me."'

By this time the busker was hung about with a festoon of assorted Jones and Tyrell children quarrelling for the honour of being closest to him. Deafy sat with his hand to his ear, and his ear nearly to the guitar. Mr. Wilks, presuming on previous acquaintance, had seated himself unasked on the companion log to the one which had provided his first introduction to his entertainer.

'"Annie Laurie",' demanded Burning Angus, forging forward to the fire.

'"My Wild Irish Rose",' shouted the Dogger.

'"The Road to Gundagai",' howled Dick Tyrell and Thirty-Bob in chorus. And 'The Road to Gundagai' it was.

'A real Australian song, that is,' Mrs. Jones was heard to declare approvingly.

Those who did not know all the words sang the line they knew. Old Jim, who had hobbled down from his hut to sit with the Tyrells, where he had been indulging in a lugubrious burst of weather prophecy, then announced that he would sing. He had been very quiet, and this sudden offer from one who had been merely a long white beard under a hat-brim took them all by surprise.

'Call that "Road to Gundagai" thing a song!' he mumbled, spitting liberally into the fire. 'Now I'll sing you a song that's a real bush song. Sung when I was a boy. You wouldn't know it.' He blinked contemptuously at the busker. 'It's the "Song of the Overlanders".'

'Well, let's have it,' the busker agreed generously. 'I'll vamp it for you.'

'No, no.' The old man waved the busker and his guitar away with a sweep of his pipe. 'I don't want none of your damned strumming. When I sing, I sing.'

He fixed his eye on Miss Phipps, who, he had been heard to declare, was 'a fine, big lump of a woman,' and broke into a quavering strain:

'When I first went exploring, I took up a fine, new run.
   I then went down to Sydney to have some jolly fun;
 I wanted stock for Queenslan', to Mackenzie I did wan-der;
   I bought a thousand head o' cattle, and then turned Over-
      lander.'

He began with spirit and vigour, waving his pipe to the time; but soon his voice faltered and sank. It was hard, seeing him then, to realise that this was 'Lachlan Jim,' a man famous in his youth as the most reckless rider in the West, with scarcely a bone in his body that had not been broken by some horse or other; the hardest drinker; the quickest for a fight; and the readiest to laugh, of those who had been young with him. And now, for all his fighting and laughing and hard, careless ways, he was come to be like an old dog, so lonely that he must creep to a stranger's fire.

'Then pass the billy round, boys, don't let the pint pot stand
    —er,
For to-night we'll drink the health of every Overlander.'

While he sang of the roaring days of the Overlanders who had cared for no one, who had thrust into the new land like spears, where now their descendants wandered landless between the barbed-wire fences, this camp might have been one of the Overlanders' camps, with the cattle lowing and the men singing in the night, had it not been for a line of baby's washing which Mrs. Postlewaite had tied from the rear of the truck to a tree.

'I scorn to steal a shirt, which all my mates can say,
  Unless I pass a township upon a washing day;
But all them little brats of kids, they sure do get my dander,
  Crying, "Mamma dear, bring in the clothes, here comes an
    Overlander".'

The spirit of the Overlanders was still the spirit of the travellers, the Apostle thought. It was only opportunity they lacked. The Overlanders' song stirred their blood. They roared again:

'Then pass the billy round, boys, don't let the pint pot stand
    —er,
For to-night we'll drink the health of every Overlander.'

Old Jim was so elated by the applause that greeted his effort that he boisterously flung an arm round Miss Phipps's waist; and Miss Phipps berated him soundly for an evil old gentleman. He ought, at his age, she asserted, to behave decently. He was far too old to go on like that.

'Too old, am I?' the old gentleman exclaimed wrathfully. 'How about Henry Parkes? Didn't he have a baby when he was seventy and something? Too old, am I?'

A roar of laughter went up at this retort. 'That's the spirit, Jim.' Thirty-Bob slapped the old man on the back. 'Give him a chance, Missus, and he'll father triplets.'

This was too much for Miss Phipps's sense of propriety. She flounced away, declaring that they were all 'most improper and degraded.'

'You shouldn't tease the woman,' Mrs. Tyrell reproved.

'Why, you can't say *anything* to her,' Thirty-Bob complained.

Old Jim, though a little dashed by Miss Phipps's reception of his overtures, now announced that he had decided to sing 'The Wild Colonial Boy' as an encore. Before he could begin, Deafy got in first, and sang it through very lugubriously and off key:

'He was a wild colonial boy, Jack Doolan was his name.
   He had poor but honest parents, brought up in Castle-
     maine;
 He was his father's favourite son, his mother's pride and joy;
   Dearly beloved by everyone was the Wild Colonial Boy.'

Old Jim, feeling that he had been slighted twice in the evening, grasped his stick, rose in righteous wrath, and said 'Good night' in a tone that left no doubt that he was wiping the dust of the camp forever from his feet. Deafy wanted to know what was wrong with Jim, and his wife and son, shouting in each ear, explained that he, Deafy, had sung Jim's song. Deafy growled that there was nothing to stop 'the silly old bastard singing, too.' It was too much trouble to explain to Deafy that no one could keep in tune with him; and the busker, realising that the bagmen were getting bored and beginning to drift back to their own camp, broke into some of the Tex Morton ballads 'Fanny Bay Gaol' and 'Rocky Ned,' which the company knew well.

'This is the best camp,' the Stray said fervently, 'that we've ever been in.'

They had all been dangerously near breaking point, and to feel that they were once more part of society, that they had a niche of their own, and were appreciated was just what they needed. Snow had broken down, the Stray realised, not because of the influenza, but because there was something in him deeply hurt. They would never have got him to hospital only for that gash on his face; but he needed shelter and rest so badly. They all needed shelter and rest.

Mr. Wilks, as he listened to the busker's yodelling, felt rather as though he had kicked a prize greyhound. Hadn't this chap come to his camp with Betty, wanting to be friendly (and he must be struck on a girl to carry wood for her), and he, Sharkey Wilks, had been, well . . . sharp was the word.

'I guess your brother must make a lot of money,' Mr. Wilks suggested, showing his yellow teeth at the Stray in what was meant to be an ingratiating manner.

'He ain't me bruvver. He's just travelling with us for a bit,' the Stray responded. 'But he makes pounds and pounds, hundreds of pounds.'

'Ah.' Mr. Wilks relapsed into thought. So the busker was just going round loose, was he, for any enterprising father to snap up? Mr. Wilks, who had a romantic mind, could see no reason why a young man, capable of earning large sums of money, should not make fitting gifts to the parents of any girl he was interested in. By all means! Visions of annexing the busker and his yodelling, of keeping him permanently attached to the Wilks family by the bond of affection rose in Mr. Wilks's mind. What were daughters for? Anyway, it wouldn't do any harm to try.

'Run back to camp, Jean, and tell Betty she can come,' he hissed at his elder daughter, a slatternly girl with a baby in her arms, a baby that had a curious dusky tinge.

Jean, with a scowl, went off on her errand. She, too,

E

was good-looking, but with a heavy, animal body and heavy features.

'I tell you you're a rat-bag,' Dick Tyrell was declaring offensively to Adelaide. His voice rose above the busker's, and it became plain that more of the audience were listening to Adelaide and Dick than to the singer.

'I tell you they're demons,' Adelaide insisted.

'And I tell you you're a rat-bag.'

Adelaide had been going about all the afternoon excitedly voicing his suspicion of two shearers who had camped near him. He was certain they were detectives, and he had worked out a most elaborate scheme, in collusion with the owner of the starting-price betting shop, to test his theory. When five men had been arrested that same afternoon, Adelaide had been triumphantly certain that the shearers were 'demons,' or plain-clothes detectives.

'I reckernised them immediately,' he asserted. 'The big feller used to be in the police at Holbrook. They go about pretending to be on the track and picking up information. Besides, that's a p'lice car they got.'

'I tell you them chaps are dinkum shearers.'

'I tell you . . .'

What further information would have been divulged was uncertain, for at that moment a voice from out the darkness said 'G'night,' and the two shearers or 'demons,' whichever they might be, loomed up.

Adelaide glowered and muttered; all the company felt awkward. To cover the embarrassment the busker burst into another song. They were spared the decision whether to invite the strangers to a seat. There were no seats. But the strangers, overlooking the chill in the atmosphere, stood on the edge of the circle unperturbed.

'I've got no time for crawlers and bloodsuckers,' Adelaide said loudly and with meaning. 'What I say is that it may only be a camp, but it's your home, isn't it? A man's got a right to his own camp.'

Adelaide was all the more angry as there were some uncaught opossums across the river. He regarded them as his 'possums, and the thought of two plain-clothes demons camped cheek by jowl with him made him almost mad with rage.

The mention of detectives, the presence of two who might be detectives, caused all those present to draw into their shells. From Burning Angus and the Dogger, who had some little experience of the police force and thought that all the powers of capitalism were vastly interested in them, to the busker, who knew he had no licence, an uneasiness spread over the whole party. References to 'crawlers' and 'informers' uttered in a loud voice left these latest visitors impervious, either because they really were shearers, or because it was not to their interest to let their real occupation be known.

One by one the circle of listeners began to wilt away. Burning Angus and the Dogger were the first to go; then Adelaide, with a final thrust at his suspects. Mrs. Tyrell went off to put the children to bed, and Mr. Wilks melted into the darkness, driving his two daughters before him.

'I'd be a bit fussy if I was you,' he called back to the busker. 'A man's judged by his pals, y'know.'

'What's up with them all?' one of the shearers asked in seeming surprise. He sat down on the box vacated by Mrs. Tyrell.

By now only the busker, the Stray, and the family of the Apostle remained. The busker decided to treat the two unwelcome guests as though they were shearers. After all, Adelaide had apparently a reputation for crazy ideas.

'Make yourselves at home,' he said none too graciously.

It was an awkward problem in etiquette, but one cannot order two men out of a camp without a reason. The busker searched his mind for some way of concluding this un-happy visit. All his friends had taken flight, and now he would be left to the cross-questioning of these men.

'We were just about to have some hymns,' the Apostle suddenly announced.

It was difficult to say whether the busker or the two shearers were the more startled. The busker put a brave face on it, seeing that the Apostle had produced a little pile of hymn-books. But the two shearers shuffled uneasily, then rose as one man.

'We were just on our way back to camp,' the bigger one said hurriedly.

'So long,' the other shouted over his shoulder, as they departed.

'That was a darn good idea of yours to get rid of those coves,' the busker chuckled.

'Indeed it was,' the Apostle replied gently. 'And now we will have a few hymns. That is, if you don't mind, just before we turn in?'

'I thought you were frightening them away,' the busker said, lugubriously, wondering whether the Apostle was not as socially undesirable as the two supposed demons.

'I succeeded. Now we will have the hymns. Do you know "Shall We Gather at the River?"?'

They had the hymns.

Chapter IX

I

JUST before dawn the shearers drove off in their car. Adelaide, who had been roused by the noise they made getting away, turned out to watch their departure and exult. So he *had* frightened them away! He woke his wife to boast that those hints and sneers of his at the busker's camp had driven the demons from the river. They knew he had found them out! His wife grunted sleepily and told him not to wake the baby.

The dawn broke cold and drizzling wet; but worse than the weather was the discovery that every horse along the river-bank had lost its mane and tail. Under cover of darkness the shearers had appropriated the whole standing crop of horsehair; and horsehair was selling at three shillings a pound! The language of the horses' owners was enough to singe their eyebrows. It was not only the monetary loss, but every man was proud of his horse and believed it 'the best on the track bar none.' The clipping had been done, if appearances were any indication, with a blunt pen-knife, and the horses had a most woe-begone look.

'That'll teach anyone to take any notice of Adelaide,' remarked Mrs. Flaherty. (The Flahertys had a motor truck, so they could take an objective view of the tragedy.) 'A man that got three shillings from the Reverend Mother and spent it on wine!'

The travellers were furious with Adelaide. 'Him and his detectives!'

'It just shows you've got to be careful who you mix with.' Mrs. Tyrell echoed Mrs. Flaherty's sentiments.

The river-bank was in a savage mood. Even the Dogger, who had no horse, gazed out at the rain and growled to Burning Angus that the Apostle was probably a social fascist or worse.

Uncle sat about and quoted Shakespeare until they could have murdered him. Miss Phipps, who was usually at her worst in wet weather, relieved them of her society, and sat in the van all day, smoking the tobacco Snow had left behind him. Now she had time to rest, instead of being whirled madly on across the plains by the impetuosity of the Stray and the busker, by the necessity of covering the distance to the next dole-station. Miss Phipps was determined that, after the brutal treatment she had received, she would no longer camp with Dancy and the busker. She would go on her own way. Going her own way involved choosing another party to whom she might attach herself as parasite; and at the moment she was hesitating between the Postlewaites and the Tyrells. True, Mrs. Tyrell had with her a group of rough, beastly men and a crowd of squalling brats; but Miss Phipps felt she could overlook these inconveniences more easily than she could the 'cant and hypocrisy' of the Postlewaites.

'Cant and hypocrisy' were Miss Phipps's terms for any form of religion.

It was not only their 'cant and hypocrisy' that Miss Phipps disliked. There was also Mrs. Postlewaite's eye always regarding her as though she were some strange ghost. No, she could not bear Mrs. Postlewaite, to whom everyone referred as 'the lady.' Why should people defer to Mrs. Postlewaite and hush their voices and stop swearing when she came by? They never bothered to do any such thing for Miss Phipps. No, the Tyrells would be more suitable as hosts. It was lucky for the Tyrells they did not know what was in store for them.

About dusk Sam Little, from the dark people's camp, lounged up with a few of his friends, and after the usual conversation about horses in general and the Horehound in particular, invited the busker to 'a bit of a beano' which the dark people were holding that night. Adelaide, Jones, Wilks and Dick Tyrell were all within hearing, so they had to be invited too. 'Anyone who likes to come,' Sam Little shouted back as he moved away. 'It's an open go.'

'Thanks,' the busker called. 'I don't know yet.'

The dark people were by no means disinterested in their invitation. They had gathered in the shadows at a distance to hear the singing last night, and among themselves agreed that Duke would be an asset to any party. They were hoping to have Black Olly, who played a piano accordion on the street corners for a living, but it was always a gamble whether Olly would be sober enough to play. He might just settle down in a corner of a hut and go to sleep, and then where would the party be? Black Olly had some vague relationship with the Littles and Murrays, which gave him proprietorial rights over any humpy in which he found himself. The dark people always welcomed him, for even if he did not play his piano accordion very well, music was, to them, music, even when it was only a cheerful noise, something that served to shut out the feeling that they belonged to the garbage tip, that they were not human beings, but 'blacks.'

The busker's vanity had been flattered by the invitation, but he had no liking for the position of understudy to Black Olly, whom he regarded as a business rival. To all queries whether he would be present at the dance he returned evasive answers. He would see about it. His friends were all eager that he should go. Fun was not so plentiful that they could miss the excuse to accompany him.

'G'wan, Dukesy,' the Stray pleaded. 'Don't be a nark.'

'These boangs are all too matey,' Thirty-Bob grumbled. 'If a bit of trouble starts, it's a case of one in, all in.' But he said it with a sparkle in his sharp, little, grey eyes.

'I don't see why we shouldn't have a bit of fun,' Dick Tyrell declared. The aim of his big, blundering existence was to come on 'some fun'; any sort from a fight to a frolic, and preferably both.

'You ain't going down to any Nigger's Heaven,' Mrs. Tyrell told her son sternly in response to an invitation to join them. 'And as for me, I've got more respect for meself. A drunken, quarrelling, fighting lot. I'm telling you, Dick, I'm telling you, Thirty-Bob, no good comes of mixing with niggers.'

She stared stonily at Jean Wilks's brown baby, which that young woman was rocking placidly.

Jean gave Mrs. Tyrell an impudent, half-angry grin, that said plainly: 'I know what you mean, and to hell with your opinion.'

'Dad and us is going,' she announced. 'So's the Joneses. You come too, Adelaide. Bring your missus along and have a good time.'

Adelaide, who had been severely snubbed all day, was only too glad of something which would raise his drooping spirits. 'I dunno about taking the missus,' he said virtuously. 'Not if it's a rough turn-out. But I might just look in meself to see what's going on.'

This was the attitude even of those who had not been invited. Several of the bagmen under the bridge were deciding that they might as well just look in on the revels despite the sour attitude of Burning Angus and the Dogger. It could not do any harm just 'to look in.'

'None of them lares under the bridge,' Mrs. Little had stipulated, when her husband wanted to invite the busker. 'And no drink,' she added, as though this were as much a crime as inviting the bagmen. And it was in her eyes. Inviting strangers led to fights, and drink led to fights. Both together would be fatal.

Mrs. Little was as fond of music as anyone; she agreed that this young chap with the guitar might be the makings of the party, but the fewer his mates the better. She was a big, warlike woman, as well she might be after nine years with Sam Little, former middle-weight champion of the district. Mrs. Little's style was not as orthodox as Sam's, being more of a catch as catch can. She could even lay about her with a club if necessary; and whenever the Littles and the Murrays gave a party, she found her prowess with a tent-peg of more use than any other social grace.

Soon after darkness fell, two motor-trucks of assorted dark people, and some white and brindle people, came bumping down the road to the garbage-tip amid much talk and laughter and general uproar. Black Olly, his accordion slung across his chest like an outsize in decorations, descended into the midst of his admirers.

He was an enormous, fat man, black as a burnt log, his face shining with smiles, his eyes glazed, his white hair as saintly as his felt hat was disreputable. Behind him came a tall, melancholy, black young man, answering all greetings in monosyllables. He was as sad and sober as his father was happy and drunk.

'Hiyah, hiyah,' Olly called. 'Old Olly with the music, trust 'im, trust 'im. I said 'e'd come. He got 'ere, didn't 'e? Didn't 'e get 'ere? Tired? Dah, dah. Tirty times I tell Alec, "No, Alec, I'm too tired. I can't play, Alec." But 'e brings me. Alec bring me. Music, Alec. They want the music.'

A very drunk, very lean white man had begun tap-dancing on a board, flinging his arms about like an animated marionette, and even at that distance the busker picked him out as Mr. Wilks. The noise of shouting voices, the roar of the truck starting, the howls of encouragement to the tap-dancer, all blended with the unmerciful shrilling of Alec's gum-leaf, and the blare of Olly's piano accordion.

'"Wilt thou have music?"' Old Uncle quoted gently. '"Hark, Apollo plays".'

'They'll be fighting drunk before the night's out,' Angus prophesied. He was going up to the Apostle's camp to talk over the union.

The Stray fidgeted impatiently about, eager to be off. The busker also was suddenly burning to be over there in the centre of it all. From the camps all up and down the river, figures, groups, mothers with children by the hand, could be seen heading casually down past the garbage-tip, where they could pause and look on, and gradually join the circle round the dancers. Only Mrs. Tyrell stayed resolutely in her own camp; and, of course, the Flahertys would never dream of associating with black people.

'We might as well drop over.' The busker seized his guitar. 'No sense just sitting about here.'

'I won't go,' Miss Phipps said stubbornly.

'Well, Dancy and I are going.' By this time the busker had learned how to handle Miss Phipps. 'You wouldn't like to be left here alone with all these rough men about.'

Miss Phipps stood undecided. 'Perhaps I had better accompany you deah people.'

'That's the ticket. They asked for you specially.' The busker glanced up at the sullen clouds and decided that the worst of the rain would hold off. Impatiently he found himself hurrying ahead, overtaking Mrs. Wilks and her daughters, Jean with her baby in her arms, and little Betty as usual with the rosella nestling on her shoulder.

Mr. Wilks had started tap-dancing again, and seemed determined to go on until he wore out the board. His feet made a monotonous pattering sound like castanets. Every now and then he would let out a whoop to encourage himself, or, if he showed signs of flagging, would be urged on by the derisive cheering of his backers, who had apparently bet him drinks that he could not dance a stipulated time.

The visitors made their way in single file along the bank to the road-bridge and then down the other side to the garbage-tip. As they came up the little rise on which the blacks' camp stood, the noise gradually rose to a deafening height. An epic dog-fight had just broken out on the stretch of beaten earth intended for a dance-floor. It was plain that Mrs. Little's edict about drink had been disregarded. Added to the uproar were the howls of two small children who had just been smacked for disorderly behaviour, and a baby disturbed in its slumber.

In the firelight the barbaric reds and blues of the women's dresses, the dark faces, the flash of white teeth, the tall trees behind leaping taller with the uncertain firelight, all mingled in a whirl of shadows and colours, confused, eddying, uncertain. But for the unholy din they might have been figures in a dream. The tap-dancer fortunately collapsed and was half-assisted, half-dragged, to a truck, where he leant, wiping his streaming brow, absorbing refreshment, and arguing as to whether he had won his wager. He was dissuaded with difficulty from starting again. The rest of the crowd wanted to dance themselves.

'Come on, Olly,' they demanded impatiently. 'Play us a waltz.'

'Yes,' there was a general chorus. 'Music, Olly.'

'Dah, dah, I'm tired,' Olly protested. 'Olly's tired.' He fastened his glazed eye on Miss Phipps, approaching unconscious of her peril. 'Oh, lady,' he called. 'It's the lady who sings, ain't it? Like an angel she sings.' He beamed at her and began to coax. 'Sing for Black Olly. They all tell Olly about you singing along the river. I tell I won't play.' He looked around triumphantly. 'Let the lady sing. Then I'll play. Yes, yes, please.'

He beamed on Miss Phipps again, who now found herself the centre of a mob all bellowing at her in various tones of good-humour or drunkenness. To tell the truth, Miss Phipps was too scared to refuse, and the grinning busker shouting 'I'll get you on the streets yet, Phippsy,' raised his voice with hers. It was Miss Phipps's intention to retreat swiftly as soon as the song was done—she was afraid of 'aboriginals'—but there was no opportunity to retreat. She had to stay with a good grace as a kind of popular hostage. Black Olly, as soon as he missed her, refused to play again for the dancing until she was found. For the rest of the evening she sat perforce at Black Olly's elbow, very popular with everyone, detesting these 'awful people' and too terrified to do anything but smile coldly. She refused to dance, and Black Olly supported this decision warmly. He was not going to have his 'lady' removed from his side, and they had to humour him.

Men outnumbered the women three to one, and the women were mostly heavy-built matrons who preferred to watch and nurse the children rather than stumble about in the ruts and be trodden on by heavy boots. So the Stray found herself besieged by would-be partners. She was giddy with being whirled round and round. In her eyes was an alternate flashing of firelight and blurring of shadow, spinning like day and night in a chaos. Over the road to the town a car sped now and then, boring tunnels of light before it.

'Look at the way they slows down to watch us,' Thirty-Bob yelled in her ear as he revolved. 'You'd think they'd have something better to do than watch a lot of common unemployed. After all, they've got halls to dance in. They don't have to dance on dirt.'

It was all very free and happy and hilarious. As the night wore on, the moon, like a lost sixpence in the crack of a floor, gleamed through a fuzz of black cloud. Hospitality in the form of cheap wine was pressed upon the busker and his friends; and at first they refused politely because it was not etiquette to drink other people's wine. The hosts might not have enough to go round. But when it became apparent that the camp was running with the stuff, and the invitations became more pressing, it seemed a pity to waste the rare opportunity.

'Keep off the plonk,' Thirty-Bob said in an undertone to the Stray. 'They just spilt some on my boot and it burnt a hole.'

But the Stray, recklessly happy, forgetting her responsibilities for poor Miss Phipps, who was watching her desperately and longing to escape from this evil, fat, black man, forgetting even poor Snow in hospital, forgetting everything, was already at the stage when she resented Thirty-Bob's solicitude.

'Can look after m'self,' she said with dignity, lurching a little. ''S no use tellin' me.'

Thirty-Bob, who could drink even raw wine and stay sober, decided that it was about time to get her back to camp. The busker, with a silly smile on his face, was playing and singing in the centre of a group of admirers who demanded one song and still one more song. Sharkey Wilks had gone to sleep. Dick Tyrell was nowhere to be seen, and neither was Jean Wilks. Many of the elder women and children had already retired.

Thirty-Bob, earning her eternal gratitude, firmly detached Miss Phipps from Black Olly, who was offering her his hand, his heart, his accordion, and a share of the tin hut he occupied. Miss Phipps was only too glad to go home. Thirty-Bob saw Dancy and Miss Phipps on their way, then turned back to the dancers, sorting out the river-men, trying to get them back to camp. He knew when a dance was working up to a dangerous pitch, and already a group had gathered round Olly, who was calling his son every name he could remember. Presently, from the noise, it would appear that Olly had knocked Alec down and was entreating him to rise.

'Get up, Alec me bo y. I didn't mean to do it. Your father loves you, Alec. Get up, me boy.' Then, his voice rising to a yell, as Alec decided to get up, 'You would, you devil; take that!'

The tone of the party was becoming more dangerous every minute, and to add a final touch, Sharkey Wilks had awakened, refreshed and ready for battle.

'Who topped off Chigger Adams to the cops?' he shouted angrily, endeavouring to free his arms from his coat-sleeves. 'I'll eat the bastards. Lot of stinking, dirty niggers. Who topped off Chigger?'

'My bloody oath!' Sam Little, with glaring eyes and bared teeth, thrust his face within an inch of Mr. Wilks's face. Even this did not help that gentleman to focus any too clearly.

'Let me get at him,' he insisted, still struggling with the flapping coat-sleeves. 'Hold me back, someone, before I hurt him.'

Mr. Wilks, sober, was well known for a lack of common courage. Drunk, he would challenge tigers, or even, as now, the more dangerous Sam Little, who could have eaten him alive.

The busker, full of benevolence, staggered in between the two in the role of peacemaker. The more drunk he was, the more the busker was at peace with the whole world.

'Now then, sports,' he said reprovingly. 'All frien's. Jus' a little friendly gathering.'

'Who sold the fight to Billy Miles?' Mr. Wilks demanded with spirit, referring doubtlessly to some regrettable incident in the past of Sam Little. 'Dirty lot of nigger bastards,' he added as an afterthought.

Sam Little was a big man, and Sharkey was a weed; but Sam explained later that he wasn't going to fight Wilks, he was going to kill him. He leapt on the swaying Mr. Wilks, got him down, and jumped on him.

The campers from the river-bank, however much they might dislike Sharkey, could not see him thus manhandled without protest. They moved in on Sam Little with the idea of removing him from Wilks's body. The dark people, convinced that their champion was being mobbed by the scum from the river-bank, flung themselves with howls of fury upon the travellers.

No one ever knew who threw the bottle. It caught the busker on the side of the head, and it was lucky for him he had a thick skull. As it was, he went down unconscious beneath the trampling feet of the scrum as it swayed backwards and forwards. He knew nothing of a small, thin body in a dull red dress pressed tight over his, taking the kicks. He never knew how Mrs. Little thrust her way like a great warship into the fray and cleft the combatants and helped Betty draw him out. Driving her own men one way and the travellers another, Mrs. Little had the mess cleaned up and the blood hidden and the signs of battle removed just the split second before the police car came racing out along the road to the garbage-tip.

The busker came to with a frightful pain in his head. He could not remember at first where he was, and strove to rise, only to collapse with a moan.

'Shish!' someone said beside him. 'Keep quiet, till they're gone.'

'Who're gone?' the busker asked presently. It took him a long time to think.

'The p'lice. Lie down behind the log again.' Betty peered out round the butt of a big, dead tree. 'They're going now.'

There was a whirr of wings, and from the darkness something like a rocket shot past the busker and alighted with a soft chattering in her hair.

'Oh, Bitsey! I thought you was dead.' There was almost a sob in her voice. 'Poor little Bitsey!' She stood up listening. 'They're going.'

The busker moaned. Someone had bandaged his head, and he felt it must be Betty, because the bandage was the coarse stuff of her dress.

'You ought to get a proper bandage,' she said, seeing his hand go up to his brow.

'What happened?'

'One of them caught you a crack with a bottle. Come on. We'd better be getting back.'

'I can't,' the busker said feebly.

'Here, lean on me. I'm strong, I am.'

She hitched one of his arms over her thin shoulders, and the busker presently found himself staggering along under a dim moonlight that made everything fantastic and shapeless. He was dizzy and sick, and but for the girl would have fallen.

'You're very decent to me,' he said faintly.

'Well, you was good to me. So that squares it.' Her voice was practical, hard. She said presently: 'Why don't you chuck it in?'

'Eh, what d'you mean?'

'Living on the track. You could do well for yourself. You don't *have* to travel.'

It was true, he thought—he had just drifted along, not caring much.

'You had a better start than most chaps. You ought to do better than just knocking about.'

Why was it, the busker wondered, that a woman— a girl, if you like, for she was too little to be called a woman—always had to be moving a man on, just as though she was a cop on a street corner?

'That's right,' he said sullenly. 'Pitch into me. Pick on someone your own size, can't you?' They had come to the bridge where only yesterday evening he had carried the log for her. 'I can walk now,' he said, still sick and faint. 'I won't forget this, Betty.'

'Good-bye.' There was almost a sob in her voice. 'You ought to give up travelling and go back to the city, see?'

A light showed where Thirty-Bob was coming along the river-bank. 'Cripes!' he exclaimed. 'You'd got me nearly out of me bloody wits. I thought you was in boob by now. Here, give us a hold.' And hitching the busker over one shoulder like a sack of coal, he bore him unceremoniously to the tent and dumped him on top of

Miss Phipps, who shrieked in horror, thinking it was Olly returned.

'Snap out of it,' Thirty-Bob commanded. 'Here, Dance, come and give me a hand to fix his head.'

They were soon busy by the light of the hurricane lamp. Perhaps being so drunk had made the busker less capable of feeling pain. He had got a nasty bruise and gash where another man might have got concussion.

'I never seen anything like it,' Thirty-Bob declared. 'That little kid pullin' you out of the middle of the gang like one of them little black ants with a big lump of bread.'

In the morning, the busker thought, he would do something about it—in the morning. He hated being grateful. Still, he must say 'Thank you' to the kid. That was the least he could do. He closed his eyes.

'We'll sleep in the van,' he heard the Stray tell Miss Phipps.

It was noon when he woke fully. He had tossed and turned and drowsed off again, but now he was awake. Thirty-Bob thrust his head through the tent-flap and said in Black Olly's guttural voice: 'Get up, Alec me boy. Yer father loves yer.' And the whole of last night came back to the busker bit by bit.

'I must go along and tell that kid I appreciate it,' he said rather condescendingly, yawning and rubbing a chin that felt like barbed wire. 'Have a shave first. Couldn't go like this. Frighten the little wretch.'

'They're gone,' Thirty-Bob said blandly. 'Sharkey was frightened blue. He put the horses in first thing and went for his life. Scared Sam Little 'ud come down and finish the job.' He eyed the busker curious as a magpie on a fence-post. 'She's a nice little shiela, that Betty.'

There was no answer.

'Ah, well,' Thirty-Bob said, 'she might have tried to fasten on to you. Can't tell with women. Go around getting a hold on a bloke, dragging him out of a row. Why, you never know but what she did it on purpose.'

He winked one eye. 'Nobody tried to stop me getting me ribs bashed in.'

The busker reached for his boot, and Thirty-Bob ducked quickly out of the tent.

So she was gone! Oh, well! it didn't matter much; but he would have liked to say thank you, and ask her what it was she said last night when they were labouring home. There was something she said that escaped his memory. Something about work. Perhaps he might recollect it later, but he had a dim feeling that it was something unpleasant, not really good to recall.

The busker (perhaps it was the drink of the night before and the blow on the head) felt very depressed. It was as though he had been just on the point of grasping something and it had slipped through his clutch, as though his ticket had been one remove from the winning number in the lottery. Not that it had anything to do with a girl who carried on her shoulder a tiny red and blue parrot. Nothing at all! He just felt fed up—fed up with travelling, fed up with the river camp, fed up with everything. He would go off on his own, go and find the show-people, his own people. To hell with this kind of a life!

II

The whole unpleasantness might have blown over, if it had not been for the children. Children, particularly the shrewd, wiry children of travellers, know everything their elders think as well as say. By mid-day, some of the Tyrell young banded with the Joneses, and even the respectable Flahertys, were playing at being 'blacks and whites.' Then, finding this uninteresting, they sallied down the river-bank armed with chunks of cow manure and ambushed an innocent group of infant Murrays and Littles who were driving home a cow.

They found this great sport, and whenever a small boy sallied from the dark people's camp, they fell upon him and drove him home howling.

'I won't have it,' Mrs. Little declared, her eyes flashing.
'First that Wilks fellow comes up here and busts up our
dance and brings the p'lice in, and now they're attacking
the kids. I'll speak to that Tyrell woman. I'll teach her
to let her brats tear into my Billy.'

So it was that Mrs. Little bore down on the Tyrell
encampment, dragging her small son along almost at a
run, so that he hung back like a dinghy in the wake of a
yacht. With Mrs. Little had come several sisters-in-law
and cousins, determined to see fair play. They appeared
over the rise like an ominous cloud.

The opening of the preliminary encounter had all the
icy politeness of those 'conversations' which precede the
bellow of the big guns.

'This'll be the third time, missus'—the attacking party
halted at a hostile distance—'this'll be the third time my
little boy's been hit by that cowardly little rat of a Johnnie.
You ought to be ashamed.' With a baleful glare at Johnnie
cowering behind Mrs. Tyrell, 'You ought to be ashamed
to pick on a little boy not as big as you are. And this
time'—her voice rose—'he's not on'y hit him, but he's
took his roller-skates that his father brought him home
not two nights ago. I won't'—her voice reached a scream
—'I won't have my kid bullied and knocked about and
thieved from and called a nigger by any little bastards
what take after their elders.'

'Don't you call my kid that!' Mrs. Tyrell was roused.

'Well, you tell him to give Billy back his skates. I want
them skates, or I'll have the p'lice on you. You give the
kid his skates, or I'll get the p'lice.'

Mrs. Tyrell turned on Johnnie.

''Ave you got Billy's skates?'

Johnnie shook his head violently. 'Never seen 'is bloody
skates.'

'There you are. He ain't even seen 'em.'

'Well, he's a liar. Don't you think you can put that
over me!'

'Don't you call my Johnnie names, woman.'

'Who're you calling a woman, you big. . .'

Mrs. Tyrell seemed to swell with wrath. 'You get out of my camp, you p'lice pimp.'

'Pimp, am I? I know enough about your mob to see yous all behind bars. That horse thief of a Thirty-Bob an' your old man with a van that he never paid for.' At this point Mrs. Little noticed a menacing murmur going round the group about the Tyrell tent. She retreated hurriedly, shouting as she went: 'Pimp, am I? Why, you dirty lot of rotten thieves. . .'

Mrs. Tyrell turned virtuously to the audience. 'Did y' ever hear anything like it? Well, I didn't answer her back. I'm glad of that. It's always better to say nothing.'

A ripple of uneasiness had spread visibly.

'Those boangs are all too matey with the police,' Thirty-Bob grumbled. 'Not that I care a damn,' he added hastily. 'But we don't want any trouble.'

'No, we don't none of us want any trouble,' Deafy Tyrell said with a double emphasis.

There was a general murmur of agreement.

Nothing more was heard until Sam Little, father of the injured Billy, came home drunk and bad-tempered, and heard that his wife had been called a police pimp. He tore off his shirt and staggered towards the Tyrell camp, yelling that he would eat them alive, beating his breast as he came and reciting his past victories. He was accompanied by a group of mates confusedly dissuading, arguing and encouraging.

Dick Tyrell met him half-way with a band of Tyrell supporters and hit him violently on the chin. He had the advantage, since he was sober and Sam was not. The infection spread, and a general *mêlée*, in which there was more shouting than actual bloodshed, took place. It was terminated by Mrs. Tyrell swooping down with a tent-peg and hewing her way through the press, doing much more damage *en route* than all the other combatants combined.

'It's disgraceful,' she kept repeating, 'for a woman who don't want any trouble and waiting for a baby.' Tears stood in her eyes. 'You get back there, Dick Tyrell, and you, Thirty-Bob. I won't have it.' She drove her own before her, and left Mrs. Little's contingent to retire to their huts.

A lull descended, broken only by shouted insults and deliberately loud conversations when any of the partisans happened to be passing each other's camps. In the lull the distressed Apostle journeyed to and fro without avail, urging peace and getting himself a bad name alternately for being 'hand in glove with them dirty blacks,' and 'one of the Tyrell gang.'

Duke and the Stray found themselves perforce Tyrell sympathisers, but they kept as far as possible to their own camp. The lull continued until it became obvious that the Tyrell dogs were sickening of some strange disease, and a search revealed a bait carefully hid in the grass. By this time it was too late to save the lives of three of the Tyrell dogs; but what most enraged the white campers was the fact that the baits were so close to the camp that, as Mrs. Tyrell heatedly pointed out, 'the babies could have picked them up.'

'Murd'rers, that's what they are,' Dick Tyrell raged, bending over the body of a greyhound bitch that had been his one hope of future affluence. 'Murd'rers, every one of them.'

A council settled down to consult on ways of getting even. The only suggestion put forward that met with universal approval was that of throwing a lighted torch into the Littles' hut by night and burning it to the ground. Dick was all for going down and 'cleaning up' Sam Little; but as Sam could give him a stone and a half, he allowed himself to be dissuaded.

At this point in the hostilities the Littles lost their nerve. At least, the Tyrells always claimed the Littles were responsible, although it was possibly some other interested party, perhaps the Flahertys, who privately dropped a word to the police that the feud was going too far.

The day after the Tyrell dogs expired, the police-car came rapidly out from the town with the constable at the wheel and the sergeant sitting beside him. They did not hesitate, but made straight for the Tyrell camp, which was a picture of industry and peace: Mrs. Tyrell whirring away at her sewing-machine, Deafy mending harness, Thirty-Bob and Dick sitting in the sun.

It was Deafy who looked up with a slightly surprised air and said: 'Afternoon, sergeant.'

'Afternoon.' The sergeant wasted no words. He was a big, heavily-built man with an overbearing manner. 'Ever since you've been here, Tyrell, there's been complaints. It was the same when you were in the town before. You're always in trouble.'

Mrs. Tyrell burst in dramatically: 'Trouble, is it? When we've been having our dogs poisoned, and our children half-murdered, and insults shouted, and abuse and quarrelsomeness, and that's not half of it with a mob of. . .'

The sergeant addressed himself to the men and she fell silent. 'I've had enough of this, I tell you. You're not allowed to camp on the river-bank, anyway. I'm telling you to get out of town as quick as you can, or I'll put you where you won't get out.' He turned to the little group of listeners, to the busker and Dancy. 'That goes for all of you. You won't get any more rations in this town.' He turned towards the car.

'But we're waiting for my mate to come out of hospital,' the busker protested.

The sergeant was unmoved. 'Your hanging about here won't help him. You can come back and pick him up.'

'And we can't go either,' Dick said sullenly. 'Mum come here to Logan 'cos she likes the hospital. She come here to buy a baby.'

'A baby!' the sergeant exploded. He gave his constable a glance that said louder than words: 'What! again!'

'She's got a right to stay,' Mrs. Tyrell's eldest son protested angrily. 'She's going to have a baby.'

137

'So are the Littles. I've heard that tale. And Mrs. Little was here before you came.' He shrugged impatiently. 'I can't have you here at each other's throats, fighting all over the maternity ward. No, you Tyrells have got to move on.'

The outraged Mrs. Tyrell had risen from her stool to front him. 'D'you mean to say,' she demanded, 'you'd hunt a white woman for the sake of a nigger? Let them go to the mission. That's their place.'

'That's a fact.' The constable, who had been silent all this time, spoke now sympathetically. 'Let the black go to the mission, sergeant. The woman's right. It isn't fair to drive her away when she's in that condition.'

Mrs. Tyrell, encouraged by this unexpected support, took on a pleading tone. 'Don't hunt me, sergeant,' she said anxiously. 'I tell you I ain't fit to travel. As true as I'm standing here. D'you want me to die on the track? Here I've made me arrangements with the hospital, and they're expectin' me any time. The birds've got some kind of a hole in a tree, and the rabbits have burrows, but we ain't got but a camping-place, and you'd hunt me from that. There ain't no hospital for fifty miles round that . . .'

The sergeant turned towards the car. He ignored her. 'Drive down to that camp,' he ordered, indicating the Postlewaites' modest truck. 'I might as well make a clean sweep while I'm about it. And don't let me hear of any more trouble,' he flung at the group. 'I'm warning you.'

He turned away from his constable, and it was obvious to that rash man that the sergeant was so angry that he could not speak. The young constable wished that he had never interfered. He knew it was almost impossible to move the numerous tribe of Littles.

The sergeant found a test of his mettle in the Apostle, who very quietly and politely declined to shift camp. He pointed out to the sergeant that he did not receive track-rations, and this was a jarring note to the sergeant. You could nearly always finish a man by threatening to cut off his track-rations.

'If you think you can come here stirring up trouble with your Red ideas,' he threatened, 'you're mistaken. I've half a mind to put you in for having no visible means of support.'

'They may not be visible,' the Apostle said, still smiling, 'but they're there. Of course, sergeant, if you prefer to send me to gaol, I'm quite prepared to go. But, at the moment, although I have no definite plans, I don't think I will be moving on for a week or so.'

'We'll see about that,' the sergeant said righteously. 'Camping is prohibited here. And I'm warning you.' He turned to his car with a victorious air. 'Get off by to-morrow.'

The Apostle smiled to himself. As soon as the police-car had disappeared, he strolled over to the Tyrells and heard their version of the incident.

'And what are we to do?' they chorused.

'Stay,' said the Apostle.

'But suppose he puts us in? Or cuts out our rations?'

'Stay,' the Apostle nodded. 'Don't worry. It will be all right.'

'I guess I'll be going on,' the busker said thoughtfully. He calculated that the show he had planned to join could not be more than fifty miles ahead.

Deafy and his sons were inclined to agree with the Apostle; but Mrs. Tyrell was nervous and frightened. 'I don't want any trouble,' she kept repeating.

'Well, the sergeant's got to feed us,' Thirty-Bob commented. 'In or out, it makes no difference to me, and if he tries to put us all in, he'll have to stretch the walls of his gaol.'

'I did fink,' the Stray said wearily, 'that wiv Snow in 'ospital we could get a bit of a spell. It ain't fair.'

Chapter X

I

DANCY, in her perplexity, turned to the Apostle. She felt that she had no one now that Snow was in hospital. The busker would be going to join the show-people, and Miss Phipps was no use at all.

The Stray was full of a loyal anxiety. Someone must stay to look after the turnout and sulky. Someone must feed and water the Horehound and Don. She was determined to wait in Logan until Snow came out of hospital. She and Bluey would be there on the doorstep the day he emerged; and he must not be told of this exodus, or he would want to come out of hospital earlier. While Snow thought Duke was looking after the horses he was content; and he would worry if he knew Dancy was single-handed.

Thirty-Bob was offering to sell the Horehound and the sulky. He would get the best price possible and not retain a penny for himself. But the Stray hesitated even to ask Snow. She could go with the Tyrells, of course; but no, she would wait for Snow. But how? If she couldn't get any dole, how was she to live? It was all so muddled and uncertain.

She dawdled over to the Postlewaites' encampment, hoping that Mrs. Postlewaite would not be at home. The Stray stood in great awe of that quiet, strange woman, who never swore or yelled or smoked or cracked a joke. Mrs. Postlewaite smiled sometimes, but that was all. The embodiment of the Apostle's cast-off respectability, she followed him like a worn-out but persistent shadow. The other camps were just camps; but Mrs. Postlewaite always made her temporary residence into a home. Even the dead leaves seemed to be tidied away from her vicinity, and the language of the travellers spruced itself as she came by.

The Apostle, noticing Dancy hovering about, hailed her for news of Snow. As he did so, Mrs. Postlewaite, to the Stray's disappointment, emerged from the tent.

'Nice day, missus,' the Stray saluted her. As soon as the lady had turned back into the tent, the Stray took a seat and rolled herself a cigarette. Mrs. Postlewaite's presence always gave her an impediment in her speech.

'Wot d'yer think of these 'ere bloody p'lice tellin' us to move on?' she asked; and without waiting for a reply, poured out all her difficulties. 'Strufe, Harry,' she concluded, 'I dunno, what wiv one fing an' anover . . .' She broke off dejectedly. 'It's bloody awful.'

Mrs. Postlewaite suddenly projected her head from the tent-flap like a bogey, and enquired: 'Why don't you get a job?'

The Stray regarded her amazedly. Mrs. Postlewaite must have been listening, and listening with interest.

'Well, I dunno, missus,' Dancy said nervously. 'It never struck me.' She turned for reassurance to the Apostle. ''Sides, there ain't no jobs. What cud I do, anyway?'

'It's not a bad idea,' the Apostle observed cheerfully. 'Just until Snow gets out of hospital.' He had never favoured his wife's approval of work for its own sake. 'You could look round.'

'But where'd I look?' the Stray asked dubiously.

Again it was Mrs. Postlewaite's head, projected from the tent like the head of some weird oracle, that supplied the answer.

'Mrs. Marks at the dairy wants someone to come in while she's sick. She'd let you put the horses in the paddock. Why don't you ask her?'

Only that morning Mrs. Postlewaite, going to the dairy to buy milk, had been offered work. People were always offering Mrs. Postlewaite work because she was so lady-like and respectable.

'Well, I dunno.' The Stray rose to her feet. This was help with a vengeance.

'Why don't you go and see this Mrs. Marks?' the Apostle advised. 'It can't do any harm to see her.'

'Thasso,' the Stray agreed, moving away. 'Thanks.'

The more she thought over the novel idea, the more it pleased her. She had always regarded all forms of settled employment with deep suspicion, but it couldn't do any harm just to see the Marks woman. Besides, Dancy thought, suppose she did get a job? How proud she would be boasting to Snow. This would show him she was worth something. A girl who could go into a strange town and land a job was worth travelling with.

'A bloody toiler, me!' the Stray murmured to herself.

She went back to the camp and dressed carefully, borrowing some face-powder from Mrs. Jones, and darkening her eyebrows with a piece of charcoal from the fire. She twisted up her straw-coloured hair under her hat and borrowed Miss Phipps's stockings.

'If I only had me teef,' she mourned.

A wistful vision of that beautiful trunk full of clothes rose before her eyes. If only she had them now, instead of these old things she had been given by the Methodist minister's wife! It was a bright, windy afternoon, and the gusts fluttered her badly fitting dress so that she had to hold it in her hand.

The dairy's nearness to the camp was one reason why Dancy decided with so little hesitation to ask for work there. It was only over the next rise, a mere quarter of a mile's walk. She trotted away without saying a word to any of her camp-mates, her heart full of fear and hope.

The house stood back from the road under some pepper trees. The land round it had the bare, worn look that feeding cattle give the most luxuriant pasture, if it is over-stocked. A thin, hard-faced woman opened the door.

'You Mrs. Marks?' the Stray asked. 'I 'eard you was wantin' someone, and me old man's in hospital, so I thought I'd come up. 'Orse bloody near kicked his face in.'

She regretted the adjective, but it had just slipped out. She won't have me, she thought sadly, she won't take me now.

Mrs. Marks regarded the figure on her doorstep narrowly. Girls were hard to get. She opened the door a little.

'Come in,' she said.

The Stray took heart. 'Thank you, missus,' she said, stepping across the threshold.

The kitchen had an air of being over-worked, as though one meal were no sooner finished than another was in progress of preparation. The flies were as much at home as at the travellers' camp. It was hot and smelt of stove-polish and bread.

Dancy had a feeling that this woman wanted her to work there, but at the same time disapproved of her, suspected her, was peering for a vulnerable place through which she could dart on some hidden weakness.

'The place is in a bit of a mess,' Mrs. Marks said, as though it was the kitchen's fault that this was so. 'Men tramping in and out all day and night. And I been sick a good while.' But lest the Stray take advantage of this admission, she added: 'I'd only reckoned on paying ten shillings and keep—of course you not staying long would make a difference—if you was regular, now. . . .' Her voice was toneless as she went on adding one set of words to another dully, as though she were washing dishes or drudging at some job she did not like. ' . . . And how long would you be here, did you say? Ah, your husband's sick. Well, well, and you don't know when he'll come out? Of course, you mightn't suit, not having the experience. . . . Yes, you could put your horses in the paddock, I suppose. If you like to try, I'll see what my husband says.'

The woman was obviously calculating that she could get more out of this wreck of a girl than from someone with more resources. The Stray was so near to unemployable that she needs must be remarkably cheap. It was only

143

when Mrs. Marks spoke of her own ailments that she really showed much interest.

She spoke lovingly of the 'pains in the back and kidneys.' What Dr. Alfred said last time he came was that she should just drop everything; but with George shorthanded and managing as best they could. . . . When the cows go dry, you've got all the cost of feeding them, and nothing coming in. . . . She seldom finished a sentence just as, the Stray was to discover, she never finished a household job, dropping it in the middle, or pushing it negligently out of sight, as she pushed the thin, greying wisps of hair that fell round her face.

Dancy knew that, if she came to this place, she would be underpaid and over-worked. Everything she saw told her so, but the realisation did not offset her triumph at the thought of announcing to Snow that she had a job. The fierce possessiveness she had displayed towards Snow had deepened since he went to hospital. She would show him she was worth travelling with. She would save those ten shillings. . . . It was almost an insult to be offered such a sum, but she would take it and save it as a surprise for him. Perhaps he would not want to take it and would give it back to her to get her teeth. That was if she stayed long enough. She gave the woman before her a long look, and a flicker of power ran through her. She could manage this frayed old dish-rag of a woman, she had no doubt of that. Mean and a whiner, was the Stray's verdict.

They agreed that the Stray was to start early next morning. She could move her belongings, on wheels and hoofs, into the paddock as soon as she liked. She was shown her bedroom, a lean-to built on to the side of the scullery. Back in the kitchen, she looked round with the eye of possession. It did not matter that the kitchen officially belonged to Mrs. Marks, if she, Dancy, were in occupation. She had not realised that she had craved a house ravenously, as though it were some desirable food, that she had a longing for four walls about her and safety. To-morrow night, she planned, she would heat water and have a real bath. She listened with only half a mind to Mrs. Marks's reiteration of the sudden stabbing pains that she got in the small of the back so she couldn't bend, and the slow aching pains that came on 'something terrible' when she lay down at night.

A figure rose from a stool by the fire as the women re-entered the kitchen, a tall lad with a vacant look who edged towards the opposite door as though the stranger frightened him.

'This is Mrs. Grimshaw, Charley,' the lady of the house explained; and as soon as the lad had mumbled something and slouched out, she turned to her new employee. 'He was always top of the school,' she remarked drearily. 'Such a clever boy! But it comes of working too hard, if you ask me, though they say the meningitis did it.' She nodded after her son, as though accepting his lack of sanity, just as she accepted the dreariness of the kitchen. 'He's gone to see the train out,' she explained. 'Maybe you'd like a cup of tea, Dancy? Was you christened that? Funny name, ain't it? I known a lot of Nancies, but never a Dancy before.' Her voice trailed across the name, seeming to leave a track behind it, such as a snail might leave. 'Yes, poor Charley . . . ever since he got that meningitis he thinks he's in charge of all the trains. It don't do no good to keep him at home, because it makes him worse. Down to the station he goes to wave them out. Thinks they can't start without him. The men have got that used to him they just say "All right, Charley," and he says "Right. Let her go," and pretends to blow a whistle and wave the flag. It's good of the station-master not to mind.'

She turned from the trouble of Charley to a grievance against a neighbour who had borrowed a horse and had an accident in which the horse broke its leg and had to be shot, and to a complicated piece of litigation between the Marks family and the owner of a market-garden into which their cows had strayed. Over these topics the woman's voice left the same faint trace of its passing as though they wilted.

She might have continued to talk until darkness fell, had not her other son Joe and her husband, big men, loud-voiced and impatient, come in demanding a meal. They looked at the Stray with a half-insolent appraisal, as they might have regarded a heifer that was not good for much. Dancy went away from the dairy with an angry feeling that she had known all too well of old, a feeling that people were trying to 'down' her. Snow had not tried, nor the busker, nor the Tyrells, nor that queer old 'Postle. But as soon as you came near people who had houses or shops or businesses, they looked at you as though you ought to fade off the earth. They made you feel small and not worth the money.

'Ten shillings!' the Stray growled, spitting vigorously. 'Ten bloody shillings!'

There was no mention of this humiliating under-payment when she boasted at the camp of her success in getting a job.

'She says to me: "That's a lot to ask, ain't it? Thirty-five bob?" and I says, "You can take it or leave it, missus. It don't matter to me."'

They all listened respectfully to her, and if there was a flicker in Thirty-Bob's eye, the Stray refused to see it.

'You ought to let me sell that jib of yours, Dancy,' he suggested. 'I've got a chap coming up first thing to look at that stallion of mine, and I'll see what I can do with the Horehound.' Dancy looked obstinate. 'Stands to reason, girl, you can't manage both of them. I'll get rid of the sulky for you too.' Then at the cautious look of Dancy, Thirty-Bob lost patience. 'Christ Almighty!' he exclaimed. 'Anyone 'ud think I was trying to pinch the filling from your back teeth instead of doing you a good turn.' The fact that the Stray had no teeth rather spoilt the poetic metaphor, but his sincerity was obvious. The Stray repented her harsh thoughts.

'All right, Thirty-Bob,' she replied: 'You sell 'er.' And then handsomely: 'I don't mind.'

Thirty-Bob reflected that you should never expect

gratitude from a woman. He had taken a liking to Dancy, and had already remarked in her hearing that 'a man travelling was always out of luck unless he had a woman to battle for him.' This tender sentiment left the Stray cold, as Thirty-Bob's previous remark had been to the effect that he thought he would get him 'a good little gin; they beat the white ones holler when it comes to work.' For this statement he was unmercifully guyed by his friends who pointed out that Thirty-Bob, if he ever did get a wife, would probably swap her away for a good-looking mare, and ask 'thirty-bob to boot.'

II

Burning Angus, man of action that he was, would not tamely creep away. He called a meeting of the travellers that same night. They all came, the men with families, the men without families, and they listened in silence while Angus laid before them his plans for a Bagmen's Union.

'What kind of a life is it for men like us? The sergeant can order us off the river, and there is no other place for us to camp. They can order us out of town, and we've got to go, like slaves, like dogs. Here's a man so inhuman that he can turn a woman away from the town just when she needs the things that civilisation can give her. For all the police care, we can die on the road; yes, and we do die on the road—of starvation, and cold, and despair. If it wasn't for the help of other men and women, who've got nearly as little as we have, there'd be more notices of old men—unidentified, destitute, died of malnutrition, which means starvation. . .' His voice rose. 'I tell you there's no one cares a damn about the men on the track. It's up to us, ourselves, to do something about it; and the only thing we can do is to make ourselves heard . . . appeal to the townspeople. . . .'

Mrs. Tyrell rose from the audience in great indignation. 'If you think you're going to make a show of me in the town, Angus, I'll let you know I've got a good name on the road, and for all the sergeant says, this is the first trouble we've been in, barring a bit here and there. . .' They pulled her back and soothed her down. 'Well, I won't have him going around the town talking about me,' she was heard to declare indignantly. 'I'd sooner just go away at once.'

'Now that's just where you're wrong, Mrs. Tyrell,' Burning Angus argued, with great politeness. 'We're all ready to stand behind you, aren't we, chaps? The police can't do anything to ye, Mrs. Tyrell, and if they send us to gaol—well, we're used to it. It's a matter for direct action. What's more, if we can get some of the men in the town to take up our case . . .'

'Crawlers, the lot of 'em,' from somewhere in the audience.

'I'm saying *if* we can get them to take it up. And to-morrow we'll go round to all the clergy and see if we can't enlist their help.' Burning Angus positively steamed with energy, so that his glasses grew moist and he had to take them off and wipe them. His hard blue eye shone with the light of the crusade. 'We want to show that this union —our union—the Bagmen's Union, can take up a case and enlist public opinion—and win. We'll beat the police by simple passive resistance. It'll bulge the walls of the sergeant's gaol if he tries to arrest the lot of us.'

'I remember once in Orion,' the Dogger said reminiscently, 'the sergeant said to a young cop who'd just brought in a batch of train jumpers: "What d'you think this is—a gaol or a boarding-house?"'

There came a murmur of agreement. 'He's got to feed us. In or out. It don't matter to us.'

'Why, the best tucker I ever ate,' Snake chimed in, 'was in a little gaol back of Condobolin. When I'd done me week, the sergeant's wife asked if I'd like to stay and do some gardening. So I occupied me cell another week, and she gave me a quid and a mother's blessing when I left.'

'Was that the place where they put up a slide at the pictures: "Will all prisoners please return to gaol? Inspector arriving any moment"?'

The audience was ready to illustrate, with a wealth of experience, just how gaols differed in towns from the borders of one State to the next. Burning Angus waited impatiently. He knew that, once started on the subject of sergeants, it was hard to stop his little following.

'As I was saying'—he raised his voice—'as I was saying, it may not come to a show-down. It's just a matter of resisting this high-handed police action some time. And now we have as good a chance as any.' His eye swept the little circle like a blue searchlight. 'I'll take a vote on it, duly and in order. Will someone move a motion?'

The Dogger proposed a long-winded and very compli- cated motion which had been written out beforehand so that he would not get tangled up in the clauses. The 'inner group'—as he proudly termed himself, Angus, Uncle and Snake—had been composing the motion all that evening on a scrap of wrapping-paper. It wound on and on, through 'whereas's' and 'fascist tactics of the local police' and 'we, the undersigned' and grand statements about 'justice' and the 'demands' of the 'travelling unemployed for shelter, decent treatment and the right of localisation.'

'Put in we need firewood,' someone suggested.

The Dogger ignored the amendment. 'We therefore are determined to resist the order to vacate the river-bank, and we hereby affirm our resolution to stay on the river- bank in a body until next dole-day.'

'And raise hell,' from another interjector.

'And do all in our power to enlist the sympathy of the townspeople in the present harsh and unsympathetic tactics of the local police.'

'Is that all?' someone asked, wondering whether the Dogger had merely paused for breath.

'Anyone second that?' Burning Angus snapped.

'I will,' purred Thirty-Bob.

Angus turned, startled, for he had arranged that one of the inner group should second the motion. Uncle, as usual, had fallen into a kind of dream, and was probably back in the seventeenth century.

'I will,' Thirty-Bob said again, hitching up his disreputable trousers and leering at the assembly. 'And because why? Because I'm going to see the sergeant's got something more to put me in for than just sitting on me arse on a river-bank. When I was in Bourke once,' Thirty-Bob grew reminiscent, 'the John took me up for tearing his uniform and using insulting words. And I hadn't called him a thing! I told the magistrate that. I says: "Yer honour, what I should of called him was a . . ."' Thirty-Bob reeled off a horrifying genealogy that traced t e constable's lack of ancestry for several generations. 'And I damn well said to meself, "That's the last time a cop puts me in for nothing." So I'm all in favour of us sitting on the bloody river-bank till we put down bloody roots.'

'Motion seconded,' Angus snapped. 'Anyone against?'

'I am,' Mrs. Tyrell said decidedly. 'I told you before, Angus, that I'm not going to be made a by-word in this or any other town.'

Her husband pulled her down, trying to soothe her in an undertone.

'It's not only you, Mrs. Tyrell,' Angus said in his most conciliatory voice. 'It's the principle of the thing. And, I may say, while I'm on the subject, that the seconder of the motion seems to have forgotten that this is to be a peaceful demonstration. We don't want any violence. We'd have a much better case if a few of those here to-night had remembered that earlier.'

'They picked on us,' Dick Tyrell said indignantly. 'How would you like to have a lot of blacks jump on your ribs?'

'I'm not talking about the rights and wrongs of it. I'm saying it looks bad. Anyway, let's get down to the motion. Where were we? Oh, yes, I'll put the motion. All those in favour?'

'How about reading it over again?' Deafy called, propping his hand to his ear. 'I didn't get it the first time.'

Angus gave a weary sigh. 'Read it again,' he ordered.

The motion was read again in all its unwieldy length, and when the Dogger concluded, the audience sat silent, as though dazed.

'Well, I'll take the vote,' Angus announced. 'All those in favour of staying right here on the river-bank?'

'Aye.' Those who did not agree did not vote.

'Against?' There was only a silence.

Angus rubbed his hands. 'Now, while we're here,' he went on, 'I'll ask Comrade Simpson'—that was the Dogger—'to give you some idea of the aims and objects of the Bagmen's Union, which is officially taking up this, its first case of victimisation.'

The Dogger rose in grim dignity. 'Friends,' he began, 'all those here present know the rotten conditions we are up against on the road. They know . . .' He stopped dead. Bobbing towards them along the river-bank was a circle of light from an electric torch. 'I'll bet it's those Johns again,' he said resignedly.

And sure enough the burly figure of the young constable broke into the circle of light.

'I'm sorry to disturb you'—he was rather breathless and awkward; by nature a polite young man, a trial to his superiors—'but I'm afraid there's going to be a flood.'

Angus glowered at him. 'It's just another dodge of the sergeant's,' he said savagely. 'Well, it won't work. We're staying here, and you can shift us out by force or not at all.'

The young constable began to lose patience. 'I tell you we've just had word through from Jasmine. There's been a cloudburst.' He did not relish this job of reasoning with so many stubborn, angry travellers. 'You'll see for yourself soon enough. They've flashed a slide on at the picture show. Look.' He pointed to the road bridge. 'Look at the cars going home.' And sure enough a stream of cars were spanking away in procession as fast as cars could go.

The farmers who lived along the Gunnar River were racing madly home.

Angus was still obdurate. 'We know the sergeant 'ud dig up the river if that was the only way to stop people camping on it.'

Mrs. Tyrell could bear it no longer. How dare they stand arguing there wasting time! 'Oh, the children!' she screamed. 'The children! Never mind standing there talking your heads off. Deafy, Dick, Thirty-Bob, get the horses in.'

There was something so piercing in the terror of her cry that it, more than anything the young constable had said, carried conviction.

'I tell you, you've got no time.' The policeman seized his advantage. 'It's coming down now. Now, I tell you. It's a flood.'

All in a minute the meeting was broken into its several elements of worried fathers snatching up stray infants and rushing off down the bank, their wives beside them, running swiftly, frenzied with fear. Few of them did not know the terrors of a flood or, in their fevered imaginations, could not envisage a great wall of water roaring down what had been but a shallow trickle, hurling great logs, boulders, debris before it as it came.

'Oh, the children! the children!' Mrs. Tyrell screamed again. 'Dick, Tom, get the horses in. For God's sake! get the horses in.'

Now, above the crying of the roughly-awakened children, the shouts of the men, working with nervous haste to bring down the tents, there came the stamping and snorting of startled horses, the chink of hobbles, the jingle of harness, and the whinnying of the Horehound, who objected to being separated from a sociable group of her own kind. She had had everything else happen, and to be put into harness at nine o'clock at night was too much for her temper.

'I ain't going to drive her,' the Stray muttered in the busker's ear. 'Not if I know it.'

'We'll shove her in the van. I'll drive the cow.'

'If she smashes up the van, Snow'll kill you.'

'Will you shut up!' Duke growled.

He was trying to do three things at once, and all Miss Phipps did was stand by and say: 'Really, this is preposterous. I refuse to be disturbed.'

'Where to, 'Postle?' the busker shouted, as he heaved his hard-won firewood into the van, and threw in on top of it, helterskelter, the tent, tarpaulin, the cooking-pots. From force of habit he found himself putting out the fire, then remembered that the flood would soon put it out for him.

'Up to the show-ground, I suppose.' The Apostle's tone was doubtful. 'We'll just have to camp along the side of the fence.'

The Apostle's little family worked much more efficiently than the others, Bryson and Whitefield busily gathering up trifles that are so apt to be overlooked where there are no methodical small boys. Thirty-Bob was cursing Adelaide's intricate wire harness, and poor Adelaide, whose van had stayed so long in the one spot that it was stuck, was dancing about impatiently from one foot to the other.

Now and then they all cast panic-stricken glances at the river. Already it seemed to be lapping higher. The young constable, reinforced by a body of citizens who were helping the Flahertys to move their furniture, went from one group to another, hurrying them, encouraging, even lending a hand.

'Won't the sergeant cheer!' the Dogger said bitterly.

'Ar! what do we care? Come on.'

'Where to?'

'Show-ground, I s'pose.'

'We'd better give a hand to those horse bagmen. Poor cows! Listen to the kids crying.' They turned in a body up the river-bank, and were soon busy taking in Mrs. Jones's washing, pushing Adelaide's van, helping bring down the Tyrells' big tent.

The Horehound, rearing and snorting and plunging, had been taken over and driven as far as the road by Thirty-Bob. Then the Apostle's truck refused to start.

He had his wife and children packed in and was frantically turning the crank-handle while the efficient Bryson trod on the accelerator. Nothing happened. Men clustered round the truck. The river was visibly higher now.

'There's nothing for it, Harry,' the Dogger said grimly. 'We'll have to push her.'

A team of bagmen set their shoulders to the truck.

'Heave.'

They heaved. The truck did not budge.

'There's something wrong.' The Dogger looked inside. 'Why, damned if he hasn't got the brake on.'

The next effort started the truck rolling towards the highway with the bagmen pushing and Angus steering. The Postlewaite family trudged behind their helpers, Mrs. Postlewaite nursing the baby, and the Apostle apologising gently for his forgetfulness.

When they reached the road, they found the busker and the Stray waiting, and after three more attempts, the policeman, who was a bit of a mechanic, succeeded in starting the truck.

'You want to clean those plugs,' he advised, taking back his torch from the bagman who had been playing its light on the engine. He swept it round. 'Everybody off?'

'Yeah. Looks like it.'

Having gone once more down the bank to make sure, the constable was able to chivvy Miss Phipps away from the fire where she was sitting with a blanket round her and every intention of imitating Canute. He was only just in time. The waters did not come down in a cream-lipped welter, but silently, swiftly, treacherously rippling up higher and higher, swirling faster and faster, mounting the roots of the she-oaks and willows, rising, as though the trees helped them, in little swirls round the trunks, running up slopes of the bank and coming round circuitously from the rear to attack the fires, that hissed a defiance and spat from their white ash.

Men who had gone to warn the Chinamen came back to the raised safety of the road to report.

'How about old Jim?' someone asked.

'He won't come. Said to leave him alone. His hut's on a bit of a rise.'

'That won't help him much. How high does it come?'

'One year,' Mr. Flaherty told them, 'it was four feet in our place.'

'Here,' Thirty-Bob announced, 'I'll fetch the old cuss. Come on, Dick.'

Jack Tyrell was driving the cart, so Dick sprang up in Thirty-Bob's sulky.

'Where you going?' Mrs. Tyrell called. 'The water 'ull be over here soon.'

'You go on, Ma,' Thirty-Bob shouted back. 'We're going for old Jim.'

They swung off the road and drove along the bank through the water, which was now swirling deeper and deeper. As they leapt from the sulky and, heedless of Jim's dog barking around them, pushed into the hut, the water was already across the clay floor.

'Jim!' they shouted. 'Hey, Jim! You'll be drowned!'

Old Jim was lying in his bunk, and although he was awake, he regarded them indifferently.

'Come on. Get your stuff. Quick! Hurry!'

'The Chinamen ain't gone,' Jim argued, 'and I guess if a Chow can stay, I can.'

Thirty-Bob and Dick, cursing furiously, bundled him off his bunk and dragged him to the door.

'What about that?' Dick howled, pointing to the darkness. 'Water all the way and getting deeper every minute.'

'What's the use?' Jim said slowly. 'I ain't got nowhere to go. I might just as well stay.'

They shoved him into the sulky, grabbed his dog up, bumped it down under the seat, and leapt in, swearing at Jim and each other.

'Should have let the old bastard drown,' Thirty-Bob contended. 'He ain't worth getting our feet wet.'

The sulky swayed and lurched over the uneven ground, and had it not been for Thirty-Bob's driving, would have overturned and flung them into the river. He wheeled his big red horse in a narrow space, and brought it trembling and snorting along the bank, and up the incline to the road. Even when he was drunk, Thirty-Bob could drive better than most men.

A little group of townspeople greeted the local weather prophet.

'Thought it wasn't going to rain much, Jim?'

'This water ain't ours,' Jim retorted. 'It come down from Jasmine. Won't rain properly till to-morrow night.'

As the sulky rattled towards the show-ground, Thirty-Bob asked: 'Where was you thinking of staying the night, Jim?'

'How the hell do I know? Come dragging a man out of his bed. Might as well have left me where I was.'

Thirty-Bob cut in on his grumbling. 'Well, I guess you can share my nap, Jim. 'Tain't everyone,' he admitted liberally, 'I'd allow to do it, and if you was, say, a pretty little shiela'—he leered wickedly at the disgruntled Jim— 'I'd like as not let you get rheumatism and plant your carcase under a shop verandah. But seein' as it's *you*, Jim . . .'

Chapter XI

I

ALL THE next day the town was full of an unusual friendliness, levity and excitement. The population had only half a mind on business, and all conversation was about the flood. The river swept people from their everyday life, as though they had been straws along its edge. They swarmed out like excited ants across the railway bridge that now remained the only link between the beleaguered town and the higher slopes. Cars spanked in with excited tales of escape over the only road left uncovered; and, as the flood deepened, a group of stalwarts set off in a boat to rescue a family who were sitting on their roof, congratulating themselves that they had shifted their sheep to higher ground.

The unsettling thing about the flood was its movement. The old landmarks—trees and windmills and houses—were still there; but between them, the land, seditiously mingling its red-yellow with the alien flood, had got up and was rolling away. The warden fences, that had laid their wire knouts across the backs of the fields, were drowned; lucerne stacks floated on the current as carefree as icebergs, masterless and anonymous. It was landscape reverted to anarchy; and the town, isolated on its eminence, had the look of a fortress taken by surprise. The spirit of defiance and lawlessness, instigated by the mutiny of so much mud, spread imperceptibly to the human beings. Small boys took a delight in pushing off such lucerne stacks as stranded on the shore, so that the full stream should bear them away and submerge them. Nothing, if they could help it, would be salvaged, unless it was edible or loot. They waited hopefully for hours to pounce on someone's property, but nothing valuable came floating by.

'Remember the time she was in flood when all the water-melons was ripe?' one freckled infant shouted. 'Gee! we was eatin' water-melons as if we was doin' it for a bet.'

'Wish they were water-melons 'stead of lucerne,' another boy responded.

'You come off there, son,' a railwayman advised one of the crowd, who had just jumped down on to a stack of lucerne. 'Nobody wants to get wet dragging your body out.'

The river's flood would be a fixed date in the slow-moving mind of the community. Men would say: 'That was six months after the river rose over the bridge and the

Bartons were washed out.' There was a superstition current in Logan that if the river rose, it would be a 'good year.'

'There's going to be some work cleaning up, anyway,' a bagman called Dark remarked to his mate Jim, the same who had commented on Miss Phipps's dancing.

'Aw, the locals 'ull get it all,' his mate responded disgustedly.

Even with the excitement and friendliness engendered by the flood, the bagmen still held aloof from the residents. They talked among themselves of other rivers they had seen in flood, of washaways out beyond Bourke, and the monsoon rains of the Gulf country. This was not, for them, The River; it was only a creek temporarily swollen to self-importance. But, for the townspeople, those brown waters encircled the world, as eternity encircles time; and the greatest thing in life for them that day was the arrival or non-arrival of the only train, due at three-thirty—a toy train, known as the 'Tin Hare', which always came in growling and panting and bristling with the self-importance of a Pomeranian dog.

When the 'Tin Hare's' whistle was heard in the distance, even those conscientious citizens who had pretended to carry on as usual, dropped everything and ran. The train shunted very dubiously to the far side of the bridge, and the driver and guard came forward to confer with the stationmaster and porter. They met in the middle of the railway bridge, and they made an effective group with the misty sun behind them. The police had cleared everyone off the bridge and the railway line; but the people crowded up the flour-mill siding; they stood on the back verandah of Harrison's Hotel; they shouldered and edged forward so that they might miss nothing should the train plunge to its doom.

The water was a couple of inches below the bridge, and after a further discussion the driver and guard walked solemnly back to their charge, and a murmur of surmise rose from the crowd. It would be too disappointing if the train just backed away. But the train had no such intention. It grunted belligerently, trembled, crept forward and came rattling across as if nothing had happened.

A cheer broke out. Men waved their hats, women their handkerchiefs. The few passengers waved back in a proud, aloof way, admitting all the dangers they had been through, but deprecating public ostentation.

After that there was nothing to do but go home. The river would not rise much higher, and if it did, would not look very different. It would begin to go down to-morrow, and all this delicious tension would be over. The towns-people of Logan knew their river. It might venture into their backyards, but it had never yet come boldly down the main street.

Amid so much excitement who was there to notice the sad little procession that had wound its way out of town early that morning by the only road that still remained open, the road that led up through the hills? First, Adelaide, with his appalling harness and his decrepit van, soon overtaken by the turnout of the Tyrells; and with them, Miss Phipps, a fat cuckoo in a nest of children, her face turned disdainfully from Logan, a town she was leaving behind, she hoped, for ever. Then the Joneses worrying about the rim-bound wheel. Past the humble procession roared the great truck on which the busker had got a lift that would take him to his destination, to the far-looked-for goal of the tent-shows.

Where the road branched, the Joneses with Adelaide and his family went one way; the Tyrells, with cries of farewell, another. Far away behind them, at the foot of the mountains, lay Logan, the water-logged, self-satisfied, rich town, which had never known they existed. Only Dick and Thirty-Bob had stayed, camped together in a back lane, defiant survivors of the cataclysm which had sent the travellers wearily journeying on, pacing the treadmill of their lives, going out to loneliness again, as unnoticed as the green grass-parrots that are one day in the wheat, then vanished no one knows where.

The farewells of the busker and Dancy had not been long drawn out. It was just: 'So long, Dance, might see you down at the fruit-picking. Anyway, I'll be at the cannery for Christmas. See you then for sure. Tell Snow I couldn't wait.' Miss Phipps merely said: 'I'll have those stockings back, if you don't mind, deah. Don't be unkind to the horse, and try not to swear. It is most objectionable.'

The busker helped Dancy harness Don and put him in the van before they parted. The dawn was cold and grey, and there was a drizzle of rain. Horehound, now so gladly resigned to the care of Thirty-Bob, was with the Tyrell horses, her hobbles chinking, her nose worrying at the grass-roots. She did not even lift her head to see Dancy go. The ridiculous bunch of tail that was all the horse-hair pirates had left her, stuck straight up and waggled derisively, as though she was pleased at some wicked jest of her own.

The dairy was already busy when Dancy put the horse in the paddock that had been pointed out to her yesterday. Charley Marks came running out and helped her to chock up the wheels of the van in a corner of the same field. How long, Dancy wondered, would the van stay like that, patiently waiting? It was Snow's van. The Horehound was his, and the sulky too, for he had bought them; but he had never seemed to care much, and had told her that any money that came from their sale would be hers, so that she had left them with Thirty-Bob untroubled. It was a good thing she had left Bluey behind with the Apostle. The dairy dogs included a nasty big Alsatian, all teeth and suspicion.

The Stray was aroused from these idle thoughts by the sharp voice of her new employer: 'You're late,' Mrs. Marks snapped at her.

'It was the flood, Mrs. Marks, and seein' me mates off.'

'Well, now you're here, you might as well start on them

dishes. Then there's the kitchen and the rest of the house, and the washing piled up that I ain't been able to touch because of me back . . .'

'Right-o, Mrs. Marks,' the Stray responded cheerily enough; and applied herself with vigour to a large pile of greasy plates that the flies had already found.

All day long there were men tramping in and out wanting food; and Mrs. Marks's voice going on and on like the buzzing of a blow-fly, settling first on one topic, then on another, and always ready with some suggestion for further toil.

'Now, when you've finished that pumpkin, Dancy, you might clean out the separator. I don't believe Harry's done it. After that there's the wood and all them big cans.'

The Stray found that her work included, not only the house, but odd jobs about the dairy. It was lucky she had never learnt to milk and was afraid of cows, or Mrs. Marks would have seen to it that her spare minutes, if she had any during the night, were occupied milking. She seemed to think sleeping an undesirable vice. By the end of the day Dancy was so tired she could have wept. She was desperately anxious to keep this job, to show Snow, when he came out of hospital, that she had money of her own. But her legs ached, her back hurt her, perhaps from the weary hearing so much of Mrs. Marks's 'little crawling pains.'

Mrs. Marks sat about all day in a dirty, faded wrapper, and told Dancy what to do; and after tea, the Stray was too tired and dispirited to walk all the way back to the camp and find out what had happened about the sale of Horehound. When, she wondered, would she get time to go to the hospital to see Snow? She was timid about asking when she would have a day off. It might look as though she was lazy to ask so soon. From Mrs. Marks's programme, there did not seem to be any day off in sight. It was eight o'clock when she finished the last of the washing-up and wiped the damp hair back from her forehead.

Now, perhaps, she could have a bath, and then it would be time for bed. It would be marvellous to sleep in a bed again, even in the rickety stretcher in the lean-to.

Charley, who had been watching her from his seat by the fire, a seat that he hardly ever vacated except to perform his self-appointed task of seeing the trains out, shifted aside as she staggered to the stove with a kerosene tin of water to heat. He watched the way she swung the heavy tin on to the stove top, then said: 'You work hard, don't you, Mrs. Grimshaw?'

The name startled Dancy for a minute. The Marks family, all except Charley, called her by her Christian name. Then she answered: 'Too right I work hard, Charley. A toiler, me!' She congratulated herself on omitting the usual adjective and gave him a smile that embraced the clean kitchen, the plates she had washed, the comfort and warmth of walls and roof over and around her, and the thought of all her mates sitting to-night by some small fire, cold and unprotected. Charley liked her. She knew that from the way his eyes followed her as she bustled about. He said, almost in a whisper, with a glance towards the sitting-room where the rest of the family were congregated,

'Would you like to be rich, Mrs. Grimshaw?'

''Strufe, yes,' the Stray responded with a chuckle. 'You found a gold-mine or sumfin', Charley?' She sat down on the opposite side of the kitchen stove, perching on the wood-box like some queer hobgoblin with straggling fair hair and big blue eyes. 'Halves, Charley. Tell me where it is.'

Charley refused to notice her chaff. 'I like you, Mrs. Grimshaw,' he said seriously. 'You're good.'

This made the Stray feel awkward. Even from a poor idiot it sounded funny to hear such words. 'Don't you believe it, Charley,' she said cheerfully. 'It's a rumour.'

But he refused to relax his earnestness. 'I like you,' he repeated. 'I'll tell you what I wouldn't tell Mum or Dad or Joe. They're always worrying about having no money.

They think about it all the time, they talk about it.' He nodded mysteriously. 'What would they say if they knew I was a millionaire, eh? That'd make them sit up, wouldn't it?' His eyes shone. 'I've got plenty of money, plenty. But they'd only laugh if I told them.' He bent forward to whisper. 'It's being the manager of all the railways. Hundreds of thousands they pay me. Well, they have to. The trains wouldn't go without me.' He shook his head; the proud confidence of his voice gave place to a doubtful tone. 'But I have trouble with the banks. They don't like to have all that money taken out of them.'

'They wouldn't,' the Stray agreed, oddly stirred to pity by this wreck of a young man. Charley must have been a fine, handsome boy, she thought, before his brain went wrong.

'I want to make you rich,' he said impulsively. 'I'll give you a cheque for a thousand pounds if you like.'

'Don't you bother, Charley,' the Stray said hastily. 'I got plenty meself. True, I have.'

'I'll give you a cheque,' Charley repeated, 'for a thousand pounds. You don't mind waiting to cash it until to-morrow, do you?' He spoke so much better than the other members of his family. That part of his brain had remained unaffected. If it had not been for the wandering eye of him, you could almost believe what he said.

'It's kind of you to fink of it, Charley.' She hoped the water would soon be ready to lift from the stove. She felt a sudden repulsion from Charley that made her move over to the other side of the kitchen.

Charley followed her, whispering urgently. 'They get so mixed up at the bank. They write down how much money you have in a book and a man stamps it, and then they give you a piece of paper. That's all money is. Even rich people like me—we've only got bits of paper, even managers of railways.'

He went over to the meat-safe for the account-book, which lay on top with a pen and a bottle of ink, and brought them over to the table. With a lordly disregard of what his father would say, Charley tore out half a sheet of paper and scrawled across it: 'Pay Mrs. Grimshaw a thousand pounds,' and carefully signed his name 'Charles Marks.'

'There,' he said, smiling proudly, 'you take that to the bank—the white one on the corner of the main street—and they'll give you a thousand pounds.'

'Thank you, Charley,' the Stray found herself saying. 'Thank you.'

'Good anywhere,' Charley emphasised, coming so close to her that he was towering over her. 'You only have to cash it.' His fit of excitement seemed to pass, and he settled down again on his stool by the stove. 'Rich,' he murmured, 'all of us rich.'

The repulsion that Dancy had felt so strongly only twenty seconds before passed from her and pity returned.

'Gee, you're kind, Charley,' she said admiringly. 'Look, I'll show you what I'll do. See, here's a safety-pin. Well, I'll pin that cheque of yours inside me dress like this, and then I'll know, if ever I need it, it's there. I won't cash it right away, see. I'll just put it by for a rainy day, and I'll take it out and look at it, and remember how good you was to me.' She beamed at his pleased expression.

'You don't laugh,' he said. 'You're good.'

The Stray lifted down the heavy tin of water. Charley sprang up at once. 'Let me carry it for you,' he cried eagerly, almost snatching it from her hand, so that water slopped on the floor.

Again the Stray had that qualm of nausea at his closeness, but she only said: 'Thank you, Charley.' What else, she reproached herself, could she say? You couldn't be unkind to a poor chap who had lost his wits. She was afraid of Charley, almost as afraid as she had been of the Horehound. In her little lean-to bedroom she had an uneasy feeling that he might prowl in when she was asleep; but she laughed herself out of that fancy. As she took off her dress, she looked again at that pitiful scrawl on the torn paper. 'Pay Mrs. Grimshaw a thousand pounds.'

She wasn't Mrs. Grimshaw, and it wasn't a real cheque. Oh, well, she would keep it. She would wear it for luck. Life owed her something, and maybe the cheque would remind whoever the teller might be in the bank of life that Dancy, who wanted to be Mrs. Grimshaw, was an unsatisfied creditor. 'Pay Mrs. Grimshaw . . . Pay Mrs. Grimshaw. . . . She ought to be paid . . . long-overdue account.'

Chapter XII

Mɪss Phɪᴘᴘs quitted Logan with the Tyrells. She did not particularly care for their society, but she felt that to travel unchaperoned with the busker would not be proper. Everything about the Tyrells she disliked except their van, and in this she ensconced herself, heaped round with bedding and children. The backs of Mr. and Mrs. Tyrell, broad and determined, shut out the view in front. The Tyrells did not mind her added weight, for they had a waggon with a pole and a pair of horses, dappled grey and 'the best on the track bar none.' They also owned a third horse which Dick considered his special property and which pulled the cart he drove, a cart the Tyrells were always going to sell or trade away and never did.

Deafy had intended to travel very slowly, out of consideration for his wife, but as the day wore on, her groans became increasingly agonised. Mrs. Tyrell was not a woman to make any kind of fuss, and the fact that she groaned worried Deafy more than if another woman screamed. He made her lie down in the van, and gave Miss Phipps the baby to hold on the front seat, an imposition that Miss Phipps treated with hauteur. She was half tempted to remind him that she was a guest and wished to be treated as such, but Deafy seemed in rather a forbidding mood. As for his wife, Miss Phipps sincerely

hoped the creature was not taken ill on the road. Not
that it would not serve her right. Miss Phipps regarded
Mrs. Tyrell as 'disgusting,' not to be mentioned in company, and the anxiety that the woman's grown-up son
had openly expressed about his mother, the manner in
which he had referred to her distressing complaint, as
though the whole affair was not shameful in the extreme,
struck Miss Phipps as just another example of the de-
pravity of the lower classes. Here, she reflected, were
people who obviously had no right whatever to children,
even one or two children, and they were indulging in
children to an extent that she considered bestial.

Deafy was nearly out of his wits with worry. They had
covered half the distance to Gargendra and the road was
harder if he turned back than if he went on. There was
nothing for it but to go on; but would his wife last the
distance? Her words to the sergeant returned to haunt
him. 'D'you want me to die on the track?' He set his
teeth. Not if he could help it! He'd get to Gargendra,
and get there in a hurry.

'Hang on, old woman,' he said tenderly. 'I'm going to
put on a bit of pace.' And he set the two dappled grey
ponies that were his pride trotting rapidly. 'If the old
woman's took bad,' he yelled to Miss Phipps, 'you'll just
have to stand by. I guess you know how it is. Got any
kids of yer own?'

'How dare you!' Miss Phipps exclaimed. But Deafy
did not hear her.

He nodded his head. 'Good,' he said. 'I'll do me best
to Gardendra, if I have to founder the horses, but if we
don't, I'll jus' have to leave it to you.'

It had occurred to Deafy that a woman might be handy,
and he had made no demur about Miss Phipps accompanying them. She looked matronly.

'Glad I got you with me,' he yelled, cracking his whip
over the backs of the startled greys. 'Bringin' kids into
the world ain't a man's job.'

Never before had Miss Phipps regarded a man whipping horses with so much tolerance, not to say approval. As long as she did not have to act as midwife by the roadside she did not care how cruelly this dreadful man beat the horses. She was resolved never again to travel with a woman who was likely at any moment to have a child. Disgusting!

Always Miss Phipps's ultimate standard of good and bad was 'Would such a statement, such conduct, be allowed in the World Feminised State?' This State, it must be remembered, was the one Miss Phipps intended to set up herself when her merits were recognised, and she was, solely by virtue of her qualities of leadership, benevolence and wisdom, acclaimed to the sole rulership of the whole world. This desirable state could not, of course, be brought about while there were men surviving to disturb the flow of 'mental harmony and psychic value, rhythmic and purposive trends,' which must ultimately triumph. To put it more bluntly, the presence of men jarred.

Worse even than those arch-horrors, men, were the creatures—she would not call them women—that would be staining the name, who had become so brutalised and degraded with the lower values of men that they had become even less than these much-to-be-despised beings. To these women Mrs. Tyrell belonged. She would have been ruthlessly extirpated from the World Feminised State, not only for her moral corruption in bearing children—for Miss Phipps recognised that children were a sign that the woman had deserted psychic harmony for the lower values of male animalism—but because Mrs. Tyrell was definitely unaesthetic. Only the beautiful, Miss Phipps often repeated to herself, deserved to survive. Did she not strive herself for perfect beauty in every detail of her person? Had she not cared for her skin and hair in the most trying circumstances? A Real Woman never forgot these details. It is the details that count.

As for Mrs. Tyrell, Miss Phipps felt, of course, a certain pity for the creature as she lay there looking very unaesthetic indeed, with the sweat running down her face and her hair tumbled untidily. But she had brought it on herself, hadn't she, by deserting The Higher Values for the low standards of a man-made world? She *would* have children. She ought to have learnt her lesson long ago; and with great repugnance Miss Phipps cast another furtive glance at the moaning creature.

'Oh, Alf,' Mrs. Tyrell groaned, 'I feel so bad.'

'Stick it out, girl,' her husband shouted. 'We've got nine miles to go. Hang on to that damn kid for Chrisake.'

Miss Phipps had rarely prayed before, but now she put up a carefully worded petition as one potentate treating with another: 'Please allow this dreadful woman to reach the hospital and spare me the nauseous details of a confinement and I will certainly endeavour to obtain work at the next town.'

The prayers of Deafy or Miss Phipps found a mark, for the greys were presently speeding towards a settlement that looked as though the small farms had drawn closer together. It was scarcely so much a town as the country congealed into a clot. The greys had foam on their coats, they were galloping now, and the old van swayed and pitched so that the children clung fearfully to their mother. Deafy drove as though he was pursued by wild Indians. He slowed down to yell at a man on horseback who was passing: 'Where's the hospital, mate? Quick! Me wife's took bad.'

'There ain't no hospital,' the man yelled back. 'There's the Bush Nurse. She'll help. I'll go and tell her.' And galloped on ahead.

He was presently to be seen again as a dust-cloud rolling towards them. Wheeling his horse, he shouted to Deafy to follow, and with a reassuring wave of his hat, thundered ahead once more. Half the little township seemed to have appeared on its doorstep to watch their triumphal entry, and Miss Phipps was terribly discomfited as people pointed her out as the poor woman who was being rushed to 'the Bush Nurse's place.'

The tiny cottage in which the Bush Nurse resided had

168

only about four rooms; but patients were hurriedly cleared out on to the verandah to give Mrs. Tyrell one of the rooms to herself. The friend and guide trotted up where Deafy was waiting by the gate and asked sympathetically how the missus was. He heard the whole story of the Tyrells' exodus from Logan, and his indignation knew no bounds. He went off to spread the tale, with the result that the small settlement could not do enough for Mrs. Tyrell's family left motherless. While Deafy waited anxiously, cheered by the remarks that the two patients on the verandah called to him comfortingly from time to time, a farmer came hurrying over to offer him the use of a paddock for as long as Deafy stayed. There was a shack that was not doing itself any good, the man explained, standing so long without anyone in it. The farmer's wife would see to the children, and, if Deafy did not want to leave the 'nurse's' place until his wife was over her trouble, then the farmer would drive the turnout over, get the horses out and give them a feed and good rub-down.

To all these words beating about him Deafy responded with nods dazedly. He stood switching at the grass with the whip that had brought the horses to Gardendra, he hoped, in time. The past few years his wife had not been strong. With his face set like iron, he nodded and murmured his thanks without really caring if the children were never fed or the horses fell in the road. He would always dislike this baby, even if it was a girl, because of that nightmare drive. 'If ever I get back to Logan,' Deafy vowed silently, 'I'll make that sergeant wish he hadn't been born. I'll smash him.' Then he remembered that these were hopeless threats from a man whose wife and children would go hungry if he went to gaol or lost his dole, who, because of his deafness, could not get work any more.

The baby was a boy, a healthy infant of eight and a half pounds. But its mother was very ill. Deafy was allowed to tiptoe in to see her, and that was all. She just said:

'Hallo, Alf,' in a dim way; and he said: 'Good old girl,' and stroked her hair with his rough brown hand as though she had been a horse.

'I'll get over it,' she whispered. 'I'll be all right.'

Deafy understood her. 'You ought to be,' he responded with a touch of his old spirit. 'You've had enough practice.'

He felt as though he had wakened from an evil dream. It occurred to him that he should send word to Dick and Thirty-Bob, so he asked if anyone was going over to Logan. The baker was going next morning to see the manager of the Logan flour-mill, and to him Deafy entrusted his message. Then he looked round vaguely.

'There was a big fat woman come with us,' he asked perplexedly. 'Where the hell's she got to?'

He had not heard Miss Phipps thank him for the lift and hastily gather up her goods and chattels—the dirty little black billy, her skipping-rope ('so good for the figure'), her foodstuffs, and her face-creams—in a burst-apart handbag tied with string. She had slipped away as soon as the turnout drew up in the grove of gums before the Bush Nurse's door. She had gone waddling away from that scene of shame as quickly as she could, while sympathisers half-carried Mrs. Tyrell into the cottage. She coldly disregarded the questions the women asked her, as she made her way out the opposite side of the settlement to that which they had entered. She was so upset and demoralised by the horrors she had just escaped, that she allowed a friendly lorry-driver to give her a lift to Oriho, and did not reprove him more than three times for unseemly behaviour.

She shuddered frequently to think what she had endured. Those dreadful people! Ugh! They ought to be put into a lethal chamber. True to her promise, as soon as she arrived in Oriho she sought work. She did not even stop to find a camp. She found the local Labour Exchange instead and told a pitiful story of her sufferings while on 'a walking tour.' The agent was so impressed by her recital that, despite the fact that she had lost her references, he took her home to his wife, and next day solicited a position for her at the biggest of the local hotels, a position it would be an over-statement to call 'pot-walloping,' since it was, even more than Dancy's job, connected with washing and scrubbing.

Nevertheless it was work, and if it had not been that she knew the Stray could not read properly, Miss Phipps would have sent her a letter to put her in her place. She was losing pounds daily as she toiled over an enormous furnace of a range, but she did not care. She was away from the dreadful people on the track. She had a roof over her head. She might not have had it long, had the hotel not been extra busy while the picnic races were in full swing. But the licensee and his wife put up with Miss Phipps because she had had such a terrible time travelling the roads and had kept herself pure and unspotted through it all. A real lady too! Even the kitchen-maids, until they found her out, cleaned up their language in her presence.

Chapter XIII

As the busker beheld the country whizzing past him at fifty miles an hour, he heaved a sigh of enormous relief. He was done with the slow crawling of vans and sulkies that had chafed his free spirit ever since he joined Snow's party. He had always travelled fast, and it irked him more than the others could imagine to see cars going by in a cloud of dust, trains that an active man might 'jump' steaming off without him. To hell with the Horse! This was the age of speed, and he was part of it. He did not intend to end his life as the personal attendant of any horse, particularly the Horehound. The only use he would have for a horse henceforth would be as a race result. But some worm of conscience intermittently gnawed the fair flower of his content. It was leaving Snow that bothered him; he had no qualms about deserting the Stray.

After all, she had meant nothing in his life. He might have attempted a mild philandering, if she had been better-looking and not quite so absorbed in the impervious Snow. But then, again, if he had attempted anything, the busker reflected prudently, it might have spoilt the tone of the camp. Dancy was one of those girls a man could never trust. She would as likely as not express her dissatisfaction, if a man so much as made a pass at her, by cracking his skull with an empty bottle. He had seen her whip off her shoe and aim a blow at an unfortunate bagman who had been over-demonstrative, that, had it landed, would have laid him unconscious. The way she used her fists had more than once precipitated an ugly situation into which he or Snow might have been drawn. No, the busker reflected virtuously, although she had her good points, he was pleased to see the last of Dancy.

He had told Phippsy terrible stories of the show-people to deter her from accompanying him and spoiling his freedom. Nothing, not the finest voice in the world, would persuade him to endure Miss Phipps's company again. She was the nearest thing to a vacuum he had ever met; and the busker, like nature, abhorred a vacuum. She drew everything into herself and gave nothing in return. She sucked all the good out of life, and her absence was a positive joy.

But he felt mean when he thought of Snow lying in hospital, thinking the busker had the turnouts in his care. He had let Snow down. But, oh hell, life wasn't long enough to be always shouldering your fair share of responsibility. Everything would turn out for the best. With this metaphysical boot-sole the busker sought to crush that ever-gnawing worm of conscience.

By the time the houses began to thicken into streets and the mile-long main thoroughfare of the great city of Walfra opened before him, he had no thought but of the show, of returning to his own people, the show-people. He

scented from afar the strange atmosphere of mingled saw-
dust, chewing-gum, hot fairy-floss and perspiring crowds
that was the breath of life to him. He tugged at the lapels
of his best suit as a horse might tug at its reins. He
fidgeted. He almost neighed with eagerness. When the
lorry-driver set him down in the main street, he even
refused a free beer, so eager was he to hurry off towards
the show-ground. His ardour was somewhat damped by a
young policeman who had seen him alight and came
strolling over with a glint in his eye.

'We don't want any travellers in this town,' the law
announced without preamble. 'You'd better get out as
quick as you came in, unless you want to see the inside
of our new gaol.'

The busker made no direct answer. He felt that both
dignity and safety counselled silence. This specimen of
the genus police was a very large, very well-developed
specimen. He towered over the busker in a way that
youth did not like. The busker mumbled something and
started to walk away, but the policeman showed signs of
accompanying him.

'You got it all wrong,' the busker explained. 'I've come
here for the show.'

'So've seven thousand other bagmen,' the policeman
observed, not without a trace of bitterness. 'The population of this town is usually eighteen thousand. And now,
show-time, there's twenty-five thousand, and most of
them,' his tone was severe, 'crooks or bagmen, or both.'

'You have a bit of faith and trust,' the busker advised.
'Come round to the show to-night, and maybe I'll get
you in free.'

The policeman eyed him coldly, but let him go, while
he slowly pondered whether he should tell this flip young
man that policemen got in free anyway, or whether he
should keep that knowledge to himself.

Over the Main Street of Walfra, pendent between the
roof of the garage and the hotel verandah on the opposite
side of the road, was a calico sign which announced in

large letters of black and red: 'Welcome to Walfra. The City with the Civic Spirit.' When this banner became old and tattered, the townspeople would have grown so used to it that they would not even notice when it fell to the ground like some overripe fruit of civic progress. At present it made the townspeople feel important just to look at that sign, for Walfra was still in the self-conscious stage of cityhood. After all, is a city a city when you can stand on one side and see right through it and out the other? Such doubts were loyally suppressed by all except unpleasant and discourteous visitors.

Like most other inland 'cities,' Walfra had started as the ford of the river, and worked its way up as the marketing centre for a rich wool and wheat-growing district. There were any number of farmers, their lambing over, and shearing not yet begun, who would come riotously into Walfra and treat their children to a ride on the merry-go-round and their wives to shilling seats at the tent show. If any of their sheep won a trophy, they might even go so far as to buy the wives new saucepans.

On the outskirts of country towns there are always mysterious bald patches, sometimes with a fence, sometimes without. They can be either a racecourse, a cricket-pitch, or, when they are not bogged, an aerodrome. They also serve as a sports-ground, and, when a grandstand and sheds are erected, a show-ground. On Walfra's bald patch, tents were being erected in a negligent way, as though it did not really matter if they went up this week or the next. Chiefest of these was a big marquee in which the main show would be housed, a marquee branded and stamped all over as the property of W. Jasprey. A large, yellow motor-van was also so labelled, proclaiming itself as belonging to Jasprey's Giant Show.

The busker had timed his arrival well. The show would start on the morrow, so a seedy-looking man who was tugging on a guy-rope informed him. There was very little indication that anything unusual was toward. The show-ground was the usual bare, scraped patch in the box-

174

tree scrub, with the usual group of tin sheds for 'exhibits' and the usual tiny grandstand. It might have been Logan all over again, except that Walfra was bigger.

The busker's high spirits drooped a little. He did not know anybody. These were strangers, but he still felt fairly confident that he would find his niche. He could always return to street-singing as a last resort. He was wise enough to know that the show-ground or the camps beside it were the last place he would find the 'big bugs' of the tent shows. They would be in the bars of the hotels. He regretted now that he had turned down that free beer the lorry-driver had offered. But the man might have expected him to shout back, and the busker had only a shilling in the world.

He strolled back down the Main Street, deciding which of the boarding-houses looked the best for free board and lodging. They would probably all be crowded, but his appearance in his best maroon suiting with the green hat would stand him in good stead. He looked prosperous—in fact he had been startled that the policeman had spoken to him. Probably had not the policeman seen him descend from the lorry, he would not have picked him for a traveller. His musings were interrupted by a raucous hail 'Hiyah, Dooksey!' and the next minute he was pumping the hand of his erstwhile mate, the jockey George Walton, and George was leading him by the arm towards the bar, talking as he went, all as though there had never been any regrettable rift between them or black eyes or bruises exchanged. George also looked prosperous. He was wearing brown trousers, a vivid yellow knitted sweater and a new blue tweed sports coat. His brown hat sported a little blue feather. For all his affluence, he seemed more than pleased to see the busker.

'Where you been?' George asked, when they were standing with a couple of mugs at their elbows. 'I expected you to show up days ago. I been putting in a good word with Jasprey—just digging round his roots— so's when you came he'd give you a break.'

'What a pal!' the busker exclaimed fervently. Forgotten was that large bruise on the cheek-bone that had been George's parting gift.

'I figured it out,' George said importantly, 'that with your voice and my brains, we could knock 'em cold.'

The words seemed somehow familiar to the busker, but he felt it would be impolitic to enquire: 'What brains?' as he was tempted to do.

'What's Jasprey got on his board for a line-up?' he asked instead.

'He'll fix you in all right,' his friend assured him. 'Surest thing you know. I'm geeing for him, and I'll fix it.'

The busker's spirits fell again. In the show world a 'gee-man' or 'micky finn' was socially on the level of a duck's feet. He is the man who goes out in the crowd and touts for custom with such inspiring cries as: 'Come along now. Come and have your fortune told. Madame Sara! All the way from Egypt! Stay on Rocky Ned for five seconds and ten shillings. Try your luck on Loop-the-Loop. Roll up and see the Bearded Woman!' That is a gee-man. He hastens the slow pace of the bucolic population which would otherwise never get within spending distance of its money.

'There's Jasprey now,' George whispered. 'Come on. Let's put the hard word on him.'

He edged up to a stout man with a cigar, a circle of listeners, a very quick, unpleasant way of speaking, and a yellow face cut into deep wrinkles.

'He comes over here, see?' Mr. Jasprey was saying, illustrating with the cigar, 'and I ask him what the bloody hell he's up to. "You Jasprey," he says, "Mr. Walt Jasprey?" "Yes," I says, "and what the bloody hell . . ."'

''Scuse me, Mr. Jasprey.' George had wriggled within interrupting distance. 'Could I see you a minute?'

'Get to hell, what's-your-name,' Mr. Jasprey responded without change of tone. 'Later. See you later. Busy as hell.'

'I got that friend of mine I was telling you about. The yodelling drover. Listen, Mr. Jasprey; he's just over here, if you could spare a minute. . . .'

Mr. Jasprey shot a shrewd glance in the direction of the busker. 'Nothing doing. Got a yodeller. Tell him to get back to his bullock-punching.'

But the busker had joined the fray. Without waiting for the outcome of the interview, he had produced his guitar and unleashed his voice in a torrent of sound that even a Swiss cataract would have envied, if it had the privilege of rivalling that incomparable yodel on some mountain peak. To the ear of a music critic the busker's voice would have sounded as though all the cats in creation suddenly yearned their passion aloud, but Mr. Jasprey, being a showman, knew the power of the yodel, the spell it binds over the farming populace. He listened almost respectfully for fully five bars. Then his normal impatience reasserted itself.

'Skip it,' he shouted. 'Come up to the truck in about an hour and I'll see what you got. Lemme alone now. Busy as hell. . . .'

But the busker went on squalling of his love for some girl in the west who had been foolish enough to entrust her heart to his keeping. Mr. Jasprey, with a weary muttering, snatched up his beer, his circle of listeners and his cigar, and wafted them into a private sitting-room. Even there he could hear the plaudits of the audience in the bar, where the publican was standing the busker beer. The busker knew he was as good as engaged.

'There you are,' his friend George said, thumping him on the back. 'I fixed it for you, didn't I?'

When the busker interviewed Mr. Jasprey he certainly found himself hired. He would get four pounds for the week the show was in Walfra, and as the busker had not touched four pound notes for a long time, although he had a lurking feeling he was being underpaid, he did not take long to accept the offer. He spent a considerable effort afterwards endeavouring to convince Mr. Jasprey that he was worth more. Mr. Jasprey, who had been congratulating himself aloud on his own generosity, turned a cold eye on his new hireling, and wanted to know if the busker were sick or out of his mind. He added that the busker would be expected to take his place in the line-up outside the tent before the show began and also to help with such chores as grooming the bucking mule, holding the tight-rope tight while the Human Fly walked along it, dressing up in a coating of black cork as the assistant of Aladdin the Wonder-Worker, and helping to eject anyone who wanted his money back. The busker removed himself before Mr. Jasprey could think of more odd jobs. His new employer had a fertile mind when it came to finding work for other people.

Having thus hired himself to the tent show, the busker made a tour of the sideshows to see what pickings he could find. He chummed up with the guardian of the merry-go-round, who introduced him to a lean, melancholy person who was running Fosdick's Ten-in-One-Show. The Ten-in-One consisted of a long-tailed pheasant from Japan, a stuffed orang-outang, a crocodile in the same condition, the handcuffs with which Legs Diamond was apprehended, the original bloodstains and revolver of the Bloodbath Murder, some very sleepy and disinterested carpet snakes and other 'Horrors.'

The busker pricked up his ears when he heard the merry-go-round owner 'ribbing' Fosdick on the number of lodgers he was taking in nightly; bagmen who, for a few shillings now and then, helped with the show, bringing water and wood and erecting tents. The night before a carpet snake had curled up on one of the lodgers as he was sleeping peacefully in the tent; and now Fosdick complained that 'just for a little thing like that,' the sleeper had vacated his claim for accommodation. The busker, always ready to save money, and realising from several 'knock-backs' that he had little hope of lodging in the town, immediately pre-empted the vacant sleeping-place. Mr. Fosdick was agreeable, provided the busker would 'ampster' for him. The busker, since his own show did not coincide with the Ten-in-One, saw no reason to refuse.

The ampster's is an easy job. He stands in the front row of the listening crowd registering intense interest and enthusiasm while the showman 'spruiks.' Meanwhile other members of the troupe collect a crowd. This they do by taking up their place on 'the board,' a platform by the entrance of the tent, and raising a great commotion over the fact that: 'In one minute Daredevil Phil will shoot the apple off the lady's head' (not that he ever does), or that 'The Wonder Worker from Ceylon will now cut this beautiful girl in halves. Roll up! Roll up!' The crowd duly rolls up because it thinks that something free is about to happen, and the lure of a free show is always potent. As soon as the showman begins to shout: 'All right, the show is commencing. Roll up! Roll up! They're starting right away. No waiting. No delay,' there is a whispered order given: 'Ampsters to the fore,' and the ampster rushes eagerly up to the ticket-window and says: 'Right-o, mister, I'll have a ticket.' He pretends to pass his money over, and is handed a ticket. His brother-ampsters form into an impatient queue behind him and file into the tent at the head of the multitude, who, like sheep, will follow the leader, but will not be the first to pay their money. If it were not for the ampsters, there would be no audience. Having seen as much of the show as they feel they can stand, the ampsters slip out, to reappear just as the next performance commences and repeat their necessary part.

His future thus settled, the busker began to look about him for distractions other than the traditional showman's holiday of 'going down town, getting drunk, and getting pinched.' He first enquired anxiously if anyone had been killed on the Northern Run that year, for the show-people are superstitious. His mind was set at rest by the reply that a bagman who was 'geeing' for Jasprey had fallen off the bumper bars of a train and had his body cut in two. Reassured that the showmen's year would be a successful one after this propitiatory sacrifice, the busker decided that what his soul required was feminine society. He cast a roving glance over what was offered; but the fortune-teller was a stout, elderly lady with a moustache, and the woman wrestler had her husband travelling with her, and he was nearly as big as she was. Several of the wives and daughters of the showmen looked possible; but it was George Walton who told the busker of the really alluring daughter of the milk-bar proprietor whose refreshment tent was just near the gate of the show-ground.

The busker cruised in the direction of this milk-bar; he even sampled the beverage, which struck his refined palate as very much like the water a milky glass had been washed in. The daughter, however, was incomparable. She was as sweet as the milk-bar proprietor was sour. She could not have been more than sixteen, but she was a flowery blonde with a skin of peaches and cream, the brains of a guinea-pig, and a most entrancing giggle.

The busker had not been among those present for ten minutes when he decided that, not only had he a job and a place to sleep, but he was already a leap and a half ahead of all the other he-persons on the show-ground, and in process of acquiring a girl as well. Every able-bodied male had been in to sample the curious fluid that tasted a little like milk and to try their luck with the proprietor's daughter; but it was obvious that the busker was out in the lead. He was, as he said himself, a good mixer; and when it came to telling lies, particularly of his own deeds of daring and skill, he shone.

He was dragged away from the damsel to take part in a parade through the town, a parade which the local authorities, with their customary obtuseness, had refused to permit. It was a beautiful parade, with trucks and loud-speakers, and damsels in gaudy spangles, and wild-looking men weaving snakes about their torsos, handbills galore and a band. The busker, in the borrowed trappings of a Red Indian brave, roared through a megaphone while a gentleman in purple tights beside him beat a large gong.

The police had received a mysterious message that a big fight was about to take place in a paddock some convenient distance out of town, and had naturally driven out to stop it. Strangely enough, the time the fight was supposed to start was the same that the procession wound its way unmolested down the main street, creating a delightful and disorderly row.

'This is the life,' the busker breathed to himself. He found no reason to alter that view during the following few days, which were bubbled to the brim with good luck and fun. In the first place, the policeman who had warned him off in the main street doubted that John Sampson, the Strong Man, did really drive a six-inch nail through a three-inch board with his hand, and vowed he could do it himself. Challenged to make good his words, the policeman had smitten the nail, which, instead of going through the board, had gone through his hand.

Then there had been a really glorious fight between the members of the boxing troupe and a gang of half a dozen 'illy-wackers' who had been unwise enough to play poker with the heavyweight. An illy-wacker is someone who is putting a confidence trick over, selling imitation diamond tie-pins, new-style patent razors or infallible 'tonics,' altering cheques obtained by fraud from, say, £10 to £100, 'living on the cockies' by such devices, and following the shows because money always flows freest at show time. A man who 'wacks the illy' can be almost anything, but two of these particular illy-wackers were equipped with a dart game. The board had a steel back, so that the dart would drop off, unless it struck on one of three or four holes, which had been liberally provided to allow a fair chance for anyone desirous of collecting the gift box of chocolates, which was the prize of the successful dart-thrower. The others were 'high-up' men, billiard-players who had put up at the hotel in style and were busily reducing the bank balance of the local billiard-players.

On the second night, a gang of assorted showmen broke into the temporary bar which had been erected at the show-ground and the camp indulged in a general 'beer-up.' You could not lift the flap of any given tent without disturbing a little nest of bottles stowed away for future consumption. The police went round making enquiries, but they could not pin the crime on anyone, partly because the field of choice was so wide. Practically the only individual to escape suspicion was Fosdick's stuffed orang-outang. Even the skipping dog had kept guard.

Then there was the unlooked-for excitement, when the gong fell off the bull's-eye in Greenhorn Mick's Shooting-Gallery, and one sportsman's shot went clean through the hat of a farmer in a nearby tent and another killed a parrot on a tree just outside the show-ground fence. For a while Mick just stood and swore, and the customers swore, too, because they were sure they were shooting bull's eyes, and no gong rang to record the shot. They complained that the show was crooked. Finally, Greenhorn Mick, in imminent danger of his life, crawled along the back of the canvas and replaced the gong while the customers were firing. He dared not let them know the gong had fallen off. There would have been a riot.

The sharp-shooter attached to the Jasprey show challenged a fellow-showman to a duel. They were both half-drunk, and when they had shot apples off each other's head and cigarettes out of each other's mouth, they decided to blaze away, shot for shot, at ten paces, to prove that shooting a man through the body would not really kill him. They were restrained by force from carrying out what seemed to them a reasonable experiment.

Emboldened by the success of the showmen's raid on the bar, a gang of bagmen broke into the rear of the grand-stand which housed the ladies' fancy-work exhibits. They were not as lucky nor as careful as the more experienced showmen. One of them, when captured, was still wearing the fancy knitted sweater he had abstracted, a beautiful exhibit in green and crimson wool, which was visible for a quarter of a mile. The police arrested everyone in sight, provided he looked sufficiently like a bagman or could give no clear account of his movements. The busker thanked his lucky stars that he could prove he was a bona-fide member of Jasprey's troupe. He had two pairs of hand-knitted socks and four sets of ladies' underwear stowed away in a safe place.

It had been the busker's intention to present the underwear to Jessie, the daughter of the milk-bar proprietor. But after witnessing the round-up of his associates, he thought better of it. He could always dispose of the underwear at a profit when the hue and cry died down. At the moment Jessie seemed quite in a melting mood, even without any presents. To be sure, her father took no favourable view of the busker's suit, and had ordered him out of the milk-bar thrice, the last time with considerable acrimony. He was deaf to the charms of the busker's yodelling, although Jessie could listen to it for hours, and even the busker's new suit, on which he had spent all the advance of his salary, had no effect. He requested his daughter to have nothing to do with that 'lazy, skulking little tom-cat.' His ill-advised command that Duke should 'get out of the milk-bar and stay out' only meant that Jessie was now obliged to slip away at odd moments to see her suitor, instead of flirting with him while she served drinks.

The night before the show was to leave Walfra, the busker, after some pleading—for she was fearful of her father—persuaded Jessie to come for a walk with him after he had finished his turn in the tent. Leaving the tight-rope walker to walk a rope that was anything but tight, the bucking mule to enter the ring without the iron burrs under his saddle that made his turn such a success, and the magician without any assistant to hold his fire while he swallowed it, the busker made off into the scrub with the lady of his choice.

If there was one thing the busker could congratulate himself on, it was his knowledge of the terrain. Even in a flat, dusty place like Walfra, where there was nothing to see but a muddy river or the stockyards by moonlight, the busker could find some comfortable little parking-place that was neither coated in cow-manure, full of bindi-eyes and other assorted prickles, nor the home of ants. He could keep a girl out until half-past one in the morning in a dusty paddock full of sheep and almost convince her that she had just been looking at the view. It was a pity his salary had not extended to a wrist-watch, for by the time they wandered back to the show-ground, even the poker-players had gone to sleep. The camps were plunged in darkness. Jessie snivelled nervously about what her father would say.

'I can't go home at this hour. He'd just about kill me.'

The busker scratched his head in doubt and hesitated. 'Well,' he said at last, 'I guess there's nothing for it but for you to share the tent with the rest of us. Then in the morning we can go and square your old man.'

'You don't know my old man. He's a regular terror.'

The busker reflected irritably that it was a bit late to think of that now, but he only responded: 'Well, there's no sense getting frozen. Look out where you put your feet, or you'll tread on some of the mob, and if they wake, they'll give us blue murder.'

Luckily his place of repose was at the far end of the tent, a little removed from the chorus of snores that greeted them as they lifted the flap, letting in a weak ray of moonshine on the row of bodies. The two late-comers tip-toed cautiously down to the far end of the rows and the busker made an equable division of the blankets. He was tired, and in no mood for further philandering. After all, he had had a hard day, and would be up at dawn helping to dismantle the tent. He fell asleep with the ease that comes of a soft heart and a hardened conscience, and was awakened by what he thought must be very bright moonlight shining on his face. It happened to be the torch of his old enemy, the very large, very unpleasant policeman who had met him on his first entry into Walfra. Beside the policeman stood the proprietor of the milk-bar, and he was holding a shot-gun in a way the busker did not like.

'So,' said the policeman, surveying the row of sleeping forms with interest, 'this is what they call a Ten-in-One Show!'

Chapter XIV

MISS PHIPPS, at the Hotel Stainford, was becoming more and more familiar with the manners and customs of the Australian aristocracy. It was an opportunity she welcomed, for she had always felt that among any aristocracy she would move as to the manner born. Were not the English Chester-Phippses expending thousands in a long and involved legal dog-fight over the Chester-Phipps millions that were locked up in Chancery? Miss Phipps always regarded herself as the heiress to those millions, even though her despicable father had roared with laughter when she suggested the possibility, and refused to put in even a claim to them, saying that he would not waste the twopence on the stamp. She hated her father as much for this cheating her out of her millions as she did for his laziness, drunkenness and general refusal to provide for his family. The last time Miss Phipps had left home she had signified her dislike by hurling a kettle of hot water over her father, and she felt that should she return, her welcome would be anything but genial. Besides throwing the hot water, she had deliberately hurled rocks through every window of the house. That would teach him to put in a claim for the Chester-Phipps millions!

It was with some curiosity, therefore, that while polishing the floors and removing dirty linen, Miss Phipps observed the behaviour of moneyed people: people whose photographs appeared in the papers; young women whose clothes caused her a gasp of envy; young men who owned aeroplanes, race-horses, and expensive motor-cars. The hotel was crowded with the *élite* who had come into town for the week of the picnic races. Stories of the gay parties 'thrown' by the station-owners who had rented the more presentable houses in the town at an exorbitant figure, were daily gossip in the kitchen. But it was around the hotels, and particularly the Hotel Stainford, which catered for the most exclusive and expensive trade, that the noisiest and fastest set of the revellers centred their activities.

They were light-hearted, they were young, the wool-cheque would be large, and what was money for but to spend? The hotel staff shared the fun; they had been lavishly tipped. The hotel-keeper, Saxe, and his wife—a woman who put the fear of the Lord into Miss Phipps—went about smiling. They knew that last year Tolly Sampson's bill for breakages had been a hundred and eight pounds, and this year they expected him to eclipse his previous record. To have the son of one of the richest men in New South Wales staying at the Stainford was alone a promise of plenty. Tolly brought with him his friends, those light-hearted fellows who saw in him the golden calf to be sacrificed to an enormous thirst, for Tolly Sampson was drinking himself to death, and they were there to help him do it.

It was their habit to begin the day with some jest, such as stripping one of their number naked and locking him in the linen-closet for ransom, or waiting until the maid had cleaned out the rooms and then raiding them, turning the wardrobes upside down, throwing the mattresses out of the window, tying the sheets into knots and generally making merry. A mild protest might have had the effect of driving their custom elsewhere, so it was seldom made. The waiters and the maids were just instructed to clean up the mess and look pleasant. They would not lose by it. 'Boys will be boys,' as the cook said benevolently, when Cissie, one of the waitresses in the first-class dining-room, complained that for the second time that evening one of the diners, in a sportive mood, had up-ended a loaded tray she was carrying. Cissie refused to be drawn into the general jollity. There were bits of broken crockery and turkey and soup and assorted vegetables all over her clean dining-room floor. 'I'd like to rub their noses in it,' she glowered. She did not mind young men ruining each other's dinner-suits, squirting soda-water, or anointing their friends' hair and clothing with tomato-sauce, but it broke her heart to see her dining-room, usually so immaculate, turned into a pig-sty.

Miss Phipps said nothing, even when she cut her hand cleaning a mess of broken glass out of the lounge fireplace, which was swimming in champagne that had been thrown there with the glasses. Her first feelings of curiosity and interest had given way to disgust. She felt frightened and bewildered. Behind her now, all the time, was a fear of being turned out on the road again penniless. Better endure without protest the riotous behaviour of the guests, the sharpness of Mrs. Saxe, the swearing of the cook, than to lose this her security, meals three times a day, a roof over her head and a bed in the small, stuffy attic she shared with Cissie. Her hands were soft and pulpy from the eternal washing-up, and stained from peeling potatoes, her feet swelled from the constant standing on a cement floor in the scullery, and her back ached from the carrying of big, heavy iron pots. But she worked harder than she had ever worked, because she was afraid. She scrubbed and polished, she cleaned and scoured. She was very slow and unhandy, and nearly drove the cook mad, but, for a wonder, she hardly opened her mouth or asserted an opinion. She was gracious and pleasant to everyone, even her habitual bad temper for once under control. She wanted to stay where she was safe, where there were no wild people who might murder her or threaten her in lurid language. Not that either the cook's language or that of the rest of the staff was much above the level of the travellers'. They swore with almost every breath they uttered. Sid, the barman—a small man with a fat, greasy face and a facetious manner—was worse than anyone.

The first sign that Miss Phipps was reverting to form was when one morning Sid came gaily into the kitchen and smacked the tempting target Miss Phipps presented as she stooped over the oven. Miss Phipps rose and smote him open-handed across the face. Sid was furious that she should so misinterpret his friendly gesture. He was just being pleasant and matey, he explained, no offence given and none taken. The look of Miss Phipps was enough to turn the milk sour, and he was just cheering her up. After her behaviour he refused to fling her even a good-day. The sour-faced bitch did not appreciate fun, he declared; she spoilt the cheerfulness of the kitchen.

Sid always brought down the spicy bits of news, and Miss Phipps would remove herself ostentatiously as far from him as she could, so that she missed most of them.

'The boss is as mad as a hornet,' Sid confided to the cook, stuffing his mouth with jam, the morning after the misunderstanding with Miss Phipps. 'Young Tolly Sampson gives me two quid, see, and says to keep the mob away from him, 'cause he wants to get a bit of sleep. He's been up all night on a jag. Anyway, I word everyone to tell his pals that he's gone out, and so on. And he locks his door. I goes down to the bar, and next thing the boss or I know is that his pals have come to take him to a party and found the door locked and broken it in.'

'Lor,' one of the maids giggled. 'You don't mean they've broken the door down.'

'Busted it clean off its hinges. You can go and see for yourself. They just collared young Tolly and carried him out to the car, two at his head and two at his feet, like a bleedin' corpse. He'll come back tight as an egg.' Sid deftly abstracted another slice of turnover. 'Last night they was all playing chasings up and down the main street in their cars. Not a copper in sight, you bet your boots. Wouldn't they look funny locking up Tolly Sampson or his cobbers? Now, if it was me or you playing chasings at one o'clock in the morning, smashing up people's cars . . .'

'Ah, well, the bosses can afford it.' The cook, ever a stickler for privilege, beamed tolerantly. 'After all, if you don't have a good time yourself, it's nice to think someone else is; that's how I look at it.'

From the rest of the staff came a murmur of hearty agreement.

'That's all very well,' Sid replied argumentatively. 'But that young Tolly'll catch it when his old man gets here. That's why the kid wanted to get some sleep. His Dad must have got wind of the way Tolly's carrying on, and he's coming up from Sydney to-night. He'll fix young Tolly—bung him back on the station likely as not. Serve the damn fool right. He's got no more head than a hook-worm.'

'If you ask me anything,' Cissie agreed, 'it's those friends of his. Getting all they can out of him. It's just too bad. That Ivor Jamieson and Jimmy Holstead. They're all the time getting him drunk and winning his money.'

'The women are the worst,' Sid claimed—'the bunch in Number Nineteen and the Blue Suite: Sheila Brendall and those two fast pieces she invited up with her, the Cliprell sisters. They may be film stars, but by God, they're stars at another game I could mention. As for Sheila, if I had a quid for every time I've seen a man . . .'

The cook dropped a spoon and Miss Phipps missed a word . . . 'I'd be a millionaire meself. I take up the drinks, and they always calls "Come in"—sweet as you like.'

The cook for once was shocked. She shook her head amazedly. 'But you don't mean they carry on like that while you're there? Surely they'd stop . . .'

'Stop! Hell! Why should they worry? I'm only the waiter.' He winked at the cook.

Miss Phipps curled her lips in contempt; but she could not dismiss Sid's words from her mind. It was beautiful spring weather, fitful and mild, with the scent of new grass and eucalyptus and briar rose loosening its petals by the roadside. The few lilacs in the town gardens came into flower, and a shower of rain filled them with wet drops. The privet trees in the hotel backyard looked as though a snowstorm had fallen overnight, and were a-quiver with

189

beetles, their yellow backs striped with black, humming and burrowing and tumbling in pollen. There were roses in the gardens of the big houses, roses everywhere flowering, and the fruit-tree flowers giving place to young green leaves.

But to Miss Phipps, who had ever taken a silent delight in such things, there came only the smell of boiling cauliflower and dirty dishes, of mountains of food for ever vanishing and renewing, and the steam of dish-water all around her in a hot, grey mist. Miss Phipps's special delight was always birds. She had in her girlhood wanted to be an ornithologist. She had spent hours watching birds, reading books about birds. But instead she had been sent out to domestic service and had grown crankier and more selfish and poisonous every year. She liked to be alone in fields with birds and other small creatures, and she could tame them when she had the chance. Her laziness, her sitting still, had helped.

She sniffed with her little snub nose at the smell of the heady privet in the back-yard. It would be pleasant to have a lot of money and drive out in a big car with a pair of binoculars through which one could really see, and lie for long hours in a sun-warmed place, making notes on birds and their ways, photographing them with an expensive little camera, finding nests. If she had money, she would not waste it throwing champagne glasses into the fireplace in a stuffy hotel lounge. When she had the rulership of the World Feminised State, she would take away all the money from these wasteful fools of men, and distribute it to people like herself who wanted to lie out in the open and watch birds or do other useful things.

That night Miss Phipps was left alone as usual after her work was finished. She sat up late, with the window of the little attic where she slept wide open, for the room was hot and stuffy. Cissie had gone off to a dance, and so was not present to object to the inrush of fresh air. Miss Phipps leaned out and inhaled the fragrance of a million flowers. She thought how soon Snow and the Stray and all those other dreadful travellers would be going fruit-picking. Fruit-picking! Think of being in the open all day picking great red cherries, eating as many as you wanted, in the leafy shade of the trees. This poetic vision had in it nothing of dirt or heavy kerosene tins to be carried full of fruit, or flies, or heat, or aching arms and shoulders. Miss Phipps had even spread a green carpet of buffalo grass beneath the cherry trees for the benefit of those pickers who felt more like lying in the shade. There is no doubt she would have been among their number.

Just as she had arrived at the vision of herself picking cherries into a dainty little china bowl, with a cool house in the distance and cream on the ice as a fitting accompaniment for the cherries, someone switched on a light in the room directly beneath hers and a woman's voice said: 'I bet you I'd get it, didn't I?'

'If you want fifty pounds, why didn't you try Tolly?'

Miss Phipps recognised the second voice as belonging to one of the Cliprell sisters, and deduced that the first speaker must be the other sister. She drew back cautiously on the window-sill, but not too far to hear.

'Tolly be damned! You can never get anything out of him except, "Let's have another drink." No, I knew at once that old Joey was my man—these stout red-faced old guys always think that every woman falls for them.'

'When did you word him?'

'This afternoon I put on that new blue rig-out and I got him alone in here, and I cried like the devil. I told him I had to have fifty pounds, and that my husband was coming up from Sydney. I'd lost fifty pounds on the races, and the bookmaker was dunning me. Always tell a man you've lost money on a horse, Ann. It's something he can understand. If you said you'd spent it some other way, he'd just think you were wasting it.'

'You're a gem, Mary.'

'He parted up like a lamb. I got out without a ladder in my stocking.' The voice suddenly broke into laughter. 'I told him I had to pay the bookmaker right away, and dashed out before he'd time to more than make a date for to-night. That's why I want you to hang around. If I can stave him off to-morrow, we'll be gone Thursday. Good God! Look at that shoe-buckle. I'll have to stitch it. Damn all! The only pair of evening shoes I brought.'

'Did you see Sheila's gold cigarette-case? Jimmy Holstead gave it to her. She says it was easy as falling off a log. You can get anything out of him when he's drunk.'

The other voice sounded bored. 'All very primitive this, Ann, don't you think? After all, I'll be glad to get back to the city, away from these louts behaving like a lot of kids. Going swimming in the river at this hour of the night! Give me a man who can hold his liquor. They think they're a wild crowd. Leaving young Tolly to walk home without any clothes!'

'That's not so. Someone gave him a pair of pyjamas and bet him he couldn't get back to the hotel without being spotted. If he's fool enough to have it on . . .'

Miss Phipps did not want to hear any more, not because eavesdropping troubled her conscience, but because she was depressed by the knowledge that even if she had the money to move among the aristocracy, she would be just as much an alien in that state of society as in the one to which it had pleased God to call her. She felt a sudden impulse to go out for a walk. She would get away at least for a little while from the atmosphere of this hotel, with its reek of drink and moral dirt. Perhaps things would be better when the fast crowd who had come to the Stainford for the races departed, taking their loud jollity and their cards and drink and big cars with them.

As she waddled down the back stairs, she snorted in her old contemptuous manner. She would like to tell these wasters what she thought of them. It became clearer and clearer to her that by remaining at the Stainford she was condoning undesirable behaviour. A set of human leeches! That's all they were. And she despised them. They might pass her without a glance, but they could never take away that feeling of superiority, that superhuman contempt of all humanity, that was her comfort, her motive power. As she reached the bottom of the steps, a voice breathed in her ear from the darkness, so that she started.

'Hey, auntie,' it said. 'Give a fellow a hand, will you?'

Miss Phipps switched on the light. It was the drunken and abominable Tolly Sampson, the golden calf, his fair hair flopped over his flushed face, clad only in a suit of pyjamas. He sat with his head in his hands.

'Turn the damn light out,' he said thickly.

'Don't you use such language,' Miss Phipps replied angrily. 'You may to your friends, but I'm not one of them.' However, she switched out the light.

'Aw, don't be a nark,' the boy stammered. 'Be a sport and help me upstairs. I'm all in. True as I stand here.' He was actually sitting on the bottom step. 'Anyone can tell you're a real sport, auntie, a real true-blue sport.'

'Don't you call me auntie.' Miss Phipps was secretly pleased to find someone elevating her to even temporary importance. She had been snubbed by everyone on the staff, and her vanity, always ready to burgeon like yeast, swelled at this slight tribute. She allowed Mr. Sampson to drape his arm over her shoulder and assisted him panting up the stairs and along the passage to his room, first scouting ahead, as he instructed, to see that no one was about. He reeked with whisky, and his proximity filled her with distaste.

'Thanks,' he said thickly. 'Knew you were a sport.' They had reached the door of his room.

'I won't come any farther,' Miss Phipps declared stiffly. She would not trust herself with such a libertine. The rooms of this hotel had a bad reputation.

'Wait a minute,' the golden calf said slowly, and staggered inside. Miss Phipps waited. He came swaying back. 'Here,' he said, ''s for you. Good old auntie. Gotta get a little sleep.'

The door shut. Into Miss Phipps's hand he had thrust several crumpled notes. She stood there a minute bewildered and rather indignant. Giving her money as though she was a servant, giving it to her in the casual manner that wiped her from all consideration as a human being who had helped him because he needed help. She, a Chester-Phipps, the heiress of millions, to be so treated by a mere stripling whose father had made his money rearing sheep. She, a member of the aristocracy, to be tipped by a swell-headed, jumped-up farm-hand. All desire to go forth and savour the beauties of the night had left her.

As fast as she could, she waddled back to her attic and, seated on the narrow bed, she smoothed out the notes with a trembling hand. She never had a penny left from her wages by the time she had bought herself some face-cream and cigarettes and stockings. All the things she could buy with three pounds! She was prepared to overlook the insult of his giving her the money when she thought of what it would buy. She fingered the notes, getting a little thrill from the unexpected windfall. Then something strange about the look of them drew her attention. She brought them up in front of her short-sighted eyes and peered at them. They were—her breath caught in her throat and she felt as though she was choking—it couldn't be possible that they were fifty-pound notes. Three notes of fifty pounds each—surely it wasn't possible! But these big gamblers did carry notes in large currency sometimes. The hands that held the notes shook. She laid them on the glaring white quilt as though they might sting her if she was not careful. It could not possibly be true. Yes, it was; she had a hundred and fifty pounds in three fifty-pound notes.

A vivid exultation that was half fear seized her. She rushed across the room and locked the door. She could not sit still but trotted to and fro, making little distracted movements. She must hide the money. She must go away quickly before the man found out his loss. Why, he'd never even remember her. It had been dark—but he must have known she was one of the staff coming down the back stairs. He must have recognised her as someone vaguely

familiar to call her 'auntie.' He'd think he had lost the
money. He was drunk. Go away, go away quickly, one
part of her brain advised.

She felt hot and feverish. Leaning far out of the window
inhaling great gulps of air as though every breath was
precious, she could still hear the chatter of those two
creatures in the room below. She did not care to hear
their talk, probably about some man who was fool enough
to associate with them. A scrap of the conversation she
had heard drifted through her mind: 'Easy as falling off
a log. You can get anything out of him when he is drunk!'
Charming words from young ladies who moved in the best
social circles!

Miss Phipps had just sniffed contemptuously, when a
horrible thought struck her. Suppose she were on the level
of such women, she, the queen, the super-woman?
Suppose—— She put the thought from her firmly. The
Ruler of the World Feminised State had a *right* to confis-
cate wealth that was being put to undesirable ends. She
was confiscating that hundred and fifty pounds. No, he
had given it to her; a free gift. She would not give it back,
she had a right to it, she needed it.

Even while Miss Phipps was repeating over and over
that the money was hers, she had folded it in her hand and
gone downstairs, sadly but firmly. Sid was so surprised
when she asked which was old Mr. Sampson's room that
he told her. She knocked on the old man's door with the
stern determination of a gaoler. The father of Tolly
Sampson had gone to bed hours ago. A big, silent, grey-
bearded man, he still retained the habits he had learned
when to be up at daybreak was a necessity rather than a
curious and unusual whim. He thrust out his head and
growled sleepily: 'What d'you want?'

'Mr. Sampson?' Miss Phipps had drawn herself very
erect. She was savouring a triumph. Almost her grandeur
rustled behind her like a taffeta train. 'I would like to
speak to you for a moment. I am sorry for the lateness of
the hour.'

The old man shot a shrewd glance at her under his shaggy brows. He did not know her, that was certain. What, he wondered, was her game? 'Go ahead,' he grunted.

Miss Phipps, her snub nose very much tilted, explained that she had been forced into the position of assisting his son upstairs. 'I thought it would be better to return these to you,' she said, suddenly dropping her drawling, elaborate sentences, and while the old man was still wondering what she was talking about, she opened her hand and held out the fifty-pound notes.

It was curious to see the old man's face change. 'You say he gave them to you?' he asked.

'He confused me with one of the staff,' Miss Phipps replied haughtily. She was speaking to this rich man as a superior; she had the right to talk down to him, and it pleased her to do it. 'Might I say that it is not in his best interests to encourage him in this wild way of living?'

'Come in,' the old man said suddenly. He flung open the door, and Miss Phipps, to her surprise, found herself obeying him. 'Sid-down.' He stood looking at the notes in his hand almost absently, as though they were some bitter message of death. 'I'm much obliged to ye,' he repeated, as though to himself. He sat down opposite her, an old man clad in a dressing-gown and slippers. 'I'm much obliged,' he said again.

'I am only pleased that I had the opportunity of assisting your son,' Miss Phipps responded graciously. She sat there in her old black dress, with the air of a duchess. 'It is a shame to see a young man go to pieces.'

'You're right,' the boy's father said abruptly. 'You're right.' He held out his enormous horny hand in front of Miss Phipps's eyes. 'See that hand? Ye do? Well, with it I've grafted for over fifty years one way or another so that boy should have everything. Jim, I says to meself, he'll never have to starve and fight and sweat as you've done. He'll never know what it is to have men down him and kick him when he's down. I've got the name of a hard man, and I've made money, and it's for him. And he throws it away with a set of fools as big as himself . . . and scoundrels. Bloodsucking . . .'

'Leeches,' Miss Phipps finished for him. They nodded in complete agreement.

'And there's nothing I can do,' the big man went on. 'There's not a soul in the world cares a damn. I beg your pardon, madam.'

'Granted,' Miss Phipps said sweetly.

'There's nobody cares but me. And I can't do anything.' He seemed suddenly to realise that this interview was unusual and peculiar. He moved uneasily. 'I can only say I'm much obliged.' His keen eyes swept over her. She looked like a working woman, her hands were rough and red, though her speech was educated. She could probably do with a few quid. Sampson had been a working man himself, and some fine instinct in him warned him that there was no opportunity of offering money.

Miss Phipps rose in a gracious and stately manner and bade him good-night. They parted with further thanks and apologies on his side and a very grand and condescending little movement of protest on hers.

'If I can ever do anything,' he said earnestly, 'to show I appreciate the interest you took in Tolly . . .'

'Not at all. I was only too pleased. Good-night.'

'G'night.'

Miss Phipps walked away as though the whole hotel belonged to her. She looked with disdain at the door-handles she had polished only that morning. She thought with contempt of the getting of breakfast, of dish-washing. She had been afraid, but she was afraid no longer. The giving back of that money had freed her from the haunting dread of loneliness and insecurity. She was once again Ruler of the World Feminised State. She decided suddenly she would leave this despicable hotel. It was spring-time and she was free, white and well over twenty-one. She would go cherry-picking. She was not afraid of the road. She was not afraid of anything.

From her window she could still hear the murmur of voices of those two women below her. Disgraceful creatures! She leant forward to hear what they were saying.

'And there was Joan standing with the clothes half ripped off her. "Mr. Morrison wants his hat," she said . . .'

Miss Phipps took a shoe belonging to Cissie, leant far out of the window, and flung it with an aim developed by her earlier practice as a window-smasher.

'Stop that disgusting conversation,' she said in a loud, clear voice. Miss Phipps was herself again.

Chapter XV

I

ALL SNOW's illness was a haunted struggle to escape from nightmares that had to do with barbed wire tangled round him, gashing his face, rending his flesh. He was wrapped in it, helpless. In his dream he would try to step across a fence, and the wires would trip him and wind round him. Or he would be driving along a road, and the fences would close in ahead of him, whichever way he went.

He spent uncounted years, it seemed to him, looking for an open space to camp, for an open road to travel, and as soon as he found one, the wire would come up round it.

He saw the wire cobwebbing the country, holding it down in plotted squares of wheat or pasture or fallow; and the railway lines shrieking their way across the humbled hills, climbing and boring through high places like grey snakes, panting over the level, binding the land in a tether. Even the telegraph wires hummed to themselves: 'Mine, mine!'

He was a fly, crawling on a sticky plate without an edge, an unending plain without water or tree, wandering in a gaol that had for walls a thousand miles of flat surface; and however far he crawled, he would never come to the limit.

On and on he laboured over an ash-heap of a country, glaring and glaring like a dead, fly-blown carcass, with maggots harvesting its ribs. He was parched so that he could not cry out. There was no escape, but to die, and he could not die. There was only the road; the red, narrow prison with walls laid flat a thousand miles each way and bound with barbed wire; the walls of other men's land, going on and on to the world's end. He was in gaol, and he must escape, and he could not escape.

Then he had come to the weir over the Lachlan beyond Condobolin. The river dripped across it, jade and milk-white. A yellow-and-green willow hung over the upper reach, and white cockatoos with yellow crests were crying in the gum trees. He could bathe his face, he could lie in the cool water and let it pour over him. But as he went towards it the fences sprang up, higher and higher in front of him, barring the way.

He was down by the Murrumbidgee—that grey, greasy river, hot, flickering, with silver lights across its rapid flow. A thousand birds sang in the shadows of the leaves high above him, but the fences still warded him off. He was walking over the green, gentle grass, smooth as a lawn, towards the water-tower at Deniliquin. Surely there he could camp! The boys played football on those green spaces on a Sunday; the golf links stretched smooth and shaven near by. The Edward River wound its shining curves round Deniliquin, so that the town lay twisted like a snake with its back broken. In all those curves of the river there must be some place for a man to camp. But everywhere was the wire.

He was beside the Namoi, red as cayenne pepper, with steep, treacherous, clay banks, red-hot as a river that flowed from Hell. There was no shade, and he lay in a bed of nettles tangled in rusty barbed wire, and the sun glared down at him, and he was bitten by red-hot ants.

People came to laugh at him. Molly was there and the boys; even Jimmy did not care. Everywhere were people, cruel, hard, hot as clay, watching him pitilessly. A nurse, with the cynical autocracy of nurses, asked him if he felt better, and then, in the same breath, told him not to speak. The doctor came, inspected him with satisfaction, and informed the nurse that an inch higher and he would have lost his eye.

Snow went to sleep again. He was not interested. He was watching a map of Australia, the kind of map they had hanging on the wall at school, that looked like some great sluggish beast, with the mountain backbone running down the coast, and ranges of ribs running off; a sprawling shape, it seemed, something like a sheep with green wool, folded into the wrinkled skin of the ranges. There were running red sores of towns and inflamed patches, spreading out in scars and scurf through the green wool. There were tiny, dark creatures, crawling and repulsive, swarming all over the hide. If only the animal had put up a fight!

'No resistance,' he heard the doctor's voice say. 'Don't talk to me about these great hulks. They go down to it. Then again, underfeeding. . . .'

The chattering of visitors to the man in the next bed awakened him. He lay there, very weak and tired, but able to talk when the Apostle was ushered into the grey and white ward, with its rows of beds in an ordered hush, and its faint smell of sick men overpowered by the strong odour of anaesthetic. The Stray had been refused admittance the night before, but the Reverend Mr. Postlewaite, with his worn best suit, his accent, and his courteous timidity, had not so much impressed the nurses as made them feel sorry for him.

He edged into a chair by Snow's bedside, and without any preliminaries, drew forth a small prayer-book and began licking the leaves, meditatively searching for the prayers for the Visitation of the Sick. The Apostle never waited to be asked to pray. He would have waited a long time. He just launched out, and it was no use shouting in his ear or plucking his sleeve. He prayed obstinately, in a rapid, monotonous mumble, rubbing his head every now and then, his eyes tight shut.

Snow and the Apostle were old acquaintances. They had once spent a long afternoon on the banks of the Darling, discussing the interesting problem of whether fish think, and what kinds of bait were best. So he waited until the Apostle had finished his mumbling; then he croaked:

'Lo, Harry. How's the wife and kids?'

'Fine.' The Apostle rubbed his head again dubiously. 'Mrs. . . . er . . . Dancy . . . sent her love.'

'Everything all right?'

'Yes. Quite.' The Apostle had been warned not to worry Snow with any news, even such joyful and heart-warming things as Thirty-Bob selling the Horehound, and the farmer returning her the same afternoon with a demand for his money back. Thirty-Bob refused to return the money. 'I sold her to you, sport. Ain't that right? Well, now, you try and sell her to me.' In the end Thirty-Bob had bought the Horehound back for considerably less than the farmer paid, and was joyfully preparing to try the trick again.

'Good.' Snow's eyes strayed to a ragged bunch of roses and bamboo sprouts. 'Who put them weeds there?'

'It's Dancy,' the Apostle said apologetically. 'She brings flowers every night she can.'

'Oh,' Snow was silent again. 'Everything fine, eh?'

'Yes, yes.' The conversation looked like fading away. The Apostle edged closer to Snow. 'You nearly got away,' he said, shaking his head seriously. 'But you couldn't, of course. No man can escape his life before he is allowed to go.'

Snow stared at him silently. He had heard of the Apostle's queer ways, but he had never met him in this mood.

'I know how it is,' the Apostle went on. 'Everything conspires against you. You can't even die.' As he rubbed his head excitedly, the coat sleeve fell away from his bony wrist. 'Disease and evil are only humanity swimming against the current of the Blood.'

Snow broke in suddenly: 'Harry!'

The Apostle's eyes lost their glitter. 'Yes, Snow?'

'How much does it cost to get a divorce? A real good one that gives you the kids.'

The Apostle became almost practical. 'I am no lawyer,' he said. 'But I think it could be done for twenty pounds. I'll find out for you if you like.'

'And you'd better find out how a chap stands, travellin' the way I do. Would I have to settle down to get it?'

'I don't think so.'

'I'd be willing to pay extra, mind, to get young Jimmy. I'd like the other kids, but I want young Jimmy, if I don't get nothin' else.'

The Apostle was his reasonable self, interested, trying to be helpful. 'If it isn't too much strain on you, Snow, perhaps you could tell me the position. I'll write to a lawyer I know, but he'd want a lot of information.'

Snow, in a whisper, told him all about the homecoming to Molly; and the Apostle wrote it down in his black notebook. 'I'll send a letter,' he said briskly.

'Thanks, Harry. Much obliged.'

'You'll have to go now.' The nurse came bustling up to the bed ostentatiously. 'I told you not to talk.'

'Twenty pounds, eh?'

'I'm sure that would be plenty.'

'Harry.' The Apostle had turned to go. 'Any shearin' yet?'

'They've started out at a place on the Crumwell Road.'

Snow turned over on his side wearily. 'Well, if I don't get no shearin', I've a scheme up me sleeve that ought to bring in a bit of dough.' He was careful not to explain to the Apostle that it was cyaniding opossums he had in mind. The Apostle was hardly likely to look favourably on the slaughter of opossums. He refused to drive a horse, though it was cheaper than the truck, because he hated to think the horse was pulling while he rode. 'I'll fix 'er.' Snow's thoughts reverted to his wife. 'I'll teach her to call in her flamin' relatives.'

The Apostle said quietly: 'What about Dancy?'

'Well, what about her?' Snow's tone was sullen. 'She can look after herself, can't she? I'm just goin' on without her, that's all.'

'You can't do it?'

'Oh! can't I?' Snow was roused. He tried to sit up, but dropped back weakly. 'You'd be surprised. You just watch me.'

'I say you can't do it,' the Apostle repeated. 'She has a claim on you . . .'

'Not a one.'

'A claim, I say. If you'd give her a chance . . .'

'You give *me* a chance. I've got enough worries.'

'You may leave her behind, but you'd always be sorry. She has a great loyalty to you, a generous, brave spirit. I tell you'—the Apostle bent his brows at Snow—'these things constitute a claim. However much you try to leave her, you never will.'

Snow held his peace. He could see the nurse coming to eject the Apostle.

'You wouldn't believe,' he said later to the man in the next bed, 'that that cove's loony, would you?'

'Why don't they lock him up?'

'Search me.'

'Influence, that's what it is,' the other man asserted. 'There was poor old Jack Riley used to camp year after year at the 'sylum gates, so that when his son come out at week-ends he'd be able to see him and have him at the camp. It beats me,' he added, 'how many loony chaps there are about. Though you could hardly pick that chap what came to see you. You sure he's mad?'

'Mad as a snake,' Snow asserted.

II

Two days later came Dancy. She had to show a great deal of determination to wrest her afternoon off from the clutch of Mrs. Marks, and was not in any mood to keep Snow from hearing the news. She had a long tale of woe to tell, the burden of her lament being that 'them bloody Markses was workin' her poor'; and she would be thankful when Snow came out of hospital and they moved on. She had learned how to make jug-covers, and this would help out between dole-days.

Snow said nothing. Now that the busker and Phippsy had gone, he saw no reason why he should still be saddled with the Stray. Where she got the idea that she was going to travel with him, he did not know. Not if he could help it! He had had enough of women for keeps. Snow's lazy nature was turning hard. The scar on his face might be healing; his coughing and gasping bronchitis were over; but his mental turmoil was cooling into a firm determination to keep clear of women.

'What kind is this Mrs. Marks?'

'Ain't I just told yer? She's like a yard of pump-water, straight up and down, wiv 'er 'air skimped back, and an eye like a dead fish. And mean! She'd skin a flea for the hide and taller.'

'How much's she payin' you, Stray?'

The Stray hesitated. She had boasted so loudly to the other campers. 'Twenty-five bob,' she replied.

'Well, that's not good, but it's not too bad.' If the woman was sweating the Stray, it was her look-out. Snow might not have left the Stray behind if she had no job; but now that she had, it was very opportune. All he wanted was to get out of this hospital as quickly as possible and be on his way looking for work for himself. The idea of work obsessed him. He must make some money, and make it quickly, so that he could get his divorce and get Jimmy.

'Thirty-Bob got slung in for drunk and resistin' arrest,'
Dancy was saying. 'He and Dick Tyrell both. And Sam
Little got slung in the same night, and they fought all over
the bloody p'lice-station. Mrs. Tyrell had the bloody
baby just as they got to Gargendra, and Deafy's waiting
wiv 'er there. The bloody 'Postle's fick as fieves wiv all
them Littles. 'E sits and yarns to 'em all the bloody day.
Burning Angus and his mob are shearin' out towards
Crumwell in a bloody cocky shed.' She sat there, in-
nocently pleased with herself and the news she had gar-
nered, and let the adjectives drip. It was a pleasant relief
after keeping guard on her tongue so long. Suddenly she
asked: 'Hey, mister, how's the bloody time?' And the
man in the next bed, who had a watch, told her. 'Christ!
I got to walk all the damn way back, an' I won't get there
till tea-time. Oh, well! To hell wiv 'er! 'Twon't be
long now, will it, Snow? We'll get Thirty-Bob and Dick
out of quod and all have a big booze-up to celebrate.' She
gave Snow's arm a squeeze as she rose to go. 'Hooray for
now, Snow.'

'Hooray,' Snow responded rather sullenly, as the Stray
swaggered off down the ward, limping a little in her old,
broken shoes.

'Gawd! she's a trimmer,' the man in the next bed
commented with a chuckle.

Snow did not want to talk about the Stray. He wanted
to dismiss her altogether from his mind. She belonged to
the city, to a kind of life that was nothing to him. All he
wanted was to get well.

But as he began to get better, his head cleared, and he
felt only an immense weakness and weariness. Why worry?
He might just as well lie there without thinking. Whenever he thought, it hurt him. His mind turned to Molly
and the boys. Why had he walked away and left her in
possession of the boys? He was too weak to fight. He only
wanted to get away. To keep on wandering on, finding
new camps, and meeting old mates, and never staying
in the one place. That was because he had been on the

track until it got into his blood. The travellers had a saying: 'Once you get on the track, you're on it for life.' They said that a bagman never settled down. He might stay in the same town for years; but he would get up again, even when he was old, and go on a 'walk-about' like a black-fellow.

It was funny, Snow reflected, how the travellers were getting to be like the blacks. They might pretend to despise them and look down upon them; but the travellers were just as much a separate race, distinct from the people who lived in towns, as the blacks were. The white 'dole-chasers' went about in families and little tribes, with a language of their own, a code of their own that forbade their refusing food or shelter to any like themselves. The women worked and sold things in towns, but the men hunted, or tended horses, and sat in the shade. Mostly the men danced and the women looked on. They had councils to decide which way they would go, and though everyone had a voice, the eldest carried most weight. They were a new sort of people, the travellers; and he belonged to them. He did not belong to the Hourigans, who scratched a little plot of land, to the 'cockies,' anxious and hardworking and greedy. He was a 'battler.'

All along the coast, sheltered to the west by the high wall of the mountains and to the east by the sea, the cities lay; where people could live in flats and have central heating and air-conditioned houses and refrigerators; and forget about the barrens and the barbed wire over the ranges. They could talk tariffs and exchange rates and stock-market quotations. Maybe, if they went on talking war and business long enough, something in the way of an apocalypse would come of it; they would be strangled, swallowing their own tongues. A faint disgust took Snow as he thought of streets of concrete and asphalt, and roaring trams, and people jammed together as though they were gummed to a fly-paper. White ants, crawling, shapeless jellies in dark, underground tunnels and cells. No more bones, no more stamina than white ants. Maybe, if they kept squealing in the cities long enough, there would presently be just a whiff of poison gas blowing over the tall human ant-heaps; and a deadly silence and grass in the streets.

But there would always be battlers. The blacks had been driven away from the coast; killed, shot, poisoned like wild beasts; mowed down in thousands; but they were hanging on. If another sort of people than the white—say, yellow people—landed on the coasts and mopped up the jelly-livers in the cities, they would still have a job on their hands cleaning out the battlers; men and women who could face a desert and live off the country, travelling in small mobs not enough to drink the hidden wells dry. Any invader would have a hard time with the real Australians, who were so dark brown they might as well be black, and so tough they might as well be leather— people who were like the shadows of a cloud going over the fields. They would hold out, as the blacks still held out in the deserts and barrens. Being without water frightened people; they stayed near the rivers and along the sea-coast. But out west there was dry country, thirsty, hard and hot. Even after the city-people had been poisoned off or bombed out, the travellers would be going from one camp to the next, slowly travelling round their territory as the seasons changed; hunting, fishing, dancing, quarrelling, making love. This wasn't really a tame country. It never would be unless the city politicians spent some money building dams; and they were not likely to do that while they could build an aeroplane factory instead.

To hell with the lot of them! The trackmen were the real people. He didn't want, Snow decided, to live in a place like Blimdagery. He didn't want to live in a city as Dancy had done. He would always go on and on, to the end of his life, travelling about and following the sun north or south. Funny how a country shaped people to its ideas more than they shaped the country. The blacks had always travelled about; and now the whites did the same. You saw it even in the city people. They were restless at the change of the year, and invented excuses, even if it was only the Melbourne Cup, to trek south. In winter they went on a walk-about north to Queensland along the Barrier Reef. They didn't settle. They wandered round. And the travellers wandered most of all, because they were closest to what the country was thinking.

Now that he was getting better, Snow had a mad craving to get out in the open; but the nurse refused to give him his clothes. He got very angry about it. Despite the fact that he collapsed twice, he insisted on stalking round the hospital in his pyjamas, and gave a lot of trouble, and would not be persuaded back to bed.

After three days of this he became so threatening, that he was given his clothes, and as soon as he had them, he walked straight out of the hospital and down the town, staggering a little, and resting now and then, but fiercely determined to go out and get a pen at one of the shearing-sheds.

Chapter XVI

ON that beautiful spring morning which saw Snow, like some weak creature new emerged from a chrysalis, crawl into the sunshine and sit trembling for a while, as though to harden his body and strengthen it for the ordeal of facing life once more, the Apostle, back in his old camp by the river, was enjoying a quince with a hornet.

It was a big, yellow, juicy quince, which one of the Chinamen had given him, for he was a great favourite with the Chinese gardeners. He would take a bite and hold out the quince, and the hornet, which had been circling and waiting for its turn, would land on the quince, and very delicately, nervously, put down its proboscis and sip the juice. Then the Apostle would take another bite, and the hornet would circle round and wait its turn again. As the last morsel vanished, the Apostle wasting not even the seeds, which he bit with great satisfaction, the hornet made a landing on a corner of the man's mouth and began to clean up a trickle of juice which was running down his chin. The Apostle waited politely until the insect had given a satisfied buzz and departed, before he rose from the log on which he was sitting and prepared to go up to the hospital to see Snow.

He had been thinking about Snow, weaving him into the pattern of his thoughts as a recurring thread that jerked in and out uneasily through all other preoccupations. Snow had wanted to die; and the only thing that had held him was his fierce determination, his hate and anger. He wanted to hurt his wife. He wanted to take his son from his wife, not from any affection as much as for revenge. Every affection in Snow seemed to have withered and hardened.

The Apostle glanced round at the river-bank, a transformed river-bank with a coating of mud inches deep. Debris and dirt choked the crotches of the trees like old, untidy birds'-nests. Festoons of dead weed and hay and willow-twigs hung like garlands from the fence-posts.

Snow's mind, he thought, must be in much the same condition—covered with a muddy anger. But, after all, from that anger, from that mud, something rich and living might yet emerge, some action good in itself. The Apostle intended to move on to-morrow, but before he went he would once more see Snow, try to talk to him, perhaps to get him to realise the wastefulness of his bitter brooding. The Apostle had stayed in Logan longer than he intended, not from any defiance of the sergeant, but because he had in charge Dick Tyrell's cart and horse, Thirty-Bob's sulky and stallion and Snow's dog Bluey. Dick and Thirty-Bob would be out of gaol to-day and they could take back their property.

Everything this fair morning was struggling out of the prison of winter. There had been two warm, sunny days, and the wattle was coming shyly, apologetically, into bloom, fluffy as yellow wool. The peach trees had their flowers screwed into tiny pink knobs as though they wore curl-pins. The early light made promises in a language the birds and trees understood. A desperate longing in all living things commanded the air to be calm, the sunlight to be more caressing. A dumb demand thudded up the boughs with the beating of the sap, asking: 'When? when?' and the light wind soothed with its reply 'Soon.'

Little black-eyed daisies flooded the fields with pale gold. The dandelions stood up to meet the Spring, and tender, new green leaves shivered against the pale washed blue of the sky.

But as the Apostle made his way over the flats towards the town, he was thinking of cruelty. It was a problem he had never really settled in his mind. Could cruelty be part of God? For there was surely nothing that was not. Or did cruelty only seem to be cruelty? The thought flashed at him startlingly that he was cruel to his wife to keep her dragging about the country with him. But how many times had he pleaded with her to go home to her brother, who disliked him so? Would it be cruel to send her back? Her presence, and that of the children, disturbed him, though he tried not to show it—hampered his movements. Women did not understand love—that dark tide that swept humanity along, holding them, embracing them, part of them. They thought of love as being close to someone, touching them, feeding them, mothering, possessing them. Surely it was possible to love someone at a distance loyally and steadily. Was it? Could a man love God if he felt He was distant instead of being close at hand? But, then, if the universe were all one medium through which consciousness flowed, what difference did it make? What was near or far, past or future?

As ever, he found these speculations beginning to excite him, as though something glowed in his head, making it feel tight about his brain. Without realising what he was doing, he leant dreamily over the fence of a farm, and stared at a large sow and her litter which were rooting there.

'Is time the fourth dimension of space?' the Apostle asked the sow. 'Ah, that is the question! If only we knew just what time signifies!'

The farmer's son came out to the kitchen door and watched the Apostle suspiciously. The Apostle's seeming interest in the sow was something the lad could interpret in only one way. A traveller had taken an interest in the sow's last litter, and the following morning there had been two promising piglets missing. He came strolling down towards the Apostle, who seemed not to notice that the calm of the morning was ominously charged with distrust.

'G'day,' the farmer's son said, leaning over the gate.

The Apostle nodded absentmindedly. 'You have no doubt often wondered,' he observed, 'that the sacred Blood should flow from the Wound. But it was not real blood, such as you or I might shed. Evil sheds the Blood. You agree'—he fronted the young man sternly—'that evil we know to exist, particularly the conscious will to harm that we call cruelty, despite sophists, who tell us that evil is a misunderstanding, a mistake. We must admit the reality of evil.'

The young man's mouth had dropped open. He retreated a pace, but the Apostle leant forward, hooking a finger in his shirt, politely but firmly, and his audience was too frightened to detach itself.

'The heart of the universe is good and wise and loving,' the Apostle continued, a little excitedly, 'and the Blood of the universe, the whole stream and current of life, flows into that sacred heart, flows towards eternal Love. Evil, then, is the human will breasting against the great current. I think you agree with me?' He fixed the young man with a glittering eye.

'I got me work to get done,' the other mumbled, suddenly wrenching himself free of that hypnotic gaze. He beat a hasty retreat up the yard, not looking back until he reached the door, where he stood to wipe his brow on a handkerchief as large as a dish-towel.

The Apostle took the escape in good spirit. 'Just a friendly discussion' he said to himself as though he was explaining to his wife.

Snow, weak and uncertain, was pleased to see the shabby figure of the Apostle coming to meet him. The Apostle had an unmistakable walk: a kind of quick shamble, as though he was escaping, dodging someone. He hurried along, stopping abruptly every now and then to take off his preposterous cloth cap and knuckle the grey curls on his forehead thoughtfully, his eyes on the dust at his feet or on some leaf-blade, some glance of light by the roadside.

He came up to Snow as though not at all surprised to see him there, and all the way back to the river he talked of nothing but cruelty and the possibility, which was a certainty to his way of thinking, that within the next few days there would be a war on the other side of the world—a great war. Snow listened impatiently. All he wanted was the loan of Thirty-Bob's horse and sulky to drive out along the Crumwell Road to see if there was any chance of 'getting on' to some shearing. Most of the shearing was done by big contracting firms who brought their own men from the city and worked all the year round. They might shear for fifty sheds in the one district. But there would still be small cockies, Snow hoped, who would need him. Even if he got on only as a rouseabout, it would be something.

'I'll drive out with you,' the Apostle suggested. 'Then I can bring the horse back.'

Snow sat and drank cup after cup of the strong tea that Mrs. Postlewaite set before him. He cursed the hospital for making him so weak. He was even relieved at the Apostle's suggestion, although he knew that the Apostle's idea of driving was to let the horse go where it pleased. If the Apostle ever got home with Thirty-Bob's stallion in the shafts, it would be a miracle.

As he watched the attempts of Bryson and the Apostle to harness the stallion, he wished Thirty-Bob could see them. Weak as he was, Snow was impelled to stagger over and do the job himself. He took the reins from the Apostle and climbed into the sulky. He didn't wish to go back to hospital again, and he had once seen the Apostle drive a horse.

The country curved up its green, rolling waves, all the greener for the recent rain. In the wide, arching heights of the sky a hawk was at home, quivering as a cinder might on a breath of air, light as an ash of burnt love. They passed an old brickyard where a pool of water lay in a hollow of yellow clay, and then another pool under the trees, black, full of old leaves. As they mounted into the hills, the country became poorer. Instead of the rolling green, there was only a splintered waste of burnt and ring-barked timber, and tufts of grass like a badly-worn mat, white where the wind pressed them.

The two men, so oddly unlike, sat silent, side by side, the Apostle still pondering on war and cruelty, Snow thinking of shearing. Farm succeeded farm, a house on every rise, the paddocks rolling round them in a flood of grass where trees stood like scattered enemies, some fallen, some ready to fall. Farmers have a hatred of trees. The sight of one reminds them only of the labour and sweat of clearing and burning off, the uncertainty and misery of a man making a start on an inimical forest. The trees the farmers tolerated were tame, like a mop upon a stick—kurrajongs or acacias useful for reserve feed; they had no wild strength or promethean courage; they were mute captives of the conqueror.

'Here we are,' the Apostle said. 'This should be the place where Angus and the Dogger got on.' Snow reined in the horse. 'If you just leave the horse with me,' the Apostle suggested, 'I don't mind waiting to see how you get on.'

So they tied the horse to a post, and the Apostle lay down on his back in the grass with his arms under his head.

The homestead, like all other homesteads, stood well back from the highway; but the shearing-shed, a long, grey building, built of split slabs, together with the men's bunkhouse and cookhouse, were close to the road for convenience in carting the wool. Beside the shed the little engine spat jets of steam 'Put-put-put,' as it ran the machinery working the shearing-blades. A mob of sheep had just been driven in by one of the farmer's sons. Their wool was a red-yellow, and they were cross-bred. Snow, regarding them critically, decided they were a poor lot.

He asked to see the boss, and was told he was in the shed sorting. Snow hung about, waiting for the mid-day break. It was close on noon, and the spell was about due. The whirr and racket of the machine, the thump of the engine, made him feel weaker than ever. Inside the shed it was dim and cool. The men, in a row, stooped over their sheep, hardly lifting their heads. Now and then one would take a swig from the billy beside him, or straighten his back as the shorn sheep scrambled down the shoot.

The shearing was rough, Snow considered; the sheep were all chipped about and bleeding. Every one of them was a mass of raw gashes and long, raking scours where the blades had bitten in. The farmer's son, a fair boy with a soft down on his face, would gather up the fleece and run with it to the board, holding it spread before him like a sail. As it fell, his father would sort it and throw it into one of the bins; and another boy would run up with another fleece.

'That's three sons he's got working,' Snow thought, 'and I'll bet me last zac most of the others are uncles or nephews.'

He hung about until the noon whistle went, and then collared the boss and asked if he was wanting a shearer. The boss instantly denied any such need, and turned away rather abruptly to give his son some directions about the sheep. 'Fair enough,' Snow thought. He had expected a 'knock-back,' but he had at least tried. He slouched over to the kitchen and touched his hat politely to a stout woman who was cooking for the shearers—an aunt of the boys, by the look of her. That was the worst of these small cockies. They always gave any job to relations.

'How is it for some tucker, missus?' he asked in his most courteous voice. He was feeling, not only loose in his joints, but very hollow in the middle. The shearers were already sitting down with mugs and plates of meat before them; and unwritten law demanded that Snow should be invited to share. But the worst of town women is that they know little of unwritten law; and the cook had been imported from Logan, where she usually helped in a shop.

Her eyes snapped at the importunate tramp. 'I've got no time,' she said irritably, 'to be feeding damn bagmen. There's enough to do without that.'

A deadly silence fell on the diners. It was as though a mob of cattle had raised their heads and were gazing thunderstruck from Snow to the cook to see how this breach of etiquette had arisen. Burning Angus recovered first. He sprang up from the head of the table and pushed his plate away.

'You heard that, mates?' he demanded. 'Have any of you ever heard a shearers' cook that spoke like that before?'

The cook stood her ground. 'I'm here to cook for you men, and not for any lousy bagmen that come biting tucker.'

The Scotsman glared at her. 'If you were a man,' he said, 'I'd know what I'd do about it.' He turned to the men at the table. 'I'm a bagman meself, and I won't have a chap that comes looking for a hand-out turned down. I said we ought to vote for our own cook, didn't I? I said that if we let the boss hire the cook, we were breaking the union agreement, didn't I? Well, wasn't I right?'

'Oh, shut up, Angus.' One of the men looked up for a minute. 'Give it a rest.'

But Burning Angus was too angry. 'A chap's got to stand up for a mate when he's out of a job,' he declared. 'I'm going to see the boss about this. I'm asking you others who are bagmen to come with me. You, Dogger, and Uncle and Snake.'

The three obediently put down their knives and forks. All through the Scotsman's tirade they had been shovelling in food as though this was their last meal. Wiping their mouths, they followed him across the yard to where the boss was still talking to his son about the sheep. There followed a long, wordy, wrangling argument, the upshot of it being that the boss refused to sack the cook— she was his wife's sister, and he was afraid of what his wife would say—but he tried to soothe Angus, a hard man to soothe. One word led to another, and the Dogger returned to an earlier grievance, that the sheep were as poor as 'damn race-horses.'

This fired the boss's blood. He was not too proud of those sheep himself. He knew they were hard to handle and poor enough; but he would not have them disparaged in his hearing. It ended with his saying: 'All right, then, if that suits you. You can get your time as quick as you like.' And he went off to get his cheque-book.

The Apostle showed no surprise at the sight of Snow returning with Burning Angus and Uncle in his wake. Snake and the Dogger were coming later on the wool-truck. All the way back to town Angus expressed his views on the A.W.U. organiser, who, he claimed, was never to be seen except when he collected the ten shillings levy and the twenty shillings for the union ticket; who hob-nobbed with the bosses and drove round in a big car, and didn't care a hoot in hell what the conditions at a shed might be like.

It was Uncle who insisted that, as Snow was just out of hospital, they should all stop at the first hotel and get him a 'face plaster.' The Apostle dropped them there, courteously declining a drink. He got his from the river, he declared, and it was much the same colour and taste.

'You'll be camping down by the bridge,' he called, as he drove away. 'If so, I'll see you later.'

'We'll be camping down by the bridge.' It would take more than an official edict to shift the bagmen off the river.

It was dusk when they came down the bank, laden with bottles, and reinforced by the Dogger, Snake, and two bagmen known respectively as Dark and Jim. Dogger and Snake had also been breaking up their 'silver cheque' into a more potable form, and they were all very merry.

Dark and Jim had spent the day clearing the graveyard of a vigorous growth of marshmallow which had sprouted after the flood, and not only were they being paid ten shillings a day, but they had been working in the midst of a set of unpaid sentimentalists and chattering school children, composing a volunteer working bee, with a Ladies' Committee taking round afternoon tea.

'And didn't we just wop into them big slabs of cake with cream in the middle?' Dark exclaimed.

'But the funniest of the lot,' his mate broke in, 'is when Dark's scrapping away those weeds—they're up to our waists—and he sings out: "Hey, Jim, here's a copper's grave."'

'"Well, don't clear none of the weeds away from *him*," I says. "He's bludged on bagmen all his life." And I goes over to have a look, and strike me, if it don't say: "Trooper Harold York, Fought at Gallipoli." That damn fool of a Dark thought trooper meant he was a copper. So we cleaned up his grave better than all the rest put together, and the mayor, when he comes down to have a look, gives us five bob each, because this Trooper York's his brother.'

'That means a new tyre for the back wheel of the bike—nine bob, and a shilling left to play round with.'

The rest of the party was also pleased with itself; Snow because he was out of hospital and in good company; Angus because he had told the boss what he thought of him, and his mates because they 'never wanted to shear no flamin' jumbucks, anyway,' and were 'glad to get away from the smell of them and the damn cocky's relatives.'

'Here comes the bloody 'Postle,' Dark said, with the touch of affectionate contempt and exasperation which so generally greeted the Apostle among the bagmen. They felt the Apostle was 'putting a roughie over them.' A parson ought to have a rectory or a presbytery and stay in it. Why did he want to go wandering round pretending to be just a human being? And if he was one of themselves, why did he break out every now and then pretending to be a parson?

'How's the war, Harry?' Angus hailed him.

'Very close, Angus,' the Apostle responded in a low, grave voice.

They settled down to talk international politics. 'The papers say' or 'I was reading the other day' began every second sentence, for most bagmen pride themselves on their knowledge of general affairs, and Angus and the Dogger in particular were always calling at the post-office for bundles of papers sent on to them by friends.

'If it comes, it'll be the First Oil War,' Angus prophesied. 'I tell ye, we'll see the world divided up like a cocky's back paddock.'

The Dogger was not in agreement. 'It's a sign the democracies are waking up,' he announced. 'They see the menace of Hitler at last. The first job of the workers is to crush Hitler, and any country that goes to war against Germany gets all my support.' From the way he said it, you almost waited for the hysterical cheers of relief from the darkness as England and France learned that the Dogger was with them.

'If it comes off,' Snake cried, 'I'll be with the first to take a bayonet and have a jab at old Hitler.'

'You're a mug,' Angus said with biting contempt. 'Let the capitalists fight their own wars. That's the line for the workers.'

But he was in a minority. They turned on him furiously and tried to convince him that he was wrong.

'This is a justifiable war . . .'

'Lenin says . . .'

'Look here, Angus, you're out of date. I read only the other day . . .'

Across their jarring voices the words of Uncle came so

quietly that they could hardly be heard; but something in his tone stopped their wrangling dead.

'I fought in the last war,' he said, 'and while I was away they buried my father in a pauper's grave. With a body above him and a body below they threw him to rot, and I never knew until months after.'

There was a silence. Then Snake said impatiently: 'Let's have a drink.'

'I thought of him lying there,' Uncle went on gravely, as though he had not heard. 'And I thought of all the other dead men I had seen. But always I thought of him again. He trained me to be loyal to King and country.'

The atmosphere, which had been so full of hilarious jollity a few minutes before, felt now as though a clammy, grey mist had crept from the river, oozing around them, laying unseen, wet hands on their faces.

'When I was dossing at the Salvation Army joint,' Snake said in a low voice, 'there was two men died. One old chap had heart trouble and he kept asking for brandy, but they wouldn't give him any. He died about eleven o'clock, and they just wrapped him in a couple of blankets and left his body there all night. There were fifty-eight chaps sleeping there. The other chap . . .'

Snow could stand it no longer. 'Ar, cut it out!' he shouted angrily. 'What about that drink?'

His violence had the effect of jolting them out of their thoughts. Snake served the beer into tin mugs.

'Here's mud in your eye, Harry,' the boy said, raising his mug to the Apostle. 'I'd sooner get a bullet in me than doss with the Sallies again.'

But Angus and the Dogger were staring at each other as though they were strangers.

'Dogger,' Angus said in a strained voice, 'you don't mean you'd lead the workers astray on this issue?'

'Lead them astray! Hell! It's you who'd lead them astray, with your anarcho-syndicalist tripe about not fighting Fascism.'

'Dogger,' Burning Angus said again, 'we've had our disagreements from time to time, but we've worked together, and we've done what we could to get a bit of unionism and self-respect into the chaps we met. You don't mean you'd chuck it in to become the serf of capitalism?'

The Dogger began to be angry. 'I don't know what you're talking about.' His voice was hard. 'I've fought Fascism here, and I'll fight it abroad, if need be.' His voice took on a tone of solemnity. 'It's the party line, and I follow it.'

Angus was silent for a minute. 'Well, this is the finish,' he said at last. 'I never thought I'd see the day when we two couldn't get along together. Here we've been organising this union. We've just got to show Snow here into it . . . we've got the chaps interested—and now you'll drop it all.'

The Dogger sat sullenly, saying nothing.

Burning Angus rose with dignity. 'Come on, Uncle,' he said. 'I can associate with the dupes of capitalism, but not with chaps who'll mislead the workers on an issue like this.' He ostentatiously gathered up his swag.

'If that's the way you feel,' the Dogger said sternly, 'I can only say that where I can work with you, Angus, I will. But when it's a genuine fight against German Fascism, it's up to us.'

They were both on their feet now: big, grim Dogger and little, sandy Angus, who had worked and quarrelled together for years.

'If you can't follow a line that's laid down,' the Dogger went on angrily, 'you're nothing but an individualist.'

'I'm not,' Angus retorted, enraged by this awful insult. 'I follow the line of the British Independent Labour Party.' He almost shouted it. 'No support from the workers for capitalist war.'

'And where the hell do you think that's going to get you? Do y'want to see us all in German concentration camps?'

Angus fell to laughing bitterly. 'That's good! Who showed me the debate in Parliament about putting the chaps into labour camps right here in this country?'

The Apostle tried to make peace. 'Why don't you wait and see?' he suggested. 'There mightn't be a war. If it comes, it may be a good thing in a way,' he added reflectively, 'the beginning of a more desirable state of affairs, the end of civilisation. After all, civilisation is an unnatural state for man: it puts too much strain on him. Far, far better to revert to the state of wandering tribes who cannot upset the balance of nature. Humanity was meant to be just a collection of little farming villages and hunting tribes, anyway. Perhaps we might then see men developing instead of an export trade.'

Snow dimly felt that all this had happened before. Somewhere he had heard those words, seen this firelit group. Even the broad seat of Jim's trousers, as he bent to pick up a bottle, had the permanence and significance of a monument.

'You and Tolstoy,' the Dogger said scornfully, 'you give me a pain.'

The Apostle only smiled. He had heard the Dogger's views on the benefits of industrialisation, and the Dogger had heard his on the benefits of its absence. In fact, they had come to a deadlock so often that it did not seem worth while to go over all the old ground again. It would only end with the Dogger's telling him he was a 'pacifist reactionary' and his asking the Dogger if a more efficient manufacture of bombs ever made a man kinder to his fellow-men.

Angus returned to the attack. 'The Dogger and his gang,' he shouted, 'have been misleading the workers for years. Talking about democracies being better than dictatorships, when here, in our own country, they want to put the unemployed into labour camps as though they were criminals. He's turning the workers' eyes to tyranny abroad instead of at home, I tell you. And if there's a war, that's what it'll do. It'll smash the unions, set up Fascism right here, and the disorganised, misled rabble 'ull be powerless to stop it. And why? Because men like the

Dogger have been preaching for five years that the workers must fight Fascism abroad.' His voice echoed along the silent river. He pointed his finger accusingly at the Dogger across the fire. 'He's a menace, I tell you.' And shouldering his swag and signalling Uncle to follow, he strode off into the darkness.

The Dogger watched him go, his eyes narrowed, his mouth stern. 'Good riddance to the pro-Hitlerite,' he said sententiously.

'Hear! hear!' Snake echoed. 'Let's have a drink.'

But the party had been spoiled. Dark and Jim muttered something about turning in, and went off to their own camp.

'You'd better come up and sleep in the truck with the boys, Snow,' the Apostle said quietly.

But Snow was experiencing such a flush of anger against the Apostle that he could hardly speak.

'Y-y-you!' he stuttered, shaking his fist under the Apostle's nose. 'You did it.' The Apostle did not move. He sat frowning at the river. 'They was all as happy as Larry till you come down talking bloody war. Can't leave chaps alone, that's your bloody trouble. Always stickin' your nose in. Why? Why? Where does it get you? For two pins,' Snow roared, 'I'd smash your face in.'

The Apostle still watched the river disinterestedly. Snow felt his anger evaporting. He tried to spur it, but it was no use.

'Separateness,' the Apostle said, as though to himself. 'It is in that that man finds his life rather than unity. Without being apart, being different, there would be no such thing as consciousness. Yes, yes, I see that now.' He rubbed his forehead. 'What were you saying, Snow?'

'Arr!' Snow had sunk back on the ground. 'Forget it.'

A dreadful weariness beset him. He was baffled by the Apostle, baffled in his search for work, baffled by the emptiness of life. He felt a hand on his shoulder. It was the Dogger's, who, now that his own irritation had gone, was smiling. 'Old bloody Angus 'ull be back in the morning,' he said, 'large as life.'

Snake nodded. 'He always goes off that way, and back he'll come and abuse us.'

'One thing about Burning,' the Dogger said thoughtfully: 'he may be a pro-Fascist and a bloody fool, but he's worked hard for this union.'

'That's so,' Snake agreed. 'We'd better humour him. I think I'll just stroll along with what's left in this bottle,' he added casually. 'They might want a drink before they turn in.

'If you care to join up with us,' he said, 'I'll just give you an idea of what we plan to do.'

As he spoke two figures loomed out of the darkness. Uncle and Burning Angus, without a word, spread their blankets in front of the fire.

'If you think,' Angus announced, in an awful voice, 'that we're going to set about finding firewood at this hour when half this fire's rightly ours . . .'

'Anyway, we'll be moving on in the morning,' the Dogger said ironically. 'One more night within smell of me won't make so much difference.'

'That's so,' Burning Angus agreed non-committally, and then, 'Meebee I was a bit hot with you, Dogger. You can't help being misled.'

'You can't either,' the Dogger replied.

Solemnly, like Livingstone meeting Stanley, they shook hands, the trackless jungles of policy encompassing them, but a small glow of friendship in the clearing.

Chapter XVII

PURE cowardice on Snow's part induced him to bring Angus and the Dogger with him when he went up to the dairy to take away his van and his horse. He knew he would have a hard struggle with Dancy, who would inevitably want to come with him.

'I tell you I'm coming too,' Dancy insisted.

'Now see here, Dancy; I can't take you. I'm going to help these coves organise a union, and there ain't no room for you sticking your oar in. Besides, the road ain't no place for a woman. Thirty-Bob's got the money for the sulky and the Horehound. When you get it, you can pay your fare back to Sydney, if you don't want to stay on here.'

It was the longest speech the Stray had ever heard Snow make, except his memorable dissertation on work, when they had just met. She stood, sullen and desolate, a small figure in an old print apron at the paddock gate, while the three men harnessed Don, and Snow climbed on the seat of the van. She even held the gate open for them.

'Where you headin' for, Snow?' she asked almost in a whisper, as Snow paused to say good-bye.

Snow hesitated. He knew the Stray, and while he did not want to be cruel, he could not have her following. And she would, as soon as look at him. So he hedged.

'Well, I don't know yet. I thought maybe I'd head out through Dubbo and Bourke. See you down at the cannery at Christmas, maybe.'

He gave her a smile because he was afraid she might cry and disgrace him, but she only nodded quietly. She knew he was lying about heading west.

'O.K., Snow. I'll be seein' you.'

'I'll be seein' you, Stray.'

Snow felt mean and rather ashamed of himself as he drove the turnout back to Logan. The Stray had behaved well. She hadn't whimpered or made a scene, and when she wanted to make a scene, there was not her equal on the track. She had just taken it on the chin. Oh, well! He couldn't be worried about the Stray. She could look after herself.

Back at the dairy, Dancy was explaining to her employer: 'Me husbing's heard of a job over in Dubbo, and he says if I can stay here, it'll suit 'im till he sees whether he'll give this job a go or not.'

'Well, I must say, Dancy, you're acting very queer. I'd be much easier in me mind if I knew I'd got someone permanent. Only the other day Mrs. Higgs's girl said she'd come for seven-and-six, and if I do keep you on, I can't be paying you more than I'd be paying a permanent girl. I'll think it over and ask Mr. Marks what he thinks.'

For two days Dancy went through her work dully and indifferently. If her eyes were more red-rimmed than usual, only Charley noticed it. He tried to comfort her timidly:

'Don't you worry, Mrs. Grimshaw. Your husband 'ull come back all right.'

'It's this smoke in me eyes,' the Stray grumbled.

As she went about the house, she was conscious all the time of a terrible weariness. Her legs seemed to have lost power to move. Her throat ached, and there was a pain in the middle of her chest, as though some heavy lump was lodged there. Her eyes were sore from crying so much to herself at night, and when she swore, it was in a dispirited and hopeless fashion without any ginger in it.

'Ain't no damn man any good,' she muttered. 'Not a single one of 'em. I 'ates men.'

She was still in this mood when the Apostle left his rickety little truck at the gate and asked to see her. Dancy was so pleased to see his friendly, gentle face, that she could have cried.

'If you like to come with us, Dancy, my wife and I would be only too pleased.'

'It's all right, Harry,' she said listlessly. 'I dunno what I'm going to do yet.'

'Don't cry, Dancy.'

'I'm not crying.' She wiped her eyes.

'If you can just remember, Dancy'—the Apostle hesitated—'if you can just remember that fretting and willing and worrying and planning are just a waste of time. Try to trust life. I know it hasn't given you much reason to trust it, but go with it, not against it. Just know

225

that you are watched and guarded and . . . loved. Then it doesn't matter what men and women do to you.'

'O.K., Harry,' the Stray promised.

The Apostle pressed her hand. 'You're as safe,' he said, 'as if you were the cherished daughter of a rich man. Safer. Think of it as a kind of luck. Whatever happens, just trust to luck. And come to us if you need help.'

'Thanks, Harry,' the Stray said. 'You're good.'

Mrs. Marks was not so sure. 'I can't have you bringing the riff-raff of the road here all hours of the day and night,' she snapped. 'It's got to stop.'

But the very next day Dick and Thirty-Bob drove up and called Dancy out to the gate. Mrs. Marks, whose curiosity was always her strong point, pattered about on the verandah, trying to hear what was said, and pretending to water some neglected geraniums in half kerosene tins along the verandah's edge.

'We brought the dough,' Thirty-Bob said cautiously, passing over four limp banknotes in which some silver had been wrapped. 'The four quid is for the mare and the fifteen bob for the turnout. I could of got more if I'd of hung on for a few days, but me and Dick want to get off. An' lemme tell you, Dance, you're damn lucky to get this. The flamin' coppers tried to fine it off us.'

Dancy did not even count the money. She knew that neither Dick nor Thirty-Bob would cheat her. She was 'on the road' like themselves, and while it might be legitimate business to fleece any farmer or townsman, 'to take down' a woman who had 'no come-back' was something they would never contemplate.

'Thanks, Thirty-Bob,' she said. 'Which way you heading?'

Thirty-Bob switched idly at a spray of godetia which had thrust its head through the garden fence. 'Well, we're going to catch up with Ma first thing, and have a look at the kid.'

'I wanted it to be a boy,' Dick beamed. 'Didn't I say it'd be a boy, Bob?'

'Thasso. Dick here's keen to see his young brother. Well, from there, we don't quite know where we'd head. Might go after Snow through Mt. McDonald to Crookwell. Though why he had to go that way, damned if I know.' He winked at Dancy. 'Comin' along, Dance?'

Thirty-Bob had noticed the look of exultation on Dancy's face without realising that it was due to his indiscretion in revealing where Snow had gone. So Snow was heading through Mt. McDonald to Crookwell! Oh, indeed! And he'd told her he was going to Dubbo and Bourke, the black-hearted . . . Dancy added a few descriptive nouns under her breath.

'Yeah, if you want to come along,' Dick grinned, 'we'll give you a lift. Better than campin' here with old fishface on the verandah. Pity her poor cow of a husband. Fancy having to sleep with that!'

Dancy's first impulse was to accept the invitation, but she hesitated. She did not want to travel with anyone but Snow. He'd be sure to hear sooner or later that she was on the road with Dick and Thirty-Bob, and she wanted only Snow. Determinedly and tenaciously she was resolved to acquire Snow as her own property, and anything that stood in the way of that could not be considered.

'Aw, I dunno,' she said. 'I guess I'll hang on here for a bit.'

'We're not asking you to travel with us on our own,' Thirty-Bob complained. 'There'd be Ma. She took a fancy to you, and it'd be company for her to have you along.'

Thirty-Bob had also taken a fancy to Dancy. He had plans to acquire her for himself, but he had been too open about them, making a joke of his intentions.

'Have it your own way, Dance. See you at Orion for the cherries or down at the cannery for Christmas.'

'Yeah. Fanks all the same.' Tears had come into Dancy's eyes, and she hurried away to hide them. She was ready to cry without any real cause these past two days. She even went out into the yard to wipe away the

227

tears when Mrs. Marks had snarled at her over some broken eggs; and now she wanted to cry because Thirty-Bob and Dick were kind to her.

'Don't think you can get off the road,' Thirty-Bob called after her. 'If you once take to the road, you come back to it sooner or later. We'll be seein' you, Dance.'

The visit had given the Stray three comfortable things. One was the money; the other a sense that somewhere she was welcome, if it was only in the camp of the 'Tyrell mob'; and the third was the actual knowledge where she could find Snow. So he had gone through Crookwell! And he thought he had ditched her! Huh!

Snow, plugging along with the spring weather, heading south-east with the birds, felt soothed and relieved to be by himself again, without a 'big mob,' as he characterised his three ex-passengers. Few travellers ever went through Mt. McDonald, because the road was too hilly, but he had messages to deliver for Burning Angus at Wyangala Dam, and another message at Bigga. It might be hard going for Don, but that could not be helped. If he could pick up work, it would mean money, and money meant he would get a divorce from Molly and claim his boys.

Sometimes, when he felt a little lonely, he thought it was the boys he was missing. Actually, it was his three pests, the busker, Phippsy, and, most of all, the Stray. The van didn't seem the same somehow, after the first thrill of exultation and freedom wore off. This took about a week, by which time he was well on his way. He missed the Stray's childish tempers, and her no less childish pleasures, her enormous lies that no one believed, her real generosity and hard work. She was a battler, Snow admitted; impudent, hardy, cool, and she could take a 'knock-back' as though it didn't matter, and come up to meet the next blow, with perhaps a curse, but at least come up and meet it. She wasn't a whiner. She was a good mate and a good toiler, and he wished her luck, whether she stayed at the dairy or went back to Sydney. He wondered some nights, sitting by his fire alone, just what the Stray was doing now. Probably getting drunk in some Sydney bar-parlour and swearing herself into a fury.

The Stray lasted all of a week at the dairy after Snow left. She was suffering from shock, and it was the sort of shock that numbed her mind and made her incapable of thought or decisive action. She went through the housework and cooking and washing in a daze. But on Sunday afternoon the warmth and kindness of the air tempted her. She would go up to the camps and see if there were any news of Snow. Someone might have come through the way he had gone and seen Snow's turnout.

The afternoon was a glass bowl in which the scent of the briar rose boiled like some invisible, intoxicating liquor, simmering in heady gusts, that overpowered the roads, the fields, the ditches, in an unreal brilliance. The trees shone, the sky shone, everything glowed and shimmered with a marvellous beauty. Even the garbage-tip, with its dirty piles of old tins and refuse, seemed less of an eyesore, and the beaten-out kerosene-tin humpies of the dark people's camp merged their rust with the dead-brown earth, the chequered lights and shadows of the thin scrub, as though they had a magic and might vanish altogether. Everywhere there were clumps of briar that had been shabby and leafless, but were now gay in their new green. Their frail petals delicately stained with rose, light as a breath, drifted freely over heaps of rubbish or the close-bitten grass, more freely than they might have done in a garden. The briar is always on the point of being declared noxious, a ruin of fields, a home for pests, the refuge of rabbits and small birds, its thorns sheltering other lives than its own. The briar that travels the roads and leaps the ditches to prowl in a farmer's field and spread itself under his very nose uncaring, is the battler's flower, and its smell is the best in the world, if you except bacon cooking over a fire of black cypress boughs.

The familiar stretch of ground was almost tentless. Dick Tyrell and Thirty-Bob were gone; the Apostle had gone.

There was a family she did not know camped where the Apostle's little truck had rested.

Farther along the bank prowled a curious figure, searching around the blackened patches of bygone camp-fires, a figure well known on the tracks, stooped half-double, as though an invisible swag always pressed on his shoulders, with a long grey beard and long grey hair, and very dirty, long black finger-nails.

The Stray had encountered George the Bower-bird before, and feared him not a little, although he bore the reputation of being perfectly harmless. He was mad, a 'Hatter,' always chattering and mumbling to himself; and he had the habit of searching camps for discarded trifles or bits of rubbish. He would eat stale bread-crusts with great content; and old boots or clothes that the travellers threw away he gathered up as though they were priceless treasures.

'How goes it, George?' the Stray greeted him affably. She was always very polite to frightening people.

George chattered and mumbled. 'Burning good clothes,' he said excitedly, shaking out a piece of mouldy cloth from the ashes. 'That's Sharkey Wilks's mob for yer. Sooner burn good clothes than let anyone else get 'em. Arr.' He shook his head angrily. 'Ought to be burnt up themselves.' He came very close to the Stray, so close that she could smell the noisome odour of his rags. 'Burn them all up,' he muttered, glaring at her. 'You see. Put a match under them.'

'You do, George,' the Stray advised, shivering. 'Good idea.'

'All them farmers'—he took a box of matches out of his pocket, and shook them at her—'they ought to have their stacks burnt. If I had my rights, I'd be richer than any of 'em. Burn them up. That's what I say. Don't let a man sleep in their shed.'

'I've gotta be going.' The Stray looked round for an excuse to escape. It was funny, she thought, how she seemed always to be meeting mad people. There was the

Apostle, and poor Charley, and this horrible old Bower-bird. 'Mrs. Little's wanting me,' she said. 'So long.'

And indeed the Stray's appearance had caused quite a stir in the dark people's camp. Mrs. Little, carrying a new baby, hurried up the river-bank, beckoning her excitedly.

'Hey, Missus Grimshaw,' she called. 'Come over 'ere a minute.'

The Stray went. Mrs. Little was plainly trying to be friendly.

'Your little boy come 'ere, missus, asking for 'is Dad. Said 'is father was in 'orspital kicked by a horse.'

The Stray regarded her suspiciously. Maybe this was some new trick on the part of the Littles.

'My kid come here?' she demanded.

'Yeah. 'E slept here last night. I couldn't see a little feller like that stay out in the cold when his father had gone. He went up the 'orspital last night and they didn't know nothing. I told 'im you'd know where his Daddy was, and sent him out to the Markses. Just now, it was. You must of passed 'im on the road.' The woman was full of excitement and curiosity. 'It's such a shame to see a little feller travellin' along by himself. The Welfare people 'ull be on to him like a shot. It's a wonder the p'lice haven't got him before this.' The other women murmured agreement, their dark faces shining with sympathy and interest. 'Jimmy Grimshaw, 'e says his name is. 'E come all the way from Blimdagery.'

'I better go after him,' the Stray said hurriedly. 'Thanks for looking after the kid.'

'I couldn't do no less,' the woman answered loudly. 'I'm not one to hunt kids.' This was a dig at the absent Mrs. Tyrell. 'I wouldn't see a kid left. Or anyone else for that matter, poor little beggar!'

Mrs. Little had a shrewd suspicion that Dancy was no more Mrs. Grimshaw than she was. Jimmy's declaration that his mother was back in Blimdagery had been a sweet morsel of scandal. But Mrs. Little had saved the Stray's face. She could have blurted it all out and shamed the woman who had sympathised with her enemies, but she had called her 'Missus Grimshaw.' She had not shown that she knew different. Mrs. Little, when her temper was not roused, or her husband drunk, had a notable kindness. Besides, the Littles were making ready to take to the road, and it does not pay to have too many enemies. Perhaps her friendliness to the Stray might a little mollify the Tyrells, though she doubted it. No Little would be safe on the same reserve with a Tyrell now.

Dancy hurried back the way she came. This new development had taken her completely by surprise. What was Snow's kid doing here? Poor little beggar! he must have come all the way from Blimdagery by himself. Of course he would get lifts, but even so it was a long way for a boy of eleven. The Stray knew all about Jimmy. He was one of Snow's favourite subjects of conversation. What was his mother thinking to let him go? Of course she would have put the police on his trail. It was a wonder, as Mrs. Little said, that they had not got him before this. Molly might have been afraid to start the police after the kid for fear they sent him to a home; but no, she would not think like that. It was only people like the Stray who hated and feared 'homes' and the whole process of justice and regeneration, who would sooner die than call in the police.

There was no sign of Jimmy on the road; but, then, she would not know him if she saw him, and she had not noticed whom she passed on her way to the reserve. Hold on a minute! There had been a boy, a gingery-headed one with freckles, lurking about in a paddock, who, she thought, was bird-nesting.

Dancy was hot and moist when she panted up the incline from the dairy gate to the garden gate. Her mind was still in a puzzle. There was no sign of Jimmy sitting on the edge of the verandah, as she had half hoped. He might have been scared and gone away. If he saw Mrs. Marks, he would be. Dancy hurried into the kitchen to find Charley, who was, as usual, crouched beside the stove.

'Seen anything of a little boy asking for me,' she panted—'a little boy called Jimmy?'

'Yes, Mrs. Grimshaw,' Charley whispered. 'I told him not to wait, Mrs. Grimshaw. You wouldn't be back, I said.' He eyed her craftily. 'I said you didn't want to see him.'

'Oh, Charley!' the Stray exclaimed desperately. 'What'd you do that for?'

'He said you weren't his mother,' the idiot replied. 'You don't want to see him. He wouldn't grow up to direct a railway.'

But the Stray had darted to the door. She was standing on the verandah, her hand shading her eyes from the afternoon sunlight, when Mrs. Marks came out from the dining-room. She was dressed in her best black, and there was a malicious glitter in her pale eyes. Her whole attitude had changed. From a whining hypochondriac she had become suddenly malignant and ominously powerful.

'Oh, there you are, Dancy!' she said. 'I've been waiting for you. A child came here asking for you.' Dancy could see at once that some secret triumph was exciting her. 'I thought: the best thing is to ring the police at once, and then I thought: No, I'll take him in myself. He's run away from his home. I gave him some cake, and he told me . . .'

'Where is he?' Dancy demanded.

'I've got him shut in the shed,' Mrs. Marks answered, still very pleased with herself.

The Stray flared. 'You got my kid shut in the shed,' she stormed furiously. 'Who the hell told you you could shut up my kid in any shed? Talk about p'lice! My kid comes out to see me, and you shut 'im in a shed! I'll have the p'lice on you, see if I don't.'

The woman retreated a little before the menace in Dancy's tone. 'That's no way to speak to me. You ain't his mother at all, my lady. She's back in Blimdagery. You ain't even the wife of the man you come here with. If you ask me, you'd better watch out, talking to me like that. I'll thank you to keep a civil tongue in your head, and you can take yourself out of my house as soon as you like.'

The Stray swallowed with an effort at control. 'I'll tell you how it is,' she explained. 'Jimmy don't want people to know all his business, so he tells them I'm back home. He thinks that makes it all right, see?'

Mrs. Marks was unconvinced. 'You ain't got no wedding ring,' she said with great virtue.

'Didn't I tell you I pawned it when me and me old man was hard up?'

'You told me that all right. But the whole thing's just a tale. You try and explain it to the police. Why, I wouldn't sleep safe in my bed with a lot of cut-throats always driving up to the house and asking for a woman as ain't married at all. And then one night I wake up and find me bed's been stolen from under me.'

The Stray thought deeply. Her first inspiration to strangle Mrs. Marks had been discarded as lacking in subtlety. Mrs. Marks had Jimmy locked in a shed, and was obviously very pleased at the thought of all the things a virtuous woman could visit on one who had no legal or economic status.

'You got it all wrong, Mrs. Marks,' Dancy said patiently. 'All I want is to take Jimmy with me and go off after me old man. 'S a matter of fact, now the kid's come, the sooner I leave the better.'

'I always knew you'd leave me in the lurch just at a busy time.'

'Well,' Dancy bargained, 'seein' I'm leaving sudden like this I won't be wanting me last week's wages.' She saw the glitter of avarice in the woman's eyes. 'If you start callin' in the p'lice for my kid—an' I can prove he's mine—you'll only get yourself in a mess, and I'll sue you, sure as I stand here, for contamination of character. But I can see you ain't got no place for me *and* the kiddie, so

I'll go to me husbing.' The woman still hesitated. Dancy, she knew, had always had more strength than she. The assurance of her manner took all the starch out of Mrs. Marks. 'Gimme that key,' Dancy demanded. 'Locking *my* boy in a shed, indeed. I'm going this very night.'

Mrs. Marks very slowly and reluctantly produced the key from her handbag. 'It's a pity my husband isn't home,' she observed. 'He'd deal with you.' But the thought of saving Dancy's wages was too much for her. 'I'll come with you to see that nothing's missing.'

'You stay right here,' Dancy declared. 'He's my kid and I want to talk to him a bit. Nobody ain't going to take any of them rusty old bits of harness. They ain't worth it.'

She sped over to the shed and let herself in. A small, ginger-headed boy made a sudden break for the door from behind a pile of old machinery.

'Jimmy.' The Stray caught at him, and he struggled to free himself. 'It's all right, love. I've come to get you away. We'll go and find your Dad this very minute.'

'You lemme go.' Jimmy still struggled. 'You lemme out of here.'

'Listen, Jimmy, not so loud. Old fish-face 'ull hear you. She wants to put the p'lice on you. We got to get out of here.'

The urgency of the Stray's tone stilled the boy. He looked at her searchingly. 'Where's me Dad?' he demanded. 'He wrote to me from hospital, and now they say he ain't there.'

'He's gone off to Crookwell, Jimmy.'

'Where's that?'

'Well, I don't exactly know from here, but I guess we'll find it. And listen, Jimmy, for cripes sake pretend I'm your muvver. This old devil's set on gettin' the p'lice. Gawd knows why, but if you pretend I'm your muvver, she won't dare. Understand?'

Jimmy nodded. He had a sharp, decided manner, that was much more his mother's than Snow's. 'All right. What's your name?'

'Dancy. But you better call me Mum. Come on now. And don't forget. We're goin' after your Dad, and I'm your muvver.'

They emerged to find Mrs. Marks approaching the shed with a renewed intention to interfere. 'Don't you go away without signing the time-book,' she snapped. 'I don't want you getting away from here, and then saying I didn't pay you.' She drew herself up virtuously: 'I won't have you saying things like that about me.'

The Stray almost exploded. 'Get out of me way,' she said rudely. 'Jimmy, you come and help Mummy pack.'

'Right-o, Mum,' Jimmy responded woodenly.

'So she *is* your mother now,' Mrs. Marks commented sarcastically, diverted from her intention of smacking the Stray's face. 'You know what happens to boys who tell lies.'

Jimmy made no answer. He followed Dancy to her lean-to, while she gathered her few garments into a gunny-sack and put on the shabby old coat she had been given by the Methodist minister's wife. She thanked heaven silently for the four pounds fifteen shillings she had from the sale of the horse and turnout. Mrs. Marks didn't know anything about that, didn't know what a secret source of comfort and strength it was to the Stray.

'Come on, Jimmy,' she said, flinging in the last of her rags. 'Mummy's ready.'

Mrs. Marks had been standing offensively near, inspecting everything that went into the sack. 'Good riddance,' she exclaimed, every line of her outraged. 'Speaking to me as I have never been spoken to in my life. Lying and thieving and . . .'

'Look here, missus, you get out of my way before I regrets it. I want to say good-bye to Charley.' This Dancy did, with Jimmy tagging after her, and Mrs. Marks bringing up the rear.

'Don't forget.' Charley nodded at her mysteriously. 'You know.' He was referring to the piece of paper, the 'cheque for a thousand pounds,' that he had given her.

'I'll remember, Charley,' the Stray promised. 'You're a kind boy.'

'I'll come with you, Mrs. Grimshaw,' Charley said, reaching for his cap. 'I'll be going down to the station now, and I'll walk with you.'

'Don't show your face inside my gate again,' Mrs. Marks shouted to Dancy as the trio reached the garden gate. 'You and your nameless brat.'

The Stray took no notice. They walked fast, Charley because he wanted to be in time to wave the train out, Jimmy and the Stray to put as much distance as possible between themselves and Mrs. Marks, still standing on the verandah like a black figure of hate.

'Where'd you leave your things?' the Stray asked. She knew Jimmy would have some little bundle.

'With Mrs. Little.' Jimmy was limping because he had a nail in his shoe; and the Stray was pleased for his sake when they reached the reserve.

'Well, good-bye again, Charley,' she said. 'You've been very good to me.'

'I've got to hurry, Mrs. Grimshaw,' he said rapidly. 'Don't forget. If you ever want money, just get in touch with me.' He shambled away, and Dancy watched him go a little sadly. Poor Charley!

'He ain't a bad sort,' she said to Jimmy. 'The best of them mongrel-faced Markses, anyway. Her and her ten bob a week!'

Mrs. Little had obviously been waiting for them. 'You found him!' she called before the Stray could speak. 'That's good.' She was all smiles.

'We got to be getting on, missus,' the Stray said hurriedly. 'I want to catch up wiv me old man.'

'You can stay here the night,' the woman advised. ''Tain't much, but it's better than bein' out in the open.'

'We ought to go now.' The Stray glanced nervously over her shoulder. It would be just like Mrs. Marks to phone the police and say there was a runaway boy about.

The beautiful afternoon was dying in a mist of rose,

delicate wisps of cloud feathering the sky with the colours of a galah's wings; but to Mrs. Little it meant only that it would soon be dark.

'Ain't you got no nap?' she asked. 'Here, wait on a minute.' She hurried inside her dilapidated tin humpy, and presently reappeared with Jimmy's little bundle, an old dirty blanket, and a sugar-bag full, as they found later, of such necessities as tea, sugar, bread, a tiny bit of butter, and half a tin of treacle. There was even some raw bacon and matches with an old knife. She held also a little billy-can. 'Here,' she said, thrusting the bundles at them. 'Good luck.'

Dancy tried to refuse, but the woman urged the gifts on her. 'Maybe you can do the same for me some day. If you're going, you'd better get along before it's too dark.'

'Which is the way to Mt. McDonald, missus?' the Stray asked.

'Mt. McDonald?' The woman was surprised. 'Why, you go through Woodstock, but you ain't going there.'

The Stray realised her mistake. 'You won't tell anyone, will yer?' she asked anxiously. 'Not that I've got anything to hide or that. It's the kid leavin' his home. We don't want no trouble with the Child Welfare.'

Mrs. Little knew all about the Child Welfare. She nodded reassuringly. 'Don't you worry. They may say I'm a p'lice pimp.' Her face flushed angrily, as she remembered the unforgivable insult. 'But I wouldn't have nothing to do with the p'lice.'

'Good on you, missus. Come on, Jimmy.'

Mrs. Little stood a long time looking after them, until they came to the turn of the road that led through Logan, and from Logan south on the first long stretch towards Woodstock, and Crookwell a hundred miles away; two tiny dark figures, lonely and insignificant under the swelling, rosy wings of the sky.

Chapter XVIII

I

THE Woodstock Road leads out from Logan through gentle land, with willows leaning to drink the creeks. Rolling miles of wheat ripen towards harvest, showing every shade through cream and buff to the colour of dry cedar-berries; and there are ploughed paddocks, fallow land, grazing ground, hard out-croppings of rock where the trees still hold on grimly, with other outpost trees scattered through the fields as shade for cattle and sheep. Wide, open, generous country, with the free winds flinging thistle-down. The iron roofs of homesteads shine like polished silver in the dark knot of the homestead trees. The road loiters from neighbour fence to neighbour fence like a contented farmer coming home from town.

Drovers with their sheep; cattle-men riding behind a herd of white and red steers; cars that swirled past in a cloud of callous dust—all these took the road with the Stray and Jimmy on Monday morning. The two had sheltered the night under a bridge, and they awoke to see the water smoking among the reeds, as though the early light had set it smouldering.

The Stray was first awake. She rolled over and rubbed her eyes; then she lay for some time watching a group of little waterhens fussing like middle-aged ladies at a sale. They had crocodile-skin shoes; grey, silk stockings; black coats and skirts with a smart white strip down the tail; and little red crests tipped over their eyes. Something about them reminded the Stray of Phippsy, and she laughed. Jimmy woke up and regarded her questioningly. He did not quite know what to make of Dancy; but he already liked her; so he smiled a little, though he did not know what the joke was.

They each ate a crust of bread, and shouldered their bundles. Both were dirty and aching and stiff; but walking, or rather limping through the glorious morning raised their spirits. Smoke was rising over the farm roofs and a dog barked. Pale yellow butterflies floated about their own affairs. An old kookaburra in a nest in a hollow branch was in trouble with a group of sparrows. They had set on him and were making his life a misery. The willy-wagtails were teaching their young to fly; the little blue-wrens tittupped along the fences and over the green wheat that was turning gold. Dandelions were growing gaily beside the road; and presently the two wanderers passed an old orchard, hot and breathless in the arms of the hills.

'We ought to get to Woodstock to-day,' the Stray remarked hopefully. 'Maybe we'll get a lift, Jimmy. Seems to me we're going to be lucky. Don't know why, but I got a feeling we're lucky.'

She turned and hopefully surveyed the way they had come. There was nothing in sight but the empty road and the walls of wheat, and, farther away, the dark line of hills. Around the next turn of the road a drover came jogging towards them; and the Stray stopped him to ask if he had seen a van the way he had come, a brown van with a brown horse; but the drover had joined the road a few miles back and had been travelling across country by the stock route.

'I would've missed it,' he said, twitching his fly-veil, and regarding the two kindly. 'I guess they can't be far ahead, eh?'

He was an inquisitive man, and wanted to know all about the Stray and Jimmy; but they evaded his questions and hurried on. Presently cars began to pass them. Commercial travellers in big sedans, the back seats piled high with luggage, were hurrying through these little 'dumps' of towns contemptuously and racing to the big centres; men who drove a hundred-and-fifty miles a day, and interviewed customers in towns fifty miles apart; go-getters with no time to waste on a girl and a small boy trudging along. Big trucks roared past loaded with goods, and at these the Stray looked more hopefully. But each was a fresh disappointment. Presently, foot-weary, the travellers flung themselves under the trees, and wiped their faces, dislodging a horde of flies that rose buzzing from the packs.

''Strufe! but I must be cartin' about a ton of these flies,' the Stray grumbled. 'They got wings. Why don't they fly? We got to walk, ain't we?' She broke off a small bough and swished it in front of her face.

'Means it's going to rain,' Jimmy said, weather wise.

'Who says so?' the Stray demanded, surveying the cloudless sky.

'Uncle Hegarty.'

'I guess the flies don't need no excuse,' the Stray replied. 'They'd do it, rain or no rain. Geeze! if they was money, we'd be millionaires.'

Money was a subject very much in her mind. Her four pounds should last herself and Jimmy for food for some time. They would not need to ask for anything at farms, and so be remembered should enquiries be made that way for Jimmy. Snow had only a week's start. He would have to wait for his dole at Cowra; and by going to Woodstock and not waiting for dole themselves they would be cutting off part of the road. The road from Cowra joined the road from Woodstock at Mt. McDonald. If Snow was going through to Crookwell, by Mt. McDonald, then there was only one road he could use, a steep road, according to all accounts, that wound up and up to Mt. McDonald, that town of dead gold-mines, then down the other side of the mountain to Wyangala Dam; and then up again over the mountain and down again to Reid's Flat. From there he would go either to Bigga or Rugby, probably Rugby, because the road was better for a horse.

'It's going to rain,' Jimmy said again; and he was right.

They got a lift from a farmer that took them as far as Woodstock, out of which they climbed again in the early afternoon. The clouds were dragging purple skirts over

the hills that were no longer rolling gently, but humped
like so many camels for the storms to ride. Far down the
slopes in the valleys tiny trickles of water ran; but up on
the road, winding round the great shoulders of the mountains, the Stray and Jimmy were thirsty.

'Here she comes,' Jimmy announced, looking towards
the rain with all the satisfaction of the successful prophet
of disaster.

'And tell me we ain't got no luck,' the Stray responded
jubilantly. 'Here comes a car.'

They halted expectantly, waiting, but the car flashed
past. Then, a hundred yards farther on, it halted.

'Come on.' The Stray pulled Jimmy by the hand. 'He's
stopped for us. I said we was lucky.'

Jimmy did not need any urging. They hurried forward.
The driver of the car had jumped out, seized a stick, and
very efficiently despatched a large tiger snake in the middle
of the road. Jumping into his car again, he was off before
the Stray could do more than gasp:

'Hey, mister, wait on.'

The two stood forlornly watching the car recede.

'Well, one way we're lucky, Jimmy,' the Stray attempted to comfort her comrade. 'We might of stepped
on that snake.'

Jimmy's mind was on the problem of shelter. 'We
could make for that old shearers' hut,' he suggested. A
weather-beaten hut on top of a hill had caught his
eye.

The heavy drops were spattering down and, despite
their weariness, they almost ran. By the time they gained
the hut, which was locked, the rain was roaring on its tin
roof. Luckily a verandah projected over the beaten earth
by the front door, and under this verandah the two took
refuge. Darkness came down in a roaring spate of water,
and there was no wood to light a fire. Cold and shivering,
Jimmy and the Stray crouched under their one thin
blanket on the cold earth, and ate some bread and jam.
Presently they fell asleep. It must have been three hours

later that the movements of some unseen animal awakened the Stray.

'Oo!' She drew closer to Jimmy. 'There's a great rat bigger'n a cat.'

'It's a 'possum,' Jimmy said, half contemptuous.

The creature approached them adventurously. The boy put out his hand, and the opossum promptly bit it.

'The shearers must have tamed it,' Jimmy remarked.

It was plain the opossum was not afraid. It came scampering round, and when the Stray slapped at it with her hat, that was all part of the game. It tried to scratch open the sack in which the bread was wrapped, and had to be beaten off. After every discouragement the opossum would retire round the corner of the hut disheartened, and presently come lumbering back for more. All night long it sniffed and scampered and raced round them; and when the Stray put the bread under her head for a pillow, it bit her ear with its sharp teeth. Towards dawn the 'possum realised at last that neither of these big things wanted to play or had biscuits to give, so it went off in search of other sport.

The morning was bright and clear, and Jimmy and the Stray were off early. They had walked for three hours when a baker overtook them; and, although his car was piled high with fresh-smelling loaves, he beckoned them to stand on the running-board. In this manner they came to Mt. McDonald among the peaks of the ranges. The baker, a good-natured man, gave them a loaf of bread, and called to all the people he knew, asking for Snow.

No one had seen or heard of him; and, certainly, in this lonely place, where ice lay in winter, and the winds blew most of the year, a brown van would have excited some comment. Cars passed through at the week-end from all towns within a day's distance, going down to Wyangala for boating and fishing; but there were not many brown vans.

The Stray's heart sank. 'Maybe he's gone some other way?' she suggested; but they told her that was impossible. All the roads had been drowned when the big dam was built. 'Well, if he comes froo this way,' Dancy instructed them, 'you tell him his wife and Jimmy is on ahead Crookwell way, and we'll wait for 'im there.'

The baker was going down the other side of the slope to the dam, and the two went with him, exclaiming in amazement as the great sweep of water came in view. They took up their bundles at the bottom of the slope, and trudged along the high rampart of the dam and round the prisoned waters. The road led to the left along the shore, where drowned trees stood up out of the little, lapping waves that slapped in against the grass. It was hot down here, with the black cypress pines taking all the air before it eddied to the bottom of this great ditch. The rocks were grey hot, burning to the touch. Lizards flashed in the dead wood. When they came to an open slope of grass by the waterside, the Stray sank down in the shade.

'I can't go no farther, Jimmy,' she said weakly.

The boy sat down beside her. 'Where d'you suppose Dad is?' he asked.

'Search me,' the Stray answered despondently. Then she brightened. 'We could make some tea.'

They built a little fire and heated some water for tea. They rested a long time; then they had a bathe, Jimmy in his trousers, the Stray in her very insufficient and ragged underwear. They rested again, and presently they felt better.

'We might get a lift in that launch the baker was talking about,' Jimmy remarked. 'Goes up as far as Bigga.' He looked round critically. 'We got to find its landing.'

Finding the landing of a launch in all those bays and curves and inlets was like looking for one scallop in the hem of a wedding garment. Groaning, the Stray got to her feet. 'It don't leave till midnight,' she reminded Jimmy.

The small boy regarded her impatiently. His confidence in Dancy had been undermined by her failure to discover traces of Snow. 'Dad might be in Crookwell now,' he said pointedly.

They could not waste time. They had come to find his father. If Snow got his dole at Crookwell next Thursday, they should be there waiting. They plodded off round the shore, looking for the place where the launch was moored. 'You can't miss it,' they had been told; but it seemed a desperately long time before they came out on a slope beside some beehives, and beheld a long jetty, running out into the water, and two motor-launches rocking placidly beside.

Here the Stray and Jimmy spent the rest of the after-noon, idly browsing, and, when they could rouse the energy, bathing. Neither could swim, and they were afraid of this great, mysterious stretch of water, where trees grew up out of the waves, as though they were on dry land. There was something uncanny about the trees growing so freely half in the water, going lower and lower until their tops were submerged, like people slowly going down into a mist.

The moon rose over the sharp, black shoulder of a hill, and the silence and strangeness of everything made them eager for sleep. Dancy was glad she had Jimmy with her. She could never have endured to be alone in this great pit between the hills with that big moon glowing down and lonely blackbirds flying and calling remotely. They lay at their little fire and talked in undertones; Jimmy about things a boy knows; the finding of nests; fishing for yabbies; horses and their ways. The Stray told him about the city, the streets and the roaring of trains, and bridges. Jimmy said he wouldn't like so many people.

The Stray admitted she didn't like the city either. 'I liked it travellin',' she exclaimed. 'But I'd like it best if I had a bit of a place to settle in like, a place of me own, green and little. . . .' She broke off abruptly. 'Aw, what's the use?'

'If I had a rabbit-trap,' said Jimmy, after some thought, 'I could catch us a rabbit.' He was a boy with a very practical mind. Jimmy never bothered to speculate. He liked to be doing something all the time, if it was only rolling up their packs in a new way. He was very old for eleven and very shrewd. He had decided to join his father and had just gone off without a word. With Jimmy to think was to act.

The Stray was wakeful because her supply of tobacco had run out. This was partly due to the fact that Jimmy smoked, and he had been smoking her tobacco, having none of his own. They dropped to sleep at last, and were awakened by the bright lights of a car dazzling their eyes, as it came almost noiselessly over the grass from the road. It contained passengers for the launch, and was driven by the launch's owner, of whom they immediately begged a lift. But he shook his head. The launch was not going to Bigga. It was going up the opposite shore of the lake, many miles from their hoped-for destination.

'Well, we'll just have to walk,' the Stray decided gloomily; and they settled back to sleep again.

Walk they did, all the long, weary, hot pull up the mountain, where the road wiggled like a snake through the thin trees, and small springs gushed through the grass below the last high rim that cut off the world on one side of the steep from the world on the other. A cold, bitter wind blew towards them as they paused for breath, and saw below the farms rolling again, on and on, as they rolled everywhere, chrome and burnt sienna and ochre and madder, umber and dun, and chocolate-coloured earth, and green wheat, and dried stunted trees, and grass for grazing, and trim farmhouses with fly-proof doors and windows and wire fences and corrugated-iron roofs; all as though they had been turned to a pattern, and the pattern laid out even on top of a range so high that it seemed when you were climbing that you were clawing your way up the steep gables of the world.

They descended on to a long, level plateau, and presently stopped to bathe their feet, for they had been walking since dawn, where a little stream ran by grey granite boulders under willow trees. Mint grew wild along its grassy edge, and, as they crushed the leaves, the mint smelt pleasant and cool. But a big leech, with gold stripes on his black velvet, came out in the stream to investigate their toes, and they hastily replaced their broken shoes over the blisters.

'We might as well have a bit to eat, Jimmy love,' the Stray suggested.

Jimmy eyed her approvingly. He was always hungry himself.

It began to cloud over and the chilly wind grew colder and colder. They trudged on, not talking much, for they were very tired, and it seemed as though such things as shelter and warm beds, while very desirable, were fantastic and incredible things. The freezing grey hilltops, waiting for the rain, lowered round them, and the wind was roaring now, scudding and thundering in miles and miles of thick forest that lay ahead, forest through which the road clove like a knife. Even the flies had taken cover; everything had taken cover but the two who moved on because there was nothing else to do. Speculatively they eyed haystacks and farm sheds as they passed, always half-deciding to ask for shelter, and then once more agreeing to push on to a 'better place.' They did knock at one door—that of a storekeeper by the roadside—but the man could not hear them for the wind.

Whenever they thought of approaching a house to beg for shelter, they were seized with the panic timidity that, sooner or later, overcomes all those who travel the road. The very thought of a stranger's house makes them uneasy and suspicious. All dwellers between four walls are enemies, hostile, uncaring and incalculable.

Far overhead, an aeroplane kept them company for a short time. They watched it eagerly until it disappeared under the roaring grey arch of the storm, which, risen now to a hurricane force, was tearing off the boughs of the trees and flinging them contemptuously after the travellers.

Now, if they could have seen any houses to ask for help, they would have asked; but there was nothing on that

247

desolate road. They could have cried, they were so hungry and tired and desolate.

'Jimmy, are you any good at prayin'?' The Stray had almost to yell against the wind.

Jimmy thought. 'Who to?' he asked deliberately.

'Anyone you like, love. I'd have a shot at it meself, if I thought I was any good at it.'

'St. Christopher,' said Jimmy, 'looks after travellers. Father Sheehan told me that.'

'Well, you word him, Jimmy'—the Stray had a superstitious nature—'that we could do with a bit of lookin' after. You might give it a go.'

'No,' Jimmy said sullenly. Then he thought. 'But I'll promise him a candle.'

'Me, too,' the Stray agreed. 'Two candles.'

They had stopped for a minute to rest, their backs against a rock, and now it seemed that someone was shouting to them. They saw a man over in a field waving his arms, beckoning, and they limped across to him. He was an old man with a grey beard who was, he explained, doing a bit of fencing. His mate emerged from a tent to survey the two newcomers.

'If it ain't a shame,' he said, removing his pipe, 'to see a woman and a kid on the road. And by themselves, too.'

The Stray explained that she was going to join her husband, and the old men exchanged a glance of indignant pity.

'Come in and sit down,' they invited. 'You look as though you could do with a rest.'

The two old men, kindly and silent, knew from having lived long years together what each was thinking. They made their plans in a murmured undertone. The girl and the boy were 'knocked up.' They could not possibly go on. The Stray must have a portion of the tent screened off. They explained apologetically that they could not sleep out, because it would probably be a heavy storm. The Stray and Jimmy were only too thankful for company and kindness and shelter. They did not care what kind of shelter.

It seemed that the sky, tortured by the wind, had broken into a passion that was almost horrible. Great, swirling wisps of livid vapour raced below the higher, darker passes of the sky where, dull, formidably, the curdled wrath of rain towered up and up, writhing. Then the water crashed down in a cold, howling, driving spate, as though a dam had burst above, as though the tiny tent lay in the vent of some celestial drain-pipe, whose black mouth jetted an unholy spray.

As the four huddled close around the hurricane lamp, the Stray, weary and frightened as she was, had a feeling of immeasurable delight and comfort. Through all her miseries there had come to her the sudden, blinding certainty that something was looking after her.

It might be Jimmy's Saint Christopher, it might be just the 'ghosts' she was so afraid of, but something had brought them to this little tent out of the lightning that crashed blue fire over the rocks, out of the threat of the thunder and darkness.

She closed her eyes the better to enjoy this contentment that wrapped her round. 'It's me Luck,' she whispered to herself. 'I'm lucky, that's what it is.' Perhaps cheering Jimmy on with this assurance, she had convinced herself, but this huge, vague, shadowy Luck towered over her as definitely as the storm towered over the tent.

The wind was now a tremendous, sustained uproar. Its note was a howl so malignant that even the thunder faded before it. The tent bellied outwards suddenly, swayed, and, as the two old men vainly scrambled up to stay it, blew away.

In the roaring darkness the Stray heard the old men shouting about a bridge not far off. Slipping and stumbling, they set out for it, carrying such belongings as they could find.

Here once again the two hosts courteously insisted on rigging up a little partition with a blanket for their lady

249

guest, so that one half the bridge, which dripped dismally, was hers in privacy and decency.

'Course I don't mind about the tent,' the Stray assured them, when they apologised for the fourth time for the inadequacies of their deserted dwelling. 'We're lucky we got a bridge to shelter under, ain't we, Jimmy? Lots of people haven't a bridge.'

II

For three days the cold rain lashed down; the wind blew a gale; and the roads ran mud. Through the gaping, eroded wounds in the hill-slopes the earth came tumbling. The soggy grass squelched underfoot as though the ground were swollen with water. Farmers who had bemoaned the dry weather now cursed to see their wheat-fields threshed flat by hail. The owners of orchards where the blossom had been mashed into an unsightly brown mess of petals wondered how they would live, even if the bank should help them. Many a gaunt man who had fought the country for a bare living for years saw his hopes of a good harvest lying ruined in the paddocks. The bitter lines deepened in the farmers' faces, just as the eroded lines of the slopes deepened under the downpour.

At Crookwell, it snowed. Not much, but just enough to show that it was possible for the weather at Crookwell to do anything. The Minister for Water and Drainage, who had come up officially to open a new reservoir, had to stand in a torrent while he did it; and his speech on the benefits of water was testily altered at the last minute.

Meanwhile Snow remained snugly in a prospectors' camp a few miles from Woodstock. He had turned off the road to carry a message to three gold fossickers, friends of Scotty, and had decided to stay until the weather cleared. While the rain poured down, he sat by the fire in the hut, resting and yarning with Scotty's friends. It was here that messages first began to reach him from the Stray. He knew it must be the Stray when they said his 'wife.' Only the Stray seemed to have this power to upset his life and turn it aside. He had told Thirty-Bob that he was going to Crookwell, but he had not intended to go farther than Mt. McDonald. Now he would have to go through to Crookwell after all. And then the thought came: Why should he go? But the perturbing news that the Stray had Jimmy with her settled that idea. He must get Jimmy. After all, he need not saddle himself with the Stray as well. At least, he tried to comfort himself with the assurance that he did not *need* to saddle himself with the Stray. Something told him, however, that the Stray was fate, a rather bedraggled and vigorous fate in the body of a girl who refused to be left behind. He could no more be done with her than he could be done with his own nature, which had been reproaching him for his desertion of that outrageous little bit of feminine flotsam.

The message had come, like most country news, through a mailman who was a friend of the baker's. The Stray and Jimmy, desolately toiling past isolated farms, had aroused more interest than they would ever imagine. 'I wonder what became of that poor woman and the boy,' one farmer's wife would ask another over the telephone. 'Did they pass your place? I nearly went out and invited them in. I'm sorry now I didn't.'

'The mailman may have seen them. I'll ask him.'

So that the progress of the two lonely wanderers was watched from farm to farm, as two free, swimming fishes might be watched by limpets under a protective shell.

'Haven't heard anything of a cove with a brown van and a brown horse Woodstock way?' the mailman asked gloomily from farm to farm. He was a laconic man, who always looked as though he might have some secret engine trouble, and he had an air of listening for a knock in the pistons while he drove.

'Well, I seen a cove go past here with a brown van Friday. He turns off past Pierce's place and down to the left where them fellers are prospectin'. It might be him.'

Sighing wearily, as though the burden was too much to bear, the mailman had driven a long way down the rutty, dangerous track to carry the message to 'the cove with a brown van' that his wife and boy had gone through to Crookwell and were waiting for him there. The mailman had no incentive to go out of his way for any unknown boy or woman, but he was used to delivering messages or going errands, and the habit was just too much for him. Besides, the whole countryside wanted to know how the Stray and Jimmy fared. Their story spread like ripples in a pool.

Before Snow had travelled twenty miles on his way, the Stray's message had been delivered to him five times by interested farmers; and he had begun to curse this friendly interest in his affairs. His coming was heralded. The mailman, going ahead on his daily round, announced it. The word was passed along from Reid's Flat by a lorry-driver who pulled in and hailed the Stray and Jimmy, where they were having their blisters nursed by a bridge-building gang.

'Your old man's coming along, missus. He ought to be here to-morrow. He's coming along behind.'

The Stray and Jimmy had explained to everyone that Snow had left them with a friendly family in Logan while she was laid up with some mysterious ailment, and that he had intended to call back for them; but, the Stray recovering earlier than expected, the two had set forth to find 'me husbing' somewhere along the track. Everyone accepted the story for what it was worth, and they were kind enough to the young woman and the boy who was obviously too old to be her son.

The mailman became the curse of Snow's life. He pulled up again on his trip back from Reid's Flat and said despondently: 'They're waitin' for you at the bridge, Joe Banks's camp, on the Bigga Road,' as though this were a tragedy in which Snow had all his sympathy. The mailman's passengers encouraged Snow and took an interest. Even the two cages of parroquets that the mailman was transporting to town for a friend seemed to take an interest. The bags of flour and groceries and mail had a sentimental air, as though they were saying to each other:

252

'It doesn't matter what your position may be in life. The heart is always the same, isn't it? Fancy that poor woman and the boy coming to find the father! Fancy, now! Such a sullen, unpleasant-looking man, too.'

The very men to whom Snow came with tidings of the formation of the Trackmen's Union greeted him with the news that 'your wife and kid were through here looking for you a day or so ago. Stopped and had a bit of tucker with us. Good kid that.'

Snow, who had seen himself travelling a lonely road, a secret emissary of the new union, found that he was far from being either lonely or secret. Everyone was watching for a brown van and a brown horse, and as soon as they saw him in the distance, they had to gallop up and verify his existence and tell him all over again about Jimmy and the Stray, wanting to know his whole life-story, inviting him to put his horse in the farm paddock and shelter in the farm shed, boil his billy over the fire, or sit in the kitchen until the rain stopped. The shyness that had prevented the farmers' wives extending hospitality to the Stray and Jimmy had melted, and all their kindliness that caution had dammed back was showered on Snow. Never before had Snow known such a friendly lot of farmers as there seemed to be in this district, and considering that they were recently ruined for at least the eleventh time according to their own reckoning it was all rather mystifying. He did not kill one sheep. He did not need to. Someone was always giving him eggs or meat or bread or sugar. He had only to ask, and often it was offered without asking. He felt as though the whole countryside was shoving him irresistibly towards the clutch of the Stray. There was no turning back. She had Jimmy as hostage, and she had announced to the whole world that she was Mrs. Grimshaw; and to all intents and purposes it was clear she intended to remain Mrs. Grimshaw, whether he liked it or not. He might just as well give in and accept his position of pleased husband and father journeying to meet his dear ones.

Snow, however, was a stubborn man and set in his ways. He had cast the Stray off; and it annoyed him that she refused to be cast off. He brooded over the problem as the slow old van moved on. There was nothing to *make* him travel with her. There wasn't any law that could force him to do it. He sulked.

It was a good thing the Stray and Jimmy had progressed beyond the orbit of the mailman, or he would have given them a lift back the way they had come, and landed them on Snow as though he was delivering two bags of groceries. And Snow did not want them dumped on him so. His hatred of interference was linked with his dislike of gaol. He no more cared to be penned in to a set course of action than to a confined space. He wanted to be free.

As he drove along, the face of the Stray seemed to float in front of him: the big blue eyes, the sunburnt fair skin, the tight funny mouth of a toothless old woman, the flossy hair like pale silk, the loose, badly-fitting print dress that covered her small, thin body—her whole hobgoblin self persisted before his mind like some vision that could not be banished into the limbo from which it had risen. Jimmy had sunk into unimportance, although, of course, he would be pleased to have Jimmy again. But the Stray had spoilt his plans of working and making money and getting a ship-shape divorce and taking legal possession of the boys. She had snapped all his carefully woven future aside like a cobweb, with her customary vigour and mettle. She could remind him that his track-card was still made out for a wife, and that they were her rations he had drawn at Cowra as well as his own. But the Stray was not mean. She would not do that. She would want to ride in the van, share his life, share Jimmy, probably share his bed as well, and this thought gave Snow a distinct uneasiness.

There was a strain in him which, if not exactly monastic, took a certain pleasure in a physical isolation. He was a born monogamist—that rare creature, a man who felt little of the casual attractions which seduce the drover from his matrimonial loyalty. Marriage with him was a matter of habit. He was used to regarding himself as married to Molly. She might not be either a satisfactory partner or a very loving one, but he was fixed in his attitude. She was his wife, and that settled it. He did not think of the Stray as his wife, and behind all his plans there lingered the faint hope that Molly might still change her mind and rejoin him. Jimmy's desertion might soften her. Suppose Molly should turn up some day and say: 'Theo, I'm sorry. It was a mistake. Will you have me back?' What could he say, if the Stray was obtrusively thrusting herself into the picture?

There! He had thought of her again. He could not prevent his mind nervously shying away from the idea of the Stray boldly claiming the right of sleeping in his arms. He couldn't throw her out of the camp bodily, could he? But again, he couldn't see himself making love to her. 'It's a matter of breaking in,' he muttered aloud. He had been broken in to Molly. You couldn't train a plough-horse for a trotter, and a racer was no good ploughing. To these rather disconsolate and apprehensive images, particularly the one of the Stray curling up like a kitten, sleeping in the curve of his arm, his mind reverted again and again. He had a paternal liking for the Stray, an elderly indulgence of her tantrums that were so like those of a spoilt small girl.

Oh, well, whatever happened, he couldn't help it. It was as the Apostle said: Life just flowed along, and it didn't matter a damn what you wanted. You just paddled the way you were meant to go. Already he was half resigned to his lot. If he had to have the Stray, that was all about it.

The vindictive ghost of winter risen like conscience was bitter company on the road. Everywhere was the crying and calling of ewes, for it was still lambing time in these parts: a desolate, weak crying they made, full of the knowledge of sudden cold and the death of new-born lambs with the frosts on their fleeces. The grey stones

255

stood together like sheep, and when the sheep moved, it was as though the rocks had stirred and walked restless with the cold. The road wriggled forward uncertainly over rises and down hollows as though it tried to escape into the green fields and was forever driven on like a worn-out drudge, its yellow ribs bare and staring. Towards him along that yellow road laboured the figure of a small boy.

Snow looked again, astounded. Yes, it was Jimmy right enough, coming down a long slope and across the level. But where was the Stray? He flicked Don into a faster pace.

'Hallo, Dad!' Jimmy called excitedly. 'I said I'd come, didn't I?' Triumph shone in his eyes. 'I got here.'

His father helped him into the van. 'Where's the woman?' he asked abruptly.

'Dancy got a lift. She's gone on. Said to tell you, now she knows I'm all right, she'll be on her way. Hey, Dad, Bluey knows me. Look at him.'

And, indeed, Bluey was wagging his tail and fawning along the ground and stretching himself on his chain until he nearly strangled himself in his efforts to express joyful welcome. But Snow seemed abstracted. His firm determination to have nothing to do with the Stray seemed to have weakened on him, and in its place the urgent necessity of finding her was settling itself like a welcome guest.

'How far ahead d'you s'pose she'd be?' he asked presently, when Jimmy's flood of news had a little subsided.

'Not far, I guess. She on'y got a lift from a farmer in a sulky, and he said he was turning off at the cross-roads.'

Snow urged Don onwards. 'I guess we better try and catch her up,' he said with an effort. 'Don't seem right to leave a woman footin' by herself.'

'She said she'd be all right. To tell you she's got some money.'

But Snow was hurrying Don in a manner that set the van creaking and groaning. Jimmy looked at his father sideways.

'I can stay, Dad?' he asked anxiously. 'You won't go sending me back?'

'You can stay, son, I guess, if your damn mother don't put the police on me for having you; we'll get along.' He was peering ahead as though he expected to see the little, thin figure of the Stray around every new angle of the road.

'She's a nice lady,' Jimmy said presently.

'She ain't no lady,' Snow grunted; but his tone was not one of reproof.

With all the pain of the sharp pebbles on her broken shoes and broken blisters, the Stray was plodding on; and she was, much to her own surprise, neither sad nor down-hearted. When it grew dark she might feel afraid, but the bitter afternoon held for her a strange exhilaration. At the last moment she had abandoned all her plans. She had left Jimmy—impatient, eager Jimmy—to walk back to meet his father alone. She had gone on, to what destination she did not know, but with a new confidence in herself. She was not going to let Snow think she would be a drag on him. If a man didn't want her, she wouldn't be hanging round him; and thinking it over, she had come to the conclusion that Snow would be happy alone with Jimmy.

'I guess I can battle for meself,' she had said stoutly, but rather uncertainly. She would not be afraid. She sang to herself, a little discordantly, a scrap of a tune remembered from some past age of reluctant and compulsory church-going: 'How beautiful, how beautiful upon the mountains . . .' Over and over again she sang it. She did not know any more, but it seemed to her a very fitting tune: 'How beautiful, how beautiful upon the mountains.'

Between two high-rolling masses of purple vapour that menaced the afternoon with more rain, a weak shaft of sunlight struck down, as though powerless to bless, but willing. It laid its light across the long curves of wooded hills; the ploughed, dark fields; the green slopes, scattered with grey granite boulders; and on the figure of the Stray limping along by herself.

She came round a bend where before her the road wound down and down, and then up the ample curves and swellings of another hill that soon she must climb. The Stray stopped to stare:

''Strufe!' she said admiringly.

Through the rift in the clouds the sunlight poured down and lit the nearby hills, leaving those behind in a dimness of shadow; and in the flare of that light the hills showed a mass of purple flowers, a carpet of them, a brilliant torrent of flowers, pouring down the side of the road in colours of crimson and blue mauve, violet and opal, opening curious throated bells like snapdragons. They rushed up the far hill, overpowering everything—the paddocks, the pasture, the roadside grass. It was as though the clouds had rained crimson and blue and it had mingled in an indelible dye.

The Stray sat down on a rock and loosed her unwieldy pack. She simply sat and looked at the flowers. She also nursed her feet thoughtfully. 'I won't forget,' she thought gravely. 'Not even when I'm old.' Two nails had worked through the heel of her left shoe, but only part of her took note of it. She was busy glancing about, drinking in the shades of crimson and purple; pleasure and weariness making her a little unsteady, as though this beauty were some dangerous red wine. 'I won't forget,' she repeated. 'When I get back to Sydney, I'll have this left.' If she had never come out on the track, she would never have seen this unknown flower flaunting its colours over miles of hilly ground.

She was still sitting there in a half daze as Snow and Jimmy and the turnout came clopping round the bend of the road.

'Get up,' Snow commanded accusingly, sternly, as though she had done him some wrong.

'We seen you,' Jimmy remarked. 'And we shouted and waved and you didn't take no notice.'

'You got the staggers like an old horse,' Snow remarked, as she settled into place between them. 'Sittin' down every few yards.' His tone was censorious, as though she had, by her very sluggishness, forced him to overtake her. 'What was yer sittin' there for?'

'I was looking at them flowers.' The Stray had hardly greeted him. 'What they called?' She waved her hand at the purple flowers.

Snow gave them a disparaging glance. 'Patterson's Curse,' he announced gloomily.

'Geeze, it's pretty!'

'That's you all over.' Snow was determined to find fault. 'It's a bloody weed. Sit there gawping at a weed that's driven many a man off his land. Ain't no use burnin' it.' He was rather glad to have something to talk about besides the fact that they were there together again, sitting in the old van, just as they had sat many times. 'Some farmer's daughter went out and picked a bunch of the stuff. Brought it home to stick in a vase. Chucked it out when it wilted, and of course it sprouts up lively. Next thing they knew they was fightin' it like it was a fire. Ends by drivin' them off the place.'

The flowers flared up from the ground unconquerable. The unrepentant gaiety of the weed, the burning blues and crimsons, set the hills glowing.

'It's a plant that's struck it lucky,' the Stray said thoughtfully. 'It hasn't got no right, but it's there.'

Oh! she was glad that she had come out into the country. She could never otherwise have seen the weed that ruined a land royally and like an army with a million bugles blowing. She would never have heard the lambs crying to the ewes; limping on white, bent legs, like four props that might buckle under them; trotting along painfully like a girl in high-heeled shoes.

The rain was sweeping towards them over the tree-tops that thinly covered the crest of the rise ahead. With the rain came a sigh, as though the suspense of cold and waiting had been lifted. Soon it would be dark, and the rain would possess all; soaking the cracked, yellow lips of the creeks afresh; running along the sharp ridges of the road. The rain was coming down the slope as though it fought the flowers; as though its grey could beat out the crimson flare and wipe the purple stain into oblivion, into the mud. But under the lash of the heavy drops the flowers swayed undaunted and remained.

'Five miles to Crookwell,' Snow observed gloomily. 'An' rainin' like hell; and you sit gawping at the worst sort of land a man ever had the hard luck to farm! I ain't sorry for cockies as a rule, but I'm sorry for the poor bastard's got that land.'

'If you give me a lift into Crookwell, Snow,' the Stray suggested humbly, 'I can get along all right by meself.'

Snow gave her a long glance. She had not altered much. Her fair hair lay lank about her face, and her blue eyes were as big, as startling as ever. But, he supposed, he must have got used to her, or something, for the sight of her made him happy.

'Of all the warby ideas,' he said, and in the spite of the rain and the prospect of a wet camp, in spite of everything, he was smiling at her, 'the warbiest is you going on your own. I guess Jimmy and me can give you a lift down to Orion for the cherry-pickin'. What say, Jimmy?'

'Yeah,' said Jimmy proudly. 'We don't mind another one.' He was not jealous of Dancy. He was rather proud of her as his own find.

'Suit yourself,' Snow went on casually. 'We ain't no bed of roses, me an' Jimmy, but, I guess, Stray, you know what you're in for. Take it or leave it.'

The Stray was unwontedly humble. 'I learnt how to make jug-covers, Snowy,' she suggested. 'I can fake jug-covers round the towns and make a bit that way. And I've still got the money for the horse. Jimmy and me didn't spend no more than seven bob. But I ain't goin' to have you sayin' I shoved in on you. You've got Jimmy.'

'Ar, don't be a bloody mug,' Snow said warmly.

And Jimmy echoed: 'Don't you be a mug, Dance.'

And, to her intense astonishment, Snow, the undemonstrative and laconic Snow, put one arm round her thin shoulders. Jimmy, sitting proud and possessive on her other side, no less warmly put his arm round her waist.

'Don't you worry,' he said. 'We'll look after you.'

The Stray was quite overcome. There were tears in her eyes. ''Strufe!' she said, gulping a little. 'I won't be no trouble, Snow. I can battle . . .'

'Shut up,' Snow said, not unkindly. 'We got to camp before dark.'

Chapter XIX

I

THE CHERRIES that year were early. By the end of October word was travelling along the roads that the cherries in Orion were early, and towards Orion there began a gradual rift of tiny specks of flotsam and jetsam; tiny, isolated smuts that the road carried as an eddy of slow air might carry soot. The pickers were coming in answer to that mysterious telegraph. They came from the city, stripling boys, men and women; from the farms of the district around; south from Victoria; north from Queensland. They were all classes; all breeds; all tongues; all drawn by one thought: to earn money— money that meant so many fulfilled hopes, so much freedom, so much of added life. Only to get a job, only to join with other men and women in the great moment when silver passed from someone's hand to their own hardened palms!

Some carelessly, some anxiously, they strained towards Orion, the rich town, the fruitful town coming to harvest. They came laboriously and by many ways; and most of them from dole-station to dole-station. Burnt black by the sun, grimly trudging, pedalling their bicycles, whipping up the lean horses, cranking the old trucks! The great wide country tossed along from crest to crest with a little foam of trees on their tops. Sometimes the brown-green waves of fields seemed to rear and topple as a great breaker rears on the shore. From under the enormous heads of the Apennines, mile after mile of vertical sheer so steep that only clouds climbed there, over the roaring hills that sweep up to break against Canobolas, came the pickers, breasting towards the deep, green pools of country where tree-tops swayed in an underseas peace fathoms down.

To stand on the smooth, high, green hills and gaze down on Orion was to look on a curve of rich land where the Lamb River flowed almost in a semi-circle. In the old days, the gold-miner had scooped out great shallow patches and holes from the yellow earth; and the deep hole in which Orion lay might have been just such another claim where a gold-seeking giant had dipped his dish and rinsed the riches of the river and splashed them over the hills. For this was not a 'dead' gold town as so many old towns were dead. From the chequered roofs by the silver creek Orion flowed up in a mass of living green. Here were some of the biggest cherry orchards in the world; peach orchards; apples, oranges, figs, grapes, all growing side by side. The regular green stripes of the orchard trees followed the slopes; patches of green peas and wheat, of clover, all the riches of the earth brimmed from that bowl in the hills.

It was not perhaps only the lure of quick ready money that turned the sunburnt, hopeless stream of landless men towards Orion. Here, at the cherry-picking, life quickened, if not into a harvest song, at least into a whirl of dancing, drinking, love-making and fighting, that made the year-round inhabitants of the town raise their eyes to Heaven. A little sourly they regarded this yearly influx of lawless persons and the riot they brewed; but, being God-fearing farmers who plugged on season after season, always moaning about their losses and envying the man next door, they did not blame the pickers as much as they blamed Waldo. And they were right.

The reason why life moved to a different tempo in Orion was all Waldo's doing. Vladimir Waldo had for the past fifty years occupied in the town the same function that a mediaeval baron might have filled in that unpronounceable town of Central Europe from which Waldo had arisen in the dim past before he burst on Orion. If one citizen met another in the main street, he would be sure to ask: 'Have you heard the latest about Waldo?' With his flaring black moustaches, his flaring temperament, Waldo at the age of seventy was as vital as he had been at sixteen, still as ready to beat his breast, to dance, to drink, to offer a fight. He was so immensely rich, so violent, so hardworking, strange and friendly, that he was not only the town's outstanding citizen, but its favourite sport. Without Waldo, Orion would have lost its individuality. The richness of his spirit was its richness. The violent, living green, striped so tidily up-hill, had something of his overflowing exuberance and his peasant shrewdness.

His nine sons, each with a separate orchard on neighbouring hills, formed a local bodyguard for the old man. They were all sandy and drawling and Australian, and had more of the Jones in them than the Waldo blood. But they managed their sire almost as well as their mother did, and she was the restraining power of the family. They soothed Waldo's labour force; they settled his quarrels and strikes; they protected him from the results of both his benevolence and his cheese-paring meanness.

There was never any trouble about getting labour at Waldo's; the thing was to keep it. Just as there are hill-tops where the tempests brew when all the land is quiet, so there are human beings who are a magnet peak for emotional violence. Fights would break out, strikes start at Waldo's when there was peace everywhere else. And just as the turbulent throng would be shouldering its belongings and marching off four abreast down the road, there would be Jim or Bill Waldo dashing after them in a car, arguing, chaffing, exhorting until the pickers came streaming back, laughing and calling like so many children. At night mandolins and mouth-organs would set the air above the orchards quivering, and the singing and dancing and shouting would mount to bacchic heights.

'I wonder that any respectable girl will pack for Waldo,' one acid farmer's wife would comment to another. 'It's disgraceful the way they rush to get on in his shed, rather than come to a nice quiet place like ours. I don't know what girls are coming to.'

But the thoughts of girls have never notably turned to opportunities for quiet retirement. Cherry-picking meant men, young men, strange men with merry, sunburnt faces, and feet for dancing and money to spend. Would a girl with any life in her stay muffled up away from the jokes and music, the rude courtship and quick glances, the opportunities of revelry? To hell with the Church social or the Aunts' Union! Let them talk! October, November . . . the smell of ripening oats and ripening fruit, of orange blossom and briar rose, the beautiful, beautiful brim of the year; who would waste so precious a chance, to dull and dwindle in the small-farm round where fathers and brothers talked of the coating of sheep-troughs and new fertiliser? Never! A girl could earn money for herself packing cherries, money of her own, live a life of her own. The best 'facers' went to the big orchards.

It was as though the red bubbles swelling on the green boughs of the cherry trees were hope, and hope not only for the young, but something that even the oldest and most broken swag, crouched over his tiny fire on the empty plains, could feel like the spring weather warming the rheumatism out of joints stiff from poor food and cold camps. The pinched minds of the travellers expanded to the beckoning promise. There was not one of those hundreds making their way, singly, in groups, or in little families, along the road who had not innumerable plans ready for fulfilment the moment he or she could 'snatch some cherries.'

Darkie and his mate Jim, as they pedalled their bicycles sturdily against a gritty head wind, disputed the need of lights for the bicycles against the more dazzling prospect of laying in a stock of articles to hawk from door to door. The Dogger, Snake, Uncle and Angus had various views on the uses to which cherry-picking money could be put. The Scotsman and Dogger yearned to send to Sydney for pamphlets 'exposing' such institutions as the landed oligarchy, the steel combine, the sugar combine, the oil, tin, rubber and other assorted combines. Snake, that tall, fair, weedy youth, was wondering if he might not send home some money to his mother. She needed it badly enough. Uncle's hopes extended no higher than a pair of new boots, and, perhaps, a few shillings to carry him on. He was a singularly quiet and dignified old man, his quietness perhaps due to his association with Angus, but his dignity was an integral part of himself. From Orange came the Tyrells, quarrelling among themselves because Mrs. Tyrell wanted to stay in Orange and Dick wanted to go to Bathurst, where lived one of the several young ladies on whom he had set his heart. From the west, Miss Phipps and the busker, unknown to each other, were converging on Orion, Miss Phipps in the back of a bottle-oh's van, and the busker in the front seat of a comfortable sedan.

Through Wombat, Snow's brown van rolled patient and slow; Jimmy, Snow and the Stray walking behind it, because they had picked up a man and his wife whose feet were so broken and blistered that they could walk no farther. Beside the van waddled a lean old dog keeping a careful eye on Bluey. It was the dog who had prevented the footsore couple from getting a lift before. Car drivers looked askance at dogs who scratched their leather up-holstery; but: 'Buggered if we're goin' to leave old Joe at home, if we have to walk every inch of the way. Nine years he's been with us, and we won't ditch him now. Four times we've walked out of Sydney with not even a blanket, but we've never left old Joe.' The O'Briens had been going to Wagga, but Orion, forty miles out of their way, was the nearest dole-station. 'And anyway, we might get a married couple's job in Orion, if we don't get on picking.'

For them all—for the Tyrells, the O'Briens, for the Littles, for every one of those anonymous atoms drawing towards Orion—the hope was there, glad, courageous, singing above the anxiety and desperation that so miserably encompassed them. The promised land of plenty lay before, the golden bowl brimming to their lips. 'Why, a real good picker might make a pound a day and more!'

This fabulous wealth, if they could clutch only a moiety of it, was no fairy gold. It represented solid things like meat and shoe-leather, a new wheel for the van, drink, tobacco, tools or harness.

'If I got a job pickin',' the Stray asked anxiously of Snow, 'd'you think I'd make enough to get me teef?' For the money from the sale of Horehound had by this time dwindled to vanishing point.

'Enough teeth for you and a team of draughts,' Snow assured her magnificently, although an unskilled picker seldom made more than a few shillings a day.

Through the gentle October weather, that was by day mellow and by night a concourse of great stars, the wage-hungry horde of humanity swept down on Orion, scrutinising critically the laden boughs of the orchards, settling in side lanes and little plots of waste land, rubbing shoulders with other travellers, making friends, begging, finding water, gathering scraps of firewood, turning out the horse to feed, getting drunk, fighting and generally settling in to wait until the cherries should be ripe.

II

Among those who were heading towards Orion was a large, stout man in a big green car, an imposing and vigorous man. As he drove he hummed absent-mindedly under his breath, for he had a hard job ahead of him. His duty it was to convince all those hundreds of pickers that they could not touch a single cherry, that their best interests lay in turning their backs on Orion, penniless as they had come, and going somewhere, anywhere else. It rested with this large, stout personage, soon to become so important in the lives of all the travellers, to lay the Union taboo on every cherry within many miles of Orion, to blight not only the cherry crop, but all the pickers' hopes. Men have descended into the dens of raging lions, but they did not hum under their breath as did this astonishing man, Christopher Crane. With his mind full of leaflets and the hiring of a hall and meetings and plans for feeding strikers, with the snarling face of enmity, abuse and defeat confronting him, he hummed almost casually as he whirled his chariot of judgment upon the stiff-necked ranks of the orchardists.

His visit had come about through the sudden lizard-like awakening of a Court that all concerned had thought, if not dead, at least slumbering. A few months before, the Australian Workers' Union had decided to submit a log of claims to the Arbitration Court for cherry-picking at Orion. The growers, seeing in this only a political move, and taking legal opinion that the claim would not be heard before the cherry harvest, had allowed themselves to be lulled into a comfortable contempt. Imagine their anger and alarm when they found that not only was the case heard before the picking, but that the judge had ruled that the award in force for Mildura, where cherry-picking was carried on on a similar scale, would apply, and would apply then and there, that year! If the growers at Mildura could pay a minimum wage, the growers at Orion, the judge reasonably suggested, could do the same.

This sounded fair enough to everyone except the Orion orchardists. In vain did they argue that the judge's decision would mean one hundred per cent union labour where they had never engaged more than seventeen per cent; in vain did they plead the unfairness of paying by the week instead of the basket, especially of paying keep or extra money, when their labour was mostly itinerant, un-skilled, and almost unemployable. A basic wage of three pounds sixteen shillings for men, and two pounds ten and fourpence for women, was the verge of ruin. All the old happy-go-lucky hire-and-fire ways would be gone for ever. A powerful union was the last thing they wanted. Meet-ings of the growers vowed, with clenched fists and angry oaths, that they would never submit to anything as unfair as an award wage. Let the Union members insist on their award. They would employ only travellers and locals who were not unionists; and, what was more, every picker must sign a declaration that he was not a unionist and would not join the union while on the job. That would settle this (*adjectival*) union and its (*adjectival*) award. Since the award applied to unionists only, there would be no unionists for it to apply to.

Sympathy, however, need not be wasted on Christopher Crane, driving so stoutly towards the wasps'-nest that awaited him, a wasps'-nest of infuriated growers, incensed 'gun-pickers,' who under the old terms could have earned a pound a day, but who now found themselves on the level of the rank-and-file whose daily earnings were no more than a few shillings. Christopher Crane, in long years as the battling organiser of the Agrarian and Harvest Workers' Union, and then of the Australian Workers' Union, had emerged safely from more nasty situations than most men had ever entered. He had the kind of tough, rubbery, disposition from which crushing blows bounce back; and he would have echoed Mrs. Tyrell's inspired words that 'you can get used to anything,' the slings and arrows of outrageous fortune, and the no less frequent slings and arrows of outrageous human beings.

III

The regular pickers, sure of a job, sure of themselves, put up at boarding-houses and hotels. Some of them even paid their way instead of getting credit from the landlord until they went out to So-and-so's place as soon as he began 'spotting out.' But by far the most popular camp was, as usual, down by the show-ground, where water could be taken from the tanks behind the sheds. To camp by the river would have been more pleasant, but the river had long ago been fenced off into the back paddocks of the residents, and there was no more chance of camping there than in the vestibule of the Town Hall. There were from fifty to sixty camps around the show-ground, so that Snow after one glance declared for 'the Three-Mile, out the other side of the town.'

'At least we'll get a bit of feed for the horse,' he grunted, when the Stray complained against being marooned three miles away from the town. 'There's no chance of having it on our own. The Tyrells'll be there, and Gawd knows how many more.'

He indicated to the O'Briens that they could either come out to the Three-Mile or go their own way, and the couple decided to stay and camp on the show-ground.

'You been real good to us,' Mrs. O'Brien declared with voluble gratitude, 'but if we camp right near the town, we can look out for a job or a lift.'

Snow, who was glad to bid them farewell, wondered dimly why it was that he had always been able to travel unencumbered before, while now he seemed to be picking up lame dogs and lame human beings almost every step of the road. He decided that it must be the Stray's fault. The Stray liked company. She had a most welcoming way with her. She made strangers free of all his belongings; she royally invited persons, whom he would have greeted with a grunt, to a love feast, an exchange of life-stories, and even to meals. It was due to her city training. She had no nice reserves or caution. In fact, feeling herself secure and adopted, she was ready to be friends with all the world.

The hard asphalt was slippery smooth, and old Don lifted his feet carefully, feeling as uneasy and out of place as Snow felt under the hard, slippery looks of the towns-people on the footpaths. He and his horse would both be relieved to be on a dusty road once more between the fields. But with the Stray it was different. She liked to snuggle into layers of people as into warm blankets, nestling into the heat of humanity, the comforting reassurance of crowds. Snow could say this was good country, and it certainly looked greener than some she had jolted across; but sometimes the Stray felt that the landscape put on a thin sneer as real and frightful as if it had bared big, yellow, tobacco-stained teeth. Snow could talk till he was blue about apple-gums and ironbark and spotted gums, but all the trees for her had the same look, as though they had suicidally hurled themselves into the gulfs of air, and then despaired, clutching at nothing with dead, crooked boughs. Not that she put it like that. She only knew vaguely that they made her think of a man hanging himself; but the Stray's imagination was always morbid. If it had not been for the comforting presence of Snow and Jimmy, for the intermittent occurrence of towns at intervals of every twenty miles or so, she would have bolted back to the city long before.

The Three-Mile Camp was nothing to boast about—merely a stretch of mullock dumps beside the sandy bed of a tiny watercourse—but there was a dam for travelling stock, and that was the main thing: water. An unclosed patch of land where three farm fences met, about six acres of it, with a few trees and bushes and fairly good grass. What could you want more? The Stray's glance gloomily took in the usual dust-coloured tents and bicycles of the bagmen, and then lighted on the Tyrell van modestly sheltered by a group of trees. She brisked up at once. Friends! Companionship! This was better!

'Yo-ho!' she yelled, full of excitement, waving her hat, running across the grass, not waiting to help with the horse. 'Hey, Ma! Dick! Jake! How's things? Oh, look! the baby! Geeze, he's a fat little beggar!'

They had, of course, all come out to see who the new arrivals were, and there was the usual confusion of questions and answers, shrieks, laughter, barking of dogs, jingling of harness, and then the orderly routine of making camp, so pleasant, so busy and friendly. From a distance the single bagmen watched sideways, aloof, considering this hurly-burly of undesirables, these slatternly, screaming women and their sinister, thievish men, people with whom decent bagmen had nothing in common.

'Woman'—Mrs. Tyrell regarded the Stray critically—'you're looking as though the road agrees with you.' And truth to tell Dancy did look a little less like a damaged beetroot topped with straw. She had almost a trace of good looks.

'I told you, Dancy,' Thirty-Bob grinned. 'Once on the road, you're on it for life. And you die on it.'

'What's the chance of getting a bit of pickin'?' Snow turned to Thirty-Bob and Dick Tyrell.

'Well, Waldo will be starting next week, and I saw Bill Waldo, and it looks as though there might be a chance there, though most of the gun-pickers'll make for Waldo's. There's Hacker's . . .' Snow made a face of disgust. 'Yeah, Hacker's a cow, but he's startin' and that's more'n the others are yet. There's a few little places out on the North Road coming along. They'll be wanting pickers about the middle of the week.' Thirty-Bob seemed dubious. 'There's a chap telling me there's going to be a strike.'

'What's that?' Mrs. Tyrell had caught the ominous word. 'Who said anything about strikes?'

'Chap was tellin' me to-day, Ma. They're holdin' a meeting to-night in the Southern Cross Hall.'

Mrs. Tyrell turned on him lowering. 'Don't you let me hear anything about no strikes,' she threatened. 'Who wanted to leave Orange? And why? Gawd Almighty! because the pea-pickers were on strike! That's men all over. Never damn well satisfied till they've found a way of getting out of any work that may be about. Dragging me to Orion, and here's the cherry-pickers on strike!'

'Now hold your horses, Ma. There ain't no strike yet.'

271

'Don't talk to me. The laziest set of bums on the road. Oh, I know you, Thirty-Bob; if there wasn't a strike, you'd start one.' She turned to Dancy. 'There I was this mornin'' with all the baby's washing and all the kids' washing and all their own dirty shirts, and do you think I could get them to carry a drop of water from the dam? Told me to hang the clothes out and pray for rain! That's the kind they are.'

'It's always the same,' Dancy agreed. 'You'd think, to hear them talk, they was the lords of creation. But it's the women and kids does the getting of wood and water and goes out selling, while the men sits in the shade.' Dancy was getting a lot of satisfaction in the role of a care-worn family woman.

Snow and Thirty-Bob moved quietly away. 'Know if Angus's got here yet?' Snow asked.

'Angus's mob's out at the show-ground. Matter of fact, that's who told me.'

'I ought to see him,' Snow spoke doubtfully. Some of his fine enthusiasm for a Trackmen's Union had evaporated.

'If you want to see Burning, we could go in to the meeting to-night. He'll be there for cert.'

The thought of meeting Angus again held no pleasure for Snow. He had no successes to report. All the men whom he had sounded out concerning the formation of a Trackmen's Union had been discouraging, full of the difficulties, the almost insurmountable difficulties, in the way. It needed a less diffident man than Snow to give a lead. He had none of the Scotsman's burning, obsessing faith; none of the Dogger's stout-hearted humour. He knew only that life on the road was dreary and brutal, and that there must be some hope of making it less dreary and brutal, less that of criminals on parole, as constantly under the eye and the hectoring of the police as if they were within the four walls of a gaol.

'I dunno.' He roused himself from his abstraction to answer some question Thirty-Bob had put about the road through Wombat. 'Yeah! I think the road was pretty good. Yeah, I'll come in with you to this meeting. May as well see what it's about.'

That was exactly the attitude of all the other prospective pickers. They would be there, but they would withhold judgment until they found out the facts.

'Hey, Bob!' Dick Tyrell gave a low whistle. 'Take a look at that good sort.'

He had been gazing idly across the eroded red bed of the watercourse towards a little tin shanty, where Snow also had noticed small dark children playing round the door. But his was not the connoisseur's eye of Dick. It had been for that stalwart judge of female beauty first to behold the girl who issued from the door of the hut holding a small baby in her arms. She stood now, rocking the baby, and smiling negligently at nothing, in the way of pretty, young girls who feel themselves observed. She had a small brown face and great black eyes; coal-black, wavy hair that fell over her shoulders in curls; and a broad mouth that showed tiny, even white teeth. Her hair was that black that has white lights in it. Like the tail of a little foal, Dick thought poetically.

'Not bad,' Thirty-Bob agreed; but it was Jake who lifted up his voice in ownership.

'You lay off Mary Burns,' he threatened in his boy's voice that was half shrill and half gruff. 'She's my girl. I saw her first.'

'Ar, who the hell wants a gin?' Dick answered brutally, turning away. 'You can have her.'

Jake chuckled. He had a perverse, jeering manner to Dick that sometimes nearly drove his elder brother wild. 'Hah-hah,' he chanted. 'Curry-eater, curry-eater.' He danced away from the blow Dick aimed at him. 'Dick the curry-eater. Who went after Abdullah's girl in Dubbo?'

He took to his heels with Dick in pursuit, for the subject of Dick's courtship of the daughter of an Afghan hawker was still a sore one.

The girl across the creek watched the two brothers indulgently, then turned and strolled into the hut. She could

not have been more than fifteen, but the childishness of
her was one of her attractions. Her thin, lithe body and
long, thin, sinewy legs and arms were part of her aboriginal heritage, the beauty of bone that makes white flesh
seem uninteresting and feeble. Unlike many girls with a
strain of dark blood, she had tiny feet, and she was
exceedingly proud of them, showing them off in little,
bright, cheap shoes.

'There's another mob come and camped over the other
side of the reserve,' Mary called to her mother inside the hut.

Mrs. Burns looked up from cleansing a little of the
rubbish out of the fireplace. 'Don't you take any notice
of them travellers,' she said loftily. 'You don't want to
mix with a lot of riff-raff.'

'This business of "I seen her first",' Mrs. Tyrell despaired to Dancy. 'They play it all along the road. There
was one girl in Cowra used to ride past on a big horse, a
girl in a red jacket, and she'd wave her hand and smile.
They galloped the horses poor riding into town after her,
and they never found out where she come from.' She
smiled indulgently. 'I don't take no notice.' She turned
to more business-like considerations. 'You want to ask
that Mrs. Burns over in the hut if you can go up with her
to the farm-house and get some tank-water. She's in pretty
good with the people at the house. They give her eggs too
sometimes. And the dam-water's that mucky to drink,
what with the boys swimming in it and the dogs swimming
and the horses drinking. I always say they oughtn't to go
in it till I've got the water, but they don't take no notice.'

So the Stray and Mrs. Tyrell presently moved in a
dignified embassy towards the Burns' hut and sat by Jennie
Burns' fire and drank tea and conversed politely of the
hard struggle one had to live at all and the chances of the
picking and the lack of feed for horses.

'And all the men going to a meeting to see if they can't
strike,' Mrs. Tyrell flung out dramatically. 'Women, I
tell you they'd better just take me to the meeting. I'd
give them strike.'

'Well, my 'usband ain't going, anyway.' Mrs. Burns tightened her lips grimly and nodded as though she could prevent him. 'What do they want to strike *for*?'

'It's got me,' the Stray chimed in. 'Snow had just better let me catch him.'

Shortly after darkness fell, Snow and Thirty-Bob, Dick, Jake and even Deafy, who would not hear a word of the speaker's, were trotting off towards the town, two sulky-loads of them, leaving a rather disconsolate group of women and children talking in undertones round the fire.

Chapter XX

THE Southern Cross Hall was one of those shabby, weatherboard structures in a back street, left over from a bygone era before the Town Hall was built, and given over to visiting lecturers of the lesser breeds, meetings of Oddfellows and occasional dances. The windows were used on this, as on other occasions, for the exclusion of air; and the light of a few dim electric bulbs filtering through a drift of tobacco smoke invested the waiting men in a yellow ooze like half-melted butter. Although the meeting was so late in starting, there was little impatience. Half the audience was out on the footpath, talking and arguing, and the other half was inside, talking and arguing, while Mr. Christopher Crane hurried here and there in seemingly endless consultation with first one group, then another. Almost everyone had the same idea: to go to the organiser personally, and state their views, and hear from him privately what he intended to say at the meeting. So that it seemed probable that he would have to argue with most of the audience separately before he could argue with them collectively.

The greater number were young—boys in their teens or just out of them, loud-mouthed, cheerful and full of self-assertion and blasphemy. But it was almost pathetic to

275

see the half-defiant deference with which the organiser was treated. The men pressed forward to hear what he had to say, hanging round him in a thick cloud, those on the outskirts repeating to their mates who could not hear what he was telling them. It was Crane himself who first became impatient and began urging that the meeting should begin, so that, after more lengthy conference, Mr. Crane, his assistant-secretary, and the chairman who had been elected by a casual 'Oh, well, Barney'd better open up. Go on, Barney, you can have the job,' finally climbed the low wooden platform and lowered themselves cautiously on to three rickety cane-bottom chairs.

Word having passed to those outside that the meeting was about to begin, they presently filtered in and squeezed into the back benches or stood round the walls. There was throughout a constant coming and going, a whispering and murmuring that would have daunted a speaker less accustomed to the ways of such gatherings. Nor were interruptions infrequent. Every man felt he had a right to give his views, and although on the whole the meeting was orderly enough it stirred and hummed like a hive of energetic and restive wasps.

'Order! Order!' the chairman intoned. He was a stocky young man with a thick bruiser's face but he took himself very gravely, with that dignity so many working men will show when they are following the procedure of Labour meetings. 'I have the pleasure to introduce to you to-night a man most of you fellow-workers know, Chris Crane of the A.W.U. He's going to give us the low-down about the new award and I'd ask you all to give him a fair hearing and ask questions afterwards. Mr. Crane.'

With which he sat down abruptly. There seemed to be a feeling among one section of the audience that they should applaud, but, all being too eager to hear what the organiser had to say, it came to nothing more than a tentative rustle. The big figure of Mr. Crane loomed up through the smoke like a mountain peak, and the tense, anxious silence that fell was more of a tribute than any applause. In that silence the organiser took off his glasses, wiped them, and advanced to the edge of the platform.

'Friends and fellow-workers,' he boomed, 'there's been a lot of rumour going round about a *strike*. I'm here firstly to tell you that there's not going to be a *strike*. What's more, I don't want to hear one of you use the word *strike*. That's a word the bosses in the Orchardists' Association have been using for their own ends, when they know very well that there isn't any need, any possibility, any least chance of such a thing.' He paused impressively. 'I'm here to-night to outline the awards and conditions that have been legally won for you before the Arbitration Court, and which come into force in Orion as soon as the picking starts. It's for you, fellow-workers, to see that those awards and conditions are maintained. We may have a bit of trouble with the cherry-cockies wanting to *break down* those awards and conditions'—again he paused impressively—'but, as I've said before, we don't need to *strike* to get them. We've got them already, and any farmer that doesn't like to observe them is putting himself in the wrong.'

He launched into a long harangue that took in the general situation of the fruit industry, the circumstances leading up to the application for an award, the way in which the Court had acted, and finally he reviewed in detail the clauses of the award. The men leant forward, row after row of intent, brown faces, fastening him with hard eyes that had lost everything except judgment. They were weighing, not only their own chances of obtaining the conditions laid down in the document which the organiser flourished, but they were also weighing the organiser. Would he be strong enough to oppose the united strength of the orchardists? They knew what they were up against, and the organiser knew. His words were brisk enough, but how did he really feel about it? Not by a tremor, not by a shade of uncertainty, did he crack that confident face he was putting on the business.

His assistant, a slight, studious youth with a shrill voice, had the same certainty. From the platform it poured down on them in words, gestures, looks, references to the past history of the Union, their unbeatable strength if they stood together. 'That's the trouble, they won't,' from one interjector, and cries of 'Order.' Let them only unite against any move on the part of the orchardists to beat down, to undermine this award, and after this crucial first year the terms would be established and the employers would have no other course but to keep to them. It was by insisting on the letter of the award during this cherry-harvest that they could make all the difference in the years to come.

'Of course, there's always little men trying to wriggle out of paying their pickers their just dues, there's always mean bosses ready to take advantage of their men; but I say, fellow-workers, that we've only got to stand firm ['How long's it since you did a day's pickin'?' from some malcontent] and let the cockies go against the law if they want to . . .'

There was a lot more of it, and the audience began to stir and hum. Finally, the organiser, wiping his brow where the perspiration was gleaming in a dew, retired, hung his coat over a chair, and prepared to answer questions. The meeting was settling down to business, and until the more voluble had talked themselves out and brought up every possible objection, the majority would sit solid and undecided. But there was a certain encouragement in that they still sat. Few had walked out; fewer still had interjected. It looked as if so far the organiser had the support of his audience.

'Haven't I seen that cove somewhere before?' he murmured to his assistant, as he leant back and surveyed the first speaker.

'Isn't he the Scotch chap who was keen on starting a special union for professional hoboes?'

The light of recognition gleamed behind Mr. Crane's glasses. He nodded. 'Just so, Brian, just so. I remember now.' He eyed the figure of the Scotsman shrewdly. 'I told him he'd Buckley's chance.'

'The Australian Workers' Union,' the speaker was declaring with a nasty rasp in his voice, 'has got suckers on the sole of its feet. The whole Australian Labour Movement is lousy with big, fat parasites who make a good thing out of warming a seat in Parliament or driving round in a big sedan collectin' the dues of a lot of mugs.' There was an angry murmur. 'We're asked to stand firm and united, and quite right too, when it's a matter of walking off a job and standing by the Union; but what I want to know is just how much the A.W.U. is going to stand by us when we do it?' Burning Angus swung round on his audience. 'You all know what'll happen. It's all very well to talk about the orchardists taking the responsibility if they don't pay the award. But the orchardists aren't going to be camped by the road without tucker or boots.' He swung towards the organiser again. 'I'm talking for the bagmen, men that have tramped hundreds of miles, jumped the rattler and risked a broken neck to get here. What's the A.W.U. ever done or ever intended to do for those coves? They're all right while they've got work. You'll come along and collect their dues; but when they haven't got a job they're just tramps and hoboes, and no damn good to anyone. Does the Union that tells them not to take a job ever try to stop the police hounding them when they haven't got one? My bloody oath it doesn't. The weakness of the whole Labour Movement is that it only concerns itself with the man in a job. Oh yes, I know'—the organiser had tried to get in a word— 'You're going to tell us about this conference and that conference that passed resolutions calling for better treatment for the unemployed. And a fat lot of good that's been. What the men on the track want is not a lot of big bugs in Sydney spending their dues, but a real union that'll get up and fight for them.'

The organiser was on his feet as soon as he saw his opening. His whole style changed. 'You talk about fighting! What is the Union doing now?' he demanded. 'Fighting for better wages and conditions. Here!' He flourished the award at them. 'Right here is your proof that the A.W.U.'s alive and fighting, and only asking your backing to get more. Our friend here has asked if the Union is going to stand by you.' He drew himself up. 'The Union will support any steps you take to secure the award's working, and will see that you don't go hungry. I can promise you that. And as for that car our friend here mentioned, with a big fat parasite in it' (good-natured applause), 'I've tramped the track and I've jumped the rattler, and the reason I'm not doing it still is that when on your Union business it's a lot slower. The car helps me to cover more territory. I agree with the speaker that the men out of a job ought to have a stronger backing than they have at present. But I ask you to consider the difficulties when those out of a job are drifting up and down the country six hundred miles apart. We've got to do the best we can the best way we know how. And I'd like to remind the speaker that I'm not God Almighty.'

To himself the organiser was saying: 'I must get hold of that Scotty. He swings a lot of weight with these chaps.'

Snow was aware that Thirty-Bob had been signalling to him, twisting his face in an alarming and ferocious fashion, that was meant as an enquiry if Snow was coming out. Dick Tyrell was already shouldering his way towards the door. Snow hesitated. He wanted to see Angus, but he also had a thirst.

They doubled round the corner and filed cautiously through the back entrance of a small hotel and so into the bar.

'No use staying,' Thirty-Bob explained, soulfully gazing into the depths of his beer. 'You ought to know by now that it'll be only Berghoffs this first week, and who the hell wants to pick Berghoffs anyway? Long, tough stalks and little, miserable cherries. Why, a packer'll tell you that thirty-two cases of Berghoffs average sixty cases of Early Lyons. You don't make tucker on Berghoffs. Wait till the good cherries begin to come in. Let's have another. All that bloody talk made me dry.' The Tyrell team had been working in Orange and had not yet dissipated all its earnings.

'I dunno,' Snow said slowly, thinking of Angus. 'Sometimes I wish I could talk.' He looked down at his big hands as though he expected them to speak for him—big knobbly fists, calloused and cracked. He sighed. 'If I had a bit of an education like Angus.' He smote his heavy fist on the table-top.

Angus had stayed behind to have a word with Crane. 'This will end,' he predicted gloomily, 'in our chaps getting the thin end of the stick.'

'Then I take it you're willing to pick for less than the award?'

'Me!' The Scotsman drew himself up indignantly. 'You're talking to the secretary of the Bagmen's Union with a membership of forty-three, and not one of them a scab. If you're going to make a fight of it, we're right behind ye.'

The organiser wrung his hand. 'Good on you, Angus. I meant to ask about the Bagmen's Union.' Until that moment he had not known it existed. 'You got it going, eh?'

'Oh, aye, it's going.' Burning Angus could not keep a note of pride out of his voice. 'And before we're done it's going to be the real militants' union, a battling union.'

'Well; there's one thing,' the organiser said hurriedly. He wanted to keep on the right side of Angus, but he knew the temper of Angus's men. 'Keep your chaps out of trouble with the police. We don't want any unnecessary martyrs going to gaol for bashing coppers or setting sheds on fire. That's the worst kind of publicity. The thing is to keep the men in their camps away from the town and the pubs.'

'There's no such thing as an unnecessary martyr,' Angus contended. 'But ye're right about keeping the chaps away from the pubs. None of our bunch'll start anything. I can promise ye that.'

'Good.' The organiser took a hasty farewell. 'I'll depend on you.'

Angus watched him go grimly. He was suspicious of this A.W.U. organiser, but he knew that Crane was right. Men would fight from sheer boredom, and there is nothing more boring than waiting for the other side to give in. Besides, in Orion there had always been a strong hostility between the 'locals'—men who lived and worked in the district, many of them related to the farmers—and the itinerant pickers who came to Orion merely to 'make a cheque.' Nothing much in the way of loyalty to a union could be expected from most of the 'locals,' who, if not related to their employers, were dependent on them for work all the year round. But the picking could only partly be done by local labour. If the bagmen refused to pick at less than the award wage, the growers must give in finally. At least, that was the accepted argument; but as Burning Angus and his mates made their way around the corner to the hotel, he pointed out bitterly how many surprises might crop up.

'They'll start bringing men over by the lorry from Orange,' he said angrily, 'if all else fails.' He cast a stern, enquiring eye over his loyal adherents, Snake, Dogger, Uncle, Dark and Jim, who were forging forward, as by common consent, towards the hotel's back entrance. 'We ought to get straight back to camp,' he announced.

'But you wanted to see Snow Grimshaw. This is where he'll be.'

Angus allowed the argument was valid. 'I don't suppose it matters just to-night,' he said doubtfully, but his team had already pushed their way into the bar.

With all the doors and windows shut, so that no light might show that the liquor laws were being broken, the bar was stuffier than the hall they had just left. It reeked of stale beer and tobacco, sweaty flannel and unwashed socks. The barman was having a hard job to keep the noise down to a murmur that could not be heard in the street; and every now and then the landlord, looking nervous, would hold a hurried conference with him on the advisability of turning away the custom that came none too quietly pushing down the back entry. He was urging them to finish their drink and go, but the men were in no hurry. They wanted to talk over the meeting, and now and then a loud voice would be raised, to be immediately hushed by the barman's urgent command for quiet. The men from the meeting crowded up one end of the bar away from the regular customers, who eyed them askance and exchanged remarks under their breath that were accompanied by scowls and hostile side-glances.

'Hey, Snow!' Angus beckoned from the doorway, and Snow lounged over. 'Come outside a minute.'

'Have a drink?' Snow offered, but Angus was already leading him into the darkness of the yard. He had much to talk about, and he wanted no eavesdroppers.

Angus's mates joined Thirty-Bob and Dick Tyrell, and were yarning about where they had been since leaving Logan.

'And talking about Logan!' Thirty-Bob gripped Dick's arm. 'Look who's just come in.'

Dick followed the direction of Thirty-Bob's eyes and started up.

'He's mine, Bob.'

'He's mine, Dick. I saw him first.'

Through the door Sam Little had thrust his way, followed by a group with whom he was talking and laughing. He took no notice of the barman's warning to lower his voice. He looked even bulkier and more formidable than when Dick, by a chance blow, had knocked him out in Logan.

'He's mine, Dick.' Thirty-Bob repeated in a low voice. Angus's mates exchanged glances as Thirty-Bob got up and went over to the bar. 'Well, if it ain't me old pal, Sam Little!' he exclaimed, leering up at Sam. 'Come to do a little pickin'?'

'Don't know you,' Sam frowned. He turned his back on Thirty-Bob deliberately.

'Come to support the union in its fight for the new award,' Thirty-Bob went on. 'Ain't you, Sam, old pal?'

'That's what I think of your union, and that's what I think of you,' Sam illustrated offensively. 'Now hook it.'

'Here!' The barman had leapt the counter. He knew danger signals when he saw them. 'Get out of here. Come on, both of you. Out of this.'

But he was too late. Thirty-Bob, with great deliberation, had slung his beer in Sam's face, mug and all, and Sam with a roar responded by hitting Thirty-Bob over the head with a chair. Thirty-Bob came up again and leapt at him. He was not a pleasant fighter, Thirty-Bob. He fought like a cat, with his feet, teeth—anything that came handy. The barman flung himself into the fray, and some of Sam Little's pals helped.

They tumbled out into the passage and through the hall, the barman swearing and struggling to get them out. Behind them poured the excited throng from the bar, ready to form a ring as the battle joined in the back alley. Dick Tyrell had fallen upon one of Sam's mates who was endeavouring to kick Thirty-Bob's ribs in, while Sam knelt on him and smashed his face with his fists. Angus's mates came to the assistance of Dick, who was being over-powered; and in the dark, jumbled alley there was a sudden, savage free-for-all battle that presently resolved itself into Union *versus* Independents.

On the outskirts there was an uproar of wildly excited men offering a fight or not waiting for an invitation.

'Come on. I'll take on the whole bloody lot of you's.'

'He was right to hit the bastard.'

'Who said he was? The A.W.U. is a . . . '

'Take a man's job, you mongrel, would you? Take that!'

The unionists were in a minority, and things might have gone badly with them, if it had not been for a yell of: 'Coppers, boys!' and at that call the fighters broke and

284

ran, union and non-union, stumbling and cursing; Dick
with Thirty-Bob's arm flung across his shoulder, Snow
supporting the Dogger, who had a cut over his eye.

In the rear came Burning Angus raging. 'A fine mob
you are! Take me eyes off ye for two minutes and you
try to cook the whole show.' It was he who had raised
the false alarm of police. It served its purpose in giving
the combatants time to collect their wits and cool down.

'Arr,' Thirty-Bob flung at Burning Angus, as he danced
round spluttering reproaches, 'what the hell! A man's
got to have a bit of fun sometimes, hasn't he?'

'Fun? D'ye call it fun?'

'It was good while it lasted,' Thirty-Bob grinned. 'It'll
teach them Littles to pick on us, eh, Dick?' He tenderly
felt his bruised face. 'Me girlish beauty's done for,' he
murmured.

Chapter XXI

I

Jabez Hacker had one of those hard, angular natures
that fitted his name like a plug of dynamite in a rock.
It was his pride to consider himself a strong, hard man.
He had a reputation for cunning, unscrupulous determination that made him disliked as well as feared. He was the
acknowledged leader of the Orchardists' Association, and
when he opened his thin rat-trap of a mouth to voice its
policy, there was seldom any opposition. What Jabez
knew to be to his advantage was usually to the advantage
of the rest of the big growers who dominated the Association. He had issued an edict that year forbidding any
grower to 'face' cherries, because he himself saw no profit
in wasting money and time placing a neat layer of cherries
on the bottom of every box. He had enough cherries to
'dump,' and he was going to dump them.

The small growers who wanted to 'face' cherries would be forbidden to use the Association's trucks and generally hounded for the pariahs they were in Hacker's opinion. It was that way with many things in Orion. Jabez Hacker told the big growers what he was going to do, and they agreed. He hated Vladimir Waldo because Waldo was the one man, fat, wheezy and fantastic, who was too big to be affected in any way by Hacker or anything Hacker might do.

Jabez was also at loggerheads with the local police sergeant, and the fight behind the hotel gave him just the opportunity he was wanting to bail up the sergeant the following Saturday and point out to him that a lawless rabble was trying to run the town, and he, the sergeant, would be failing in his duty if he didn't bring them to heel. Why should Orion be over-run with ugly, drunken tramps who refused to work? Jabez spoke significantly of the last sergeant who had followed a policy of 'clearing off the scum,' which meant that anyone who after a week in Orion had no work, either left the town or went to gaol.

'Why, last year I couldn't get pickers for love or money, and there were men, unemployed, working on a relief job right beside my property! I offered them work and they refused it. Refused it! Said they would have too much trouble getting back their relief again, and they couldn't make enough to support their families picking. This relief work ought to be cut out. Stop a lot of this unrest. What the hell do they want? I've paid two-and-six a basket for the last ten years, and I'm damned if I'll give three shillings to any man living.'

The sergeant listened quietly. He knew that Hacker had already told all his friends that 'the sergeant was as weak as dish-water' and secretly in sympathy with the pickers. Well, if it came to that, he did sympathize with the pickers. He had not always been a sergeant, and he had two brothers who were not in the police force. One of them was droving in Queensland, God alone knew where; and the other was breaking his heart and his back on a dried-up patch of stubble and scrub that he thought was a farm. Like many another broken 'wheat cocky,' the sergeant's brother Jim might be packing his kids and wife into his old truck any time now, moving off on the roads, looking for work. As the sergeant strolled majestically down the main street, he often thought that it must be hard on the wives and children of these slouching, hard-faced men. It would be hard on the sergeant's brother Jim, if he was trying 'to make a crust' picking.

'I know how you feel, Mr. Hacker,' he said at length. 'It's cruel to see money ripening on the trees with no one to pick it off for you. But I can't make these chaps pick for you. If they break the law, I'll see to it. But I can't drive them to work.'

He knew that this would be used against him, and he was troubled. Hacker was already rubbing in the fact that a fight had taken place without his knowledge. The sergeant knew Hacker was a powerful man. He would have to tighten things, whether he liked it or not. The first thing would be to clean up all the hotels and stop their trading after hours. Then, he supposed, he had better refuse dole to the pickers down at the show-ground. The Union was feeding ninety men there already—men who had no dole. He felt a spasm of anger against Hacker. It was all very well for Hacker to tell him what to do!

Fresh from his encounter, and furious over the sergeant's recalcitrant tone, Hacker joined a little group of farmers on the street corner. 'He's a Red,' he growled— 'nothing but a damn Red.'

'How about getting pickers over from Orange?' one of his friends enquired.

Hacker hesitated. He remembered vividly one occasion when his orchard had been declared black and several loads of strikebreakers had been set on and battered by infuriated pickers whom he had sacked. 'Yes,' he said, but not in his usual confident tone, 'we might have to come to that.'

At this point in the conversation a stout figure came

waddling along the footpath, to be greeted by the group of farmers with a mixture of deference and jocularity, depending on their financial status.

'Morning, Mr. Waldo.'

'Morning, Vladimir. How's the boy?'

'No cherries this year, Waldo. They'll rot on the trees with the first rain.'

Vladimir Waldo might have been one of his own pickers. He wore a dirty, baggy old pair of trousers, below which his disreputable sandshoes bulged, with a cut in the toe for his bunion. Around his neck, instead of a collar, was a red cotton handkerchief with white spots.

'You,' Vladimir Waldo chuckled, slapping Hacker heavily on the back. 'You big men, huh? Mek noise like little puppydogs? Me, I laugh to damn bloody hell!' He patted himself on the chest approvingly. 'I tell you, these chaps, they jus' little schildrens.'

'That's all very well, but you can't get any pickers.'

The district problem gave a wheeze that sounded like an old mattress taking a weight of twenty stone. 'Ho-ho, I have no troubles. I rejoice.' He threw his arms wide. 'I roast an ox!'

His neighbour and antagonist Hacker fell back in dismay. Trouble and disappointment had plainly turned Waldo's brain. Then, suspiciously, he came close enough to smell the magnate's breath.

'Roast an ox? Good God! what for?'

'For my pickers.' The old man chuckled. 'Good boys. Loyal. They fight a little, they sing a little. Just schildrens. They will like a bullock roasted, I think.' He nodded good-day and waddled off, still very pleased with himself.

Waldo and the ox he was going to roast had, before the day was out, become the topic of the moment, some asserting that he was crazy, others that this was another example of his superhuman cunning. By next year the growers would have fought the award in the courts and obtained some kind of a compromise. But this season they must not only refuse the extra money, but get their crops

288

off the trees. The news spread and spread. Confidence among the orchardists revived. So Waldo wasn't having any trouble with his pickers, after all. Waldo had a bumper crop, and was going to hold a dance and ox-roasting the following Saturday as a celebration.

'A lot of bolony,' the good unionists scoffed, as they rolled their swags, preparing to depart for other districts.

'I haven't seen an ox roasted since I was a kid,' one youth exclaimed to another. 'Gee! it'd be a lark to get on at old Waldo's place for the next week just to see it. Needn't do much work,' he hastened to add. 'We could just go up and ask if they was wanting any pickers.'

There was always the virtuous thought that working for Waldo would be collecting evidence for the Union that he was breaking the award. How was the Union to issue prosecutions against growers without evidence? There was a strange rush to collect evidence at Waldo's orchards.

II

In his own camp Snow was facing mutiny.

'True, I ain't breaking no award,' the Stray pleaded. 'I on'y want some money to get me set of teef.' She had found herself a job 'facing' cherries for a small farmer, one of the few who was paying the three shillings a basket, because he wanted to get his cherries to market early and reap bumper prices before the big men began to dump their crop. 'Look, Snow, there ain't anything about "facing" in the award,' the Stray triumphed.

Snow dubiously turned over the pages of the grubby copy of the new award. There was certainly nothing in it about 'facers.'

'All right,' he said at length. 'You can go on working until I see Crane. I'm going to see him first thing when he comes back from Orange. I still think a man ought to belt the hide off you.' But he was impressed by the fact that the farmer was paying three shillings for picking.

'I'll chuck it now if you like,' the Stray offered humbly.

Snow was regarding her with a chilly doubt that suggested she had sunk back in his esteem to that place she had first occupied when he found her burgling his tucker-box.

Did he think she liked standing from six o'clock in the morning until six o'clock at night on a concrete floor, until her feet swelled and her ankles swelled and she could hardly move? Several times already she had been on the point of just quitting in sheer weariness, but before her shone the vision of those pearly teeth that would make her so attractive to Snow.

It was just on sunrise when the Stray limped off every morning, a small, lonely figure, with a blackened billy-can for her tea in one hand, and a parcel of bread in the other. To reach the packing-shed she had a mile walk across the loose dirt of apple and cherry orchards, and at dusk she came trudging wearily back.

It seemed to be the Stray's fate always to be employed by people who wanted the most work for the least money, and her employers considered a mid-day break of a quarter of an hour quite sufficient. They had a new motor-truck to pay for, and they were going to pay for it out of this cherry cheque, or know the reason why. If it had not been that 'facers' were so hard to get, they would never have taken on an unskilled girl, and they were constantly talking of the marvellous 'facer' they had last year, who thought nothing of seventy cases a day. The Stray, working furiously, could never do more than thirty cases of these small early cherries that were so hard to handle, and at twopence a case, she was lucky to make five shillings a day. However, she cheered herself with the thought that, if she learned to 'face' skilfully, she might get a better job next year. But the thought of next year was something from which she turned away. To think of to-morrow was bad enough.

After five days of it, the Stray was profoundly relieved to see Christopher Crane whirling by, as she trudged back to the camp. She halloed him, and he slowed down.

'Oh, mister,' she asked fervently, 'do the "facers" have to come out?'

'What're you getting?'

'Tuppence a case.'

'Certainly. One of the worst-sweated jobs in the industry. Tuppence a case! Good God!'

'There was nothin' about it in that paper you gave Snowy.'

'"Facin'"' comes under packing.'

'Hooray! I'll stop right now. Gee! if I didn't come out on strike'—the Stray heaved a sigh of relief—'I'd a come home in a ambulance.'

'Tell Snow I've got to go back to Sydney, and that Angus will be at the show-ground if anything crops up.' A frown creased Christopher Crane's forehead. 'I don't like going, but it can't be helped. I've done all I can, and now it's up to the men themselves.'

He had had interview after interview with the officials of the Orchardists' Association. He had addressed the men; he had already more than twenty prosecutions against growers who were under-paying their pickers. Now, as he said, it was up to the men. A week, two weeks, would see the matter settled. Meantime, he must go on. He had too much work to do—work enough for six men—to remain longer in Orion.

The Stray was immensely flattered to be the bearer of a message from the organiser. 'I'll tell Snow,' she promised. 'Him and Thirty-Bob's gone to look for some peas to pick.'

With a wave Mr. Crane whirled away, and was seen no more in Orion that season. He had, as he said, done his best, and so far most of the men were holding out. The really good pickers had mostly rolled their swags and gone over to Orange, but others remained trying to get odd jobs, or, like Thirty-Bob, were out picking peas.

Thirty-Bob, if he had no native talent for keeping a job, could always find one for others. He had discovered several patches of peas, and each time came back with glowing reports of their quality and what his team could earn picking them. At first the Tyrell family turned out in force jubilantly, but it soon dawned on them that the peas around Orion were all in the same state—stunted, stricken, and almost worthless. The growls and ingratitude that assailed Thirty-Bob whenever he found another farmer with peas that needed picking were, as he said himself, 'something fierce.' No one thanked him for the opportunity of labouring all day in the burning sun, while the flies crawled maddeningly into nose, mouth and eyes. Stooping over the low pea-bushes made a man feel as though his back was broken. Picking peas was bad enough when there was a good crop to pick, but when the crop was light, a man couldn't 'make tucker'; he only 'knocked himself up for nothing.' Not even an occasional clod of earth stowed in the middle of a sack, or a few hefty paddy-melons, could make the toil profitable.

In the end it was usually Thirty-Bob and Snow who went off in the sulky, with perhaps a few of the children. Children, being closer to the pea-bushes and having small, nimble fingers, did not find the work so back-breaking.

It was with Dick that the real trouble in Snow's camp began. For the moment Dick was occupied training a greyhound he had received as part payment of a private deal, and tagging after Mary Burns in a way that enraged his brother Jake. Jake could not understand Dick's lack of etiquette. He should have accepted the convention that since Jake saw Mary first, she was his property to court undisturbed. But Dick had disobeyed the rules in a most unsporting manner, and he was making enormous strides in Mary's favour. Mrs. Tyrell, who hated 'dark blood' as she hated snakes, and with the same unreason, was already hinting that the time had come to shift camp.

'I like chaps with fair hair and blue eyes,' Mary had stated quite openly, flickering her black lashes in Dick's direction.

The Burns family ranged in complexion from light buff to dark tan, and they were all bitterly conscious of the pigment in their skins. Mary's mother had been a nurse during the first world war; a big, hearty creature with a loud laugh and the gipsy colouring. In a convalescent hospital in Kent she had met an Australian, whom his mates nicknamed 'Dark,' as they nicknamed so many swarthy men. He had promised, when they married, to take her home to his lizard farm; lizard skins, as he told her, bringing a pound each on the world market. The war ended and she had insisted on coming back with him to Australia.

Joe Burns was a good husband, and they had started a small greengrocery run, doing well for a time. When she realised that there was a difference in Australia between her kind of people and her husband's, Jennie Burns had held her head high and made the best of it. Hard times and high prices drove them out of business and on to the track, but Jennie, with an increasing tribe of children in assorted shades, still accepted things as they came.

'Of course, it isn't what I expected,' she admitted. 'But then I knew Orstrylia 'ud be different from 'ome.' In many ways life in a half-caste camp was not so dissimilar from the picture of Australian life drawn by her English relatives long ago. 'A better 'usband than Joe you could not meet,' she declared sturdily—'drunk or sober.'

But though Mrs. Burns tranquilly refused to notice such trifles as a colour bar, her children felt it sorely.

'Me, I'm going to marry a man with fair hair and blue eyes,' Mary had boasted when she was a little girl.

'Me, too,' her small sister Frances had chimed in. 'Then the other kids won't be able to say: "Go away, you dirty nigger." They'll have to play with us then, won't they?'

Mrs. Tyrell did not mind her younger children playing with the Burns children, but she hated the way Dick would lounge over to take Mary to the pictures, or just to take her walking, and she spoke acidly of Mrs. Burns's lack of care of her daughter. But Jennie Burns took Mary's flirtations with the same equable temper as she took Joe's occasional drinking.

293

'What can you expect with a life like this?' she would say. 'It ain't much for a girl.' But what other life was there for her?

Anyway, if Mary couldn't look after herself, that was just too bad. Mary was certain enough that she could. She parried Dick's clumsy attempts at love-making with a laugh. 'Why don't you do some picking?' She would tease, when Dick had no money to take her to the pictures. 'I'm working at Waldo's, and you could come and pick with me any day. You don't have to stay, do you?'

Dick only mumbled something about the others wouldn't like it.

'Why worry about them? They don't own you, do they? Why, I'm making as much as a man meself, and you could earn a pound a day, I bet—a good picker like you. Why, you'd gun the paddock!' She gazed at him admiringly. 'I bet you're as strong as a horse. We could pick together all day.'

For a time the thought of Snow and Thirty-Bob made Dick hesitate at such a tempting offer. After all, Snow and Thirty-Bob couldn't stop him. And as for his father and mother—Dick gave his head an impatient shake. He had never taken any notice of them. The thought of what Thirty-Bob would say weighed more than anything else. Thirty-Bob had a wicked tongue, and Thirty-Bob was his mate.

'I'll think it over,' he mumbled.

Next day, by ill chance, Thirty-Bob, Deafy and Snow went off to camp beside the pea-picking job they had found, taking Jimmy and Jake with them. It was too far to come back to the camp every night. They could have taken the Stray, but she was sick. Her head swam and she could not stand up.

'I'll look after you, woman,' Mrs. Tyrell promised maternally. 'You just lie in the tent and have a rest. You've fair knocked yourself up.'

'I don't like going.' Snow was uneasy. 'But a man's got to make a crust.'

The departure of the men left Dick, who had refused to go with them, bored and ready for anything. Mary had been talking of this ox-roasting that Waldo was giving for his pickers.

'If you was picking with me,' Mary suggested, 'we could go together.'

There wouldn't be any harm in getting a job at Waldo's until after this feast. It would be fun. Dick's slow blood lit at the thought of escorting Mary. There would be dancing. A chap had to have some good times, and there was something about Mary that hit him hard. He despised her at the same time that he wanted to be near her; to touch her, to put his arm about her, seemed the most desirable thing in the world. She was like a fever as unexplainable and sudden as that which had smitten the Stray.

When Mrs. Tyrell came to see if she wanted anything, the Stray saw from the old woman's face that something was wrong. 'What's up, Ma?' she asked weakly.

'It's Dick, Dancy. He's gone off to get a job picking at Waldo's. It's that girl,' Mrs. Tyrell declared bitterly. 'He'd never a done it but for her.'

'I thought you was against this strike,' the Stray said after a minute's silence.

'Dick oughtn't to go against his own people, Dancy. I don't see what good the strike's going to do; but if Alf and Thirty-Bob and Snow stay out, Dick ain't got no right to pick.' She shook her head dejectedly. 'I never thought no son of mine would turn on us like this. Wait till his father hears about it.'

But if Mrs. Tyrell could not get anything more out of Dick than an angry scowl, there was little likelihood that his father would be more successful.

'Twenty years,' Mrs. Tyrell ruminated, 'I been travellin' the track. I brought my children up to be decent. Leastways, I tried. We've had our troubles, but I've kept them together, and married off the two eldest girls decent to decent men in towns who could keep a roof over their heads. I wouldn't mind Dick takin' up with a girl who wasn't travellin'. But to take up with a girl whose folk travel, and not only that . . . *dark* into the bargain! It's just the limit!'

She pushed the streaks of greying hair wearily away from her weatherbeaten face. 'What's the use of life, anyway? You work and work, you slave to bring up children, and they shame you. It ain't no use at all, I tell you . . . livin'.' She pressed Dancy's hand. 'You get off the track, woman. Snow's a good man, and I guess you wouldn't have come on the track again except for him, would you?' Her voice was gentle; she was holding one of the Stray's small, hot paws in her own big, work-hardened hand. 'And you're a good girl. I've watched you with young Jimmy. You make Snow localise somewhere and give you a home. You're worth it.'

'Oh, Ma'—the Stray turned her head wearily—'what's the use of talking?'

She gazed out of the tent door listlessly, as though she saw her life unrolling before her until she was old and grey like Ma Tyrell. She knew Snow better now. Under his look of a quiet yokel something smouldered—something bitter and compelling and dangerous. In his own groping way he was out on a search to which this Union of his was but the clue. He was looking for something bigger than a comfortable life or work to do; he was driven on by that burning discontent, on and on; sometimes he did not know why; sometimes he thought it was to leave old wrongs behind or find a new justice and freedom; but the Stray knew that the discontent in his blood would never let him rest now, would never be purged into peace until death once and for all laid Snow's long bones in some dusty town for ever.

'There's times,' she said simply, 'when I wish I was dead.' That would be one way out of everything. Snow wouldn't really mind. He might miss her a little, but he was solitary by nature, and he had Jimmy. Jimmy would miss her more. She could not bear the thought of what lay ahead of her.

'Oh, woman!' Mrs. Tyrell was deeply shocked. 'You mustn't say that. It's my fault for talking like a fool.' At once she reverted to her practical, busy self. 'You wait a bit and I'll bring you a cup of tea. You're sick, that's what it is.'

The Stray lay thinking, her eyes shut to shield them from the bright light. She smote wearily at the tormenting flies. Some day, she thought, oh, some day, if they could only come over the brow of a hill, she and Snow, and know that the town below was their own town, and their camp that night a house of their own. Towards dusk it would be, and the smoke drifting up into the cool air from cottage chimneys, and the green fields going down into the folded hills like a green blanket wrapping the town from the twilight. Red roofs and little gardens and orchards shining under the last fading of the clear sky, and a hut waiting for them, if it was only broken weatherboard with the wind living in the cracks, and a patch of ground to grow feed for a cow and a few chickens, and a door to the house to shut out the darkness and the cold regard of the stars. Two tears of misery forced themselves under her hot eyelids. Never, never—Snow would never settle down. Oh, if she could only make him!

'I will, I will,' she muttered. 'I'll make him settle down, right here in Orion, damned if I don't.' She lay there concentrating on Snow, willing him to stay in Orion, not to go on.

Mrs. Tyrell was pressing her bulk into the tiny tent. 'And here's some tea for you, woman.' Her voice was kind. 'You sit up and drink it. I'm sorry I spoke like I did. After all, where would I be but for Tom? Where would any woman be but for her man? What sort of wife would stay behind and see her husband go off on the track alone?' The Stray made no answer. 'For better or worse it said. I had a church wedding, and I know. For better or worse, and it can't be *much* worse,' Mrs. Tyrell consoled. 'How the hell could it, with Dick going off like this?'

III

Dancy was still sick when the men came back from their pea-picking. No one knew what was wrong with her; but Snow was certain it was a touch of the sun; Mrs. Tyrell, that it was due to the dam water they had all been drinking; while Thirty-Bob, with a singular lack of reticence, plumped for dysentery straight out. A mild form of it was raging at all the camps. 'It's all this fruit,' he pointed out. 'It can't be good for you.'

Snow was so worried over Dancy that the news of Dick's treachery, while it came as a bad shock, did not affect him as much as it affected Thirty-Bob.

Thirty-Bob was furious. 'The dirty little black bitch,' he spat. 'If brains was dynamite, Dick wouldn't have enough to blow his hat off. I'll give 'im something.'

But Snow shook his head. 'Let him be a bit,' he counselled. 'He's only a kid. We shouldn't have left him here at a loose end.'

The single men on the reserve soon made it plain what they thought of the 'Tyrell mob.' 'You ask a man not to work, and then one of your own mates goes out and gets a job scabbing. Call that a fair go?' They were very savage about it, and Snow felt a slow, helpless despair take him. If only there was something he could do.

No one was speaking to Dick except Thirty-Bob, whose mouth had swelled up outrageously after the fight with the Littles. His lips were still puffed out, and he made obscene jokes about joining a tribe of blacks with Dick. 'Plenty nice young 'possum, Dick. Plenty nice young gin.' He tormented Dick until the boy threatened to make his face look even worse than it was. These days, Dick was keeping away from camp as much as possible. He had thought of going to live at the pickers' huts in the orchard, but the fear of what his mother would say made him quail. He was still a little afraid of his mother, and she was all the more formidable at times like these, when she did not shout at him.

What with Dancy sick and Dick in disgrace and no more peas to be picked, the camps at the Three-Mile reserve were far from cheerful. The chief trouble was that no one was getting enough to eat. The few shillings for the pea-picking had all gone on small necessities. It was no use expecting anything from the Union. The men at the show-ground were only getting bread and tea. Thirty-Bob was right in saying that everyone was eating too much stolen fruit. Cherry-bootlegging had always been one of Orion's chief entertainments, and fully half as many stolen cases of cherries were shipped away as there were legitimate cases picked.

'I could do with a feed of real meat,' Thirty-Bob exclaimed, mournfully regarding the leathery substance impaled on the point of his knife. The moment he had said it, he looked across at Snow, who had started up, his face alert. Now there was something Snow could do! Then he sank back again.

'It 'ud be mad so close to the town,' he said aloud. But the idea had taken root. If he didn't do something, Snow felt, he would go grey; and certainly a good feed of meat would restore the morale of his mates. Looking after the Three-Mile was his job, and buying meat was something that had always offended his principles, even if they had money to buy it.

'The night of this here ox-roasting,' he remarked to no one in particular, 'anyone that can get a leg in 'ull be up at Waldo's place grabbing a bit of beef.'

Thirty-Bob nodded. 'Just you and I,' he suggested, 'could go out and get the meat for a little roast of our own.'

'You keep out of this,' Snow said, with pretended contempt. 'Think I'm going to have you stumbling all over the paddock? One's all that's needed, and I'm the one that's going.'

Thirty-Bob protested, but Snow was determined. Now

that it was settled they cornered Dick Tyrell and faced him with a definite choice.

'See here, Dick. You don't want to be up with Waldo's mob of dingoes. We're going to have a bit of a beano of our own to-morrow night. You're not going to quit us to go up there, are you?'

Dick tried to bluff, but he knew this was an ultimatum. 'Aw, there's no harm in just going up to have a look, is there?'

'Take it or leave it.' Thirty-Bob's voice was stern. 'One thing or the other. You're no mate of mine if you go.'

'Then get to hell. Leave me alone.' Dick turned savagely away.

'I don't travel with no nigger-lover,' Thirty-Bob flung after him. It was the first time he had ever quarrelled with Dick. He had backed him in his fights, had gone out with him working or drinking or raising Cain or racing dogs, but that had all been finished by those two words. 'There,' he said bitterly, 'goes a kid that was as decent as any on the road.'

Snow wanted to get the business over before the moon rose. With a quiet word to Thirty-Bob he vanished as soon as darkness fell. Thirty-Bob gathered the children and started them singing. He teased Mrs. Tyrell until she smiled in spite of herself; he exchanged shouted jests with Deafy; he dragged the Stray from her tent, and propped her against a box.

'We're going to have a beano of our own,' he announced. 'Snow's bringing back the ox, and then what-ho.'

'Gee! he shouldn't be doing that,' Mrs. Tyrell cried. 'So close to the town and all!'

But the fact of his daring made her feel better. She got out her biggest camp-oven and filled it with dripping.

Snow, as he walked up the road towards Hacker's farm, failed to take cover as a car swung past him. It had come so fast that its headlights were on him before he realised it. Anyway, he thought, there was nothing in that. There

300

would be any number of cars on the road to-night. He would cut back across the fields after he had taken his sheep. He went quickly with his queer, long stride, and presently turned off the road and across a stretch of bush to the field he had marked down. He put the dog among the sheep, for he wanted the job done quickly, and Bluey knew as well as a human being what his work was. Bluey never pinned a sheep; he killed it. While the flock fled bleating in alarm, Snow was down on Bluey's sheep; had it across his shoulders, and had started off almost at a run. This was a dangerous, a reckless thing he was doing, and he knew it, to snatch a sheep in such a closely settled place. He had covered a mile and was coming across the last paddock before he slipped through the reserve fence, when a dark figure loomed up before him and a revolver was thrust into his ribs.

'Stop,' a voice said; and a flashlight blinded his eyes. 'Come on, boys. We've got him.'

It had been Hacker's car that had passed Snow in the road, and he had phoned the police. Hacker had always been a very astute man.

Chapter XXII

To DICK it seemed that the whole world combined against him in misery and injustice, just because he had a pretty girl, a girl who wouldn't have looked twice at Thirty-Bob or Snow. They were a couple of jealous narks, and anyway it would all blow over. Thirty-Bob and Snow would get over their grouch and everything would be all right again. The way Thirty-Bob talked, you would think he had a halo, pulling such a long face over a chap taking a girl out.

Steadily Dick refused to face the issue of his strike-breaking. He nursed a smouldering, grumbling resentment that just managed to cover a deep unhappiness. He had always been proud of the friendship of Thirty-Bob, proud that Thirty-Bob travelled with his family; and that final cut about a 'nigger-lover' had bitten deep.

There was something about Mary that fired his thick, slow blood. If Dick wanted a thing, he just put his head down like a bull and charged through every obstacle. He did not pretend to be clever or quick. Why, damn it all, what a stupid fuss they were all making about nothing! His fleshy forehead creased in three deep, horizontal furrows. He had only wanted a good time. He had only wanted Mary, with her lustrous dark hair and her light, pretty giggle and her thin, maddening girl's body. He'd like to smash the lot of them, looking at him as though he was dirt. 'Nigger-lover! By God!'

The worst of it was that he knew there was something about Mary that repelled while it enchanted him, something that made him despise her, while he was madly in love with her, and the something was the streak of a different breed from his own. Mary fascinated him all the more because she was something forbidden by all his mother's standards, by all the years that he had been taught that the dark people were to be avoided and suspected. Anyway, he had paid a high price for this confounded night out, and he was not going to have it spoiled. If he could not give Mary's elder brother the slip and snatch Mary away into the darkness for himself, his name wasn't Dick Tyrell.

And it looked as though this night was going to be worth everything. Waldo, characteristically, had invited all his neighbours and enemies. He had invited half the district. No one refused, if it was only for the sake of laughing at Waldo afterwards. Cars and trucks full of would-be beef-eaters bounced across the grass to the hollow at the back of the homestead where the bullock was being roasted, and their headlights lit up the dead, ring-barked trees, the excited crowds, already milling about aimlessly. Great preparations had been made. Stacks of logs carted. The great pit of glowing coals over which the carcases hung was so scorching as to be almost unapproachable; and when, finally, the beef was pronounced ready, it was singed on one side and raw on the other; but no one minded. Everyone crowded and struggled to snatch a piece of half-cooked flesh and bear it off triumphant. Families and groups sat round on logs, in cars, on the grass, picnicking. They yelled around the fire. They danced and sang. Someone was playing a concertina, and a good deal of Waldo's worst wine was consumed.

The hospitable Waldo moved from group to group, slapping backs, exchanging jokes, waddling over to superintend the sweating stokers in charge of the roast, encouraging the concertina, making speeches to which few listened, telling all his neighbours about his marvellous crop, about his pickers, jeering at the other growers until they were stung to boastings of their own.

The tone of the festival was that of a triumph, a celebration of victory; and it had its effect on the morale of the pickers, just as it was intended to have. So many loud-voiced, confident farmers, all talking together about how little trouble they were having and what a good year it would be, could not fail to make an impression on the gate-crashers who had found no attempt to oppose their entry. The strike had been brushed aside as an amazing trifle. It didn't count. Fully half the strikers from the show-ground were there, come to look on, and, mingling with the crowd, feeling very daring to have thus braved the camp of the enemy. Here was plenty; songs, laughter, wine, beef, big cans of tea boiling over fires and free for all, bread for toasting, sausages—all free. It was a great contrast to the hungry camp by the show-ground.

'It must be costing him something,' one of the gate-crashers muttered to another.

'Arr, he's putting on all this show just for a stunt.' But the tone in which it was said was defiant. After all, Waldo had the reputation of never wasting money. Perhaps he had got enough pickers. If so, what was the use of staying out any longer? If Waldo could get enough pickers, then the resistance was broken. A man might just as well leave the fight for the award over until next year and make the best of the present situation.

The Sydney newspapers, which had crushingly ignored the Union's bulletins and circulars, its laboriously detailed account of the exact position at Orion, were only too willing to print long articles describing 'Idyllic Scenes in Cherry Orchard' or 'Interview with Notable Cherry-Growers. Best Season for Many Years'. This feast of Waldo's, his roasting of a bullock, was something they welcomed for the magazine page. A lady journalist who had come down to Orion for copy made a very good thing out of Waldo's party. Her article was full of descriptions of the 'splendid spirit', 'the bronzed, happy faces with carefree smiles,' 'this harvest festival of the old world in this new sunny land'. It was salt in the wounds of the hungry little crew down at the show-ground when they read it.

Actually there was a constraint over the crowd that never once left it, not even under the influence of Waldo's 'plonk.' The pickers showed a tendency to draw away from the 'bosses,' so that one end of the paddock was an exclusive cluster of cars and farmers, and at the other the pickers made merry on their own. There was a feeling of unseen barriers between the men who had sold their award for a bit of beef and a good time, and the men who owned the beef.

Dick Tyrell, in particular, felt abominably lonely. Like the others, he tried to down the feeling by shouting as loud and long as might be, by horseplay and flirtation and drink. Outside the circle of cars and firelight, the moon had risen over the silver boughs, looking down on this bubble of noise breaking against the dignity of the silent hill. The firelight clawed at the faces of the throng, stripping them of sanity and identity, shifting and whirling and eddying in gusts of smoke that left even friends inhuman, savage, clutching a chunk of flesh.

The worst of it all, to Dick, was that to-night Mary,

who had appeared so desirable, who had made him hot and desperate, seemed now only a giggling child, no older, no more alluring than his young sister. His piece of beef was coated in charcoal and ash, and, from the toughness of it, there was no doubt that the bullock would have died shortly from old age, had it not been sacrificed on the altar of festival. The whole thing was stale and washed-out and false. He would sooner have been back by his own campfire with his own people, rather than with this crowd that more and more, as the night wore on, thinned and dwindled as though the moon had withered up first one group and then another. Car after car drove away without explanation, leaving the pickers in possession, a drunken and rather dangerous gathering that would need a firm hand when the time came to get them back to their huts.

Mary was beginning to be bored by Dick. He had been in a strange mood all the evening. They had given up attempting to dance over the broken, sloping ground, and Mary sat on a fallen log, Dick's head resting against her knee. At the sound of two powerful voices announcing that their 'Luv was Like a Red, Red Rose' Dick started up and displayed a sudden interest.

'Listen,' he exclaimed. 'It's the busker and Phippsy. I wonder how the hell they got here?'

'Maybe they just came.' Mary was not interested. 'There's a lot of people from other sheds.'

'We camped near them in Logan. Gee! Wouldn't Dancy run a mile! She's scared to death the fat piece will catch up with her again.' Dick jumped to his feet, and without waiting for Mary, he was making his way over to the group round the busker.

'Well, well,' Miss Phipps replied to his greeting. 'It's the young man Dick, isn't it? Ah! yes.' Anyone would have thought Dick was asking the favour of her notice.

'How's it, Dick?' The busker beamed at him. 'Good to see you. How's the rest of the gang? Seen old Snow lately? Out at the Three-Mile, are they? Good! I'll be out there one night.' He took up his interrupted strumming.

'We'll have a night together,' he called, as Dick retreated. 'Just the old gang, huh?'

The old gang, Dick thought. Yes, that would be better than this confused and savourless gathering that tasted, as the ox had, of grit and ashes. He looked round for Mary, and saw her talking and laughing with a woman who seemed to him vaguely familiar. Then, as the strange woman scowled, he recognised her as Mrs. Little. It gave him a shock to see her there. With a vague mumble he passed on and waited until Mary came strolling towards him.

'Know who that was?' he asked in a low tone.

Mary glanced at him, surprised. 'I ought to,' she retorted. 'That's my auntie.' Dick recoiled.

'What's up?' the girl asked.

'Nothing.'

'Can't I even say Hello to Dad's sister?'

'They're a rotten lot,' Dick burst out. 'Sam Little poisoned my dog.'

'I don't believe it.'

'He did, I tell you. You ask any of our mob what the Littles did at Logan. They're dead copper-narks, the lot of them.' He could not see Mary's face in the shadow, and foolishly went on justifying himself. 'Why, Thirty-Bob and Sam Little nearly murdered each other a week ago over what happened in Logan. See that?' He attempted to display a scar over his ear. 'Well, that was your flamin' uncle's boot.' He seized her hand to guide it to the spot, but Mary snatched it away. 'Don't you have nothing to do with them,' Dick ordered. 'Not while you're going round with me, at any rate.'

Mary moved out of the shadow, and at the look on her face he blinked. 'You!' she hissed at him. 'You ordering me about! Who d'you think you are? You think you're the salt of the earth, don't you? Why, you poor scum! Get back to your lovely gang of thieves. Get back to your own mob, or to hell, or to gaol. Don't you come near me again.'

She turned and was gone before he could speak. She fled to her brother, demanding to be taken home. She was crying, and he wanted to know why, but she could only shake her head. How could she tell her brother of the undertone of contempt in the boy's voice when he spoke of the Littles? How explain the peremptory way he had commanded her to keep away from her uncle and aunt? 'I hate him,' she raged. 'I hate him.' She had been a fool to set her heart on Dick because he was big and fair and had blue eyes. Never, never again. It wasn't what he said, but his tone, that had been like a blow. Why, oh why, hadn't she kept to Dad's people, who didn't fling stones with their voices and hurt you, who were kind and happy and easy-going? Never again.

Dick stood staring after her stupidly. What a way to behave! Why, he hadn't said anything! He'd only asked her, in the politest sort of way, to keep off the Littles. What was there in that to make her turn on a chap? Oh, to-night he didn't seem able to do anything right. Savage with disappointment, he went back to the gang of pickers with whom he had been making friends.

'Where's the girl friend?' one of them asked.

'Shut up!' Dick snarled. He settled down to a steady course of what Waldo called sherry. It might have been arsenic for all Dick cared. It was soon plain enough that he was looking for a fight, and he observed, with the sharp clarity that falls in certain phases of drunkenness, that people were avoiding him. No one liked him. He could have wept for his pitiful fate.

Finally he fell over a log and lay there asleep. The sons of Waldo, clearing away the last of the guests with remarkable despatch, missed him in the shadow of the log, and there he lay until the early light and the fiendish efforts of the flies to penetrate his eyes, nostrils and ears wakened him to his surroundings. He sat up with a groan and considered the blackened embers of the fire which had roasted the bullock, the embers of other similar fires, some empty bottles, and a scattering of papers and cans and bread-crusts and bits of meat over which the flies were crawling in a black welter.

All he wanted was to get back to the Three-Mile camp. If only he could bury his face in a pile of bedding in the shade of the big cool tent. Just to get out of this blinding sun and sleep was all Dick asked. He would have to walk, and across country at that. He had come over the night before in the Burns's sulky, and not until he started back on foot did he realise what a formidable distance the Three-Mile camp was from Waldo's orchard. Orion was a jig-saw puzzle of roads, but if he kept ploughing due north he would emerge on the reserve or the road that led to it. The trouble was that high walls, houses, barbed-wire fences, dogs and suspicious farmers all seemed to gather in his path. Turning aside to avoid a house, he would find himself in a ploughed field where it was less trouble to skirt round than to tramp across. Even the landscape seemed to be playing vindictive tricks, as though it knew the headache that shot darts at his eyeballs almost blinded him. He was the butt of the sun, and it played with him as a cat might play with a mouse. Fences tore at him; unseen stump-holes tripped him; and the very crows, as they flapped heavily up to sit on the trees and watch him pass, made coarse, disparaging remarks.

It seemed that he had been walking for hours, and the sweat glued his shirt to his skin. All the creek-beds were dry-baked sand and an ever-renewing disappointment. Any thin, muddy trickle would at least have moistened his parched throat. Dick tramped sullenly on, head down, switching the flies with a green branch as a bull lashes with its tail. He could have whimpered in a kind of panic. Up over the hill, and there was another hill in front. He must have lost his sense of direction. Surely it could not be so far. Then he came out on the familiar road, and his pace quickened. Only half a mile from the camp. Soon he would know the blessed relief of oblivion, the comfort of that familiar tent, never before so welcome.

First, some tea. He felt it would be just too much to bear if he had to go and get water. He would bribe one of his young brothers. But there was sure to be tea, black, perhaps, but all the better for that, in a big billy-can beside the fire. His mother would be full of dramatic reproaches, but there was even a homely comfort at the thought of Ma 'going off the handle.' He was used to it, and he never listened or took much notice. He would just growl and roll into the tent and sleep.

Sick and stupid as he was, Dick noticed that Thirty-Bob's sulky was gone. He stamped into the deserted camp and took a long draught of bitter cold tea on which floated an iridescent surface that advertised its strength. That was better. He rubbed his bloodshot eyes. Here came his mother and Deafy. They had been sitting in Snow's camp across the reserve talking to Dancy. It was not until they were quite close that Dick noticed something ominous about their silence. They walked together in step, deadly and purposeful as a regiment charging the guns.

''Lo, Ma,' Dick attempted his usual careless bluster. 'Don't I get anything to eat?' Not that he wanted anything, but he had learnt that attack was the best form of defence.

His mother said nothing, which was in itself unusual. It was Deafy who spoke.

'You!' he said, as though the word burst from him. 'You low-down mongrel!'

'Ar,' Dick snarled. 'Give a chap a bit of peace, can't you? I don't want you nagging at me.'

The set expression of his father's face was as hard as judgment. On Dick's head he poured the wealth of language that life on the road had stored for him, life in a construction camp, life with railway gangs, and there was a touch of the bullock-driver's raw force in it. Even Dick could not help wincing.

'I wouldn't want to call you a son of mine,' Deafy concluded, shaking his head in grief. 'I'd sooner think your mother had you . . .'

'Shut up,' Dick yelled at him. 'Let me alone, damn you.'

'It wasn't Dick's fault, Tom,' Mrs. Tyrell pleaded, feeling her husband had gone too far. 'Let the boy be.' She turned almost pleadingly to Dick. 'Now don't go against your father, boy. Snow's been pinched.'

'Snow?'

'The p'lice grabbed him just as he was coming back with a bit of meat.' Mrs. Tyrell this morning looked very old. All her dominance and energy had been wiped away, leaving only a haggard woman worn with too much hard work. 'Your father's been going on about the disgrace of it. To think we was going to share and Snow's got to take all the trouble. And poor Dancy . . .'

Dick clasped his head with his hands. 'Where's Thirty-Bob?' He hoped Thirty-Bob would be a long way away. He could not bear Thirty-Bob as well.

'I don't know. He went into town.'

Probably to get drunk, Dick thought. As a matter of fact, Thirty-Bob was selling his sulky. Someone ought to raise money for a lawyer, he considered.

'Thirty-Bob felt it, I can tell you. He tried to get taken with Snow. But they didn't seem to want him.'

Thirty-Bob felt humiliated, just as Deafy did, that there were two men letting a third take the blame for a sheep that they were all going to share. Once before, Dick remembered, Thirty-Bob had stepped forward and claimed a sheep that another man had killed. 'Well, how could I let him go to quod?' he had said. 'He's got a missus and three kids to look after.'

Deafy was still giving his son a considered opinion of his conduct. 'To think that a son of mine would go staying all night with a black whore while his own family . . .'

The injustice of it stung Dick. 'What could I have done?' he shouted. 'It wasn't my fault.' But even as he shouted, he knew that was not true. If he had not broken that solid little circle, Snow might not have taken such a risk. It was not like Snow to be so incautious. Dick had talked about this ox-roasting, he had insisted on going to it. Snow had wanted to entice him away to a little feast of their own.

'You could have been here,' his mother said in a low voice. 'You could have been with us when it happened.'

Dick did not answer. What was there to say, anyway? If they were going to hold him responsible just because Snow had been caught with a sheep . . . Good God! what wouldn't they hold him responsible for? 'Oh, shut up,' he said wearily. His father was still standing there raging at him. 'Will you shut up?' he repeated again threateningly. It seemed to him that his brain was on fire.

'It's this life on the road that's rotted you,' Deafy was saying. 'At your age I was slogging in a construction camp, working as you've never worked in your life. You're a loafer and a waster. At your age I was making a home and rearing a family. . . . And you . . .'

'Not if I know it,' Dick raged. 'D'you think I'd drag a woman and kids all round the country when I lost me job or they chucked me out? D'you think I'd give any kid of mine the life you've given me, you old bastard?'

'Dick'—his mother tried to deflect his mounting rage— 'don't speak to your Dad like that, boy. He's been a good father to you.'

'Oh, he has, has he? What kind of a life has he led you, never a roof over your head.'

Deafy drew himself up. 'We've been married twenty-five years, and never once has your mother had to complain of me looking even sideways at a woman, and as for spending a night away from camp with a black slut . . .'

Dick crashed his fist into his father's face. It was the first time he had ever even thought of hitting his father. He might have answered him savagely or cursed back when his father was annoyed, but to strike him was a different matter. He stood stupidly trying to take in the implications of what he had done.

Deafy got slowly to his feet. There was only one thing now. He must thrash Dick, or Dick would be unbearable, and he must settle this matter once for all. He came at Dick dangerously, heavily. Deafy was as hard as iron, and for all that Dick was so big, Deafy had the endurance, the toughness, the experience, and Dick was not in his best form.

'I'll teach you,' Deafy grunted. 'Striking your father.'

But if Dick was angry before, he was mad now. He did not care, he told himself, what happened. Everything was spoilt, ruined. It could never be the same. A dreadful desire to smash his father into a bleeding pulp obsessed him. He was through with this life for good. The old man had jeered at him for not making a life of his own. All right, he would. But first he must destroy every vestige of the old. His fist shot out in a blow he had used with dire effect before now. It caught his father on the side of his jaw just under the ear, and he dropped as though he had been hit with a mallet.

'Dick!' His mother was hanging on his arm. 'Dick, don't, don't!'

He sent her reeling. 'Get away from me,' he shouted. 'I'm through. I'll teach him. Damn him!'

He snatched up the axe. Mrs. Tyrell with a scream flung herself on Deafy's still body. He could see the terror in her eyes, but he made no further move against his father. There were little flecks of foam at the corner of the boy's mouth. His face was distorted with fear. Clinging to the still body of Deafy, Mrs. Tyrell watched speechless with horror the wreckage Dick was making of the camp. Her little table, the chairs, the treasured sewing-machine; he battered them scientifically into matchwood. He smashed the crockery to the ground and jumped on it. 'I'll show him, I'll show him,' he kept repeating. The kerosene tin of water went over with a clang as Dick's boot struck it sending a stream of brown water with a hiss into the fire. On top of what fire remained he threw the mattress and all the bedding he could find.

'Dancy!' Mrs. Tyrell screamed, but Dancy was already running towards her, weak and unsteady, but still ready to face this destructive madman who had been her big, good-natured friend.

Two bagmen, camped at a distance, who 'hadn't liked to interfere in no one's rows,' as they said later, were slowly following her.

'You try and stop me,' Dick roared, 'and I'll brain the lot of you.' The tent came down and he started on that with the axe. But his first fury had worn off. 'So long, Ma,' he shouted, and without one backward glance, he was off to catch his horse. 'It's my horse,' he repeated to himself. 'It's my horse.'

The greyhound he would have to leave behind. He felt no compunction for what he had done, only a cool satisfaction, an access of strength and clarity such as he had never felt before. One minute he almost turned, but then he had fastened the rope bridle, leapt on the horse's back, and was off.

'Oh, Dick!' Mrs. Tyrell sobbed, distractedly trying to raise her husband and to salvage the bedding, which was smouldering unpleasantly. 'Oh! Dick! My God! he's gone!'

Dick did not even turn his head when he reached the road. He was off at a gallop, riding as well as he ever rode, his head high, a half-smile on his face. He vanished round a curve of the road as completely as if he had never been there. As he clattered furiously away, the idea that had been forming in his mind became more and more a certain goal. He decided that he would be much happier overseas fighting for home and country.

Chapter XXIII

THE Apostle never believed in chance. In fact, his whole life was devoted towards combating that heresy which allows that there is no good reason why things happen or that they happen in a sequence. He would have explained that it was the nature of the stream of life to swirl past a Pharisee and a priest so that the Samaritan could demonstrate his superior kindliness to the man stripped by thieves. He was so firmly convinced of this predestination of events that he would loaf around for days waiting, as he said, for a 'pull' in one direction or another. How could you waste time, he protested, when there was eternity before you?

He had been idling so beside the Lachlan when he suddenly started up and said: 'We're going to Orion, Millie,' and to Orion they went. The Apostle was pleased to observe that the truck, under the guidance of some Divine purpose with a better skill than the Apostle's, neither broke down nor ran out of anything. He took this surprising conjunction of circumstances as an omen.

There was no doubt that the Apostle's arrival was very opportune for the little group at the Three-Mile; and no one welcomed him more fervently than Thirty-Bob, who was accustomed to sneer at the Apostle's habit of 'sticking his beak into other people's business.' Thirty-Bob had his hands full, with Dancy sick and Mrs. Tyrell weeping silently, Deafy nursing his jaw in sullen despondency and Snow in gaol. The Apostle in his rickety little truck looked to him, for the first time, like a heavenly messenger.

The Apostle's first good deed was to take the bottle of medicine which the chemist had supplied and which Dancy was dutifully swallowing thrice a day, and fling it into a clump of bushes. He asked a few shrewd questions, then prepared a brew of his own which tasted twice as nasty, but which Dancy declared made her feel much better. Perhaps it was merely her faith in the Apostle, or that the sickness had run its course, but she certainly did improve.

To Mrs. Tyrell the Apostle listened in sympathetic silence. He heard her version of Dick's behaviour about four separate times, and Deafy's twice.

'How would you like it if it was your boy?' Mrs. Tyrell demanded, woefully turning to Mrs. Postlewaite. 'You may think you can keep a family decent on the track, but I tell you, woman, sometime, sooner or later, I knew this would happen. I've dreaded it for years, ever since Dick began to grow up. It's all very well while they're little, but you'll see. Oh, you'll see how hard it is when a boy begins to drift off on his own. Oh!' she broke off bitterly. 'I want my boy. If I only knew where he was . . .'

In the Apostle she found for the first time someone who did not say: 'Cheer up, Ma. Dick'll turn up.' Instead the Apostle went into town and got on the trail of Dick. No one else thought of asking at the swimming-baths, but sure enough, when the Apostle enquired, the girl on the gate remembered a big fair boy who had ridden up and persuaded her to lend him a costume. She had even been curious enough to watch him ride off across the bridge, and the road in that direction led only south.

The news cheered Mrs. Tyrell immensely. 'We could catch him up at the next dole,' she cried. 'He's got to get his dole!' Her first thought was to break camp and follow Dick. Then she remembered Dancy. 'We can't go until we know what's to happen to Snow,' she murmured, immediately subdued.

'Nonsense,' the Apostle told her. 'You get the horses in.' He had everything settled. Dancy could come with the Postlewaites. Or, if she wanted to travel with the Tyrells, she could catch up with them at the next dole-station. Thirty-Bob could drive the turnout for her, if that would suit Thirty-Bob. He had everything arranged.

They took time arguing over this new idea, but the very fact that he had plans to offer, that he could see them going on, that he had lifted them all out of their ruin and despair, was something. While they were still discussing who would go there, the Apostle was off again to town.

'Where this time?' Thirty-Bob asked.

'To see the priest,' the Apostle responded.

Nobody had thought of that either; but the Apostle, with a breadth that did him credit, had no scruples about asking help from any quarter, and within an hour he was

315

sitting in the presbytery pouring out a tale to a big, red-faced old man whose powerful bulk overflowed his chair. From time to time Father Farrell nodded, but he let the Apostle tell his story uninterrupted to the end. Father Farrell was a power in Orion, a big Irish priest who had built a convent, a hospital and a school, where there had been nothing but a tiny chapel. He was reputed to be the one man who had put the fear of the Lord into Waldo.

On one occasion he had alighted on Waldo's doorstep unannounced. 'I've come to stay wid ye,' he declared. 'And before I leave I want a hundred pounds for my hospital; it will be well worth it to ye to get rid o' me. Ye're rolling in money and mean as a louse.'

For three days Waldo entertained him royally, and when he left Father Farrell took with him a cheque for two hundred pounds.

If he was extortionate in his demands on the rich of his parish, he spent their money on the poor. No one went from the Father's door without at least a hearing, and the help he had given to bagmen in his time had created a saying along the track: 'Like Father Farrell, all tough hide and soft heart.' But no one before had ever expected him to plead for an unknown sheep-thief.

'And what d'ye come to me for?' he demanded, with seeming irritability. The Apostle made no answer. 'Am I to be bothered with all of them? Cursing the Church when they rise up, sneering at it every day? But 'tis to the Church they turn with a hard-luck tale when they want clothes or food or shoes to their feet. It's Father-this and Father-that to me face, and "to the Devil with him" behind me back.' He tapped his hand on his knee. 'What d'ye think I can do for your mate, eh?'

'You could speak for him,' the Apostle said confidently.

'Speak for a man I've never seen?' He dropped his pretended severity, and the look that was Father Farrell's passport into heaven came into his face. 'Ah!' he cried, 'and it's speak for him I will.' He gripped the Apostle's arms. 'The time I remember it was no crime for a man

316

to take a sheep. Why, 'twas no crime at all! Help yeerself, they'd be saying. And now a man goes with his heart in his mouth and his hat in his hand to ask for a drop of water, let alone a bit of tea. 'Twill be getting to the stage when we'll be transported for trapping a rabbit, as in the old days in England.' His voice descended from prophecy to reproof. 'And them that owns the sheep, they're that mean they'd put a bent threepence in the plate. Sure I'll speak for your friend.'

'I knew you would,' the Apostle smiled.

'And his wife and boy? What's to become of them?'

'My wife will look after them.'

The priest nodded courteously. He knew the people of the road and their strange fear of supervision, whether of Church or State. 'Tell the woman to come and see me if she's in need, and bring the boy. I'll speak for the man.'

If it had not been for the 'chance' meeting Father Farrell had with the visiting magistrate and the luncheon that followed, Snow would have received the eighteen months he expected. For a man with Snow's record three months in Goulburn Gaol was a light sentence.

The anxiety with which Snow greeted the news that Father Farrell was taking an interest in Jimmy surprised the Apostle. 'What the hell did you want to drag a priest into it for?' Snow snarled at his advocate. 'Now he'll be getting in touch with Molly and putting the kid in a home.' He gripped the Apostle by the shoulder. 'You tell Dancy to get out of this, hear me? Tell her to get on the move and keep on the move till I come out. Don't let Molly get Jimmy again. Tell Dance to keep Jimmy. Tell her that.' His tone was savage. 'Tell her I'll meet her down at the cannery and she's to look after Jimmy till I come.' He controlled himself with an effort. 'Thanks for everything, Harry. I know you thought you was doing me a good turn.'

'I was,' the Apostle said gravely. 'Snow . . .'

'Well, what?'

317

'Why don't you try to think more kindly of your wife? Why not send Jimmy back to her?'

'Hell! no.' And that was all the Apostle could get out of him.

He returned to camp with Snow's message to Dancy, and found everyone still at cross purposes. Mrs. Tyrell kept deciding to go on, and then to stay and see what happened to Snow. Deafy refused to 'chase after' Dick. If Dick wanted to come back, he could, but what was the use of running after him? Let him cool down and come to his senses first.

The Apostle's wife, as usual, went quietly about her own affairs. She seemed particularly abstracted. When the Apostle asked her what was the matter, she merely said: 'It's that poor Mrs. Tyrell. That brute of a boy! I've been thinking.'

'What, Millie?'

'Nothing.' The Apostle had brought back a letter from her brother, and as she read it, he noticed her thoughtful expression had deepened to worry. 'Anything wrong, my dear?'

'No, Harry, nothing.' She passed him the letter, which was full of small items of news and the usual urgings that she should come home.

The Apostle handed it back and went off busily to see how the Tyrell baby was progressing. It had shown disturbing signs of a rash. All in all, the Apostle was in his element, helping, advising, doctoring, and, as Thirty-Bob would say, 'generally interfering.'

'There's some men,' Thirty-Bob always declared sarcastically, 'who can sit down and eat their dinner with a murder going on. But all I can say is Harry ain't one of 'em. It's a wonder he ain't been a bloody deceased corpse himself before now, the way he butts in.'

Mrs. Postlewaite, as she watched him, could not help a sad little smile. Harry never minded giving himself away. That was one of the differences between them. She would always want to retain her reserves, her own mental privacy,

318

but Harry never minded how foolish or odd he might look to other people. He gave away everything, he thought and felt with the same unconcern with which he would have dressed in public had that been necessary. He lived in the open.

Her mind went back to that time, it seemed so long ago, when she first met him. He had been speaking of missions, and she had always been fired with the idea of the mission-field. To go out and give your life in the service of God in a strange land! She dreamed of jungles and deserts and tropic islands where she, as the helpmate of some worthy man, might minister to the souls and bodies of the natives. Perhaps it was something of the glow in her eyes, as she listened to him, that had attracted Harry Postlewaite, thin, shabby and always in trouble with his rector, to the sedate sister of the senior churchwarden. And when Harry Postlewaite wanted to make friends with anyone, he was as difficult to repulse as a stray cat. Then, she knew, he had been sorry for her, sorry for the dreary monotony of her life, the round of small domestic interests and church socials. He had married her in the same impulsive and determined way that he always rushed into trouble; and ever since she had been good to him, she had cared for him even after she ceased to worship him, and discovered that he was . . . well, erratic and strange at times.

She had been a good wife to him; she had left her home, her elder brother, everything, just as she would have done had Harry felt a call to a far tropical island. At first she had believed that Harry was doing a missionary work, even if there were no tropical palms and white duck suits to go with it. She had set her teeth when they had no food and the water was bad, when the truck broke down, when, penniless and ashamed, she had to ask help of strangers. She had put up with the foul talk and fouler jokes and ways of the people he moved among, even when the foulest of these jests were directed against themselves. Scowls, threats, even open brutality, she had faced; but those words of Mrs. Tyrell had opened to her a nightmare from

319

which she half feared she might not wake. 'How would you like it if it was your boy? I've tried to keep them decent. But you can't. It's just the life on the road beats you in the end.'

Suppose that it had been Bryson or Whitefield who had beaten his father unconscious and gone away without a word? Oh, no! Not her sons! Anything but that!

It was true, she told herself, facing the fear that lurked at the back of her mind ever since Mrs. Tyrell flung the words at her. It was true that you could not keep decent in the conditions these people endured. You grew old and dirty and didn't care. The Tyrells had started out, just a working man and his wife looking for the means of a livelihood, and when they hadn't been able to find them and settle down, they had tried to keep decent. Their children had not even the standards with which their parents started out. What of her own baby who had never known a home? Suppose she and Harry went on wandering in this way for years? Oh, it wasn't fair! It wasn't fair to the boys, and Harry asked too much when he took it for granted that she should drag the children along, sacrificing them to his passion for missionary endeavour.

On a tropical island you were at least not expected to live like the natives. You had your suit of clean clothes, your own standards, your own bungalow and church into which you could retire when the degradation of a savage existence overwhelmed you. For herself, she did not care, but for the children, never . . . never . . . never. She must make Harry see that he was wrong. He had brilliance; he could get some work in the city surely: writing, perhaps; speaking over the radio; her brother would find him something. What was there for him if he went on as he was going? Only to get old and mad and dirty and degraded. And again her mind came back to the centre of the whole tornado of her revolt. She must save her boys.

She nerved herself to have it out with Harry, although she knew in her heart what the outcome would be.

Harry was as inconsiderate to his own as he was considerate to strangers. He was hard on his family as he was hard on himself. As a Good Samaritan he might be all that was to be desired, but as a father he was impossible. 'How would you feel if it was your boy?' No, she would not see her boys ruined, brought down to the level of the people of the road. They must have an education, a chance in life.

'Harry,' she said quietly, when the Apostle came back. 'I'm going home to Ted.' She said it as casually as if they had been out for an afternoon's stroll instead of years of aimless travel.

'I knew that was it.' The Apostle sat down and regarded her with a slight, anxious furrowing of his forehead. 'I knew it was coming. Just what decided you, Millie?' He did not protest. Sooner or later, he thought, it was bound to happen.

'That woman, Mrs. Tyrell. Oh, Harry, I couldn't bear Bryson or Whitefield to grow up like that.'

'But there's no reason why they should,' the Apostle returned.

She was holding her baby in her arms, and now she clutched it to her, fiercely maternal. 'No reason? Why, that poor boy—and you'd say it yourself, Harry, at any other time—was just the result of his surroundings. I want Bryson and Whitefield to have good food and clean clothes and baths. Look at all the children you see along the track. Stunted, burnt-up little animals with bad teeth and sandy blight and hollow chests. I don't want my boys like that.'

'And how about their minds? You'll take them back and bury them under the ruins.'

'Ruins?'

'Books, business, and banks. Stale ruins of other men's minds left for hundreds of years. Towns, streets, churches, all the things that make life easier and thinking harder. Cluttering up their lives and their minds. Softening in corners. Air-conditioning their flesh, getting them accustomed to accepting aeroplanes, cars, machines for

321

building more machines. Crawling about in a stinking, swarming city. Bah!' He recovered himself. 'Even at the risk of sandy blight or bad teeth (which they haven't had so far), I wanted them away from that.'

'But you came out to lead these people to a better way of living.'

'I know,' the Apostle admitted. 'Poor fool that I was! But I'm not a missionary now. I'm a refugee. I'm fleeing from a civilisation that drops bombs on its cities and fouls its nest. Give me the road any time.'

Mrs. Postlewaite could be out-talked, but not convinced. 'If that poor Tyrell boy had had a good home, and been able to meet nice girls at tennis parties . . .'

'Mary is a nice girl,' the Apostle suggested.

'But she's . . .' Mrs. Postlewaite could not say it. She knew that for her husband there was no such thing as a colour bar. But to her, natives were natives, and blacks were blacks, and no amount of talk could ever reconcile her to the vision of Bryson in a like situation to Dick's. Infatuated with a half-caste! Impossible! Or one of these terrible girls they were always meeting, swearing, smoking, depraved. No!

'It's the boys,' she said breathlessly. 'You see that, Harry? It isn't for myself.'

'I know that, dear.'

'Oh, Harry, come with me.'

The Apostle shook his head. She knew this parting was hurting him. 'You go home. Go back to good old Ted.' Ted was her brother. 'Then, when you've had a holiday, you can see how you feel.' He knew that if she left him, it would be for ever, but he preferred to give her this excuse. 'You take the boys and the baby and have a good rest. Ted will be pleased. He's a lonely man, and I . . . well, I'll miss you.' He had not realised before just how much his wife and the boys had meant. Into their loyal circle he could retire, when the misery of things almost overcame him. They were like a shade-tree in the heat, like a civilised outpost in a foreign land. Perhaps, he

322

thought, that is why they should go. So that I may rely the more fully upon the Blood. So that I may have no temptations to separateness.

'I'll sell the truck,' he announced suddenly, 'and walk.'

This matter-of-fact reception of her ultimatum hurt Mrs. Postlewaite more than anything else could have done. She had known that there was a hard streak in Harry, but he seemed almost glad to get rid of them. Tears came to her eyes.

'Oh!' she cried, 'haven't you any feelings? Haven't you any real love for the children? You're unnatural . . . that's what you are . . . unnatural.'

Had she been another type of woman she might have screamed and cursed and thrown plates at him. 'Unnatural,' she repeated through stiffened lips. So might she have reproached a missionary who had deserted his high calling to civilise the savages and had descended instead to their level of sitting under a tree all day, lotus-eating. It must be that Harry's aberrations were slowly crumbling his moral fibre.

The Apostle made a movement almost as though he saw the terrible prophecy in her mind of his gradual disintegration into a dirty, drooling idiot; as though she had tried to strike him.

'Whatever you may come to think of me, my dear'—his voice was sad—'remember that I love you and the boys more than anything on earth.'

More than anything on earth! That was it. They didn't count. Mrs. Postlewaite for the moment was jealous of God. To her husband, his family did not count, except as part of the earth, to him a temporary Hell, a bubble rolling along in the dark stream of the purpose of God. She would not have minded so much if her husband had lost his faith. That was something she could understand. Instead, that faith had grown in him like some enormous cancer eating out his normal life, leaving it a husk without savour. All his intensity had turned from human beings; he did not try to convert them, believing in a personal revelation when the subject was ready for it; he just showed them affection. His kindness to the lost and forgotten people was more in the nature of something to occupy himself, as a priest might tell his beads while he meditated. It was just a religious exercise. It did not really matter. Nothing really mattered to him that ordinary people felt.

An even more horrible idea came to her. He was wanting to die. All the time he was so cheerful and busy, 'poking his nose into other people's business,' the dark lust to be carried away, to be sunk fathoms down, drowned in his Eternal, was his real aim. The green hills were a coloured bandage wrapped around his eyes, and he would tear them away, and the light as well, gladly, to see into that terrible torrent beyond the light.

'When will you be going, my dear?' The Apostle broke the silence that had fallen while she stared at him so intently.

'It doesn't matter when.' She could hardly speak.

'I could sell the truck and give you the money to take with you.' He looked at the poor, battered little truck speculatively.

'I'll write to Ted for money,' his wife said. 'You'll need what you can get for the truck, if anything.' She forced a little smile.

The Apostle, who admired bravery and knew just what a struggle it had cost her to make this decision, tried to smile back. For a moment their eyes met, and in that moment the shabby little man and the plain woman knew such agony of grief as it is not often given to human beings to endure.

Then the Apostle looked away. 'The sooner the better,' he said, and then almost humbly, as though he asked a favour, 'I may come and see you sometimes?'

'Oh, Harry! if you only would come now! For good.'

Again the Apostle shook his head. 'When I feel I can come to you, I will.' He tried to be practical. 'I must look up trains.' He straightened his shoulders as though to brace himself against the pain of her going.

'Harry, I'll be worrying about you and wondering where you are.'

'I'll write.'

'And I know you won't take care of yourself, and you'll starve. Oh, why did I ever think of leaving you?' She was turning now to the opposite of her mind, as women do. 'I won't go. The boys will be looked after. I know they will. They're good boys. The Lord is with us here as everywhere, as you say, Harry.'

If she were willing to fling over all her resolutions just for that look in his eyes, the Apostle was made of sterner stuff.

'I must look up the trains,' he repeated.

Chapter XXIV

THE busker had come to Orion a little saddened by the experience of turning twenty-two. He had been down to Sydney and had hung about starving, because he had no fixed place of abode, and so could get no dole. In the roar of the traffic, even his yodelling was drowned, as he stood night after night on the street corners, thankful for a stray penny. Now he was on the road again, with his old jaunty assurance, his old battered guitar, and only the clothes he stood up in.

Twenty-two seemed to him a great age to be just 'knocking about,' still insecure, still with a blank scroll of fame to carve. To tell the truth, he was a little afraid. He sometimes, particularly after a hard spell of drinking, saw before him a horrible future, in which he would grow older and more disreputable, as he tried to drown the bitterness of lost opportunities. Where was the tent-show he had been so sure he would one day own? Receding like a mirage, illusive, unattainable. Perhaps if he could make some money, cherry-picking (you couldn't do anything in the city without money), he might storm the fortress of vaudeville and radio.

'Anyway,' the busker comforted himself, 'I've kept free. Never have any ties. That's the main thing.'

He was thinking particularly of a succession of enchanting damsels who had talked to him with tenderness in their voices and the clank of matrimonial fetters in the background.

It was late one Saturday night, when he was waiting for some mates of his in the Orion Hotel, that the busker renewed his acquaintance with Mr. Wilks. For a minute he could not recall that he had ever met this inebriated stranger, who hung upon him with maudlin affection and insisted he have a drink.

'Got plenty money,' Mr. Wilks confided, pulling out a handful of silver to prove it. 'C'mon, it's on me.'

Then the busker remembered the night that the little girl with the rosella had bound up his head with a strip torn from her red dress.

Sharkey Wilks was drinking with a thin, watery-eyed man, to whom he referred alternately as 'ole pal' and 'Greg'ry'. They were deep in fond memories of other days, memories that made them shake each other's hand affectionately every now and then, or even slap each other on the shoulder and mournfully shake their heads like two crows on a bough.

'Remember the time, Greg'ry, when we drank away that team and waggon?' Mr. Wilks breathed tenderly.

'An' remember the time when we drank a buggy and two sets of harness?' Gregory countered.

They shook their heads again, and gazed deep into each other's eyes. It was rather dreary for the busker, who drained his pot and, after he had 'shouted' in his turn, rose to go.

'No, you don't.' Mr. Wilks shoved him back with some violence. 'Me an' you and ole Greg'ry goin' to have a night out. Ain't that so, ole pal?'

Gregory nodded with tears in his eyes. 'We was drunk for three weeks,' his voice trembled with emotion, 'that time in Molong.'

They shook hands solemnly once more. Then they both wanted to shake hands with the busker.

'Y' comin' home with me.' Sharkey Wilks put his face so close that the busker shut his eyes and shuddered. 'You're comin' home with me, me boy. I know a little girl that ain't thought of nothin' else but you ever since Logan.' He twisted his face in what was meant to be a knowing look. 'I tried to thrash 'er out of it. But that didn't do no good.' Sharkey began to show signs of truculence. 'Comin' home with me. Hear that?' He shook his fist under the busker's nose. 'See that? Well, let's hear no more about it.'

The busker was now definitely alarmed. There was something more than mere drunkenness behind the attachment which Mr. Wilks seemed to have taken to his person. But Duke had enough dealings with drunks to know that, if he sat quiet and returned soothing answers, Mr. Wilks would presently forget whatever muddled idea he had in his head and fall asleep, or fight Gregory, or seek some other diversion.

'Greg'ry Hourigan,' Mr. Wilks said sentimentally, 'you remember the time we broke that ruddy stallion that broke Jeff Wilde's back.' He began to laugh hilariously. 'Three days we had the flank-rope on him, and a bag of wet sand on his back. Then we got him down and saddled him, and drove him through the scrub, and cut him to pieces with the stock-whips. That taught the bastard. That broke his spirits.'

'He wasn't no good after,' Gregory amended mournfully. 'Remember we gelded him so it 'ud bring back some of his spirit.' He shook his head. 'But it never did.'

If he could keep the talk to horses, the busker thought, he could presently slip away. They became immersed in reminiscences about one 'Hoppy Brown,' and his exploits in bringing a mob of draughts from Victoria to Queensland.

'Excuse me, sports,' the busker said graciously. 'There's a chap over there I've got to see. I won't be a minute.'

327

And he vanished quickly through the bar door and out across the yard.

Mr. Wilks and his friend might be drunk, but they were far from incapable. As the busker trotted out of the back gate, there they were waiting for him, howling with laughter at their own cleverness, and linking their arms through his.

'Thought you'd give us the slip, eh? Not on your life. Comin' home with us, ain't he, Greg'ry?'

And despite the busker's protests, they hauled him into a rickety buggy, whipped up the horse, and started off on a wild gallop in the opposite direction to the busker's camp, through a darkness that made their demise almost a matter of minutes.

As he drove, Gregory howled a song, in which Mr. Wilks joined him very heartily. The buggy leapt and bounded, and threatened at every moment to send them hurtling in the road. Gregory held the reins and Mr. Wilks plied the whip. The busker had never been kid-napped before—no one had ever thought he was worth it —and now he resigned himself to whatever might come: a broken neck, a couple of broken ribs. If he was lucky, when they overturned, he might come off with just a smashed rib or collar-bone.

At last, with profound relief, he realised the buggy had drawn up before a cottage, the gate of which Mr. Wilks was drunkenly endeavouring to open. The horse spanked through and round the back of the dim bulk of the house. Shaken but still whole, the busker descended. He did not know where he was, he did not know what would happen next, but nothing could be worse than that ride over breakneck roads with two drunks urging the horse.

Mr. Wilks was again draped round his neck, breathing stale fumes over him.

'We're home, Maria,' he called unnecessarily to the thin wife of Gregory. 'But if it hadn't been for me ole pal Harley—Harley's the name, ain't it?—we'd never have got here. Meet me friend Harley Duke, Mrs. Hourigan,

Maria. . . . Ah, I used to know 'er before she ever married Greg—the Lily of Blimdagery, she was.'

He flung a chaste kiss in the direction of the haggard woman, who, with one child in her lap and another whining about her knees, did not smile. She looked at Sharkey with a timid hate, and for her husband, who now staggered in laden with bottles of cheap wine, her glance was one of reproach and grief.

There was no furniture in the room but an old school bench, a table, and a rickety chair; but the busker thought he had never seen any place so bewilderingly crowded with children. Taking a count of heads there were ten in all, and their eyes were fastened on Gregory Hourigan with the same grief and reproach that was in the eyes of their mother.

'Greg,' the woman whispered, 'you promised me you wouldn't touch it.'

'Meeten ole pal,' Gregory dribbled. 'Meeten ole frien' like Sharkey. Gotta have a drink. Ain't it so, Sharkey?'

''Corse you gotta, Greg. Where's the missus, Maria?'

'She's in your camp in the shed, Sharkey.'

'Tell 'er to come up.' Sharkey gave a grandiloquent sweep of his arm. 'Gonna make a night of it.'

'I'd better put the children to bed,' Mrs. Hourigan said. 'They've got to get off to early Mass in the morning.' And with another reproachful glance, she shepherded half the children, the boys, before her, to bed them in a section of the huge stone barn which, the busker was to discover, eked out the inadequate living space of the two-room shack.

The busker sprang to open the door for her. He followed her out. He found it painfully necessary to his self-respect to explain that he had nothing to do with this situation, that he was a helpless victim of circumstance and Sharkey Wilks.

The woman only nodded her head listlessly. She led the way into the big barn, and took down a hurricane lamp and lit it, to show an interior of dusty junk-heaps,

329

old motor-tyres and tools, with several heaps of bedding on the floor.

'I don't suppose you know Blimdagery?' she said in a conversational tone.

Would he ever forget it. That flight across the plains, with Snow half delirious in the van, and the wind slicing them all to mincemeat.

'I've been through Blimdagery,' he admitted, wincing at the memory.

'We come from there.' Mrs. Hourigan had the colourless lack of interest in other people that often afflicts women whose life has been one personal disappointment after another. 'I often tell Gregory I'd like to go back. My folk all live there, so do Greg's.' She raised her voice to a sudden yell: 'Jean!'

'What?' came a sullen voice from the other side of the stone partition.

'Your father says to come over to the house.'

'Tell him to go to hell. We're all in bed.'

The busker could not restrain himself. 'Is Betty there?' he asked eagerly. He had scarcely once thought of Betty in the months that lay between to-night and their last meeting, but now he was unreasonably curious to see her again.

There was a silence from beyond the partition wall. Then Mrs. Wilks's high screaming voice was heard. 'What is it, Jean? Who's the cove out there? I can hear him. Don't think I can't.'

Jean shouted at her: 'It's a man wants Betty.'

Mrs. Wilks's answer contained the inference that she objected to being awakened by casual men who had (censored) designs upon her younger daughter. The busker's blood chilled. Muttering a hasty apology through the wall, he beat a retreat into the open, leaving Mrs. Hourigan to shout to Mrs. Wilks a description of her husband's homecoming.

'And I suppose the money he got from the girls' hard work is all gone,' Mrs. Wilks wailed.

The busker hesitated in the doorway. At any minute
Mr. Wilks and his pal Gregory might come seeking him,
and he felt that a continuance of their society was more
than he could stomach. However, he was entirely mysti-
fied as to his whereabouts, and he could not have found
his way back to the town unaided for a bet. Mrs. Hourigan was now hearing the boys say their prayers, from which
he deduced that she would be emerging soon, and then he
could ask her which way he went to Orion.

He heard the squeak of a gate, and a white form blurred
the blackness that was the back paddock. The busker
stepped out in the dim light from the doorway of the barn
and heard a little cry of amazement.

'Is that you, Betty?' he called.

'Yes.' She came towards him. 'I went down to stop
the dogs barking.' He had noticed that the din of the dogs
had stopped a minute or so before. Her voice was timid,
but eager. 'How'd you get here?'

Rapidly he told her how her father had insisted on
dragging him from town. 'And now how do I get
back?'

'It's five miles.'

'Five miles!' the busker exclaimed. The old goat!
His mortification at being kidnapped was increasing as he
realised the difficulties of escape. Listening to Betty's
directions, he decided that he was practically lost in a
neck of the woods.

'It's no use,' he said at last. 'I didn't see any big tree
when we turned to the left. And I couldn't see my hand
in front of me now.'

The girl hesitated, then seemed to come to a decision.
'I'll come with you.' The busker protested. 'Just as far
as the main road,' she explained. 'That's about three
miles. And it's just a track to there.' She vanished
inside the barn. 'Wait a minute,' she called over her
shoulder.

He could hear Mrs. Wilks's shouted threats and pro-
hibitions as the situation was laid before her. Presently

Betty stepped out again, this time clad in some kind of a dress in place of the white petticoat she had been wearing, and with shoes on her feet.

'Mum and Mrs. Hourigan say you'd better stay and sleep with the boys, but I said you'd sooner get back.'

At that moment the back door was flung open, and Sharkey Wilks called: 'Where's me pal Harley? C'mon, Harley. Give us a bit of a tune.'

The busker was pleased he had left his guitar in safe keeping in Orion.

'Quick!' the girl urged. 'Or they'll want you to stop and have a drink.'

She stooped under the wire of the paddock fence, and held it for him to follow. They followed a little track that led through acacia scrub and ant-heaps, through dry water-courses where the busker stumbled and floundered, and over a stony rise.

'Take my hand,' the girl offered.

Presently his eyes grew more accustomed to the darkness, but he retained the girl's hand as he walked by her side. The busker had a romantic nature.

'The moon will come up soon,' he suggested.

'There isn't a moon to-night.'

'Well, there ought to be.' The busker's disgust at being dragged to this hovel against his will by a couple of drunks was giving place to a sense of the strangeness of the situation.

'Every time I meet you,' he said, 'you're getting me out of something. I haven't thanked you for Logan.'

They were on the track now, and he began to tell her of his hopes and disappointments in Sydney, revealing even the mean things he had done, the tricks he had thought clever at the time, the way he had lived in a back room in a squalid street, the time he had gone hungry. It was a relief to get it all off his chest to this shadowy figure who was not a stranger, not a friend, nothing but a voice and a blur of shadows. He could talk to this girl.

'Here, let's have a look at you,' he concluded abruptly;

and before she could stop him, he had halted and struck a match.

The light almost dazzled them for a moment. Then he studied the brown face, the thin mouth with lips that had a fine curve above a determined chin. He had not noticed in Logan what a firm chin little Betty possessed. She had always seemed so shrinking.

'You've grown a bit,' he said.

The match went out and the darkness seemed all the deeper for that tiny flare of light.

'Yes, I've grown.'

Their voices had waked some bird, which called questioningly with a high, melancholy note.

He moved closer to her in the gloom of the path.

'Sit down here for a minute with me,' he suggested, his hand on her arm. 'Here, by this tree.'

The busker knew all the moves, and he felt that since he had been dragged so far out of his way, the Wilks family owed him some recompense.

'If I was you, I'd go away quick.'

'Why should I?'

He was holding her close, and even as he kissed her, he felt a qualm of uneasiness. She was so little and frail and thin. It was a damn shame to think what a life she must lead. But he was the busker, and he stifled the thought. Life was all too short to worry about other people's troubles.

'Why should I go away?' he asked again.

She made a queer little noise that was half contemptuous, half a sob. 'Because you're a mug.' She pushed him away, and this time he was surprised at her strength. 'Here,' she said. She was holding out something towards him in the dark. 'Now will you go away?' A piece of money rang in the road as she thrust her handful on the busker.

'You haven't got much,' she said. 'It was all in your left pocket.'

The busker lit another match. 'So you're a dip.' He

333

ruefully placed his possessions in his pocket. He caught her sensitive long fingers and gripped them hard. 'Where'd you learn that?' It was humiliating to have his pocket picked.

'A dark girl taught me. And Dad.'

The busker felt a new interest in her. 'It was a nice piece of work,' he commented. 'Why'd you give me back the stuff?' He drew her towards him. 'Like me, huh?'

'I want you to clear out.'

'Why?'

'Because Dad's got ideas in his head. He's trying to make you travel with us.'

'He seemed to have the idea that you liked me,' the busker mused.

'I do. That's why,' she said in a whisper, 'I want you to go, see?'

'I can look after myself.'

'You don't want to get mixed up with my crowd. They won't do you no good.'

'Protecting me again.' He tried to draw her down beside him. 'A little kid like you.'

'I'm telling you to get going.'

'Will you get into trouble for coming away?' he asked.

'I don't take much notice.'

'Wait.' The busker turned back with her. 'I'm going back with you.'

'Why?'

'Well'—he was at a loss—'I don't want you to get hurt by that rotten swine because of me.'

'Don't you be silly.'

But the busker followed doggedly. 'I've only just found you again, and you want to run away from me.'

The girl laughed, and Duke was shocked to hear the mocking ring of that laugh.

'Wouldn't Dad love to hear you?' she said grimly. 'He's got his mind set on getting you to travel with us. He thinks you'd be worth a mint of money. And I'm the bait.'

334

'He might be right.'

'If I was you, I'd go away quick.'

'Why should I?'

'Well, you know Dad.'

'I'm not scared of him. As for this idea of his . . .' He stopped.

'I'm not that low down.' She was half crying, half angry.

'I didn't say you were. But if you'd let me walk back a bit of the way. . . . I know the track now. You said you liked me.'

'I don't know you.'

'Oh yes, you do. I feel as if I'd known you for years.'

'It won't do no good,' she said. 'It's no use trying to put any soft stuff over me.'

'I'm not trying to put any soft stuff over you. I'm on the level. I look at it like this.'

The busker was surprised to hear himself saying wild words. One part of him stood back shocked, repeating, 'Keep clear, no ties.'

'I look at it like this,' he went on stubbornly. 'A chap like me, a bit careless, just drifting along, he needs responsibilities, see? ties, someone to pull him up when he's blueing his money, someone he can talk to, who'll see things his way. Now, a man's mates are all very well. But you know how they say: "Come and have a drink," and you go and have a drink. But when a bloke's got a girl or a wife, see? it keeps him straight.'

'Some men it doesn't. Look at Dad and Greg'ry Hourigan.'

'I'm talking about men,' the busker said impatiently, 'not lice. There's one kind of chap straightens up if he has someone who cares about him, someone who'd stand by him. But it 'ud have to be tight and square and fixed up properly. I'd want to be married, for good and all, see? I haven't got any money . . .'

'That doesn't matter.' She had said it impulsively, and he felt her shrink away ashamed the moment she had spoken.

They had reached the paddock fence. 'Walk a bit of the way back with me?' he asked, all the old arrogance gone from his voice.

As they wandered up and down the track, he began to know every hole in it.

'Like Dad and Greg'ry seeing each other home,' she suggested, laughing.

He told her all about his mother, and how he learnt to play the guitar—about his whole life.

'If you got to know me better,' he was saying, when the bush began to be lighter.

'The moon must be coming up.'

'No,' she told him. 'It's daylight, that's all.'

'Well'—the busker looked down at her—'you'll have to let me come home with you now.' She did her best to persuade him to go back to town, but he shook his head. 'I'm tired.' She was tired, too, and she gave in.

The shack looked different in the dim light. 'Let's not go inside,' he suggested. 'I don't want to wake them up. Let's just sit here and talk a bit more.'

They were still talking when Mrs. Hourigan came out to milk the cow, the only cow that had, so far, escaped Gregory's predilection for drinking things away. Mrs. Hourigan stood regarding them a moment, as indifferently as if they were two fence-posts.

'How I look at it is this way,' the busker was still explaining. 'I never realised that a man needs ties. Not that I mean to go getting tied up to your family—the sooner we give them the slip, the better—but I mean me and you, travelling together, we'd get a break sooner or later. With my talent and brains . . .'

Chapter XXV

I

THE Stray was trudging back to camp from her last visit to Snow before he was removed to Goulburn Gaol.

'You get out of Orion quick,' Snow had insisted on parting. 'Get on the move and stay on the move. I don't want none of them snoopers askin' where you got Jimmy. You look after young Jimmy, see?' He scrutinised her anxiously. 'That suit you?'

The Stray nodded mournfully. 'I'll look after him, Snow . . .'

'Well, what?'

He was impatient, she knew, of any long-winded lamentations or farewells.

The Stray gulped. She had been going to ask if he—well, perhaps not loved her, but just if he really considered her as his mate. Now, even now, she was afraid to ask. Suppose he told her bluntly, as he well might, that she could go to hell for all he cared, and that Jimmy could go with Mrs. Tyrell. She dared not put her fortunes to the test, but, woman-like, she so desperately wanted the assurance of Snow's regard for her. That would make all the difference between insecurity, fear and despondency, and a warm, comforting hope. If only Snow would say: "Listen, Dance. When I come out, we'll try to start all over again, just the two of us and Jimmy.' But he just looked at her and said 'Well?' in a hard, toneless voice.

'What is it?' he asked again, his face as bleak as the cell wall.

'Oh, nothing.' The Stray gulped. 'So long, Snow.' He did not like tears, and she forced them back for fear he might turn away disgusted. That she could not bear.

'So long, Stray.' Snow had reached out his hand to her in a hard, friendly grip, and that comforted her not a little. 'So long.'

That was all she had to remember; all there was to cheer her in the weary, desperate months that lay between his going and his release. She felt almost as though Snow had died. Her heart ached for him, laid away in a captivity that was as cruel to him as to a wild beast. She could not bear to think of Snow with the walls he detested closed in around him, crushing him down oppressive stone on stone. It was like burying him alive.

She had not liked to burden Snow with her worries, so small in comparison with his imprisonment. She had agreed to get on the move and stay on the move from loyalty to his wish, but she could not help wondering if he was right. As she tramped gloomily along the road, she was thinking uneasily of the kindness—the really terrifying kindness—of those nuns. Father Farrell had passed her on to the convent, and the nuns had done their utmost to find her a good home. So far the Stray's stubborn refusal to part from Jimmy, her insistence that her 'husbing' wanted her to stay with 'friends'—namely, the Tyrells—had thwarted their efforts. Until Snow came out of gaol, she told them stoutly, she would hawk jug-covers, and travel south to the cannery where he would meet her. But she was nervous and suspicious that their efforts to 'place' her would be successful. The Mother Superior had even suggested that she might work in the laundry at the hospital. All in all, the Stray considered, the sooner she and Jimmy got away from this interest in their welfare the better. The thought of being constantly under supervision, with kindness and respectability all about her, made her feel, as she told Jimmy, like 'a cat on a windy night.'

'It's good of them, Jimmy. I ain't saying that; but mi-Gord what kind of a life would we have with them rustling about every minute of the day?'

She had wanted to settle down, she admitted that, and

here was her chance to do it. But to settle down and be improved was a different matter.

They had got a lift into town, but there was no one going their way to the camp, so they cut occasionally across fields where the road took a curve, for they wanted their tea, and it was getting dark. Jimmy knew all the short cuts. He was the kind of a boy who would find a short cut across a roof-top, if it seemed to halve the distance. Now and then the Stray complained that it would have been quicker to go by road as he helped her up steep banks and through fences.

'Where are we?' she demanded, coming to rest panting on the sheer edge of a cutting.

'We go across that paddock and then out the back of that orchard, and that brings us on the road again. Come on, Dancy.' Jimmy was already off again impatiently. He treated Dancy with a combination of casual derision and protective liking. 'I'll look after her,' he had promised his father proudly. 'We'll be all right.' He was secretly thrilled by his parent's mishap. There were not many boys, he reflected, who had their dad in gaol for stealing sheep.

They came to a high bank overhanging a small, grassy patch by the road where those disinclined to camp at the Three-Mile often pitched a tent. Jimmy stopped and peered over a briar at the sound of voices, and the Stray, overtaking him, peered over his shoulder. When she saw who was below, she jerked back with an involuntary exclamation of dismay. Miss Phipps was wrathfully laying down the law to two drunken, red-faced gentlemen who surveyed her with a swaying gravity.

'I was here first,' she said firmly, 'and I like privacy. I would request you to leave.'

'Lady,' one of the two hiccupped. 'Always camp here. Don' we, Joe?'

'Thasso,' his mate agreed. 'Have a drink, missus?'

'Well, if you won't go, I will.' Miss Phipps nervously gathered her scattered odds and ends into what seemed to Dancy the same small, burst cardboard suitcase and the

339

same old sugar-bag. 'Things have come to a pretty pass when a lady cannot choose a place of retirement without . . .'

'Don't go.' One of the gentlemen clamped a large detaining paw on her shoulder. 'Siddown and have a little drink.'

'Thasso,' his mate nodded.

'We know how to treat a lady. Even me wife says that. Nobody can say we don't know how to treat a lady.'

'If I met your wife,' Miss Phipps said haughtily, 'I would tell her you drank methylated spirits when you were away from home.'

'Don' make no difference.' Her captor still retained his grip on her shoulder. 'Drinks jus' as much at home. Haven' seen her for five years. Siddown.'

'I won't sit down.'

'Siddown,' he roared suddenly. As Miss Phipps tried to wrench herself free, he thumped her roughly on to a stone. 'An' take a drink,' he added in a threatening voice. 'Or I'll belt your head off. Sayin' I dunno how to treat a lady.'

At this point Miss Phipps gave a yell. 'Dancy,' she screamed. 'Oh, thank goodness!'

Dancy realised that Miss Phipps, casting her eyes upward for help, had seen the interested Jimmy and Stray peering down at her. There was nothing for it but to slide down the bank and land almost at the feet of Miss Phipps's tormentors.

'Come on, Phippsy.' The Stray put a good face on it. 'Better come along with me an' Jimmy.'

Miss Phipps sprang up, snatched her baggage, and headed down the road. The two drunks, taken by surprise, blinked for a moment at this interruption.

'Th' lady,' the one who was flourishing the bottle observed, 'going have drink.' He turned suddenly ferocious. 'Gerrout!' He advanced on the Stray threateningly. 'I'll teach yer. Taking a lady away. Know how to treat a lady.'

'Keep off.' The Stray ran nimbly backward.

But the man still came on. ' I'll give you something for yerself,' he shouted.

'Is that so?' the Stray said grimly. 'You come a step nearer and I'll give *you* somefing too, you . . .' She was thoroughly frightened now, and spat names at him that made Miss Phipps shiver.

The man halted and half-turned. 'No lady,' he said with an attempt at dignity.

But his mate was annoyed. 'Nobody ain't going to call me that,' he announced.

The two of them turned purposefully upon the Stray, who backed slowly, bristling like a kitten. Then, as the men closed on her, she bent swiftly and snatched up the empty bottle which had caught her eye and towards which she had been retreating. With a guttersnipe ferocity she brought it crashing down upon the head of the one who had said she was no lady just as a stone from Jimmy caught his mate on the ear.

The next moment Jimmy, the Stray and Miss Phipps were speeding down the road. They ran strung out in a row, Jimmy first, then the Stray, then Miss Phipps gasping for breath and trembling. They did not realise there was no pursuit, not in fact until they were forced to stop for lack of breath.

'Well, Phippsy,' the Stray panted, 'you've got some marvellous pals.'

But Phippsy, for once, was too scared to be haughty. 'Oh, Dancy dear'—she fell on the Stray's neck and hugged her—'if it hadn't been for you, I don't know what would have happened. Those terrible creatures!'

'Well, if you will go telling blokes off . . .'

'I didn't. I wasn't. Oh! don't be so horrid to me just as I've found you again. If you only knew'—poor Miss Phipps was as redolent of trouble as an Irish stew of onion—'oh, if you only knew all I've been through. Where are you camped?'

The Stray looked cautiously at Jimmy. The last thing she wanted was Miss Phipps on her hands again. She had enough to worry her without that. 'We ain't camped there no more,' she explained. 'We're moving.'

'Well, I'm coming with you,' Miss Phipps declared. 'I never realised before, Dancy, how really valuable your . . . your methods are. I have wronged you in the past.' Miss Phipps's tone had an unusual warmth. 'I thought you rough and coarse. But I realise now that roughness may be a very present help. I would feel much better travelling with you.'

'Now, see here.' The Stray turned aggressively on her erstwhile camp mate. 'If you think I want you loafing on me, eating twice your weight, and sneering and jeering, and causing rows, you've got annuver fink coming. I wouldn't travel with you, Phippsy, no, not for quids. So you clear, see? Hoppit. Get away wherever you came from and do your own battling. We got enough trouble.'

She set off at a rapid pace along the road, but to her dismay Miss Phipps kept pace; and not only that, but she now burst into tears.

'Oh, Dancy!' she moaned. 'Oh, dear . . .'

The Stray's pace slackened. She met Jimmy's questioning look ruefully. It was no good, the Stray told herself; it was just like the Apostle said: You couldn't walk round what was coming to you. She stopped, and allowed Miss Phipps to rest her head on her shoulder. She drew her down on the side of the road and patted her and made soothing sounds and let her cry.

'You go on, Jimmy,' she directed, 'and get tea.

'There, there, love,' she said presently. 'It's all right.'

'Oh, Dancy, I'm so frightened. I'm so lonely. I'll do anything you want. Please let me come.'

'There, now,' the Stray soothed. 'Don't talk about it. I guess I didn't mean it. You can come.' She sighed a little. 'Though *where* I don't know.'

'Oh, Dancy, that is good of you.' Miss Phipps humbly planted a wet kiss on the side of the Stray's chin.

Poor Miss Phipps, the Stray noticed, had lost weight, had lost much of her old insolence.

342

'Don't you know where you are going, dear girl?'

'Just on and on.' Dancy straightened up and removed Miss Phipps from her shoulder. She had to put her arm round the older woman's waist, for Miss Phipps was, as she said, 'much shaken by her terrible encounter.'

'Anyway,' Dancy promised, 'wherever it is, you can come too.' Surprisingly, the presence of Miss Phipps had given her a renewed strength. Perhaps Miss Phipps's woebegone aspect, her dependence, was a comfort. No one else depended on the Stray, neither Snow nor Jimmy nor any of the travellers.

'Come on, Phippsy,' she said in her old rough way. 'Get a move on. Jimmy will have tea ready.'

They moved down the road, Miss Phipps leaning her weight on Dancy's thin arm.

II

Jimmy had prepared the tea by scraping a layer of black ants off the top of a tin of raspberry jam, toasting some stale bread, and getting the billy to boil. They ate in silence; the Stray and Jimmy because they were thinking hard, but Miss Phipps because she was ravenous. There never was such a woman for eating, the Stray considered.

After tea, as though their reunion had called up his wandering spirit, the busker materialised on the other side of the fire. He had slipped on to a vacant box, and was at home drinking tea, almost before the Stray had recovered her breath.

'Cheerio all,' he said, appropriating a mug. 'Here's luck. How's the girl, Dancy? So this is young Jimmy, is it?' And without further preamble he turned to Miss Phipps. 'I've just come from your camp. Dropped in to see you.'

'I don't want to see you,' Miss Phipps replied coldly. 'I told you that.'

'I like to keep an eye on you, Dora. Who got you the job you chucked away, I'd like to know? Just as well I do keep an eye on you. You ought to know not to camp with metho fiends by now.' He turned austerely to Dancy. 'And as for you, Stray.'

'Don't you dare call me that!' the Stray flared.

'Well, as for you, Dancy, I've always known you'd get yourself into trouble. Going round smashing blokes with bottles. Bottles indeed! A fine kind of life this'd be if everyone went round getting in a temper and smashing people with bottles. You could be had up for assault. Anyway, those chaps back there are very hot about it. Their last words were something about setting the camp alight.'

'Yeah?' the Stray retorted. 'Talk!'

'Maybe.' The busker nodded. 'Still, I thought I'd better bring my nap with me and stay the night. You need,' he said grandly, 'a man about.'

The Stray narrowed her eyes. She knew there was always something underlying the busker's glib flow of talk when he took this tone.

'You need a cove like me around the camp,' he went on, 'for protection. Bottles indeed!'

'A fat lot of good you'd be in a row,' the Stray remarked scornfully. 'Anyway, what's the game? You can't tell me you came all this way just to tip us off about them chaps back there. As for firing a camp, you'd have to hold their hand. Why, they're blind blotto by this. What are you up to?'

The busker did not answer for a minute. Then, 'The old firm,' he mused fondly. 'Only Snow missing, and after all there's his son to take his place. I was sorry to hear about Snow. I . . .'

'Cut it out,' the Stray ordered. 'You've got somefing up your sleeve.'

'Well, it's this way,' the busker admitted. 'I've always felt that if I had a bit of a turnout and a good little team to travel with, I could make a mint of money, just going from town to town and putting on a bit of a show. Shove up a bit of a tent. Posters. Me singing and playing and

344

Dora doing her stuff, and you could tell fortunes, or run a dart-board, or . . .'

'And me?' Jimmy demanded eagerly. 'What could I do?'

'Oh, all sorts of things. Take the money or play a drum.' The busker waved his hand grandly. 'There's money in it, and what you want is a guy like me that knows the game, see?'

'You're still the busking bum,' the Stray said in the tolerant tone of a grandmother. 'Still going to make a fortune, ain't you?' She became sardonic. 'But what you want the turnout for, and us? Why don't you go on your own, the way you always said you got along better?'

'Well, as a matter of fact,' the busker said frankly, 'there's times when even a wise guy like me can see there's safety in numbers.' He turned and beckoned, and from the shadows stepped Betty, a bundle in her hand and Bitsey on her shoulder. 'Dance, you remember Betty in Logan—Sharkey's daughter?'

'We're going to be married,' Betty said, her head high.

'And I'm not too keen on travelling with Sharkey. If you could give us a lift to Boswell . . .'

The Stray eyed Betty kindly. 'Anuvver mug,' she grumbled. 'Anuvver mug that's found a man to work for all her life.' And then generously, 'Course you can come. Why!' A thought struck her. 'The 'Postle 'ud marry you.'

The busker considered. 'I want things shipshape,' he said virtuously.

'Aw, what you worrying about? You can pay for a real legal turnout later, can't you? I guess the 'Postle 'ud do to go on with. Hey!' The Stray stood up and yelled: 'Ma! Thirty-Bob! 'Postle! Guess who's here. C'mon over. I want you.'

Miss Phipps was not the woman to see Betty throw herself away. She persisted in unwanted warnings while the rest of the gang overwhelmed the pair with congratulations.

'I suppose so,' the Apostle said doubtfully, yielding to persuasions. 'I can give you a religious ceremony, but it won't be legal, you know.'

'That's all right, 'Postle,' the busker said contentedly.
'We can't get a legal ceremony anyway until Betty turns
twenty-one, and that's a long way ahead. Old Sharkey
turned dog on us, didn't he, Bet? Said he'd get me for
abduction. So get a wiggle on you, 'Postle, I may as well
be illegal one way as another.'

Chapter XXVI

I

THEY left Orion, travelling in what Snow would
have called 'a big mob': the Tyrell family, 'Snow's
gang'—as the others called Dancy, Miss Phipps,
Jimmy, the busker and Betty—the Apostle and Thirty-
Bob. With them went a crate of fowls Thirty-Bob had
obtained by barter, Bitsey, Snow's dog, Bluey, Thirty-
Bob's Rex, Dick's greyhound, and two cattle-dogs belonging to Deafy.

Thirty-Bob had put the big bay gelding he had just
received by exchange in Dick's cart. The Apostle, having
failed in his tentative efforts to sell the truck, was persuaded to drive it to a bigger town and find a better market. 'Some of these fruit cockies down on the irrigation
might come at it,' Thirty-Bob advised. 'You leave it to me.'

Thirty-Bob had overheard the Apostle explaining the
truck's manifold defects to a possible purchaser; and
thereafter he would frequently break into an imitation of
Harry selling the truck. This never failed to send his
audience into fits of laughter, so that going along they
would shout gaily to each other in the Apostle's voice:
'And remember, the differential's also faulty.' They
needed something to cheer them up, for it was a silent,
thoughtful party that took the road.

The most thoughtful, as far as her nature would allow,
was the Stray. She had reached one of those crises when

the brain wearies and a dull, heavy cloud settles over all speculation. Perhaps it was the effect of her recent illness. Whatever it was, her thoughts went round and round: Snow, the future, Snow, the past, what was to become of her, where could she go, what was the use of living?

What was the use of wandering and wandering, never reaching any place of rest, coming to a town as strangers, and leaving it unwanted? Always going down the fenced road where the mountains, shivering in the heat or misted in rain, kept pace stealthily beside the van. Camped uncertainly on the edge of a settlement, on the edge of the road, hustled on, loitering, hungry, shrinking back from suspicion and words that hurt like a flung stone, or from the cold ignoral of safe, comfortable people who had houses about them, fences and walls and gates, who never knew what it was to lie or plead for a mouthful of meat, a stale bit of bread, and have it grudged and refused. Surely, surely, there must be a purpose that kept them so, that kept the travellers walking the treadmills of a God who ground His bread of human passions as slowly as the waggon wheels turned; whose step followed deliberate as the iron hoofs of the mountains keeping pace with the crawling cart. She thought of things like this, while her fingers flicked the gay threads, the scraps and beads in her lap. For the Stray had taken to the old stand-by of the road, 'faking' jug-covers. Her back ached sometimes with sitting; but she must have jug-covers to sell at the next town, taking them from house to house, from door to door, while her broken looks, her shabby clothes and shoes, pleaded for the shilling the jug-covers would never be worth.

'We going out selling to-day, Dance?' Jimmy would ask, and Dancy, wiping her hair back from her forehead with the same gesture that Mrs. Tyrell used, would reply: 'Sure we are, Jimmy love. I'll get these finished.'

Sometimes a storekeeper would refuse to let her have beads and net on her dole coupon, and she learned to keep

347

a few shillings in reserve for such a mischance. It was all to the good, the Stray reflected a little bitterly, that she wasn't well-dressed or had false teeth or her hair cut and waved. She was more sure of fending for herself and Jimmy as she was. People liked to despise you. It was a sort of luxury to look down on someone, if it was only Miss Phipps, who was so fat and useless. At least, she, Dancy, was a good battler, she could 'fake' with the best of them. She could care for Jimmy and herself, making a penny here, getting a little food there, some old clothes perhaps—anything that charity bestowed.

'We been lucky, Jimmy,' she would point out, 'that the police ain't asked no more questions about our dole.'

For dole-day was an ordeal. She went in dread until it was over, never knowing when some officious sergeant might not pounce down on her feeble tissue of lies and rend it from her. She had almost come to believe the Apostle when he said that 'it was so much less trouble to tell the truth. People never believe you; they admire you because they can't find you out.' But the habit of a lifetime was against Dancy making a change. A good, extravagant lie was to her like a briar bush to a rabbit. You could always slip into it and hide, then scutter and run for another patch of cover.

After leaving Orion they had turned south-west into a part of the country that had little to give, no matter how ingenious or pitiful a tale was told. While there had been heavy rain farther north, in this area there had been little rain for nine years, and now the heat of the summer was upon the place again. Already, the trees, the grass, had a dusty, ashy look, and the earth was but an anvil upon which the light beat and beat. It was a hard country, worn bare by winds as hot as a furnace-blast, only the jagged flints jutting above the surface; and the people in the same way were worn bare, grated down until only the hardest parts of them were left showing. Sometimes a gust of hot perfume would rise from the dust, as though the savour of dead herbs was in it, as in mummy-dusts. The country lay

348

in a shroud of light, wrapped in the yellow, wrinkled cere-cloth of gullies and hills.

There was no green, no gold; only the grey-brown of a scrub-turkey, the grey-black of a goanna, the black and white of a magpie. Here was a land that did without colour, did without water, did without everything but life, and that it snatched from some other creature. A place for the great black snakes, the thorny lizards, the trees and bushes hard and dry as stone.

The yellow liquid in the dams was not good for drinking, but they drank it for want of anything better. If they camped within a mile of a homestead, the women would tramp wearily up to ask for water. The Apostle had remonstrated at the sight of Mrs. Tyrell or the Stray staggering half a mile with a heavy kerosene tin of water in each hand; but Thirty-Bob and the busker told him not to be a mug. 'What chance would you and me have of getting water?' Although he might turn away a man, no farmer, however hard his heart or low his water supply, would refuse a woman or child.

'Look here,' one farmer's wife said almost desperately. 'We're not mean people, but this place hasn't had any real rain for years. Unless we get some in the next few weeks, we'll be drinking dam-water ourselves.'

Over a hook by the water-tank hung the bodies of three monstrous black snakes, victims of a thirst for water that they had never quenched. The Stray eyed them and shivered. How that woman could live here in a place where snakes came, could even, as she admitted, kill snakes, passed her comprehension. The Stray slept in the van with Miss Phipps for fear of snakes.

'It's all right for you,' the farmer's wife went on, seeing the Stray stare at her so dumbly. 'You can go on. We've got to stay here. Here!' She almost snatched the tin from the Stray's hand. 'Just this once you can have the water. Just this once, mind.'

The Stray said timidly: 'This is a hard country, missus.' She could see that the woman was nervous. Her thin face was taut with worry. 'I guess it ain't much living here.'

'We could be worse off,' the woman answered brightening. To her loneliness the Stray was a precious opportunity to talk. 'The soil's that rich it'd grow anything with rain. Why, one year we had the wheat so high, so full in the ear, we used to come out and sit in the evening and think how many bags it'd go to the acre.'

'Well, that was fine,' the Stray agreed heartily.

'It wasn't so fine,' the woman said grimly. 'A week before harvest a hailstorm came. It started just one side of our fences and finished the other. Not another property got it but ours. The wheat . . . there wasn't any wheat.'

'Oh!' The Stray did not know what to say.

'I sat down and wrote to my sister. I'd been having a real good cry. And I said: "We'll have just enough to buy a pair of socks and we'll pull them up and go on".'

'It's a hard country,' the Stray said again, for want of something better.

'You'd think so, wouldn't you?' Now the woman was quite bright and cheerful. 'But it isn't. I haven't finished telling you.' The Stray paused and set her tin down politely. 'We were cleaned out, you see. Nothing. My husband says: "Come on, old woman," but we'd been counting on that wheat. And everyone knew it—all the men farming out this way knew, and they were sorry. Do you know what they did? They got together down at the siding, and they held a little meeting and said: "One bag off every load for Jim Baker, chaps." And do you know, everyone in the district put a bag from each load to make up for our loss? Why, when they'd finished, there was more wheat for us down at the silo than we'd have from our own crop. Now wasn't that a wonderful thing?'

'It was that, missus.'

'People can be so kind.'

'They are when they know,' the Stray agreed.

Trudging back to the camp, she reflected sadly how those farmers, so kind to their own people, had sat up nights to see that the travellers took nothing, had rung each other up to say that a 'big mob' of travellers was coming through. Where one van, or a solitary bagman, might slip past without attracting attention, such a community of bad characters as themselves met with constant suspicion.

As the little troop filed past a farmer's fence, it would be made aware that just inside the owner was loitering to shepherd them past his property. He might even have a rifle across his saddle. When he wasn't visible, they were uneasily conscious that he was riding along just the other side of the hill, ready to pounce on them in any wrongdoing. They knew, and he knew, that it was the law of the track that 'a man must battle for his horse,' by fair means or foul his horse must be fed, though he go hungry. And the grass on this route was a vanished dream. There were a few tough thistles and a bit of salt bush, sometimes not even that.

Thirty-Bob and the busker would go out by night foraging in the wheat-fields, taking one sheaf from every stook, and, with a nice sense of delicacy, only from those stooks farthest from the road, where the depredation would not be noticeable. There was no sense, as Thirty-Bob said, in 'cruelling the game' for the next comers.

At Combingal the Tyrells had expected news of Dick. They went to the post office to see if there was a letter waiting for them, they combed the hotels and the camps for news. But the town seemed to be interested in nothing but the send-off to the troops who were going away to Sydney next day. It was in a whirl of patriotic enthusiasm and over-run with young men in ill-fitting uniforms and big boots.

A little sadly, the travellers stood to one side of the street to watch the troops marched down to the park, where they were to be addressed from a flag-draped platform by the mayor and other notables. There was to be a band and a roll-up of Boy Scouts and little girls from the Junior Red Cross, and proud, tearful mothers and

351

sweethearts and sisters in their best dresses. The sunlight glittered on the silver and brass of the band, on the leaves of the trees, the waving flags and bunting.

'Arr, come on,' Thirty-Bob snarled. 'What the hell's it got to do with us?'

The little main street, the little town in its pride and stir, reminded him too much of the town from which he came, and a pang of impotent fury and contempt shot through him. As these young men were, so he might have been, raw, simple, proud. He could not go back to the simplicity of these boys in their hot, mustard-coloured uniforms. He was outside all that, 'on the outer,' as they would say. He didn't want to go back. Why, it hurt him even to watch 'a lot of mugs looking like sheep in a sale-yard.' But dimly he wondered why it hurt him, whether somewhere there might not be in his case-hardened person a remnant of the lad he had left behind when he marched off so young to battle with life. He could laugh at these kids, but they had something he had never possessed: a belief in the purpose of their lives, a belief in something bigger than themselves. And even if the belief was a mistake, what of that? It was the feeling that you had a purpose that mattered.

'Come on,' he said again impatiently. 'Let's get back to camp.'

His companions refused to stir. Their lives were not so exciting that they could miss the interest of a free show. There were the officers, chipper young cubs from the militia with smart uniforms, throwing their weight about, and ordering the police sergeant to clear the way; while the impassive old sergeant, who had known most of them when they were little boys, refused to be bullied and made his own arrangements with an unhurried air. There was the rank and file, as rough and tough a body of men as ever growled about their officers; old 'diggers' who had seen service in the last war, veterans with seamed faces and work-hardened frames; young men who thought of the 'jaunt overseas' much as they would of ranging off to the

Gulf country to shoot alligators and buffaloes or of a droving trip with cattle. They saw no reason why these smart sprigs of 'cockies' sons' should order them about, and they let their officers know it in no uncertain manner.

They were seething with wrath, not only at the insulting airs the young militiamen gave themselves, but over the confusion and muddle of the whole business. A good part of the district's unemployed had joined in a body, joyous at the thought of good food, good clothes, self-respect and money to spend. They found themselves issued with old uniforms that had been left over from the last war; the very same coats that, dyed black, had been issued to them with their dole as clothing relief. They found that no sooner had they signed up than they lost their dole; and their pay did not begin until they reached camp near Sydney.

In the middle of the mayor's peroration about 'this land we love which you are about to defend from the horrors of tyranny and oppression,' there was a shout from the ranks: 'Hey, what about our dole?' and a chant of 'We want our pay!'

A murmur of disapproval and amazement went through the crowd. The mayor, put off his speech, concluded hastily and signed to the band to strike up. The officers glared furiously. The girls tittered. And Mrs. Tyrell, in a piercing shriek, cried: 'It's Dick! It's Dick's voice, I tell you!'

She was with difficulty restrained from breaking through the ring of Boy Scouts and little girls in fluttering white, and flinging herself on Dick's stalwart figure in the ranks. 'It's Dick,' she kept repeating. 'Oh, my God! He's gone and joined up.'

Sure enough, as soon as the parade was dismissed, Dick made his way towards them, a smile all over his big, stupid face; and hugged his mother just as if nothing had happened. He seemed to think that now he was in training for a hero, it wiped out any little misunderstandings

353

there might have been. He even patted Deafy on the shoulder to show he forgave him.

His small brothers and sisters clung about him; the busker shook him by the hand and dragged Betty forward proudly. Only Thirty-Bob held aloof.

'I always told you it was a mug's game,' he growled. 'And you go and fall for a lot of guff. You've got a fat lot of land to defend, ain't you?'

'Aw, don't be a . . .' Dick struck him heartily between the shoulders. 'Come and have a drink? Got any money, Ma?' His mother eagerly, gladly, produced a few shillings, which Dick pocketed. 'Come on, Dad. Let's go and have one. So long, Ma.'

'But Dick'—his mother caught his sleeve—'you won't go away again without . . .'

'That's all right. I'm coming back to the camp with Dad and Thirty-Bob. Been sleeping in a shed two nights. Gee, it nearly crawled away from me, the rats that was in it.'

The women found themselves standing alone on the pavement while the men pushed their way through the swing door.

'And have something to eat,' Dick called over his shoulder. 'I could do with a bit of tucker. K-e-r-r-ist!' he said with a sigh when they got their beer. 'What with not being allowed to stouch any of the coves in charge of this turnout, and no pay, and no dole.' He drew a long draught and wiped his mouth. 'It's tough, I tell you.' But he was smiling delightedly at his own superiority.

'You big, flaming mug!' Thirty-Bob swore at him for a while, but in a friendlier tone than he had used for some time. 'That's all you're good for,' he ended up. 'Just to be a home for bullets.'

Dick was inclined to be injured. 'Ar, lay off,' he pleaded. 'I on'y get till to-morrow night. Fill 'em up again. Your shout, Dad.'

Deafy was reflecting his son's glory. He had forgotten, almost, that lift under the lug which laid him out. He shook Dick's hand after the third pot of beer. He patted him on the shoulder after the fourth. By the time they all piled into the cart and trotted back to camp, they were singing, the busker's soulful yodel soaring up into the bright light of the later afternoon.

They ate, they went back to the hotel again, returning drunk and hilarious at midnight.

'Well,' Deafy defended himself from his wife's reproaches, 'it only happens once that the boy joins up.'

And Mrs. Tyrell, despite the dwindling of her reserves, was overcome with the logic of this argument and her own affection.

'He might as well have a good time while he can,' she told the Stray. 'Poor Dick! It's only the other day, it seems, that he was a little feller selling with me round the houses and pinching fruit.'

It comforted her to feel that Dick was back again, if only for a few precious hours, demanding money from her in his old way, making her feel she had some share in him. Her heart overflowed with mingled grief to see him go, and pride in him, so big and strong and careless.

Dick was trying to persuade Thirty-Bob to enlist too. 'Look at the time we could have. Why, there's half a dozen of us got it all planned to meet that bastard of a lieutenant after dark and bash his face in.'

But even this lovely prospect failed to tempt Thirty-Bob. 'Arr, it's a mug's game,' he said over and over again; but each time with less conviction. The thought of Dick going off without him, seeing new things, getting into new brawls and beer-houses, with no Thirty-Bob to jeer and argue and lie their way out, was too much.

'You need a flamin' wet nurse,' he said at last. 'A man ought damn well go with you to see you don't get into no trouble.'

Dick grinned. 'C'mon.' He seized Thirty-Bob by the elbow. 'You're yellow as . . .' He made an unmentionable comparison.

Thirty-Bob pretended to be furious. 'I'll show you,' he spat. 'You bastard!'

Next morning they went off arm in arm to persuade the enlisting officer that Thirty-Bob was going with the squad to Sydney, if he had to ride the buffers.

The new excitement threw the camp into a flurry. Thirty-Bob wanted to sell his horse, the Apostle's truck and Dick's cart, and 'make a clean-up' before he went. Luckily he had to forgo any such idea, as the lure of the hotel was too strong, and he and Dick were constantly in and out providing against the horrors of a dry canteen when they should reach the city camp.

Thirty-Bob left the horse for Deafy to sell, with many injunctions not to part with it under a certain figure, and more advice about disguising its age.

It was almost a relief when the train pulled out with Thirty-Bob and Dick hanging out of the window, waving as though their lives depended on it. Mrs. Tyrell cried all the way back to the camp.

'Poor boy,' she kept saying. 'Why didn't we tell that there enlisting man that he's only eighteen?' She was deciding to interview that officer the very next day, when the thought of Dick's fury dissuaded her. Then she cheered up. 'He'll probably enjoy himself,' she said, wiping her eyes. 'After all, Bob's with him.'

At the next town, the Apostle, as the person most likely to call at the post office for letters, found a telegram waiting. It read: 'Don't let Deafy sell horse. Coming back. Wait for me. Thirty-Bob.'

They waited, perplexed. They waited four days in all before a very tired, dirty Thirty-Bob arrived at the camp. All he wanted to do was to sleep off the effects of several days' solid drinking. They pestered him with questions, and he answered as briefly as he could.

'I got there all right, but they says I got flat feet. Wouldn't have me at any price. Well, put me on a horse, I says. I never use me feet anyway, if I can help it. The cows just chucked me out with nothing but this here

356

uniform and a return ticket. One poor cove what had a weak chest they did the same, and he's sold his bike and his camping gear, and he's back on the track with nothing but the uniform.'

'How about Dick?' his mother asked anxiously.

'Oh, Dick's all right,' Thirty-Bob yawned. 'He's in clink already.'

He had had a good time in the city, seen all the sights, drunk all the drinks, free, fought three policemen and had been discharged sympathetically by a patriotic magistrate; then, becoming fed-up with the city, he had sold his return ticket and jumped the train back to his natural haunts.

The lurid pictures he drew of camp life deterred many a traveller from joining. 'Four showers for two hundred of us; the food so putrid they had to chuck half of it away; raining all the time and water leaking through the holes in the roof. Half of them down with dysentery; no decent boots; no uniform; and the damned officers' mess planting a rose-garden round their quarters because the place looked so bare.'

'It serves Dick right.' Deafy took on a paternal sternness. He had had time for the exhilaration of Dick's send-off to wear away. 'He needs a bit of straightening up.'

But Mrs. Tyrell went out begging wool. Dick should not go overseas without enough socks. She sent off all the money she had to him at once, lest he should need anything.

One thing Thirty-Bob did not tell them. It was something so secret that he could not tell anyone. He was relieved, overwhelmed with gratitude to the kind fates that gave him flat feet. Not that Thirty-Bob was by any means a coward. He would have reached for the trap-setter and felled anyone who so much as hinted at such a thing. No, what he felt was that he had escaped as an animal might escape from a snare.

On his first night in camp he had been prowling about restlessly when he realised what was wrong. The camp was

357

enclosed by six strands of barbed wire. He went up to it curiously, touched it with his hand, stood looking at it as though he had never seen it before; and the horrible realisation came over him that he was inside! A curious panic had seized him at that moment, a claustrophobia, a horror of being fenced in, unable to get out. He would be like this for years, cooped up under guard, ordered about, drilled, without a mind of his own or a way of his own. He could have blessed the doctor who refused him, he could have flung his arms about his neck and kissed him. Thank God for flat feet!

That night as he looked up at the kindly stars, glinting down at him through the frail, crooked twigs of stringy-bark, as he enjoyed the hard ground under him, and the freedom from walls, from ranks of snoring men, he felt such a love for this hard, hot country that he could have patted the very grass. If anyone wanted to fight for the place, he decided, they could come and fight him here, on his own ground. He'd fight; no doubt about that, if he had to fight with his teeth. Sooner than give up one inch of the stretching plains and valleys, the high hills of the country he owned, he would die many times. But thank God for his flat feet!

II

They travelled slowly so that they would not 'knock up' the horses. Sometimes they would camp for a day or two where the grass was good. The country was better here; but the heat was not mitigated by furious winds, dusty and scorching, that flung dry leaves and dirt in their faces as they drove.

Always the waves of wheat flowed on, on either side of the road; and over the waves of wheat you could see the air shivering and blowing as though the wheat were on fire. To see the wind blow the hot air before it, as it quivered and shone, was a new thing for Dancy, and it frightened her a little. She had seen mirages on the plains, mirages that showed trees beside pools of clear water, but never the air afire, wavering like a curtain when the wind shook it.

They passed siding after siding where mountains of bagged wheat awaited trucks. The paroquets fluttered about, making such a din that under the stacks a man had almost to shout to be heard. The sparrows in their thousands dug in their sharp beaks, boring holes in the bags so that the wheat would trickle out. Most of them were so fat they could hardly fly. Thirty-Bob declared that they must get away with at least a bushel a day between them, but as the wheat made up the weight absorbing moisture from the air, no one worried.

At Marellan, Thirty-Bob got the offer of some bag-sewing, and he managed to work Deafy and the busker into the team. It cheered Deafy not a little to find he could still outwork men younger than himself; and the other two accused him cheerfully of 'pace-making' and getting extra money from the boss for making them work harder. In a little over a week the job cut out and they went on again.

Now they were travelling through a patch of country where the road was only two sandy ruts running between walls of mallee scrub, so thick and black that alone the Stray would not have dared to drive through it. The strip of sky above the two black edges of the road narrowed to a ribbon; the air was stifling; and when they passed the mallee and came out where the wind met them in a roaring column of red dust, the Stray was relieved as though she had passed through some danger.

'Last lap,' Thirty-Bob said cheerfully, as they took the horses out at dusk. 'We'll be in Boswell to-morrow night.'

The day after to-morrow was dole-day, and whether they liked it or not, they must push on.

The wind, that raged so industriously by day, always downed at sunset, as abruptly as if it had heard a knock-off whistle blow, leaving the loneliness for the stars and the slow clouds travelling. Always at this time the Stray, amid the duties of making camp and getting food, thought of Snow caged like a tiger in his cell, sitting with the still patience of a brute, waiting and thinking—his thoughts pacing the prison of his head. This night she watched a frail crescent moon glowing with one star above the black hills; and as she bowed to it, the Apostle came up and paused to watch her. A girl had once told the Stray that you must bow seven times to a crescent moon to make a wish come true, and someone else had told her you must turn round three times. The Stray was doing both, just to be on the safe side.

'What were you wishing, Dancy?' the Apostle asked.

'It don't come true, Harry, if you tell.' But she had been wishing that when Snow came out of gaol, he would settle down somewhere with her in a green place with a house to shelter them. It was such a fantastic wish that had there been three crescent moons in the sky, Dancy doubted whether their united strength could bring it about.

'Harry,' she asked, 'how long is it now?' The Stray had never learnt how to keep time. She was always pestering the Apostle to tell her how much more of Snow's sentence there was still to run.

'We've been travelling just over five weeks, Dancy. That makes it six weeks and three days.'

'Harry?'

'Yes, Dancy?'

'I s'pose Snow 'ud want to go on travelling when he comes out. You don't think he'd localise?'

The Apostle shook his head. 'I don't think he ever would. He's been on the track so long, it's in his blood.'

The Stray sighed. 'I was just wondering. They say once you start on the track you die on it.'

The Apostle smiled at her. 'There could be worse fates.'

Rising in the chill before dawn, the Stray doubted it. The wind was blowing again. It crept through the marrow of her bones, and she was glad that Duke had the job of putting the horse in the van while she packed the breakfast mugs away. Miss Phipps, who had been slightly less obnoxious, but was as helpless as ever, merely crouched over the fire until the last possible moment.

'What's the betting the truck breaks down?' the busker asked sourly. He claimed he had 'worked himself poor' pushing that truck. Not but that he had great schemes for buying a half share in it from the Apostle on credit, so that his troupe might have transport, whenever he collected them. He was afraid the Apostle might any day feel a 'pull' and go off to some unheard-of place, but so far he had stayed with them, mainly as spiritual support for Mrs. Tyrell and the Stray.

It was on the Apostle that Dancy and Mrs. Tyrell relied in any perplexity, and so much did they value his company that on one occasion when the truck was out of petrol, and the Apostle announced that he would just camp where he was until he found means to go on, they had begged from every garage in the little town, returning in triumph with two gallons, after hours of pleading.

'Cripes!' Thirty-Bob had said with a yawn. 'Is that all you get for a day's outing?'

They had been speechless with rage at his lack of appreciation; but the Apostle had known what their efforts meant. *He* had appreciated them.

'I bet the damn thing breaks down,' the busker grouched. 'It's just the day for it.'

As the sun rose, the wind, which had been so cold, took on its load of heavy red dust and heavy heat, and came bowling along in a succession of willy-willys that, for the time of their passing, obliterated the road, so that only the plodding rump of the horse was visible. The stinging, blinding grit filled their mouths, ears, eyes, so that every now and then they would turn the horses aside from the full blast of it, and even debated camping in some sheltered place. But there were no sheltered places. The red sand flung itself over everything, and they might just as well endure it going on as sitting still. So they struggled on, and the hurricane would now ease off, now fling itself on them again with a fresh shriek and a heavier load of dirt.

Towards afternoon they came over a low rise, and the Stray, rubbing the grit from her eyes and peering ahead, saw a line of green. Not the dusty grey-green of the gums, but a clear, lovely colour of willows, a solid wall running for miles each way.

'What's that?' she called to Thirty-Bob.

'That's the irrigation,' Thirty-Bob responded. 'We'll be there in an hour.'

As they came to the first bridge, a flock of galahs rose in a pink-and-grey cloud, shrieking above the swift, green water. Grey ibis stalked through the now vivid green of the rice-fields covered with a shallow blue flood. Pink masses of cleaner blossom hung over the fence of a house, and a hundred flowers, blue, white, purple and rose, coloured the gardens. None of the travellers spoke. They let the horses stretch their lean necks to the deep green grass of the roadside, where tiny golden daisies shone. They devoured the soft green, with their eyes pleasuring in it, as the horses pleasured with their noses buried in tender shoots.

Behind them lay the hot, wind-swept plains. Only a mile back the land had been barren as the desert of Egypt. But here the water flowed through the deep channels and all was paradise. They rested a little, then went on past orchards, rice-fields, vineyards, vegetable gardens, acres of tomatoes, acres of grain. The Israelites must have felt much the same when they came to a land flowing with milk and honey.

The children gave little shouts of excitement to come suddenly on a man leading four camels, which he had brought to the town, he told them, 'on spec,' to make money giving rides.

Last year a farmer had let the Tyrells camp by his fence on the irrigation canal. Perhaps he might let them camp there this year. Mrs. Tyrell was busy already with plans. But the Stray sat in a kind of dream. She had come to the promised land. Surely among all these riches there must be some place for her, for Jimmy, for Snow. Surely they could stay here forever among all these beautiful orchards and this cool water. How she loved water! She craved the sight of water, clear, green, flowing, as long as it was water. Surely Snow would stay here. Oh, he must! And the people they passed looked kind. The town of Boswell had a flourishing prosperity; a cleanliness; a trim, tree-planted, shady main street. If only she could stay, if only she could! She was enraptured with Boswell.

'There's the cannery,' Betty said suddenly. She was riding beside the Stray.

A group of buildings, dull red, as though they were angry, imposed on the view. They sprawled from the main street to the railway line, rows of red buildings painted with big white letters, telling the world that this was the property of the Boswell Co-operative Fruit-Growers' Society. There were sidings for the railway trucks everywhere, and trucks stood around like hens around a homestead doorstep.

They passed across the railway line; and Boswell ceased to be a neat, pretty township, and became sprawling and slatternly, a haggard stretch of goods yards, stock-yards, cannery yards, and bare, plain country beyond. Gone were the flower-gardens, the delicate trumpet vines, the glow of bougainvillaea, and green gloom of great trees. There remained only an arid stretch of bare, beaten, red earth with fences flung to mark a field from a road. And here the little company pulled their horses into a lane that formed the cross-bar of an H. On one side of them lay the stock-yard, on the other the foundations of an old store known to the bagmen who camped there as the Millions Club.

It was only a cement floor raised on pillars, but in the wet men could crawl under this shelter and stay dry; not that they needed to worry about shelter from anything except the dust.

The red dust had taken to this particular lane and was patrolling it like an officious policeman on his beat. It would come past in a willy-willy, that rolled down the middle of the beaten stretch of dirt between the railway and the stock-yard fence, twitching the few straggling gum trees, sifting a few dry straws for evidence, nodding the dead thistles. There was no corner the dust did not search out. Despairing of finding another camp, the little troupe just settled where they were in the lane. The children were tired and wanted their tea and began to cry. Red dust lay in a film on the food; it went to the bottom of the kerosene tins of water. The horses stood switching their tails, their heads drooped away from the stinging grit. The flies were so thick they committed suicide in hot tea, in anything left uncovered, and they crawled and buzzed so that it was a weariness to wave them away and a sickness to endure them.

Thirty-Bob went one way, the Apostle another, Deafy a third, each looking for a better place to camp. The dusk closed down and the wind dropped. The mosquitoes came out, at first only in squadrons of a few million at a time. Then the main army arrived from the direction of the irrigation canal.

Thirty-Bob came back with the news that the cannery wouldn't be starting on the apricots for a week, and that their old camp by the channel was occupied. The Apostle and Deafy had no better luck. Mrs. Tyrell fretted, but everyone was too tired to make any further effort. There was no feed for the horses in the lane, so in low undertones it was decided to duff them in on the banks of the canal, and get them out before dawn, when the inspector would be riding round.

It was a hot, still night. The clouds had closed down like a blanket beneath which the earth lay, a fever patient, burning, tortured, stifling, unrelieved. The clouds did not mean it would rain. They would clear away by morning, but they made the darkness and the chanting of the mosquitoes more unendurable.

Over by the deserted rice store three small fires burned, and shadows showed about them in the smoke. The Millions Club was in darkness, but the occasional spurt of a match and a low murmur of voices told that it also was occupied. Presently in the quiet a voice rose in denunciation; it was a voice like a rusty lawnmower.

'The workers!' the voice rasped, 'the workers wouldn't wake up if you put a bomb under them.'

Thirty-Bob groaned. 'Kerist!' he exclaimed. 'Ain't it bad enough with a rotten camp and heat and mosquitoes, without having Burning Angus and the Dogger into the bargain?'

Chapter XXVII

I

THE Stray went to Mrs. Dexter for information about a job in the cannery. Mrs. Dexter had worked there every season since the cannery was built; and travellers were always told: 'Go to Mrs. Dexter and she'll put you wise.'

Mrs. Dexter's camp was less a camp than a defiance thrown in the teeth of the town. There was so much furniture in the tent that there was room only for Mrs. Dexter to sit in the doorway among her geraniums and aspidistras, an implacable figure. She owed life a grudge, and life seemed to return the hostile glare with which she regarded it. Her habit was to nod her head gloomily at any piece of news and remark: 'I could have told you that—ah! and more. But I don't believe in talking.'

Steadfastly regarding the town that had turned its back on her, she sat motionless all day in her doorway, dignified, stout, permanent as a Sphinx, or, as some less poetic person put it, 'like a bump on a log.' Mrs. Dexter's grievance against Boswell was a concrete one. A worthy widow woman, she had not only brought up two sons in the sweat of her brow, but had saved enough to buy a little piece of land on which the sons, otherwise not notable for diligence, had built a house. Here Mrs. Dexter had settled very happily, only to discover that the man who sold her the land did not own it—he had a lease which expired nine months after the house was built. The land then reverted to its rightful owner, and Mrs. Dexter had nowhere to go. The unrighteous lessee had vanished with her money; she could not remove the house she had built, and she had no case for a lawyer to fight. Everyone said it was a shame; but, since there was nothing else to do, poor Mrs. Dexter had perforce to move all her furniture out by the railway fence and sit beside it, hoping that next season, if her varicose veins were not too bad for her to stand, she would be able to redeem her fallen fortunes by the same hard work in the cannery which had previously built them up.

As for her two sons, they called themselves drovers; but the only signs of their profession were ten dogs, each tied to a separate stake about the camp, each with a separate kennel and a deep hole worn in the dirt where the unhappy animal dragged its length of chain. The sons lounged about, waiting for a job to leap out at them, and despite their convenience to the stock-yard, nothing ever did. They had suggested to their mother that she go with them 'on the track'; but old Mrs. Dexter refused to leave her furniture, now sadly deteriorated by the weather; she refused to leave Boswell, which she had known before ever there was an irrigation channel or a cannery, when it was just a dusty little collection of shacks in the middle of some sheep paddocks.

After all, she could sit in her doorway tragically demonstrating the hardness of heart that was Boswell; she could advise all strangers, particularly female strangers, and condescend to them, and tell them her story, and receive much more sympathy than she could have done anywhere else. In her own way, she enjoyed it all, enjoyed being bitter and giving warnings against trusting anyone.

'Look where it's brought me,' she would say, shaking her head. 'Just being too trusting. I never thought I'd come to this.' And people deferred to her and respected her and were sorry for her.

'You'll need to register as soon as you can,' Mrs. Dexter told the Stray. 'The first to register gets on first. Last year there was thousands of women came and no jobs for them.'

The Stray's face lengthened.

'One year there's too many here, then the next year they think it's no use coming and there's not enough,' Mrs. Dexter continued. 'Though I will say, there's not such a tough crowd the last few years. I can remember when the girls at the cannery set on the union organiser and tore off all his clothes. Not a shred on him, and them laughing and booing him as he ran. A rough crowd, they used to be.'

'Why'd they do that?' The Stray was intrigued. She wondered why she had not visited this cannery before.

'They wanted to strike for more pay, and he advised 'em not to. Took off all his clothes, they did, and tore 'em up. But it's not like that now.' The light of enthusiasm in the Stray's eye made Mrs. Dexter feel that perhaps this new acquaintance was not among the nice women who now came to the cannery. 'A quieter lot you wouldn't wish to meet. Of course, there's a good deal of drinking and fighting still, but you don't need to mix with them that does it.'

The Stray hypocritically agreed.

'You'll have to buy a pitting-knife, but they buy it back from you when you leave. It's only a few shillings. Then you'll have to buy a uniform; that's only six shillings. They don't buy that back, of course.'

She gave the Stray further directions: whom to see at the registry office, and what to say.

'Tell him you haven't any money,' she advised. 'He's a very decent kind of man, and he mightn't ask anything for registering you.' The Stray was dismayed at the cost of getting a job, counting up the shilling here, the few shillings there, that she must spend.

'Some wear rubber gloves,' Mrs. Dexter advised, 'but they're no good. You can throw 'em away by evening because the caustic soda eats them. Others wrap cloths round their hands, but I don't wear anything. You'd better get a rubber apron if you don't want to ruin your uniform. The bosses like you to look decent.'

That was all very well, the Stray thought ruefully, but unless she could raise a loan from Ma or Thirty-Bob, she would have no earthly chance of getting the uniform.

'They run the peaches through the caustic,' Mrs. Dexter explained, 'and that takes the skins off. Then you take your pitting-spoon and spit the peach . . . and give the stone a twist . . . here I'll show you.' She produced a curved knife. 'This is the fastest way . . .'

By the time Mrs. Dexter had told the Stray a few more things that might be of use to her, Miss Phipps had wandered up.

'Some come to the cannery thinking they're going to make a fortune,' the old lady was saying. 'But the boarding-houses charge them thirty-five shillings for board, and a girl's lucky if she can make two pounds, to begin. Of course it's different with you; you don't have to worry about board.' She nodded at Miss Phipps. 'Is your sister going to register, too?'

'Oh, yes, indeed,' Miss Phipps cooed. 'Lovely money.'

'You want to watch out you don't slice half your hand off,' Mrs. Dexter advised. 'Of course, they've got nice rest-rooms for them who faints; and if you *do* slice your hand, they put you on compo. . . .' Seeing them puzzled, she explained: 'Compensation money while it heals. But mostly,' she added, 'a woman just gets her hand bound up and goes on working. I've seen women with their hands cut to ribbons working away for dear life. They couldn't afford to stop. You got to expect to cut yourself a bit at first.'

Miss Phipps did not seem to be as enthusiastic as she had been. 'A woman's hands,' she declared, regarding her own stubby fingers, 'should be her first care.'

''Tain't my hands.' Mrs. Dexter misunderstood. 'It's my legs. I can hardly stand up for the pain now, and what they'll be like after a week at the cannery . . .' She gave a little groan of anguish. 'But I don't want to be camped down here the rest of my life.'

At the registry office, much as Mrs. Dexter had predicted, the man in charge took one shrewd glance and said: 'Sixpence for men, but we don't charge anything for women to register.' They thanked him.

Betty had come with Dancy and Miss Phipps, and when he asked Betty's age, they all assured him that she was older than she looked.

'It's the worst of being little,' Betty said ruefully. 'But when me and Harley gets some money, we're going to buy a wedding ring. That'll show them.'

But when the cannery started, there were younger girls than Betty, and older women than Mrs. Dexter—women with white hair and grim, wrinkled faces—all kinds of women; slatternly harridans; stout, respectable matrons; flirtatious, fashionably-dressed, little things giggling to each other; girls in groups chattering; girls in twos and threes, all kinds and shapes and sizes.

Some of them had just come with friends to look over the cannery and talk to old acquaintances. They hung about under notices that said: 'Strictly No Admittance' and 'Trespassers Will Be Prosecuted.' Others hobnobbed with strangers, comparing cards from the registry office, joining the long queue that filed past a small window where a couple of harassed men strove to sort out the particulars of each applicant. Those waiting chewed gum and ate oranges. Some had brought children with them, despite the rule that no children were allowed on the premises; but they argued that the cannery had not properly started yet.

Beside a huge heap of boxes Chris Crane had established himself, with a fountain pen, a book of union tickets, and a big, thick account-book. As each woman was employed, she went straight to Crane to pay her union dues, and there were many, like the Stray, who could only pay the ten shillings required of them from their first wages.

'That's all right. Yes, that'll do,' Mr. Crane kept saying. His keen eye roved the crowd, particularly the group of men lounging and waiting around the landing outside the entry. Chris Crane had the memory of an elephant, and he was out for blood. Already he had vetoed nine men who, to his personal knowledge, had been working as strike-breakers in Orion. This cannery of the Boswell Co-operative Fruit-Growers' Society was 'A Hundred Per Cent Union'; and anyone the union vetoed, the cannery refused.

The management had had too much trouble in the past not to realise that it saved money and time if they kept the union friendly. The board of management, most of them growers, were a reasonable body of men. The cannery was a model cannery with a cafeteria room for the women when they fainted, and a matron to attend the sick, and a dormitory for girls that charged only seven shillings a week. In fact, in the workings of its welfare committee, the cannery had as good a reputation as in any other department. The cannery took pride of place over the packing-shed because it was bigger; and over the Store that distributed all the farmers' needs by reason of its more intricate organisation.

There was in the town and on all the farms around a feeling that the cannery 'belonged' to Boswell. The townspeople loved it, they were proud of it, they took visitors to see it; and the cannery basked in this affection and was reasonably kind to the eight hundred women who assembled beneath its great roof, with its three hundred men, to add their quota to the two-hundred-and-fifty thousand cans of fruit that issued daily from its maw. The very children in the town knew that the cannery had turned out nine-and-a-half million cans last season; and could talk about 'local ripe' and 'export ripe' and 'local green' and 'export green'; just as the children of a wheat farmer can tell you the rainfall in inches and points for the district.

The cannery was so big that most of the new recruits spent the day before they came on to the job in exploring. They went in and out gaily, upstairs and down, peering at the great vats where the syrup boiled; the twisted pipes and the shining taps; the piles of coal for the furnaces; the trucks shunting to and fro; the grimy engine-rooms; the great machines where sheets of metal were stamped into lids, rolled and soldered into cans, clattered away in trolleys to be filled.

Here and there someone's bicycle had been wheeled in to the engine-room or the can-making department, so that the owner could keep an eye on it, and this casual appropriation of space by a stray bicycle was tolerated as long as the foreman did not trip over it. Men hung their coats where they thought they would be handy, and were grieved if a machine chewed them up. There was a casual and friendly air, even at the most furiously busy places.

The cannery hissed and steamed with the great green vats, like ten tame railway engines rearing up to the glass roof, where lattice shutters screened off the worst of the heat. Though, as the Stray and her mates found, with a temperature of over a hundred outside, it was much more inside, and the provision of beds for those who fainted was a desperate necessity. The cannery had to work when the fruit was ripe; and this was at the hottest time of the year, the apricots just before Christmas, then, after a break of three weeks, the peaches and nectarines.

More and more the place seemed like Hell, as the weeks wore on, and the temperature rose; nerves were frayed; tempers developed blisters of hate. A simmering haze rose up over sorters, packers, canners, pitters, speckers on the belt cutting out specks from the fruit; they worked with a maniac energy, ready to drop from exhaustion, too busy to talk. As soon as the whistle went, the women would run to their corners and begin work as though their lives depended on it. Soon the sweat would be pouring off them. The barrow-men on the pitting-floor rushed up with fruit; the men pulling down boxes, bringing cans and taking them away were cursed or bribed by the women to work faster. Minor grievances developed, as a woman felt that her neighbour was given cans and she neglected; complaints and squabbles arose over someone taking a place that was closer to the supply but belonging to another woman.

The closers soldering down can-lids, the men taking off fruit as it came through the cooker, the tappers-out, the stackers—they all felt that they were being simmered in this cannery, as though it were a great red vat; their very life-blood running away and trickling from them in a syrupy sweat.

Even when Miss Phipps cut her hand very badly and was led out to be stitched, the Stray worked on, wasting not a moment. She knew that the 'fat fraud,' as she termed her companion, would now loaf round the camp on compensation. But though she cut her own hands, though she was ready to faint from the terrible heat, she clung grimly to her determination to make money. Whatever happened, she would work and work. Snow would be coming out of gaol, and they would need everything she could earn.

Little Betty worked beside her like one possessed. How would the busker ever get to the city if she did not earn the money? And he must, he must get a chance. Thirty-Bob, with his accustomed luck, had got a job wheeling a barrow at one of the packing-sheds; but the busker and Deafy could only lounge about and curse and hope for better luck when the peaches started and more men would be put on. Presently, they both found a chance picking apricots; and it was hotter and harder, they claimed, than stewing in the cannery. They had a long way to go; but they drove out in Thirty-Bob's cart, taking a fresh horse each day, so that it would get the benefit of the grazing. They even debated moving out and camping at the farm where the picking was done; but it would have been too much of a hardship for 'the girls,' so Deafy and the busker put up with the long, hot ride; while Mrs. Tyrell silently endured the heat and ants and flies of the stockyard camp, and sat sewing pot-holders and minding the children.

By the time the knock-off whistle blew, everyone was always too tired to do anything but just get back to camp and lie in whatever shade there might be. Sometimes they went mad and went up town for beer; but the Stray, always so generous, was frightened even to spend sixpence.

Jimmy and the Tyrell children ate oranges all day. They would go to the packing-sheds with a sack and take away a new load of rejects each morning. The men were only too willing to give it to them, for if the children did not eat it, it would have to be carted out of the town and buried in pits. Eating too much fruit 'upsets their insides,' Mrs. Tyrell complained. It had been the same in Orion, where cherries were easy to come by; but she was glad for the children to have the fruit, for in such hot weather they could not eat the meals she prepared—meat stews and bread for the most part, or just bread and jam. All the women wanted was tea. They drank tea by the gallon, black, with plenty of sugar. The camp was so hot, so hot and dusty, and the insects crawled and bit like a million red-hot needles, so that they could not sleep.

Even the local residents were alarmed by the weather. They were used to a climate that was a mixture of red dust and just plain dust, a dust-storm a day and no rain with it; but the heat was beyond human powers of endurance. There was something frightening about the vindictive pressure of the sunlight, bearing down like a heavy, hot weight. The Sydney papers quoted with respect the Boswell temperatures of 108 and 110 degrees day after day.

'It's got to break,' people said desperately. 'If this is what it's like now, what will it be when it warms up?' For the hottest season of the year was always January and February. The locusts had come out, and their shrilling added to the torture. The noise they made suggested they were cutting the air into zig-zags with a fretsaw. It was like a million tiny drills boring the eardrums.

The Stray and Betty ceased to congratulate themselves that they were camping and not paying board. At least the girls who occupied the dormitories or had boarding-houses to go to could get out of the heat part of the time. They did not return to a patch of sun-baked dirt on a corner of a lane, a tent where red dust sifted into everything. Betty and the Stray began to develop an expensive vice: inviting each other and poor Ma Tyrell up town to eat ice-cream in the Greek café. Thirty-Bob pointed out that for the money they spent, they could get properly drunk, but they preferred ice-cream. 'It's only just while the heat lasts,' they excused themselves and their extravagance; but the heat seemed to get worse and worse.

One relief was that Miss Phipps had left them. She had gone to stay at a cheap boarding-house until her money should be spent. 'She'll be back,' Mrs. Tyrell prophesied. And she was right. Miss Phipps found that the boarding-house keeper was 'an insolent woman'; and was back again, making life so hard for Mrs. Tyrell that that much-tried woman finally threw a tin plate at her and cursed her roundly. But even Mrs. Tyrell could not get rid of Miss Phipps. She always got over her rage and excused Miss Phipps on the ground that 'the poor thing didn't know no better.'

The Apostle was working too. He had gone out with Angus, the Dogger and Uncle 'snatching apricots', and was camped at the orchard where they all picked.

The number of women who fainted, who cut themselves, who answered back the forewoman, increased with the temperature. Finally the canning department became the storm-centre for one of the best rows of the season. There was always hostility between the girls who lived in Boswell and the others who came there in the canning season 'to make a cheque.' Some of the visitors were more expert than the locals, and on this occasion one city girl in particular was working with a turn of speed that was amazing. The girls about her were incensed that she would not talk; they said she thought herself too good for them.

They took to playing malicious tricks; and two of them, when her back was turned, deliberately slipped cans of apricots from her tray to their own. This was the last straw. Flaming with anger, the victim turned on her tormentors, and flung a whole tray of apricot cans at them. 'Take my cans, would you? Here, cop the lot!'

Friends joined in, and the two rival factions of 'City *versus* Boswell' fought until the cannery was a swimming mess of apricots; with tins flying and rolling everywhere, and a crowd of interested onlookers encouraging, and the forewoman trying to drag them apart. Eighteen women were sacked and went uptown to the hotel, later taking up the fight again in the main street.

Through it all the Stray and Betty worked on. The Stray, who took all a larrikin's joy in a good brawl, actually worked while the best fight of the year took place around her, and tins of apricots sailed past her to land with a splash and a clang in every corner of the canning floor.

'We don't dare to get sacked, Bet,' she murmured to Betty. 'It's all right for the girls that ain't got no one dependent on them. It's different for us.'

After that things tightened up in the canning department. The inspectors were more severe, small breaches of discipline were snapped at, there were more women dismissed. Poor old Mrs. Dexter collapsed and was taken to hospital.

'You want to look out,' Mrs. Tyrell told the busker. 'That little Betty's working herself to death, and Dancy ain't much better.'

But off they would go to the cannery each morning. 'It can't last much longer,' the Stray kept saying. 'There'll be the three weeks' break over Christmas, Bet.' And they looked with as much longing for that time of rest and peace as they had formerly looked to the opening of the cannery.

It was on a Sunday afternoon that the spell of abnormal weather broke. All the Tyrell camp had driven off with a lorry-load of campers who were going down the river ten miles away. Dancy was left to mind the camp because she was tired and wanted a rest.

She took the opportunity to wash, press and starch her uniform. The girls from the camps—and there were about forty of them—took a queer pride in being the cleanest and best dressed of any of the cannery workers. They would come home staggering with weariness and set to work at once to wash their only uniform, so that it would be clean and fresh for the morning. What it cost them, they only knew; but Dancy, who had never cared before how bedraggled she looked, was infected by this passion for a clean, starched overall. Having laid the garment away from the dust in Mrs. Tyrell's tin trunk, she set off uptown to indulge her passion for ice-cream. She felt a little guilty about it, for sixpence was sixpence; but the others were all away enjoying themselves, and she knew the camp would be safe enough. There were other camps about, and anyway no one would steal from a traveller. It wasn't done.

'There's going to be a dust-storm,' one of the neighbouring campers called to her, and Dancy nodded cheerfully. What was one dust-storm more or less? They had had any number of them. But when she reached the main street, she noticed a queer excitement in the few people about. They shouted and pointed and ran as though the devil was pursuing them. In the direction of their shouting and pointing, a great dun-coloured cloud was rolling up obscuring the sky. It came at a speed that was ominous, and as it came, everything was blotted out. Dancy, her need for ice-cream forgotten, stood rooted for a minute watching it. Then she plucked at a man's sleeve.

'Is it going to be a bad storm, mister?' she asked.

'Bad?' The man stopped for a moment. 'Well, last year a storm like this come up, and blew the roof off the hotel and twenty houses. Better get home, sister.'

But he had no need to tell her. Dancy was already speeding back to the camp. Her clean uniform! She could think of nothing but that uniform lying unprotected in the path of a dust-storm. How could she get to work to-morrow if her uniform was dirty. As she ran, the great cloud closed down over the sky, seeming to blot out the light of the sky. In the town the street lights were turned on, as though night had fallen. A dreadful roaring, that Dancy had not noticed before, grew louder and louder behind her; then the wind caught her and blew her along, the dust enveloped and choked her. Now, too, she heard the crash of corrugated iron, as the roofs began to go, and she flattened herself against a fence that trembled under the onslaught of the hurricane. Something zipped past; it clanged and danced head over heels; and she realised that it was a sheet of tin blowing like tissue paper. The force of the wind was so terrible that she could not stand upright. Twice it flattened her to earth. Presently she rose on her hands and knees and began to crawl. She had only a little way to go, she told herself dully. The big tent could not be far ahead. But the big tent was gone, the little tent was gone. Thirty-Bob's tarpaulin was flattened against the fence like a sail. With a sob of relief Dancy threw her body across the big tin trunk and lay there spread-eagled; her uniform, her precious uniform, and Betty's, lying beneath. She had saved them.

A new note was added to the howl of the wind, a maniacal howl that had seemed the highest note it could compass. It was the rain coming. It came pelting down on her; and with it, the hail, a stinging, lashing hail that revived Dancy from the daze into which she had fallen. Slowly she began to tug the trunk under the van. And there she lay on top of it, while the hail bounced round her in a white, roaring curtain. Now and then she would make a little rush out into the downpour and salvage anything she could snatch.

As the swift fury of the storm abated, she made more and more of these little, trembling runs, clutching up clothes that lay in pools of mud and water, sodden bread, a tin of jam half full of hail, a dirty paper of butter. A bag of flour, transformed into dough, lay in a puddle, where it had been flung when a tucker box overturned.

Presently, Bluey came crawling up, trembling and licking her face. From the direction of the Millions Club, where most of the campers were sheltering, encouraging cries were heard, and figures began to run to her help with coats over their heads.

The Stray crouched there under the van; and suddenly all the strain of the past few weeks, the heat, the hard work, the terrible fatigue welled up in her, and she began to cry. She buried her face in Bluey's neck, that smelt of wet dog, and she cried silently and terribly, as a woman cries when she is at the last of her strength.

II

By the time the half-drowned pleasure party had hurried back from the river, Dancy, with the help of friends and neighbours in the nearby camps, had succeeded in recovering most of the scattered property, with the exception of a tin dish and a blanket that had seemingly blown away. Some of the bagmen from the Millions Club put up the big tent for her and the little tent in which she slept with Miss Phipps. The sun was shining, just as if nothing had happened, and torn telephone wires and roofless sheds were the only evidence left of the storm's passing.

The fowls of which Mrs. Tyrell was so proud came pecking back, all except one which had been killed by hail. The rosella, Betty's main anxiety, had been safe in the van. Everyone shouted at once, asking questions, giving their experience of the storm. Travellers from all the camps went to and fro estimating damage and enjoying the excitement. Thirty-Bob went off early in the evening to swap a horse with a Greek farmer, and after long haggling, finally agreed to accept two kerosene tins of home-made wine as a make-weight with a young mare.

He came back with his wine, very pleased, and insisted that everyone have a little to help them over the shock. He was particularly solicitous about Dancy, who every

378

now and then had a fit of shivering. 'It'll do your nerves good,' he advised.

Dancy sipped the brew doubtfully. 'It's full of brown paper,' she cried.

Investigation proved that the brown paper was the skins of the grapes. It was very new wine, and despite the number of people who helped consume the two kerosene tins full, the potency of the brew had its effect. They were all hopelessly drunk—not just the Tyrell camp, but the other camps as well.

Dancy woke next morning with a racking headache; and was nearly late for work for the first time. It wouldn't do to be put off now. After all, the work before Christmas didn't count. It was the peaches, three weeks later, so everyone told her, that gave the piece-workers a chance for big money. She and Betty were now much faster and more skilful. As soon as the three weeks' break was over, they would return to the cannery with a greater confidence.

It was a hot three weeks. They all shifted camp to the river, about four miles from the town. Much to everyone's disgust, they could not get any dole. The police knew very well who were working and who were not. To support themselves for three weeks, even in their customary meagre fashion, took money, and chopped a frightening hole in their hard-earned wages.

'Arr, what's the use?' Thirty-Bob growled. 'It's Christmas, ain't it? We might as well have a good time.'

That was the view of most of the travellers who hovered in the vicinity of Boswell over that three weeks' break. They got drunk and they stayed drunk.

It was so hot, and there was nothing to do. Of course, you could go in swimming; in the river, if you camped there, or in the irrigation channel, if you didn't get caught. The townspeople had an unworthy prejudice against bathing in the channel which provided their drinking-water. Not so the travellers. They believed that the townspeople were not clean, because they bathed in the town baths, where you had to pay to get in and where the chlorine disinfecting the water stung your nose and eyes. Every now and then someone was drowned in the irrigation channels, but the travellers still stubbornly refused to pay admittance money to the baths.

The Apostle, when his job petered out, reverted to his old habits, and on Saturday and Sunday nights he would drive to some nearby township, or merely go up to the street corner of Boswell and harangue the loungers from his soap-box until an officious policeman would send him away. Betty and the busker turned an honest penny by going off with the Apostle and doing a 'quickie' singing round the little townships. The polyglot population, Greeks, Italians, Central Europeans, would come out and dance to the music. Betty could tap-dance well, and they liked that too. They were a good-natured, happy lot of farmers around Boswell, kind to the travellers, generous and likeable.

'I'd sooner work for a Dago or a Chinese any day than an Australian,' Deafy Tyrell always declared.

Christmas passed in an extravagant burst of gifts for the children. The camp was littered with Christmas stockings and cheap toys, and the adults were nearly driven mad by the noise of whistles and drums and trumpets.

'Well, we might as well make the kids happy,' they told each other. 'It's only once a year; and it's not much we can give them.'

They lavished money on the children that they would have grudged spending for themselves. It was a matter of pride that, even if the townspeople had cool houses, the travellers would give their kids as good a Christmas, just as good a Christmas dinner. They had tinned plum pudding and a turkey that Thirty-Bob found one dark night. They had beer and crackers and cakes. But the money drained away in an alarming manner.

'There's the peaches coming on in a week or so, and we'll make a big killing,' they all assured each other cheerfully.

But the Stray's little roll of notes dwindled, a roll that she fastened to the front of her dress by a safety-pin—the same safety-pin to which hung a frayed bit of paper scrawled with the words: 'Pay Mrs. Grimshaw a thousand pounds.'

The week before the cannery was to open, they moved back from the river to the old, dirty camp behind the stockyard. In one way they were glad to see it, because it meant the end of the enforced idleness. Angus and the Dogger and Uncle were back in the Millions Club. Snake had enlisted with the object of undermining the morale of the army; and hot disputes arose between the Dogger and Angus over the ethics of his conduct. George the Bower-bird had appeared from nowhere and was up to his old tricks, prowling around deserted camps, swooping on rubbish.

'Well, George,' the Stray called to him cheerfully. 'Going to get a possie in the cannery?'

She was always a little afraid of the dirty, hairy maniac; and no amount of reassurance could convince her that 'Old George was perfectly harmless.'

'By rights,' he chattered, nodding his head excitedly. 'By rights I own that place. I do, by hokey! I own it. But they done me out of me rights.' He came so close to her that she shrank back. 'Put a light under the lot of them. That's what I say.' He waved his hands violently. 'See them all go up in smoke. You see. You can laugh. But up! Up in smoke! That's the way.'

'I don't want him bower-birding round this camp,' Mrs. Tyrell complained. 'He gives me the creeps, with his whiskers and his hands with them long, dirty nails.' But she could not be actively unkind to George, and she left a large parcel of bread crusts where he could find them.

The cannery began to take on workers again; and there were more and more coming to the town every day. It seemed as though the far-off cities had poured out half their women to can peaches. The Stray was restless and unhappy. Every goods train that pulled in to the sheds she half-expected would bring Snow, for she knew he was not the man to spend money on train-fares. In a way, she was relieved that he had not come. If she could only make 'a good cheque' before he arrived, it would be something to lay proudly before him, a concrete evidence of her value as a partner. Counting over her small store, she discovered with a shock that she would not have enough even to get her set of false teeth. Oh, well! it just meant she would have to work harder.

She was put on again on the first Wednesday after the cannery opened, and she worked hard enough to be glad when the week-end came. All Boswell spent Saturday in its usual fashion getting beautifully drunk, and Sunday sobering up. But on Sunday morning, as they lay about idly talking, a strange phenomenon arrested their attention—a column of black smoke, so thick and strong that it might have been the column of smoke that went with the presence of God in the desert.

For a moment they looked at it unbelievingly; then the full import of that awful omen burst on them. Thirty-Bob bounded to his feet, and rushed off towards the railway crossing.

'The cannery!' he shouted, as he went. 'The cannery's on fire!'

From all directions now people were running and shouting, their eyes upturned, amazed. It couldn't happen! It wasn't possible! How had it started? They blundered into each other in their haste and excitement. Where was the fire-engine?

The great black column of smoke was shot now with flame, a flame that burned with an unholy thunder. It rose from the sacks of sugar and sulphur in the packing-sheds, and it had an unearthly green streaked with rose, that made it like no fire anyone had ever seen before. It was as though a volcano had suddenly burst below the packing-sheds, and minor craters began to shoot up from a dozen places over the great sprawling bulk of the cannery.

In front of the building a crowd had gathered: a crowd that only stared open-mouthed and stood, not knowing what to do, that surged about and demanded the fire-engine. The caretaker and the few men who always stayed by the furnaces had gathered in an excited group, waving fire-extinguishers; and presently they disappeared into the smoke again with the intention of trying to save the books and safe in the locked office. The police had arrived, and began to busy themselves keeping back the crowd. Only a small group of employees were allowed to try what they could do in the way of salvage; and these were under the command of the manager, who had dashed up in a little red car and was issuing orders with the rapidity of a Bren gun.

'Get the hose from L4 and fix it to the hydrant,' he ordered. 'You, Jim, take a gang round the back and see if you can keep it from spreading to the dormitory. Four of you help Ellis (that was the caretaker) to get as much of the stuff as you can from the refrigerating plant.'

But in the face of a volcano, what are the desperate cries of one helpless manager? The great green and crimson flower rose straight in the air, and the spreading, rolling smoke-clouds enveloped everything in a haze that blotted the sunlight and reminded the Stray of the dark hurricane that had beaten her down to her knees. The crowd murmured for the fire-engine, and moved back nervously, as a great section of the wall bent and curled outward gracefully like a petal, and another section of roof leaned slowly inward. A telegraph pole, around which little adders of white smoke had been writhing, burst suddenly into flames, and there was a white flash and an explosion as the wires whipped apart.

'Get back there! Get back!' the police shouted, pushing at the crowd.

From every direction men and women were still hurrying, tiny figures whose very voices were drowned by the dreadful sounds the fire made in its upward rush. It was all so unnatural. There at mid-day, with Sunday dinners cooking peacefully in the kitchen stove; husbands dozing with the newspaper over their faces; birds chirping in the trees; the sun shining down on the baked, ordinary railway station; the ordinary streets and front gardens and little shops; instead of the comfortable, dull, red roofs of the cannery basking like a cat, this nightmare had broken loose.

It was worse than a nightmare. There was the prosperity of hundreds of people, the very heart and soul of Boswell, built so proudly from the savings of farmers and townsmen, turned before their eyes into an inferno, a roaring, outrageous, belching horror, that nothing could defy or halt; certainly not the tiny fire-engine that now came jolting slowly from the other end of the town, the firemen struggling with their braces, with their brass helmets, some of them half-dressed, and all soundly cursing the fire chief who had refused to come until he had put on his uniform.

A roar of frantic anxiety went up from the crowd. 'Don't hurry!' they shouted, maddened by the leisurely pace of the fire-engine. But the engine crawled on deliberately, and halted while the fire chief conferred with the cannery's manager, who was almost out of his wits with anxiety.

'The safe!' he kept saying. 'The books in the office.'

The mechanic from the electricity plant was much cleverer and quicker than the firemen. He had rushed up in his truck, flung out a long ladder, and was running up it to the light and telephone wires. With one swift flick of his cutters, he had severed them, and was running down again.

'What's up? What's up?' the crowd murmured. 'Why don't they put it out?'

But the heat was too great for anyone to approach the water hydrant. The Co-operative's hose was alight in any number of places, and the men had to retreat dragging it after them. The fire hose was much too short. The seemingly endless conferences went on, and the great fountain of fire raged and sang overhead, filling the heavens with its fury. There were tears flowing down the cheeks of the most hated of the foremen, tears that he said were due to the smoke. He was a man about whom rough jokes had been made by the cannery hands, a hard, steely-eyed, overbearing fellow who, they said, would be softened 'when a stone or an old galah was cooked tender.' But before his eyes, in no gentle syrup, was his whole life burning, blackening.

There was a muffled explosion.

'That'll be the petrol depot at the back,' someone said.

'They got out all they could,' another man told him.

Now the crowd had been pushed back so far that it could see only the great stalk of fire over the roof, the blank walls of fire where a wall of brick had fallen in. The onlookers began to circle round to join others behind the cannery and along the railway line, eager to assess what damage had been done there. The fire-engine set the example by driving across the railway line and round, but here it could not approach close enough to the cannery, until a section of the crowd tore down the fence and allowed the engine to get within reasonable distance of the water supply. Now, at last, the hose could be used, but the feeble jet of water looked less against that flaring fortress than a trickle from a garden hose.

The deliberate movements of the firemen began to quicken. There was just a chance of saving the cafeteria, and the can-making shop, which stood a little removed. They set to with a will. Part of the crowd which had begun to realise that its mid-day dinner was getting cold at home drifted away, to be replaced by new arrivals who added their questions and arguments to the hum that rose from the watching crowd.

Thirty-Bob was glancing about him. 'Don't see the Bower-bird anywhere,' he remarked.

'Who the hell cares?' Dancy clenched her fists. 'What's the Bower-bird got to do with it?'

'I'd like to know, that's all.'

385

Something in his tone arrested her attention. 'You don't fink he had anything to do wiv it?'

'It didn't start itself, did it?'

Dancy turned back to watch the fire. There was something hypnotic about that core of flame shooting up out of the husk of the cannery. She suddenly felt very tired. What was the use of working hard, of trying to go straight, of striving and planning? She had just one pound note pinned with that scrap of paper to the front of her dress. She might just as well have not worked. She could have sat about and drawn dole and been no worse off. She understood now what the farmers meant by their constant attitude of pessimism, their view that, if the rain didn't ruin you, you would be burnt out by a bush-fire. You could work and work and be no better off after years of struggle than if you had sat in the shade.

The next day news came that the Co-operative Store at Brienna, fifteen miles away, had gone up in flames; and the same afternoon a fire broke out at the Dried Fruit and Raisin sheds at Mapella. There was now little doubt that a maniac was at work.

'It's the Bower-bird,' Thirty-Bob declared that night, as they talked in undertones around the fire. 'It's him all right.'

'But why? Why?'

Thirty-Bob thought. 'He's just crazy,' he said slowly. 'He's been on the track too long.'

The others nodded. They had all met these madmen who had wandered alone, outcasts from human living, until they developed a vindictive hatred of all men and women. They would murder their own mates, fall upon innocent housewives, and cut them to ribbons, all without any reason but the madness bred by isolation and bitterness.

There was a pained silence. The travellers had all suffered from the loss of the cannery; suffered as much in their own way as the manager finding his fireproof safe still intact with its contents a heap of ashes. But they could not overcome their prejudice against police. The Bower-bird, however crazy, was one of them, and anyone who voiced his suspicions of the Bower-bird to the authorities would be known as a 'dead-copper,' more to be avoided than any maniac.

It was not for the travellers to interfere. They had looked year after year to the cannery as the one sure employment they could hope for. They had turned towards Boswell as a Mecca; they had always made rendezvous there. 'Meet you at the cannery' was as sure an appointment as at the next street corner. Now the cannery was gone, a holiday bonfire for a lunatic. It was no use being angry with the Bower-bird. He had 'been on the track too long.'

Chapter XXVIII

WHEN they had all gone, the Stray stayed on. Alone in the deserted camp with Jimmy, she waited for Snow, impatient and restless to be gone. She had had quite enough of Boswell. Not for her were the beauties of its green orchards, its drooping willows, its flower-patterned gardens. A little bitterly she reflected that all this paradise had meant was long, endless hours of work in a stewing hell, a grudging camp on the dustiest outskirt of the town. It would always be like that, always the worst end of a settlement that the traveller saw. Now she had been left here alone with Jimmy. Even Miss Phipps was shaking the dust of the Stray's camp from off her feet in a fine old rage.

Miss Phipps had remonstrated with Dancy about her determination to remain and wait for Snow.

'Surely, deah,' she drawled, 'when even *I* can see that it is better to keep in with a band of people, however uncouth, rather than trust to the uncertainties of . . . of meeting with others even less refined. . . .'

'Scared someone 'ull rape you, huh?' Dancy had asked, and then reflectively: 'Do you a lot of good, Phippsy.'

Miss Phipps had drawn herself up and given Dancy an awful glare. Without another word, she departed from that place rigid and unforgiving. How dare anyone, least of all that little guttersnipe Dancy, utter such a word as 'rape' in the presence of a Chester-Phipps! She would have liked to ask for her skipping-rope which was being used as a halter, but even if she must sacrifice her skipping-rope ('Such a good reducing exercise! Skipping improves the figah!'), she would not spoil her lips by addressing that low Dancy.

Miss Phipps was the last. There had been councils and discussions night after night to decide where they would go. Thirty-Bob was heading down the Murray and 'snatching a few currants.' Mrs. Tyrell wanted to go north to Orange, where a Chinese market-gardener always gave the family work picking tomatoes. The busker and Betty were almost agreed that the great city of Sydney, or alternatively Melbourne, should have another chance to employ the busker's talent and brains.

While they were making up their minds, a messenger had arrived seeking the Dogger—an excited little man covered in dust and perspiration, who, from his air of mysterious importance, could only be a member of the Bagmen's Union. He was brimming with news, and after awful hints that his message was for the Dogger alone, he spilled it in the middle of the camp.

'Out pickin', are they?'

'Yeah. Them and the 'Postle. Lot of these farmers are going to dry their apricots, so they say.'

The little man fidgeted. He wanted them to ask about his news, and no one asked.

'Well, seein' we're all friends here,' he burst out— 'members of the Union, eh, mates?—I might as well pass the word.'

They regarded him politely but distantly. The word, whatever it was, seemed to arouse no quiver of curiosity.

388

'It's like this,' he whispered, glancing round. 'Ever been through Coiling's Flat?'

'Yeah,' Thirty-Bob drawled. 'Dirty little rat-hole.'

'But listen.' The bringer of news fairly quivered with excitement. 'There's a big boom on there. It's going ahead like a house on fire. It's the mine. . . .'

'What mine?'

'They're reopening the works for treating the ore. Mills for crushing the stuff and stamping it. Zinc, wolfram, concentrates. Plants for treating it and melting down the chunks of rock. . . .' His technical knowledge was not extensive, and he faltered. 'They're going to put up plants worth a million, and they'll be wantin' chaps at the works. It'll be another Port Kembla. . . .'

'If it's anything like Port Kembla,' Mrs. Tyrell declared stoutly, 'I'd sooner stay away. Men waiting round the steel works, so that when a chap is killed they could get his job. Paying thirty-five bob to sleep in shifts in a lousy bed. Not if I know it.'

'Well, there's goin' to be a big boom at Coiling's Flat,' the messenger insisted. 'Hundreds of men they'll need. It'll be one of these war supplies, see? I come up right away to tell the Dogger. He's wanted there. Orders from Headquarters.' He was a little ashamed at having let out this important fact, but he had been bursting with the urgency of his message. 'I'd better get out to this orchard right away.' But he accepted another cup of tea, and sat for a long time boasting of the prosperity of Coiling's Flat. 'Money pouring into it,' he cried. 'And they're going to take on hundreds of men. There'll be big money. And we want our own men, union chaps. That's why I'm after the Dogger.'

'Big money?' Thirty-Bob's tone was derisive. 'There's always big money somewhere where you ain't.'

'Well'—the visitor rose—'I must be gettin' along.'

After he had gone they sat silent, but they were think-ing. It was Duke who spoke first.

'We could do with some money, couldn't we, Bet?'

'I don't want you to get hurt in no metal-works.'

'Oh! I wouldn't get hurt,' the busker said carelessly. 'Be damned to that.' He began to see the possibilities. 'Why, if what this cove says is right, we'll make tracks for this Coiling's Flat to-morrow.'

'Ker-ist!' Thirty-Bob sneered. 'Hold out a carrot to a neddy! What the hell's the use of rushing and sweating to get work? Damned if you ain't better on the track rations.'

'Well, I'm going to see if there's anything in it,' the busker said defiantly. 'I take it you're not coming?'

'Me?' Thirty-Bob was surprised. 'Why, I'll give it a go. Might as well be there as anywhere else.'

Mrs. Tyrell obdurately shook her head, as they looked at her.

'No,' she said, her lips thin. 'No, Deafy ain't going to get no hot metal poured over him.'

They laughed at her. Deafy, when the remark was roared in his ear, was indignant.

'I can work with the best,' he asserted piteously. 'I s'pose you want to go on selling pot-holders and aprons? We're getting old, woman. No, don't you start nagging.' He checked the rising torrent of Mrs. Tyrell's words with an upraised hand. 'You battle hard enough most times. Gimme a chance.'

'You're a fool, Tom. They won't take you on.'

Deafy disputed this. 'Anyway, we're going,' he announced, 'and that's all about it.'

To the Stray, her mind still bitter, still turned towards the blackened ruins of the cannery, where scavengers were even now prowling in the heaped ashes, the sudden revival of hope in her companions seemed nothing short of a miracle. They had been just the same all the way to Boswell, planning how they would spend their money at the end of the fruit season. Now it was ore-smelting or mining. . . . Anything, as long as it gave them hope, as long as it gave them somewhere to go, made them feel that they were not merely moving slowly around the walls of a great gaol, dragged on a chain from one dole-station to the next. Their faces had brightened; they sat straighter; they talked eagerly; arguing which route would get them quickest to Coiling's Flat; where they would get their dole; where they would camp.

They went off to spread the news to friends and neighbours, and the excitement increased as the story of immense riches at Coiling's Flat, jobs for all, bigger and bigger wages, spread and enlarged itself. Even Mrs. Tyrell, obsessed as she was by the vision of Deafy writhing under a torrent of white-hot metal, began to see the brighter side.

'It's a road that ain't been faked out,' she confided to the Stray. 'We can sell as we go. That is, if some of this mob don't get ahead of us.'

For the camps at Boswell were full of people who 'faked' or 'dropped' small articles: artificial flowers, belts made of kangaroo skin, brooches made of feathers, patent polishing powder—anything and everything to bring in ready money.

'We ought to make an early start,' Mrs. Tyrell continued, brightening still more at the prospect. 'I'll get some of our stuff packed to-night so that we can get away before it's too hot. If we start about four, we can travel till ten, and then rest through the heat.' Already her mind was busy about the practical details of the move.

When the Apostle returned to the camp later that evening, they overwhelmed him with enthusiastic descriptions of the riches to be won in Coiling's Flat. He had, with Thirty-Bob's shrewd assistance, sold the motor-truck, and was come to insist that Thirty-Bob take some form of commission.

'Now's your chance, Harry,' Thirty-Bob encouraged. 'You'll be able to get yourself a gold-mounted soap-box in Coiling's Flat. The place is booming like a gold-mine.'

'Yes, I heard about it,' the Apostle said, smiling. 'So it's got you too?'

'Well, a man wants to make beer-money, don't he? Ain't you going?'

'Oh, I suppose so.' The Apostle had bought a bicycle at the suggestion of Angus and the Dogger, who both had bicycles. Why couldn't he, they asked, throw his lot in with theirs?

The idea had appealed to the Apostle. There was always room for one more in the constant cross-fire of argument that went on around the camp of the Bagmen's Executive.

'Might as well take the bloody Apostle,' the Dogger himself had declared. 'Poor old bastard's breaking up fast. Don't like to see him left. He isn't any worse to live with than you, Angus.'

'We could keep an eye on him, too,' Angus argued. 'See he didn't put over too much of that Tolstoy stuff. Keep him on the right line.'

'Yes, I'm going to Coiling's Flat,' the Apostle told the Tyrells. 'But I haven't, I'm afraid, your expectation of making high wages. I just want to be with the Bagmen's Union, and that's where they'll all be going . . . all the people on the track.'

'There'll be plenty left,' Mrs. Tyrell told him. 'There's always plenty left over. Maybe you're right, Harry, about there being no money in it. But it's something, ain't it, it's something to think about? Tom might get a job navvying or that.'

'True,' the Apostle nodded. Men, he thought sadly, were all fevered to clutch at security, to feel that they had some settled place in life, however poor, that they were not outcasts from their kind. All were deluded into the belief that security in this world was possible. He could preach to them of the cosmic plan, give them some comfort if they would take it, but how few, how very few, would listen, any more than they would listen to the Dogger's and Angus's plan for reconstructing society. They would gallop hundreds of miles to snatch at a wage, to wear themselves to death, parch in the heat, and shiver in the cold, only so that they might not be left to the tender mercies of the police and the half-starvation of 'rations' in the outdoor workhouse of the roads. Humanity seemed to him so pitifully, so heartbreakingly, hopeful.

The Stray, regarding the Apostle's thin face, echoed the Dogger's judgment that the 'poor old bastard was breaking up.' He looked even thinner and shabbier than he had been when his wife was with him. There was not much likelihood of anyone employing the Apostle at heavy labour. He looked as though the first gust of wind would blow him away.

The Apostle met her looks. He crossed over to her. 'I want to speak to you, Dancy,' he said under his breath, and drew her cautiously out of the circle of the firelight. 'Here, my dear child'—he thrust something that felt very much like bank-notes into her hand—'I want you to do me a favour.'

'Course I will, Harry.'

'Get that set of false teeth.' She began to protest. 'You must let me give you the money. I've made arrangements with a dentist—the man on the left of the shoe store in the main street—a decent fellow. He said he'd make you the set for five pounds. It's all arranged. Now, just to please me. . . .'

'Listen, Harry; you'll need this money more'n I need them teef.'

'Not at all. First things first, Dancy. Your teeth are important. And you heard what Thirty-Bob said. I'm going to get myself a gold-mounted soap-box in Coiling's Flat. Besides, I've plenty of money.'

'You're a liar, Harry. I ain't never known you when you had more'n green leaves to eat. And I bet this's all you got for that truck.'

'Don't let's argue, Dancy. You'll be giving me real pleasure if you'll just take it and say nothing to the others.' He divined, as if by telepathy, that the thought had crossed her mind that she could hoard this money; keep it for Snow. 'Now mind, you're not to save it. I'm giving it to you to get those teeth, and I want to see them when we meet again.'

393

'We mightn't meet again, Harry.'

'Oh, yes, we will.' He patted her hand. 'Now be a good girl and just put that money under the old safety-pin.' She had been almost too overcome to do more than mumble her thanks. 'And remember, Dancy, wherever you go, however hard things are, just remember. . . . You're safe, you're always safe while you can trust, we'll call it . . . your Luck.'

'Right you are, Harry,' the Stray mumbled, embarrassed. Poor old Harry! she thought; it was a shame to see him tramping and preaching. 'A chap with an edjication,' she said to Mrs. Tyrell, who was busily clearing camp. 'He ought to do better for himself.'

'He's a good man.' Mrs. Tyrell had been told of the Apostle's gift.

'He's a bloody fool,' growled Thirty-Bob.

They had all gone, Thirty-Bob driving Dick's cart and swearing at the chestnut mare he had got with the kerosene tins of 'plonk'; Betty, with the little rosella sitting on her shoulder and the busker's arm about her; Mrs. Tyrell calling to the children and shouting instructions at Deafy, who drove his two dappled greys ('the best on the road bar none') with the air of a man setting out on a triumph, the children crying 'good-bye's' to Jimmy, who stood proud and unresponsive.

'We're glad to have the place to ourselves, aren't we, Dance?' Jimmy had remarked, when even Miss Phipps had stalked away.

'I'd be better pleased, Jimmy, if your Dad was to show up. I dunno what can of happened to him.'

'Oh, he'll be here,' Jimmy said, in a very man-of-the-world tone.

But days passed and there was still no sign of Snow.

'I can't make it out,' the Stray fretted. 'D'you think he's hurt, Jimmy?'

'Not Dad,' Jimmy assured her.

On the next Thursday, dole-day, the sergeant suggested that she should move on.

'But, mister, I'm waiting for my husbing. I gotta wait for him, mister.'

'Where is he?'

The Stray hesitated. 'He's in Goulburn.'

'You told me last time that if I let you stay another week, he'd be here.'

'I gotta wait,' the Stray replied stubbornly. 'Even if you don't give me no rations.'

There was trouble, too, about Don being found grazing on the banks of the channel. Only Dancy's fervent pleadings had saved him from being pounded by an irate inspector, who made her promise to keep the horse out of the irrigation reserve. Poor Don wandered in the grassless lane, snatching hungrily at morsels of dry straw and whinnying over the stock-yard fence at better-fed animals.

Dancy was on her way back from that ominous interview with the sergeant, walking sadly, her shoulders bowed with the weight of her trouble, when she almost stumbled over a gentleman who had fallen out of the side-door of a hotel, and was sprawled in the lane. Just a drunk, red-faced, sodden, lying dead to the world in the gutter, an object to arouse the disgust of passers-by, to start enquiries why the police didn't do something about it. But the Stray stood stock-still, then flung herself on the beastly object.

'Snow!' she cried. 'Snow!'

He attempted to thrust her away, as he sat up dazedly. 'Lemme alone,' he muttered. 'Dunno you.'

'It's me, Snow. Dancy. We've been waiting, Jimmy and me. Oh, Snow, I'm so glad you've come.'

He had swayed to his feet and was looking at her sullenly, but she doubted he could see her.

'Come on, Snow,' she coaxed. 'Lemme give you a hand back to camp.'

But he turned and staggered through the swing doors. Dancy doggedly followed him.

'Snow,' she was saying. 'Snow, lissen. . . .'

He turned on her savagely. 'Lemme alone,' he said again. 'Dunno you, see? Don' want to.'

But she persisted. She even appealed to the men at the bar, who watched grinning, and to the barmaid who, with a withering glare, turned her back.

'Here, some of yous,' Dancy called, 'gimme a hand with him, can'tcha? I got to get him back to camp.'

Snow, through the fumes of drink, only realised that someone was pestering him. 'Gerrout!' he said savagely, swinging his arm in what was meant to be a threatening way.

The flat of his hand caught Dancy across the mouth, and sudden tears of grief and horror sprang to her eyes.

'Snow!' she gasped, and then, turning savagely on the men in the bar: 'Won't none of you help me to get him back to camp?'

'Yes, get the brute out of here,' the barmaid said in icy tones. 'Or I'll call the boss.'

'Here, mate.' One man, better-natured than the others, stepped up and laid a restraining hand on Snow's arm. 'You just come on outside quietly and . . .'

'Brute?' Snow yelled in a rage. 'A brute, eh? I'll fight the lot of you. I'll fight any crawler who . . .' He flung off a stream of curses and threats that might have frightened anyone less used to curses than Dancy. 'I'll show you.'

Two more men came to the rescue. They took Snow on each side and propelled him, still talking and waving his arms, towards the door.

'Here y'are, Missy?' one of them said kindly. 'Now what you going to do with him?'

'Oh, mister,' the Stray gasped. 'I want to get him to the camp—our camp down by the stock-yard.'

'Right y'are,' the man said. 'I've got me jinker here, and we'll just take him down for you. I doubt'—he grinned—'if you'd ever get him there alone.'

She thanked him fervently.

'And you'd better do something for your lip,' he said. 'It's bleeding.'

The Stray wiped it on her sleeve dazedly. There was no room for her in the jinker, so she walked back to camp. She walked as though in a trance, a nightmare from which she might not wake. Boswell was the same; the heat, the flies, the glaring sun were all the same; even the people who passed her and pretended not to see her, as they always did, because her clothes betrayed her as a traveller. When she got to the camp, she was relieved that Snow had fallen asleep. Her two helpers had deposited him in the tent, and she sat silently at the door, crouched in a heap. Beside her Bluey lay, his yellow eyes fixed on that figure in the tent; his tail waved slowly to and fro. Now and then he would get up and try to enter the tent to lick Snow's face, but the Stray kept him off. She cautioned Jimmy to be quiet. They tiptoed round the camp during the long, hot hours of the afternoon; and Jimmy kept watch while the Stray went back to collect her groceries up town.

Evening fell, and Snow slept on. It began to be dark, and Jimmy and the Stray made their usual meagre meal of bread and jam. Sitting beside their tiny fire—wood was scarce by the stock-yard—Jimmy and the Stray talked in a whisper.

'If he's on a real proper beer-up,' the Stray whispered, 'he may go on for days.'

It was not that that depressed her; but those awful words Snow had spoken: 'I don't know you. I don't want to.' How long had he been in this town? And had he been avoiding them? She could not bear to think of Snow's disowning her before all those grinning men.

'Dad never goes on the booze much,' Jimmy declared. 'He can't stand it. He's never been a bloke what drunk much.' This comforted the Stray. Jimmy came and sat close to her. 'Don't you worry, Dance,' he whispered. 'He'll be all right.'

In the morning Snow woke, groaning, holding his hands to his head to keep it from splitting apart. The

Stray was awake and had tea ready for him. He drank about a quart in silence. Then he went away and came back looking very sick but sober.

'You right now, Snowie love?' the Stray asked humbly.

Snow felt very far from right, but he mumbled 'Yeah'; then managed a sickly smile. 'How've you and Jimmy been?'

Dancy eagerly began to pour out all that had happened to them, demanding to know in return how he had 'got on' at Goulburn. But Snow would only shake his head impatiently to her queries. Bluey, his tail active, crept up and laid his head on Snow's knee. Jimmy, without being asked, gave a supplementary account of his own doings. Snow, his eyes half shut, tried to be genial; but it was an effort, with a head that felt as if it was full of hot knives. He had a fierce desire to be going, just to feel he was fleeing from his misery.

'Let's get out of here,' he demanded, rising abruptly. 'I can't stand it.'

'Now, Snow?'

'Yeah. Now.'

'Where?'

'Anywhere. Got to get on.'

'Coiling's Flat way?'

'For Chrisake don't ask me. Let's go.'

Jimmy and the Stray bustled about breaking camp. Snow, after a feeble attempt to help, sat down again and nursed his head.

'Did you notice me teef?' the Stray asked humbly.

'What teeth?' Snow carefully removed one hand from his head and tried to open his eyes.

'Me teef. Me teef in me mouth.'

'Oh, yeah. Look out for that rope.' He hadn't noticed them at all, the Stray thought sadly. Presently Snow stumbled to his feet. 'Got any money?' he asked abruptly.

'What for, Snowie?'

'Don't ask what for. What y' think? I want a drink.'

'But, Snow, we're all packed nearly.' The Stray drew from her pocket a shilling, a sixpence, and a threepence, and placed them in his outstretched hand.

'This all you got?'

'That's all I got.'

'Well, pick me up at the pub, when you're ready.'

He was off before she could ask which pub, and it meant that she had to go from one to the other asking for him. When she did find him, it seemed as though the drink had done Snow good. He was much more like the Snow of old time.

'Sorry, Stray,' he said, as he climbed in the van and took the reins. 'You know how it is.'

It was his only apology—an awkward apology, but to the Stray it made all the difference in the world. He had not meant to be cruel to her yesterday. He had only been drunk.

'You didn't mean you want to get rid of me, Snow?' she asked fearfully.

He stared at her. 'Get rid of you? Why should I?'

'She's been worrying all the time,' Jimmy broke in, 'that you'd not want her to travel with us. I told her you didn't mind.'

Snow smiled. 'Well, if she can put up with us,' he said, 'it's a deal.'

The Stray met his eyes determinedly. 'For always?'

'Yeah. You an' me's mates. For always.'

'Well, that suits me,' Dancy said joyously. 'Oh, Snow!' She would have kissed him then and there, had it not been for the grave presence of Jimmy.

'If I had a bit of money,' Snow pondered.

'We're going to get lots,' the Stray said eagerly. 'Ain't that why we're going to Coiling's Flat? Millions, Snowie. They're putting on millions of men, and payin' 'em ten pounds a week and more. All the gang's gone down there. If you don't believe me, you can ask Jimmy, can't he, Jimmy? Hundreds of fousands of mines opened, and mills and crushers and all.'

'Go on!' Snow grunted disbelievingly.

''S a fact.'

Snow still looked disbelieving, but interested. 'Well, there might be something in it,' he said slowly.

'We could settle down.' The Stray bubbled with plans. 'And have a bit of a house wiv a little paddock round it.'

Snow growled. Women, he thought, were all the same: all wanting you to settle down.

'One thing,' he said, 'I see you got rid of that bloody Phipps.'

'I'll say I did. She went off days ago. She must be hundreds of miles by now. I says to her . . .'

They had just topped a little rise; and in the hollow below a stout, familiar figure rose to its feet from beside a fire where a blackened billy was boiling. As Miss Phipps recognised the van, she waved affably. She had hurt her foot, she explained, so she had waited for them.

'So good to see you again, Mister Snow, and I trust you will stop Dancy beating the horse.'

'I s'pose,' Snow said, after a gloomy silence, 'it's the way the Apostle says: If you're meant to be a mug, you're a mug. Here, get up, Phippsy. I'll walk.'

'Oh no,' Dancy said quickly. 'You gotta drive Don.' She slipped from her seat. 'I'll walk.'

'I'll walk, too,' Jimmy said loyally.

'So nice to be all together again,' Miss Phipps remarked, settling her bulk comfortably beside Snow.

He clicked to Don in his old way, and the van creaked into action on the long pull up the red road ahead of them. That left wheel, Snow noticed, was screeching like a trapped rabbit. He'd have to take it off and tighten the rim. Trust a woman not to attend to a thing like that.

'How's it, Stray?' he called, turning in his seat to regard the two small figures trudging behind; with Bluey on the end of his chain puzzled whether to walk near them, and then making little runs as the collar pulled him under the van again.

'All right, Snow.' The Stray turned a shining, happy face to him; and Snow noticed that she looked almost handsome. He supposed it must be the teeth.

As the Stray went, she sang, discordantly, and to herself. 'How beautiful,' she sang, 'how beautiful upon the mountains,' then stopped because that was all she knew.

Jimmy looked at her, puzzled. 'There ain't no mountains, Dance,' he suggested.

'How beautiful,' Dancy sang, 'how beautiful are the feet . . .'

They went on, across the plain stretching before them with farms and fields, with trees and sheep, and windmills sailing above the bores, with a faint blue line of hills very far away before them, and the barbed-wire fences running everywhere like demented spider-webs. They went on and on.

'How beautiful,' Dancy sang, 'how beautiful upon the mountains.' At the next farm, she thought, she must try to sell some jug-covers. She had Snow and Jimmy to look after, and that silly fraud of a Phippsy. And there was now no money at all, only under her thin dress a paper on which was written: 'Pay Mrs. Grimshaw a thousand pounds.'

As Dancy thought of that paper, she smiled to think how rich she was, and how happy.

THE END

Between the Flags and other stories

JANE HYDE

etween the Flags comprises eight SHORT STORIES AND A novella, 'The Green Waving Rye Fields of Wales.' The novella records a week in the life of Nick as he struggles against the odds to keep faith in the creed of Ture Love..

'... complex characters who are equally tough and tender... [Jane Hydel] shows us this man's grief and vulnerability in a way men are seldom able to show it themselves.' Kate Veitch, Sydney Morning Herald

Kangaroo

D. H. LAWRENCE

*K*ANGAROO IS THE STORY OF RICHARD AND HARRIETT Somers, who leave exhausted post-war Europe in search of a new and freer world. Written in Australia in 1922, it is a novel of conflicting perceptions, opinions and attitudes where white Australia is subjected to critical scrutiny from an aboriginal (if not an Aboriginal) point of view. By the time the wandering Englishman and his wife leave Australia, the novel has discovered hope, not in the protofascism of Ben Cooley and his secret army, nor in the socialism of Willie Struthers, but in the spirit of a tiny coastal village and the people who live there.

Although Lawrence was in Australia briefly Kangaroo *catches the features and the moods of the Australian scenery brilliantly.*
OXFORD HISTORY OF AUSTRALIAN LITERATURE

Now that we have Raymond Southall's eloquent introduction to the Imprint edition, perhaps Aldington's unreliable and dated essay will no longer be cited as the last word on the subject.
BRUCE STEELE, MERIDIAN

This is a definitive edition containing Lawrence's corrections.